THE BLOOD GOD

THE BLOOD GOD

Joseph Mac Anthony

GRAFTON BOOKS

A Division of the Collins Publishing Group

LONDON GLASGOW
TORONTO SYDNEY AUCKLAND

Grafton Books
A Division of the Collins Publishing Group
8 Grafton Street, London W1X 3LA

Published by Grafton Books 1987

British Library Cataloguing in Publication Data

Mac Anthony, Joseph
The blood god.
I. Title
823'.914 [F]   PR6063.A118/

ISBN 0-246-13216-7

Typeset by V & M Graphics Ltd, Aylesbury, Bucks
Printed in Great Britain by
Billings of Worcester

THE BLOOD
GOD

PROLOGUE

The images were brilliant but confused. Figures and objects swirling, then disappearing. He saw his mother, grim-faced soldiers, flickering lamps. He heard screams and smelled smoke. But the worst moment arrived when they seized and forced him down into the hole. As they kicked the dank soil over him, he felt the air curdling in his lungs. He began to suffocate. Trapped under the piled dirt he knew he was going to die. In the gathering blackness, that terrifying knowledge sparked resistance. Weak at first, it gained strength and spread like a flame through his being. Miraculously, he found the power to cry out. With that sound, the spell shattered and his eyes jerked open.

He was alone in the compartment of the Amtrak train. His head rested against the window, the vibration of the speeding train drumming into his skull. He lay still, his heart thumping wildly, hardly daring to move. Outside, the New England countryside sped by in the darkness.

Several minutes passed before he drew away from the window, leaving a faint stain from his slick black hair on the glass. He lay back against the headrest. His head continuing to loll with the movement of the carriage. But his heartbeat was already slowing. And the perspiration on his body had begun to cool.

Finally, Otto Lentz raised a hand to rub his eyes. The first thing he wanted to do was exorcise the terrifying pictures of the dream. Mostly because the memories they aroused were too real. But it wasn't possible. After more than forty years, the childhood images were still too vivid.

He could still see the kitchen of his neighbour's house outside Cracow. Lit by an oil lamp that cast long shadows on the earthen wall of the tiny room. He could see his mother too, her face half

7

hidden in a scarf, whispering urgently in his ear. And again from outside the room that night, he recalled the screams and the harsh voices of the soldiers carrying on the wind.

It was the night they put him in the hole.

More awake now and in command, Lentz shook his head impatiently and sat up. It was time to put things like that behind him. He looked at his watch. It was past 5 a.m. Still more than two hours to Montreal. He got to his feet and winced at the sudden aches shooting through his knees. The cramped seating, he thought. Straightening his jacket, he reached up and pulled down his suitcase to get his shaving bag.

The dimmed lighting reflected off the varnished panels and brass fittings as he slid the door back and stepped into the corridor. He shivered in the wintery draught. Gripping the rail, he moved down the empty passageway past the darkened compartments.

Through the window, the blurred lights of a village rushed by. He glimpsed tumbling snow under the lamps of a freight yard and guessed the weather would be worse in Montreal. He hoped Gedi Reubel remembered to meet him at the station.

Reaching the end of the corridor, Lentz stopped at the vacant washroom and pushed open the door. Turning sideways he edged his bulk through the narrow opening. The clacking of the wheels was louder now, the swaying stronger.

The floor inside the washroom was stained and damp. Loose toilet paper lay crumpled in the corner beyond the upturned lavatory seat. The place reeked of cheap disinfectant. But Lentz hardly noticed. That kind of smell was not important to him. Otherwise he could not have worked in the slums of Latin America where he made most of his money. To Otto Lentz, a sense of danger was more important than a sense of smell.

Methodical, he slid the lock shut, took off tie and jacket and hung them on the plastic hook behind the door. He bent his shirt collar back and turned to the washbasin. Pressing on the hot tap, he took out his razor and shaving cream. As the water rose in the metal basin, his thoughts returned to his mother and to her last act. Putting him in the hole.

He wondered if his parents ever considered the possibility of

8

escaping themselves back then. He thought not. They didn't have the money for it. He smiled thinly. They would have been amazed at how wealthy their son was becoming. Although with their peasant mentality, they might have pleaded with him for more caution.

He shrugged and splashed the water on his cheeks. Almost absently, he rubbed cream into his darkening stubble. He wet the plastic razor and slowly drew it down one cheek and then the other. Fresh from the packet, the blade was sharp. Soon the sallow jaws were gleaming. He stretched the loose flesh of his neck and brought the razor in. Just at that moment, the train struck a switch in the track. The washroom jolted quickly from side to side. Lentz's hand jumped. Before he could stop it the edge of the razor nipped the soft skin.

'Damn!'

He grimaced at the small cut and reached for a paper towel from the dispenser. Wetting it, he held it to his neck and waited for the blood to congeal. Idly, he gazed at the face in the mirror.

Overweight, he thought. But the plump features were still almost unlined. A smile warmed his dark eyes. Not bad for fifty-three.

As he reflected on his health, he suddenly became aware of a tiny movement. For a moment he wasn't sure where it was. Then he saw it. His eyes widened. It was a red stain, a bloodstain. Spreading softly across the paper towel.

'Jesus!'

The tiny red bubbles were forcing their way through the wet paper. Even as he stared, the frothy edges blended into a single drop. It hung for a moment, swaying like a miniature ruby. Then it dropped into the matted hair of his chest. Almost immediately, a second grew. It dropped too. Then a third. Shocked now, Lentz grabbed a wad of towels from the dispenser. Pushing them under the tap he pressed the soaking paper to his neck.

Outside, a warning siren blared as the train rushed through a level crossing. Lights flashed by the frosted window of the wash-room. Lentz did not notice.

With one hand gripping the basin and the other holding the paper to his neck, he tried to will the bleeding to stop. Seconds,

9

ticked by. Water from the soaked paper plopped into the sink. No sign of further bleeding. It looked like the wet towels were holding. Lentz allowed himself a sigh of relief.

He was about to take away the towels when he spotted it. A small fresh welling, seeping out from underneath the soggy paper. Horrified, he watched as it formed into a thin thread, then grew into a tiny rivulet. Down it ran, quickening, into the white V formed by his shirt front. The white polyester reddened as the stain slowly spread across it.

Lentz gripped the washbasin. His eyes were locked on what was now a steadily widening river of blood. The narrow washroom rocked from side to side. The wheels clanged on the steel rails. In the streaked mirror he saw the growing pallor reflected on his face. Below it, the bleeding grew stronger, malevolent, as if it had a will of its own. Suddenly he felt weak. Terrified, he grabbed the handrail. His knees, those aching knees, were starting to buckle. He swayed, resting his shoulder against the wall, heart thumping, eyes searching for support. A whistling started in his ears. He could feel the pumping growing fiercer in his neck. A sickness gripped him and he felt nauseous. He knew he was beginning to faint.

Clumsily, he edged towards the toilet seat. He almost fell as he sat down heavily on the rim. Breathing deeply, he closed his eyes, seeking control. The move helped. Despite the giddiness, he was beginning to dominate his fear.

He sat still for a few moments. Then he opened his eyes again. With his head low on his chest, he was looking down at the floor between his feet.

'Oh God!'

A large red pool had already gathered on the grey linoleum. As he watched, it widened, touching the edge of his shoes. Panic-stricken, he reached back and tore white trails of toilet paper from the roller. He jammed them to his neck. Huge spots were dancing before his eyes now. His vision was clouding. Terrified, he tried to rise from the lavatory seat. But his legs had turned to rubber. The patter to the floor went on, its strength growing. A sob broke from Lentz's throat. He raised his head from hunched shoulders, streams of toilet paper festooning his body.

10

'Help!' he cried, his voice breaking. 'Somebody help me!'

But nobody heard. The clatter of the churning wheels drowned out his voice. Around him, the fittings rattled in the tiny compartment. Water slapped around the washbasin.

Lentz's eyesight was going. The darkness was closing in. An icy coldness gripped his limbs. Sounds were fading. He tried to get up again. But it was hopeless.

In those last terrible moments Otto Lentz finally grasped the truth. This was no dream, no nightmare. This was real.

'*Maman!*' he screamed. '*Maman!*'

But no one was listening. The train hurtled on towards Montreal.

She approached the porter.

'The New York train, *m'sieu*. Which platform?'

'*Vingt-et-un.*' The porter pointed to the numbered standards which ran down the centre of the cavernous station in Montreal. Gedi Reubel saw the number twenty-one, grey on white, halfway down. A policeman, his back resting against the pole, chatted with a ticket collector. Reubel looked about. No sign of Otto Lentz. Her pale face creased with worry under the fur hat. She knew if he had come and gone, there would be hard words later. It was always like that.

She hurried across the brown terrazzo, her small body almost submerged in the muskrat coat. She knew it was too large. But at forty-five, she accepted comfort over style. Even if Otto might not like it.

She approached the official at the platform entrance. He was making some point to the policeman. 'Excuse me. Has the New York train arrived yet?'

The official, a tall thin man, paused to look down at her, not pleased at the interruption. 'It came in twenty minutes ago,' he said, turning back to the policeman.

'Please.' She had to persist. 'Could any of the passengers still be on board?'

'No. Everybody's left.' He did not bother to turn.

'But I don't understand,' she said, looking around again. 'I was

11

to meet my employer here. And I know he wouldn't leave without me.'

The policeman looked at her. 'What was your employer's name?'

They took her along the cold platform to Car 2. An elderly conductor helped her up the high steel steps. Several policemen stood inside the narrow passageway. They stopped talking as she entered. She was introduced to a tall greyhaired man, an inspector, whose name she did not catch.

'This will only take a few moments, *madame*,' he said, his voice soft and kind. 'And please, remember, look only at the face. You understand?'

Gedi Reubel nodded, her mind numbed at the shocking possibility. He took her arm gently. The shadowy faces of the other policemen watched curiously as the detective led her forward. At the end of the corridor he stopped to lean close. She could smell his after-shave.

'Remember, *madame*, just the face.'

She nodded again, steeling herself this time. He let go of her arm and she stepped forward. Very tentatively, she put her head slowly around the door of the washroom.

She stopped, appalled.

Otto Lentz's small dark eyes stared up at her. Sightless, but still beseeching. His round face was ghostly among the trailing coils of toilet paper falling around him to the floor. The ample flesh was drained of colour. It might have been carved from wax.

Somewhere in the distance, an engine rumbled to life. Fragments of sound echoed in Gedi Reubel's ears. She stared down at the frozen image, at the mortal terror still etched on her employer's face. The detective tugged softly at her sleeve. Gedi Reubel did not feel it. She continued to stare, unable to move. The detective pulled again, harder this time. Without thinking, she looked down. And saw the softly swaying floor. The policeman caught her as she slumped.

They carried her forward to an empty compartment. She heard their words of comfort through the maelstrom in her ears. They stretched her out on the seat and awkwardly opened her coat.

12

Through it all, Gedi Reubel had time for only one consuming thought.

It had not ended as he claimed it would. That handshake they offered on the platform in New York was a trick, a bloody deceit.

There was treachery.

The Investigation

1

Stephen Haggerty was not feeling good. He had drunk too much the previous night and ended up sleeping on the sofa. Now he was paying the price. When a thirty-nine-year-old behaves like a kid, the cost is usually steep. Knowing that in retrospect fuels the pain.

Charged with mild self-loathing when he rose at noon, Haggerty had showered, thrown on a highnecked Aran sweater and black corduroys, taken coffee with the last wholewheat bun from the bread bin, smoked, and then driven to work.

Work was on the sixteenth floor of the Canadian Broadcasting Corporation building where he was a reporter on the public affairs show, VisionProbe. The view he caught from his office window that morning matched his mood. Not one, but two successive storms had swept down from the arctic in the past week, covering the streets with ice and snow. Now, warmer air drawn in from the Great Lakes wreathed everything in a wet clinging mist. The foggy air didn't quite obscure the downtown skyline usually visible from the window. But it did bleed away any colour that the Montreal cityscape offered. It was a depressing sight.

Gloomily, Haggerty lit a cigarette and turned away. He was just under six feet and still lean for his age. The heavy smoking saw to that. His face, which looked young when it wasn't drawn, was longish with a square jaw. His lips tended towards thinness and, along with the hazel eyes, gave him a cold, stubborn look when he was angry. That picture did not always correspond to the facts but you had to know him well to realise it.

The floor outside his office that morning was quiet. Most of the staff from the show were away on winter break. He would have

17

gone too but the disruption of the past five days had wrecked his plans. The only reason he came in that day was because it was better than killing time in his now empty apartment.

He settled down in his chair now with the *Gazette* and his second coffee. He was scanning the inside of the paper – the front page was newsless except for the weather story – when Sheila's call came through. His stomach knotted when he heard her voice.

'Please, Stephen. Listen to me.' Her opening words were hot, feverish. Damn it, why doesn't she call it a day, he thought. 'You've got to understand. I didn't mean it. It just happened ...' The words trailed away.

He listened to her painful breathing. He had lost count of the number of times they had had this conversation in the past few days.

'Sheila,' he said, weary of it. 'I don't want to talk about it any more. There's no point. Now please don't make me hang up on you. Put down that phone.'

'Stephen. Don't do it. Not like this.' She began to cry.

He knew if he hesitated he was lost.

'I'm going, Sheila.' He tried to keep his voice level. He had to do it some time. And this was as good as any. 'Goodbye.'

He put the receiver down.

Somebody had been typing out in reception. The sound died away and the floor grew quiet again. Haggerty drew out his cigarettes again, took one, and threw the pack on the desk. He had done the sensible thing. But making good sense and feeling comfortable didn't always go together. He lit up and lay back in his chair.

Everybody knew about it, of course. Producers, research staff, the whole goddamn show. Most of them were at the wrap party in Ned Williams's house when it happened. He could still picture them in the living room, sipping drinks and listening to Sheila and a pal having a carnal bump and grind in the bedroom above, knowing he was in the kitchen, unaware, chatting about boats with Ned. It must have been a hell of a giggle for them. Still he could sympathise with that. He knew he would have laughed if it happened to somebody else. But when he saw the two of them lingering on the stairs together after he returned to the living

18

room, it wasn't so damned funny. It was obvious what had happened. Sheila's white linen skirt was wrinkled and the rose she wore behind her ear was crushed in her hand. The flushed look he knew so well was still on her face. When she saw him, he caught the flash of guilty fear, quickly followed by a pouty defensiveness. Her partner, a freelance soundman, had both hands on her shoulders at the time. Like one of those conga dancers. His pale drink-blotched face and reddish eyes showed that this was no grand passion.

Haggerty remembered the surprised rage he felt then. It had lessened greatly in the five days since. But he still had trouble with the view that night of her breasts swaying loose under the carelessly buttoned blouse as she left the stairs to come towards him. And that fresh reddened mark on her white neck below her ear. It could as well have been a message on a sandwich board. When he turned away in disgust, she called out. But he didn't look back. After that, for five consecutive days, she hadn't stopped calling. But there was no way.

It wasn't the first time in their three years together. And he knew, without doubt, that if the opportunity arose again it would not be the last. Something had happened to their relationship that she couldn't help and he hadn't the power to change. So there was no point in continuing. He just wished to hell she would stop calling.

He stood up from his chair, drawing on his cigarette. Not for the first time, he wished he was back in New York. It was almost seven years now since he had left the place. Biblically, that was supposed to be a long time. But it passed so quickly. Like a mythical wind that made no noise; it just aged you. Wryly, he rubbed at his crinkled, greying hair. Part of the reason for the break-up, he thought. Sheila was thirteen years younger. And the difference had begun to show in her mind now as well as in her face. He recalled how she had glanced down between those fabled breasts at him during lovemaking and remarked that it was like being massaged by a Brillo pad.

A glimmer of a smile lit his lips. She always had a way with the bitter word.

Bitch.

19

'Steve.'

He turned. Ned Williams, workaholic and VisionProbe's executive producer, stood in the door.

'Hi, Ned.'

'Thought I'd catch you before lunch,' Williams said amiably, entering. He was a trimly bearded man in his mid-fifties who tended towards business suits at conference time and sleeveless sweaters for the rest. This morning he wore a cardigan, blue striped on grey. He held a typed sheet in his hand.

It was Haggerty's professional habit to read papers that other people carried. Even upside down. But this time he hadn't the inclination; or the opportunity because Williams was waving the sheet about.

'Don't know if this is worth much. But I thought you might be interested,' he said, finally laying the sheet on the desk. 'Came in earlier. With vacations and all I took the call myself. Don't fault the spelling.'

Haggerty pulled it over and read.

—10.15 a.m. Woman named Gedi Reubel called. Said she wanted to talk to someone about her employer, Otto Lentz (make that the late Otto Lentz). Seems he had an accident on the New York/Montreal express two nights ago (15th/morning 16th). Found dead in washroom when train arrived here. Reubel says there are suspicious circumstances surrounding his death but she wouldn't go into detail on the phone. Wants one of our people to call her and make an appointment to meet. She said she'll be home from 4 p.m. today. Her phone number is 632 3487. Her address is 236 Lally Drive. P.S. That's in Notre Dame de Grace. - NW.

'Well, how'd I do?' Williams was conscious that he was an administrator, not a player in their game.

Haggerty smiled. 'Pretty good.'

'What do you think?'

'It's a bit sparse, Ned. Still, might be something. How did she sound?'

'Nervous, I guess. But not crazy or anything like that.'

Haggerty nodded.

'Want to check it out?' The offer was tentative. Haggerty

usually chose his own stuff. Like most investigative people, he was not particularly liked as a team player. So he was left to go his own way.

Now he shrugged. 'Why not?'

Williams smiled, a little happier. 'Great. It makes me feel our wheels are still turning. This place is like a tomb today.'

He moved to the door where he paused, hand on the knob. 'By the way, Sheila called before you arrived. More than once.'

'Yeah?'

Williams looked at him, hesitant. 'Steve, I know this is none of my business, but is she all right? She was acting pretty hysterical.'

Haggerty sighed. He respected Williams and he knew this was not for gossip. It was concern. 'To tell the truth, Ned, I don't know. Something's been happening to her lately. That thing the other night. It was kind of the last straw. It doesn't make sense to live with her any more. But she's making it very hard to end it.'

Williams shook his head. 'I'm very sorry to hear that. I used to think you had something very nice going there. Listen, if there's anything I can do to help, just let me know.'

'Thanks, Ned.'

'And keep me posted on the other thing,' he said as he left.

Haggerty smiled.

'Sure.' Work was never far from Ned Williams's mind.

Temporarily inspired by his example, he re-read the memo. Lentz had died in a public place. That meant a post mortem. He pulled over the phone and dialled the morgue.

'Zossy Gingras, please.' He waited. 'Zossy? Steve Haggerty here. How's it going?'

'Pretty good, Stevie. Nice to hear from you again.' It had been months since he last contacted Gingras. Financial scandals were the current fad on VisionProbe. Personally, Haggerty preferred violent crime, like murder. With that type of offence, you sometimes helped the perpetrator's family by exposure. With financial crime, you almost always ruined them. After fifteen years, Haggerty had seen enough to be bothered by the difference.

'You got a stiff down there tagged as Otto Lentz?' he asked.

Gingras gave a dry laugh. 'Sure do. You interested in him too?'

'A party just called. What's the story?'

21

'Well, he's just about the whitest white man I ever seen. And some people here are talking murder. You want to take a look? I can fit you in around two.'

Haggerty glanced at the window at the grey, mournful day. The morgue could hardly be worse. At least it was out of Sheila's reach, if she tried calling again.

'Why not?' he said. 'It'll help to brighten my afternoon.'

After he put down the phone, he finished off the *Gazette* and left for a wet lunch at the Rainbow. A few beers would clear the cobwebs. And he was sure his interest in food would not be high later in the afternoon. Zossy Gingras might not like to hear it, but his work had that effect on you.

The drawer slid shut and Gingras pulled down the locking lever. The sound echoed through the white-tiled room with its high walls and lined steel cabinets. In spite of fortifying himself, Stephen Haggerty was still affected.

'The cops got any ideas how this happened?'

Gingras shook his head.

'They threw it back to the pathologists.' Small and birdlike in the green high-buttoned smock, Gingras led the way to the door.

'What did they say?'

'Well, they don't like to admit it but they're up shit creek on this one. It seems our friend Lentz had all the symptoms of acute haemophilia. He had no coagulent – the stuff that makes blood harden over a wound – in his system. Absolutely none. So when he cut himself shaving, he just bled to death.' Two shadowy figures passed on the other side of the opaque doors. Gingras lowered his voice. 'Steve, the problem in this case is not with the diagnosis. What has them baffled is that Lentz could not have suffered from haemophilia without showing symptoms. And he never did. That's what makes the whole business so bizarre.' They stopped by the door.

Haggerty began buttoning his sheepskin. 'I'd like to know more about him, Zossy. Who was he anyway?'

'Businessman. Ran his own company. Otto Lentz Ltd.' A twinkle surfaced in Gingras's eyes. 'Here's a twist for you. Know what his business was?'

22

'You tell me.' They passed through the tall glass doors into a long corridor, Haggerty dwarfing the little man.

'Lentz bought and sold blood. Human blood.' Gingras pulled the huge door closed behind him. 'He was what's known as a blood broker.'

'How did you get to know that?'

'Transcript. The cops interviewed his secretary. A broad named Reubel.'

'Nobody uses slang like that any more, Zossy. Can you get me a copy?'

Gingras grinned. 'I might.'

Haggerty reached into his top pocket for the twenty he had put there earlier. He dropped it into Zossy's open palm.

'Move your little ass,' he said. 'And get it for me.'

Gingras looked at the bill and shook his head. 'Cheap, Stevie,' he said. 'Cheap.'

Gedi Reubel lived in a Tudor-style house on what looked like a $150,000 street. A late model Volkswagen sat in the drive. Stephen Haggerty noticed that the snow had not been cleared and wondered if the shock of Otto Lentz's death kept her indoors. He stepped gingerly through the ankle-high drifts and reached the verandah where he rang the polished brass bell, stamping his feet to dislodge the snow. An orange light came on overhead. After a few seconds, the door opened and a middle-aged woman peered out from behind a lock chain. She was barely level with it.

'Miss Reubel?' His breath streamed in the night cold.

She nodded through the opening. Her face looked pale in the ghostly light.

He smiled. 'I'm Stephen Haggerty. I called earlier.'

'Oh, yes. Thank you for coming, Mr Haggerty.'

He waited as she slipped the chain off and opened the door. 'Please come in.' He stole a quick look as she stood back.

Gedi Reubel had a taut, white-skinned face with small dark eyes. Her face looked a little uneasy now. Maybe she was worried about the step she had taken. She was wearing a green high-necked woollen sweater with loose tan pants and slippers. A small gold cross and chain hung from her neck and her grey hair

23

was straight-combed to below the ears. Haggerty would have taken her for a schoolteacher.

He stepped onto the side mat and gave her his coat, then unzipped his boots. It was clear she approved of that. As she put the sheepskin in the closet he glimpsed a camel's-hair man's coat on the rack too. He wondered about that. The police report said she lived alone.

'This way, Mr Haggerty.'

She led him down the hall to a spacious living room. It was elegantly decorated in floral brown with soft wall lighting and a log fire in the stone fireplace. The scattered furniture was well-kept period. A set of old family photographs lined one wall and a nature study from the Canadian north that might have come from the Group of Seven hung over the fireplace. The wide bay window at the far end of the room was filled with plants, separately lit, all green and very healthy.

With a place like this, Haggerty thought, she has to be the highest-paid secretary in Montreal.

'You've got a very nice house,' he said. 'Your friends must envy you.'

'Thank you,' she said. 'Not that I have many.' She gave a little smile, still slightly uneasy, then held her hands together. 'Would you like a drink?'

He settled on vodka. Watching her at the cocktail cabinet, he noted that she knew how to pour a drinker's portion. Unconsciously, she tasted her own to get it right.

'I've been thinking about you since you called,' she said as she turned to bring him his glass. With something to do, she seemed more relaxed. 'That accent. You're the American, aren't you?'

He nodded as she settled in the fireside chair opposite. She nestled her drink in her hands.

'Were you the man who did the Firenoux case?'

Senator Claude Firenoux's downfall was one of the reasons Haggerty preferred violent crime. The generous Senator had spread his government kickbacks widely. A lot of hapless people were swept away in the fallout.

'Yes,' he said. 'That was mine.'

'Well, I'm glad they sent you,' she said, then paused. 'You're

24

probably wondering why I chose to call your programme about this affair.' The accent was definitely European. 'Rather than go to a lawyer or the police.'

'Not really,' Haggerty said. Although he could see she was still a little nervous, he liked the way she came to grips. 'It can be awkward talking with those kind of people about what are often just suspicions.' Absently, he stirred his vodka. 'I'm assuming, of course, if you had concrete evidence that Mr Lentz's death wasn't an accident, you would have told the police.' From the interview he knew she had said nothing.

'Yes, I would,' she said. 'But you're right. I have no evidence. Only suspicions.'

Haggerty smiled at her. 'We get a lot of people in the same boat. Evidence can be hard to come by.'

'Oh, it's not like that,' she said. 'You see, I expect to have evidence very shortly.'

He looked at her. 'Really?'

'Most certainly.'

Outside, the man in the hooded parka crossed the icy street, avoiding the pools of light under the streetlamps. Slipping between the parked vehicles he hurried along the sidewalk to Stephen Haggerty's Mustang. He sank to one knee and worked quickly on the lock. With a click the door unlatched. The man slid inside, reaching up to turn off the tiny interior light and took out a pencil torch. The narrow beam flickered around the interior.

Opening the glove compartment, he drew out the material inside. A street directory lay on top. The man turned over the leading page and stopped where Haggerty had written his name and address. His breath hissed as he saw the logo of the Canadian Broadcasting Corporation. He closed the book quickly and replaced the piled items where he found them. Switching off the torch, he reset the doorlock and slipped out onto the sidewalk. He hurried down the street and crossed to where a black camper stood among the line of parked cars.

The street remained silent, empty. He reached the camper and slid the side door back a foot to climb in. A short, muscular man sat inside by the darkened window with a coffee in his hand. He looked up.

'Well?'

'He's a reporter.'

'Shit!'

They stared at each other for a few moments. The heavier man finally put down his coffee. 'I better call. The man will want to know.'

In Gedi Reubel's living room, the fire crackled in the hearth.

'You know, Mr Haggerty, I'm one of your show's oldest fans. Going all the way back to the seventies.' She drank from her glass. Substantial swallow, Haggerty thought. He was building a picture. She cradled her drink again in her hands. 'I thought of VisionProbe immediately when this thing with Mr Lentz happened. But maybe I should tell you something about that first?'

'Please.'

She repeated the brief facts. Lentz's death in the washroom, the symptoms of haemophilia, and how it was impossible for him to have had the disease. No discrepancy, Haggerty thought.

'I worked with Mr Lentz for seventeen years,' she said, 'and he was not a haemophiliac. And there's no way he could have become one. Haemophilia is the result of a genetic disorder. You can't contract it. That's one of the things I learned in the blood business.' She looked at Haggerty. 'Are you familiar with the trade, by any chance?'

He shook his head.

She nodded. 'I'm not surprised. Few people are. Commercial blood only attracts attention when there's a horror story about drug addicts or drunks selling their blood to support their habits. But the fact is, human blood is a very marketable product. More than a billion dollars of it is sold every year.'

Haggerty looked at her, surprised.

She smiled. 'It's true.'

'A billion dollars' worth? That's incredible. Who buys the stuff?'

She laughed. 'Not vampires, I assure you. Normally, it's the big drug companies. They make blood products, prescription medi-

26

cines or use the plasma in lab work or for research. The voluntary donor system used by the Red Cross couldn't hope to meet their needs. So they have to buy on the open market. And they buy a lot.'

'Well, it must take a heck of a lot of donations to bring in that amount of money. Where do they get it all?'

'Well, much of it comes from the Third World. There are a good many buyers operating in Latin America and in Africa. Usually in places where the Red Cross and red tape don't stifle private enterprise.' Haggerty didn't bother to hide his view of that. She shrugged. 'I see you're not very sympathetic. Well, I won't apologise. But I can tell you that the Western world would be a lot worse off without the international traffic in blood. And so would the Third World. You see, for most of the donors in the backward countries, blood is the only resource they have left to sell. Take the Haitians, for instance. They make about $70 a year trying to scrape a living from the land. Well, they could earn twice that by selling their blood every week.'

'Hold on. Isn't it dangerous to bleed people that often?'

'It used to be. But not any more.' She rose and went back to the vodka bottle. When she raised the bottle and looked questioningly at him, he nodded. It was a quicker refill than he liked, but it was better to stay up there with her.

'We have a system now called plasmapheresis,' she said, carrying the bottle over. 'It allows you to bleed people weekly provided you return the red cells. You hold on to the rest, the plasma, which is really more valuable. The process takes longer than the normal donation but it's just as safe. Mr Lentz introduced the system into Central America some years ago.'

'Where? In Haiti?'

She shook her head. 'Guatemala mostly. His plasma was usually shipped from there to Europe through Miami. That's where he was on his last trip.' She paused at the memory, looking down at her glass.

'Maybe you better tell me about it,' Haggerty said gently.

She nodded finally and looked up.

'I should explain a little about our company first. We not only bought and sold plasma. We also dealt in specialised blood fractions for rare illnesses. Now a lot of the buying and selling in that field goes on between individual brokers. And over the years you build up relationships with people in complementary fields.' She hesitated. 'A lot of this business I'm talking about is done by word of mouth. That's because health authorities in most Western countries are extremely cautious when it comes to blood products. Sometimes that's justified but mostly it's not. Anyway, in this case Mr Lentz had built up a relationship with the owner of another blood company called the Purax Corporation. I wasn't directly involved because Mr Lentz normally kept the more sensitive parts of the business to himself. But I knew a little about it. The Purax head office was in Guatemala City but its owner also worked out of Miami. Mr Lentz and this man had a very close relationship or that's how I understood it. Until three days ago. That was when Mr Lentz called me from New York.

'He was very unhappy when we spoke, and very nervous. He said that he and Purax had a falling out. He went on to say he had been threatened. It seemed to me that he was telling me this as some kind of insurance, as a hedge against them taking action against him. That feeling was strengthened when he told me that he was depositing material connected with the affair in our New York safety deposit where I could retrieve it if any problem arose. Naturally, I found that upsetting. I was worried about his safety.

'But the next day, he called again. This time it was from Grand Central Station. Just before his train left for Montreal. He said the crisis was over. He had solved the problem with Purax and they had just shaken hands on a new deal. He said I was to forget what he had said earlier and he would explain when he arrived in Montreal.' She paused. 'And then this happened.'

'You see a connection between the first phone call and his death?'

She nodded.

'This man who allegedly threatened Mr Lentz. The owner of Purax. What can you tell me about him?'

'Well, there's not a lot. His name is Ernst Dackman and he's a medical doctor. Mr Lentz never told me much about their relationship but they did share blood bank facilities in Guatemala. Otto – Mr Lentz – had a share in a blood import business

28

they opened in Miami a year or more ago. I have an address for Dackman from that time if you're interested.'

Haggerty nodded. 'I'll get that from you later. Now look, Miss Reubel, let me be the devil's advocate here. I know Mr Lentz told you he was threatened. But we have to consider another angle. What if his death really was an accident? What if this Purax or Dackman or whatever was just engaged in the normal business wrangling? I know things like that can get very bitter but they don't normally threaten life and limb. From that point of view, this could be a harmless dispute.'

'Oh no, Mr Haggerty,' she said, shaking her head vigorously. 'I can tell you with certainty that there's nothing harmless about this.' She put down her glass. 'I didn't say this before because I was afraid you might think I was being melodramatic. But Mr Lentz said something about Purax that has me really concerned.' She looked at him with worried eyes. 'Mr Haggerty, he said that Purax were embarked on a course that was far more dangerous than anything I could ever imagine. And he said that someone very important, a very high figure, was going to die because of it.'

It was past ten when Haggerty got back to his apartment. He heard the phone ringing as he reached the door. He swore. From the previous night's performance, he knew it had to be Sheila. What was wrong with that woman? Why couldn't she stop?

Inside, the sound reverberated through the empty rooms. He went to the den, lifted the phone, disconnected and left it lying off the hook. He went to the kitchen and got a beer from the refrigerator, knowing he had to do something. He drank some, turning it over in his mind. Returning to the living room, he reconnected the phone and called Ned Williams.

'Hi, Steve. How's it going?' Haggerty told him about the Reubel story.

'Sounds as if it might be interesting,' Williams said. 'What do you want to do with it?'

'I thought I might look up this Dackman guy. Reubel gave me his address. But it's in Miami. Means spending a couple of days there.'

'You think it's worth that?'

29

'To be honest, I can't give a definite answer, Ned. But there was a threat, a man is dead, and Reubel says that someone far bigger is now at risk. As far as I'm concerned, it's worth speculating a thousand bucks to look into it. And, of course, you will be helping me a lot by sending me down there right now.'

For a moment there was silence. Then Ned Williams laughed.

'What the hell, Haggerty, you've been paying your way lately. Why not?' He paused. 'When are you planning to go?'

'Soon as I can.'

'How are you for cash?'

'I can cover it on plastic.'

'Sounds like you can't wait.'

'Amen, Ned. I'm booking as soon as you put down the phone.'

'Well, enjoy yourself, Steve. And just remember to phone in the temperatures now and then. I like to be told when staff is having a good time.'

Later, after booking an early-morning flight, Stephen Haggerty sat with a beer in the darkness of his living room, wondering about the high-level figure under threat of death that Gedi Reubel mentioned. He wondered too about Ernst Dackman. It was all puzzling, but interesting. He thought there must be other people involved. Sipping from the bottle, he wondered what kind of people they were.

2

William Masters was not a happy man. Even if the setting before him was idyllic.

On either side of the villa, the sloping hills of this Caribbean island rose green and majestic in the evening light. Along the white beachfront where the last sun worshippers held out, the shallow water was still a deep transparent blue. Farther out to sea, the colour altered as water and sky blended at a ripening pink horizon. Above it all hung great orange clouds, shot through with the last gold beams of the sun. It was travel-poster stuff.

But William Masters could not enjoy it. A snatched glimpse of nature was not going to eliminate the inner darkness. With a glass of Coke in one hand, he moved back into the bedroom, massaging his chest, restless. Although the room was not hot there was a faint sheen on his forehead.

Masters was a thinnish man and slightly above average height, with a thatch of loosely combed black hair above his narrow face. He was in his mid-thirties but his skin already had the faintly purple look of someone with high blood pressure. There were deep lines under his faded blue eyes and his cheeks looked drawn. That evening he was dressed simply in an open-necked maroon shirt, grey pants and loafers.

Abruptly now, he put the Coke glass on the side table and went to the overnight bag on the bed. He took a fresh shirt and pants from inside and laid them on the coverlet. He paused for a moment, considering, then reached into one of the smaller compartments, his hand searching. Finally, he pulled out a bottle. A mickey of rye, almost full.

Walking lightly, he carried it to the side table where he poured a small measure carefully into the half full Coke glass. Closing

31

the bottle, he returned it again to the bag, zipping it shut. Glass in hand he went to sit on the settee by the window. Resting his feet on the coffee table he sipped the drink, watching the rising shadows on the wall opposite. Even still he could not relax.

He was waiting for the call from the patio. It was something he was not looking forward to. He already knew he had made a mistake in accepting this assignment. But that made no difference now. There was no going back. Once taken, you had to go through with it. That was a Masters's house rule he liked to keep.

Even so, he felt he was not entirely to blame for what had happened. Others were at fault too. The Washington people should have known better. Putting pressure on him so soon after treatment. Any qualified person could have told them it was wrong.

It all went back only eight days to that cold Sunday afternoon in the East Potomac Park in the capital. To that meeting with Korner. Masters saw that impressive figure again in his mind's eye, striding along the path under the bared trees, the big, gaunt, white face unsmiling, the rangy body masked by an ancient pearl-grey coat. The rigid dignity of the man had left Masters feeling like a derelict in his black navy jacket. Yet they both shared the same employer. And Masters held the more dangerous job for much of that time.

Or at least he had held it. Until, quite unexpectedly, the top blew off.

William Masters had completed almost sixteen years in intelligence work when that happened. And although he never had a high opinion of himself, there were some people who said his work was good.

Certainly he did try hard.

Korner knew that. Which was probably why he tapped him for this one. Masters, dry and recuperating outside Syracuse in upper New York, came to the Washington meeting because he was curious. He had never worked for the Western Hemisphere people before. And, in his condition, he hadn't been expecting job offers. Why not, he told himself.

Big mistake.

The meeting started that afternoon on a strained note. Korner had not bothered to shake hands, or even smile. It was almost as if this were some bothersome interview that was disturbing his schedule. Compassion had no part in it. As his first brutally edged question showed.

'Can we take it that you're cured?' he asked, glancing down at the smaller Masters, who was walking hands in pockets, momentarily high and now cast low. It was dirty pool but what could he do? Nod and say yes was what.

'Good,' Korner said as if that was all that was needed. He gazed ahead as they walked. 'I know you're an experienced man,' he said. 'And I need somebody who is not on active duty at the present time. The job is not testing in terms of time or effort. And besides, Cal thinks you're up to it.'

William Masters glanced up in surprise. 'You talked to Cal?' Of course he would. They all dealt with Cal at one time or another.

Korner nodded.

'I called him and told him I needed somebody, that it was a one shot thing. I asked him if he thought it was time for you to get back to work and if you could do it. He said yes.'

Masters moved in as a jogger approached. He waited until the man passed.

'I am ready,' he said. Once again that cursed urge to please anybody with a little power. It seemed embedded in his character.

'I'm glad,' Korner said, not sounding as if he cared much. He pushed his gloved hands together. Misted breath streamed from his squared mouth. He was getting down to business.

'Tell me,' he said. 'What do you know about the situation down in Guatemala?' His large-boned skull inclined like a priest to listen to the reply. William Masters saw the tiny blue veins under the white skin of the temple. God, he thought, this is an ugly man.

Outwardly, he shrugged. 'Not that much.' His fields had been Asia, the Middle East, then south-east Europe. He didn't feel he had to be qualified on Central America. But he thought to smile. 'It hasn't been keeping me awake nights,' he said, then wished he hadn't.

But Korner seemed not to notice. He gave a short dry laugh that

33

actually had some humour in it. 'There are a good many in the administration who wish they could say that.' He nodded slowly to himself as if nursing some private memory. Then he came back again. 'You know this arms embargo that President Robson brought in to force some improvement in civil rights down there?' he asked. He must have realised he was walking too fast now for he slowed his pace to Masters'.

'Yes. I've read about it.'

'The damn thing is affecting the Guatemalan military's campaign against the guerrillas,' Korner said. 'They're losing ground. Very rapidly.'

'I haven't really paid that much attention to it,' William Masters said, 'but I guess they would.'

Korner seemed not to have heard. 'Their President, General Serena, feels he will be overthrown if the embargo continues. And he's started to fight back.'

A cold gust swept across the park. Korner raised a glove to smooth down the sparse grey hair.

'On New Year's Day, he called the White House and told the President that if the embargo wasn't lifted within two months, he would take counter measures to ensure his government's survival.'

Korner slowed and came to a stop in the centre of the path. As Masters watched he reached into the inside pocket of his coat, probing, and withdrew an envelope. He passed it with a gloved hand.

'This is what Serena meant by counter measures.'

William Masters slipped the single sheet out of the envelope. He stared. It was a State Department cable, graded for the highest secrecy. It came from the US Ambassador in Guatemala City and was barely three days old. It reported the secret arrival in the capital of a small party of Russians. William Masters read the names.

'Christ!' he said, shocked.

'You know who they are?'

'Of course,' William Masters said shortly as if his competence was in question. He handed back the message. 'They're logistics personnel. Weapons supply specialists. The very best.' He looked

34

at Korner, who was putting away the envelope. 'What the hell are they doing in Guatemala?'

'I told you,' Korner said serenely. 'The Guatemalans say they need arms.'

'But it's a right-wing regime,' Masters protested, 'Even the Russians have their principles. I can hardly see them dealing with somebody like Serena. The man's an out and out fascist.' His hands were getting cold again. He put them back in his pockets. 'Do the Cubans know about this?'

'At this moment we don't think so although you can never trust your information from down there. But whether they know or not this embargo has opened up a new and dangerous game for us in a very sensitive area.'

They moved along the path slowly.

'What's the White House reaction?'

Korner shrugged. 'The President is unyielding. He calls the move blackmail. Serena, for his part, calls it the politics of necessity.' Korner gazed thoughtfully ahead. 'So we have a conflict of national interests. Which must be resolved.'

Masters thought this was interesting. 'So what happens?'

Korner continued to gaze ahead. 'It won't surprise you to know that a select group has been examining options,' he smiled. 'Surprisingly, they've come up with a unanimous recommendation.'

The recriminations always come later, Masters thought.

'What is it?'

Korner smiled again. More widely than before. 'Their solution is very simple.' He looked at Masters, the pale eyes showing a faint amusement. 'They think we should knock someone on the head. Physically. Kill them, if you like.'

Masters gaped. That kind of talk was common in Georgetown cocktail bars. But a senior man, actually saying it?

'Are you serious?'

'And why not?'

Masters raised his shoulders. It was his turn. 'Look,' he said, 'you're not going to get an argument from me on the morality of the thing. I can go along with that. It's getting caught is the problem. You won't get away with it.'

Korner shrugged.

'I don't see why not. Anyway, that's not really your problem. All I want from you is the benefit of your experience. We already have a man who is prepared to carry out the operation. We need somebody to vet him. Someone who knows about such things and is not on the active roster.'

'That would implicate me,' Masters said quickly.

Korner looked at him coldly. 'This conversation has already implicated you. Unless you plan to go to the FBI when it's over.'

Masters bit his lip. 'Does Cal know?'

'He will be told before it happens. For a number of reasons we don't expect him to oppose it.' Korner slapped his gloved hands together. 'You realise how high the stakes are? Serena could make the announcement about this new Russian link at any time. And then the genie is out of the bottle. If Guatemala goes that will put Mexico in the firing line next. We can't let that happen. We have to stop it.' He slowed and looked at William Masters. 'Well, what do you say? Will you do this job for us? Will you vet this man and tell us if he has the makings?'

'Where is he?'

'He's on one of the Bahamian islands at present. Two hours out of Miami.' They were keeping him out of the jurisdiction. Good. 'The whole thing should take no more than three days,' Korner said. 'If you agree.'

Even now, William Masters was not sure why he had said yes. But that night after he did, he took his first drink in months. Now, eight days later, that problem was still under control. But he wished it hadn't happened.

While he was brooding on it, the bedroom had been darkening around him. Suddenly, he became aware of a soft tapping on the door. He looked across as it opened cautiously. A black face appeared in the gloom. It smiled apologetically.

'Excuse me, sir,' the servant said, 'but Dr Dackman will see you now.'

3

Vacationers crowded the main terminal at Miami International Airport. Pale families coming in, tanned going out. Stephen Haggerty, bag slung over his shoulder, pushed his way forward through the throng. Soon tiring of it, he slipped outside through the automatic doors. The warm air enveloped him like cotton wool. Pulling off his jacket, he headed for the cab rank beyond the drooping palms. The faded blue sky hung like a balm above his head, soothing, banishing thoughts of snow and ice, even mellowing his views on Sheila Blais.

A knowing judge got it right when he said that sunlight was the best disinfectant. Maybe distance helped as well, Haggerty thought.

It was still hard to believe in the transition. Last night, sinking in snow with Sheila baying at his heels. Today, in tropical sunshine, seeking out this Ernst Dackman, a shadowy medical man who settled business disputes with murderous finality – if Gedi Reubel was to be believed.

He had been thinking about Reubel on the plane. He thought he might have a fix on her. It came from her farewell statement as he stood on the verandah saying goodbye. She mentioned then that she was Otto Lentz's executor. He thought the admission was well timed. Too late for him to pursue but made, nevertheless, so that he couldn't accuse her of double-dealing.

Along with the camel's-hair coat in the closet and the expensively furnished house, it led Haggerty to believe there was more to Reubel's relationship with Lentz than she admitted. They were probably involved. If it was true, it didn't disturb him. He had known sources who were malevolent, decent, vindictive, fair-minded, thieving, mendacious, violent and upright. He had

37

yet to meet one who was disinterested. Sources in investigative reporting were like those tricky currents on a fast-flowing and usually muddy river. They led you towards your destination. But they could just as easily upend you, if you didn't watch out.

Not that Haggerty was worrying much about that today. Not with a thousand dollars credit on his American Express, courtesy of VisionProbe, some hot sun and the possibility of an interesting chase unfolding.

The airline had booked him into a motel on the airport strip. The cab journey took little more than five minutes, all peppered with complaints from the Cuban cab driver. Haggerty smiled through it all. The fare was four dollars. He handed over six.

The Miridiana turned out to be a white, neatly pleasant stucco. The constructional equivalent of the fast food business, which would leave nothing for archeologists to sift through twenty years after it came down. Scattered among its rich flowerbeds were clutches of plastic flamingos and fibreglass fountains. At the desk, Haggerty joked with the shy young receptionist, got a map and hired a car. In his room he showered and changed to light denims and sandals. Feeling refreshed despite the long plane ride, he plotted directions to Doctor Ernst Dackman's last known address on Bayview Avenue.

The slow drive under a blue sky, past shirt-sleeved people and luxuriant vegetation heightened his relaxed mood. When he reached his destination, it seemed too soon. It was also a surprise.

The address supplied by Gedi Reubel turned out to be a shabby single storey warehouse that looked more like a prime target for a demolition derby than a doctor's surgery. It was set back from the road and fronted by an unpaved parking lot. A faded 'Space to Let' sign stood by the entrance. The only car in the lot was an old Buick.

Haggerty drove across the gravel and stopped near the door. Close-up, he saw the sun scorched facade was flaked and peeling. He checked the address again. No mistake. He cut the idling motor and got out of the car. Flicking away his cigarette without concern about adding to the litter, he went to the door. It was locked. Peering through the dirt stained glass into the empty hall, he pressed the buzzer.

A few moments later, an elderly man appeared. He limped slowly to the door and stopped to examine Haggerty through the glass. Finally, he opened the door a crack. His old lined face was watchful.

'Yeah?'

'Hi there,' Haggerty said. 'I'm looking for a man who did business here. Name of Dackman. A doctor. You know him?'

'You a bill collector?'

Haggerty grinned, shook his head.

'Reporter.' He passed his press card through the crack. The old man looked and passed it back. A short grin showed a toothless mouth.

'You're out of luck on this one, young fella. He hasn't been here for near twelve months.'

'I figured that,' Haggerty said as he put the press card back in his wallet. 'I just thought you might have a forwarding address.'

The old man shook his head. 'All he left here was a pile of messy garbage,' he said.

'What kind of garbage?'

'Blood.'

'How's that again?'

'You heard me.' He seemed irritated at his word being questioned. 'He left me with a heap of stinking blood plasma. I had to get the city to haul it away.' He waved at the traffic passing on Bayview Avenue. 'Stunk up the whole place for a month.'

'Jeez,' Haggerty said.

The old man nodded, mollified. He wanted to talk. He eased the chain off the door. 'You better come in.'

Haggerty stepped through. The door was relocked behind him.

'Any idea where the blood came from?'

'From down south,' the old man said as they went down the hallway. 'Central America, I believe. In here.'

They entered a small office crowded with boxes of papers and files. The old man gestured across the laden desk and Haggerty sat down.

'Did he do much business here?' Haggerty asked.

'Not to my knowledge, he didn't. I only saw him a couple of

39

times. Mostly when they were opening up. They made a big deal of that. Matter of fact, I should have a picture that was taken then. For publicity, they said.' The old man cackled. 'Imagine advertising blood for sale. Beats me what folks will do for money nowadays.'

'Can I see the picture?'

'Sure. If I can find it.' He adjusted his glasses and began rummaging through the files packed on his desk. 'Here we are.' He opened a dog-eared file and drew out a photograph. Haggerty leaned across to look. It was a formally posed group of men and a single woman, photographed in the parking lot with the building in the background. 'That's Dackman there,' the old man pointed to a strongly built, middle-aged man with swept back hair in the centre of the group. But Haggerty barely noticed.

He was looking at a face in the rear. The last time he had seen it was in a steel cabinet in the Montreal morgue. It was Otto Lentz.

'Know anything about the other people in the photograph?'

'Only the lady there.' The old man indicated the woman. 'All the cash business went through her. She was a nurse, I think.'

'Do you have her name?'

'Should do. She was the one that paid for the garbage pick up.' He went through the file again and pulled out a receipt.

'Here it is.'

Haggerty read the standard script. 'Received from Dorothy Kreise, the sum of three hundred and twenty-three dollars.'

'She give you any address?'

The old man shook his head. 'No. But thinking about it, I'm pretty sure she was a nurse.'

The lunch-hour traffic had slackened when Haggerty came out. He drove along Bayview Avenue until he found a pay phone. The local nursing organisation was in the yellow pages. He dialled and a breezy voice answered. He introduced himself as a journalist from Montreal.

'Ah, *La Belle Province*. What can I do for you?'

'I need to talk with a nurse who lives in the Miami area. Her name is Dorothy Kreise.' He spelled it out.

40

'Let me check.' He waited, gazing out at the passing scene, still mesmerised by the change of climate. The woman returned.

'Got your party,' she said. 'But there's no employment listed for her. And I'm not supposed to give out home addresses.'

'Hell. Can you give me a break on that?' It was a career hazard common as dried ballpoints.

She paused. 'I guess for a reporter I could make an exception. Just don't say where it came from. Okay?'

'You got it.'

'347 Hanover. Apartment 784.'

Driving back to the Miridiana, he detoured by Hanover Boulevard for a quick inspection. Afterwards he stopped at a pharmacy and bought a pair of sunglasses.

Back at the Miridiana, he changed into a bathing suit and wandered down to the pool where he worked on some rum and coke, took a swim and soaked up a little sunshine. After the long flight and the first part of the work done, he figured he deserved a long lunch hour.

Two hours later, he got back to his room. Tossing the bath towel aside, he sat on the bed by the night table. He found the phone number and began dialling. It took some time before he got an answer.

'I'm sorry to disturb you, Miss Kreise,' he said when she came on. 'My name is Hamilton Rayner and I live in Apartment 231 downstairs.'

'Yes?' She had a hard brittle voice.

'My car was damaged this morning by someone leaving our garage. The superintendent said it was a Toyota Corolla.'

'I don't drive a Toyota,' she said. 'I have a Chevette.'

'Well, anyway, it was a blue sub-compact. The accident happened about 10 a.m.'

'It wasn't me,' she said. 'I leave the building before eight-fifteen every day. And besides my car is white.'

'I see,' Haggerty said. 'Well, I'm sorry to bother you. I hope you didn't mind.'

'That's all right,' she said. 'I hope you find out who did it.'

'Thank you, ma'am,' Haggerty said, 'I hope so too.' He put down the phone.

41

That evening, as he usually did when he had work on the road, he ate in his room. Small sirloin, fries and a half bottle of the Piat. He read the papers, watched some television and was asleep by eleven. He hardly dreamt or so he thought.

It was just past 7 a.m. when he left the Miridiana next morning. The lightly travelled streets were washed by early morning lemon-shaded sunlight. Haggerty felt good, really rested. His imagination was roused by the anticipation of the chase. And although he realised that Dr Dackman might be more difficult to find than anticipated, it didn't mar his enjoyment as he started across town to Hanover Boulevard.

Fifteen minutes later he entered the service road opposite Dorothy Kreise's apartment and rolled to a stop. Killing the motor he lowered the radio and lit his second cigarette of the day. It was shortly after eight when the white Chevette rode up the ramp opposite. Haggerty got a clear view of the passing Dorothy Kreise. She wore an elaborate silver hair-do piled high above her temples. Thinking she had to sleep alone to foster a creation like that, he pulled out after her. She led him north, skirting the downtown core where the poverty line was as clear as if the city planners laid it out that way. He managed to stay close without sitting on her tail, a skill perfected during his early New York years in journalism.

A couple of dozen blocks went by before the real estate began to improve. Haggerty was settled in a hundred yards behind the Chevette, always ready to sprint on a threatened light change. Still, he was almost caught by surprise when she suddenly made a right into a side street. He followed. It was lined with small stores and shabby businesses a smidge higher economically than the black ghettos they had passed. They were two minutes along the street when Kreise began to slow, her indicator flashing.

Haggerty pulled to the kerb and watched her turn into an alley alongside a store fronted, two-storey building. He waited until she was out of sight then pulled out and started after her. The sign above the battered door said Mayburn Plasma Clinic. Red lined posters in the dirt-glazed windows on either side of the door said BLOOD DONORS WANTED. Some men lounged on the

42

corner talking, obviously waiting for the premises to open. As Haggerty passed the alley, he glimpsed Dorothy Kreise entering a door in the side of the building. He drove on for two blocks then did a U-turn and slowly returned, stopping about fifty yards from the clinic. Leaning back on the seat, he settled down to wait.

Almost fifteen minutes passed before someone opened the front door and the waiting men went inside. The day was already warming up. Haggerty closed the window, switched on the air conditioning, and smoked. Take your time, his father used to caution, if the story is there don't lose it through impatience. He smiled at the old injunction. When you forgot rules like that, it was time to pack it in. That came from his father too.

Over the next hour and a half, he counted twelve men, mostly black and all poorly dressed, entering the building. Finally, one of the men who had been on the sidewalk before the clinic opened came out. He was black too and in his forties. As he walked off in the other direction, Haggerty climbed out, locked the car and followed.

The humid air carried a stench from garbage abandoned in the alleys. The sidewalk concrete was buckled and cracked. But it seemed that even the weeds couldn't make a living in this part of town. There was only a brown shrivelled fuzz between the paving.

Haggerty closed on his prospect cautiously. He didn't want to scare him. 'Hi there.'

The man stopped and turned. He looked frail and unwell, rocking as he stared at Haggerty, who stood a few yards away.

'How much they pay for blood in there, man?'

This donor looked like he'd already had a few. He grinned now, showing gapped teeth. 'Pretty good,' he said. 'Fifteen bucks a shot.'

'Hey, that's not bad,' Haggerty said. 'How much they take?'

'Dunno, man. Pint, maybe, something like that.' He was losing interest.

'You reckon it's safe?'

'Sure,' the black man said, 'ain't no problem. They got a nurse in there.'

'Got a doctor too?' Haggerty asked.

'No.' The black man shook his head. 'No doctor there, man.'

43

With a wave of his hand, he cut off further questions and shambled away.

Haggerty returned to the car. During the rest of the morning he tried two others. The replies were the same. There was no doctor supervising donors. But one man said there might be one working inside the clinic. At noon, Haggerty drove back to the Miridiana.

In his room, sitting on his bed and lunching on pastrami, Haggerty put in a call to the *Miami Sentinel*.

'Library, please.' He waited. 'Hello. My name is Stephen Haggerty. I'm a journalist down from Montreal, Canada. I'm looking for any news clippings you have on a medical doctor. Name is Ernst Dackman. He owns a Miami blood bank called Mayburn Plasma. I understand he's an importer of medical products.'

'I'll check for you,' a brisk voice said, 'but if he's on file, it's going to cost $15 an hour to research. Photostats are 35 cents extra.'

'Fine. I'll hold.' He refilled his coffee from the plastic jug on his bedside table.

The librarian returned. 'We got three clippings outstanding under the name of a medical doctor called Ernst Dackman. They involve the importing of blood from Guatemala to the United States. Is that the man?'

'That's him,' Haggerty said. 'How soon can I come down to see those clippings?'

'Morning is usually best. Can you make it around 11 a.m. tomorrow?'

'Sure.'

'Okay. And ask for Harold Leese. He's the boss around here.'

After he put down the phone, Haggerty opened the package he had brought back to the motel and spilled the contents onto the bed. A pair of worn jeans, work boots and a faded plaid shirt. The entire outfit had cost him $17.50 in a used clothing store.

He dressed quickly, drank a little rum and splashed some more on his shirt. It was almost two o'clock when he left the motel.

The Mayburn's reception room was decorated to imitate a hospital waiting room. Bright health posters decorated the walls.

Plain wooden benches lined opposite sides of the room. Three men sat on one with legs outstretched, looking bored. The place was quiet as a funeral parlour. At the far end from the door a man in a white jacket sat behind a desk under a notice outlining blood regulations. He glanced up from the *People* magazine as Haggerty approached. He looked more like a bouncer than a medical attendant.

'Yeah?'

'I want to sell some blood.' Haggerty tried a sneaky grin. The man ignored the shady attempt at friendship. He stared at Haggerty without much interest.

'You an addict?'

'No, sir.'

'Let me see your arms.'

Haggerty pulled up the plaid sleeves. The attendant spotted the Bulova on his left wrist at the same moment that Haggerty wished he had removed it. 'Nice watch you got there.'

'Present from my daddy.'

'Sure,' the attendant said dryly. He examined the unmarked arms and dropped them. 'Okay,' he said. He drew a form out from the desk drawer.

'You anaemic?'

'No, I ain't.'

'Ever had syphilis?'

'No, sir.'

'Are you taking any regular medication at this time?' Haggerty shook his head. The attendant took up a ballpoint.

'Name?'

'Hayes. Stephen Hayes. 39 Wheeler Avenue. Miami Beach.'

After taking a birth date and weight, the attendant gestured to a trolley in the corner. 'Okay, over there. We need a blood sample.'

Haggerty rolled up his sleeve. The attendant corded his arm with a rubber tube, brushed a little anaesthetic on the vein and sank the needle in.

'Tests take up to an hour,' he said, squeezing the blood from the syringe into a phial. 'Want to wait?'

Haggerty nodded. He took the offered cotton wool as the

attendant went through a rear door with the phial. Keeping his arm bent, Haggerty sat down on the empty bench. The other prospective donors examined him but soon lost interest. The attendant returned, took up his magazine again and began reading. Silence settled on the room.

Haggerty forced himself to wait for at least ten minutes. Finally he rose to his feet.

'Gotta use the washroom,' he announced. The attendant looked up, annoyed.

'Back there,' he said sourly, pointing at the rear door, 'just make sure you keep it clean.'

Haggerty nodded. He went through the door and entered a long green corridor. It seemed to run the length of the building. He walked quickly towards the rear, ignoring the washroom.

He reached the door at the end. It was unlocked. He opened it gently. He was looking into a large empty storeroom with a small mountain of cardboard boxes stacked in the centre. He hesitated for a moment then slipped through. Closing the door quietly behind him he crossed to the carton stack. A quick examination showed the boxes were empty. The cartons were labelled Mayburn Plasma Clinic in black lettering. On the bottom of each was the name of the supplier. The Purax Plasma Corporation, Guatemala City. He was on the right track. He circled the stack, searching. There were no other names. Glancing quickly about he found nothing else of interest in the room. The walls were bare except for a double exit door and a smaller door with a small glass panel on it to his right. Preparing to hurry back to the waiting room, Haggerty shot a quick glance through the glass. He stopped dead.

'Jesus!' he breathed. He stared through the glass.

A woman lay in the centre of a small, narrow room. She was in a rubber hammock suspended from four upright chrome poles on a medical trolley. What stunned Haggerty was that she was awash in her own blood. It had settled in the bottom of the hammock around her arms and legs, gleaming red in the fluorescent light. On one of the woman's hands, a gold wedding ring shone among the stained fingers. Her eyes were half closed but Haggerty could see her lips were barely moving. He realised

46

that she was praying. And close to death. He grabbed for the door handle.

'Hey, you!'

Haggerty looked back to see the white-smocked attendant at the far door.

'Get away from that door!' he shouted. 'Hey, Tony. Get down here!'

Anger swept Haggerty. 'What's the matter with you? There's a woman dying here. She needs help.'

A second white-coated man joined the first. As they crossed the floor, Haggerty turned back and began tugging at the locked door. Suddenly, he was grabbed by the shoulder, swung around and slammed against the wall. The burly attendant from the front office pinned him tight.

'Are you guys crazy? Let me go!' Haggerty struggled to free himself. 'That woman is bleeding to death.'

A scalpel appeared in the burly man's hand. Quickly, he brought the point to Haggerty's throat. Haggerty froze.

'That's it, fella.' The attendant had a hard smile behind the shining blade. 'Just take it nice and easy.'

Haggerty's mouth was dry. The cold concrete pressed on the back of his neck as he tried to hold his throat away from the knife.

'Hold it, man,' he said, heart pounding, 'I'm staying cool.'

His captor grinned.

'I'm glad,' he said. 'Now you want to tell me what the game is? Not satisfied with what you get out front, is that it?'

'No,' Haggerty said, his eyes on the scalpel, 'I'm a television reporter.'

The attendant's smile faded. He glanced at his partner. Haggerty felt the hesitation.

'What the hell are you talking about?' the other man, Tony, asked harshly.

'It's the truth,' Haggerty said. 'I'm doing a story on the blood trade in Florida. I have a crew outside.' He lowered his head as the scalpel moved back. 'You guys could pick up a heap of trouble on this one.'

The attendant lowered the scalpel.

'Don't let go of him, Mel,' Tony said warningly. Mel tightened his grip on Haggerty's shirt front.

'I'm telling the truth. I swear it, guys,' Haggerty said. 'You can see my I.D.' He reached down as if for his wallet, moving his body out from the wall. The attendant's grip loosened for an instant.

Haggerty ran his knee up, hard. He felt it slam into the soft underflesh. The attendant screamed, his grip falling away.

Haggerty's shoulder bounced off his chest, sending him crashing into the other attendant. The two men reeled back, tangling with each other.

Haggerty scrambled by them running for the office door. As he neared it, another attendant suddenly appeared in the entrance.

'Get him!' he heard Tony scream. 'Don't let him get away!'

Haggerty spun, scattering cartons, scrambling through them towards the rear exit. He reached it, hitting the safety bar. The door swung open and he reeled out into blinding sunshine. For a moment he almost lost his balance but he recovered. Turning quickly, he just managed to slam the door shut in the face of the men following. The roar of pain from inside told him he had made contact. It brought a quick grin to his face. Bastards.

Turning from the door, he sprinted down the narrow lane leading off to his left. The ground was rough and broken with random weeds sprouting along the high walls. He ran its length until it made a dogleg to the right. He rounded the corner and stopped. He was in a dead end.

'Shit!'

The crumbling walls, separating once proud family homes, were too high to climb. He was trapped. With his pursuers closing, he had nowhere to turn. Then he spotted a small wooden door barely ajar in the wall near the end of the alley. He ran towards it and found it was open. He pushed through and closed it behind him, standing against it, panting.

He was in a small well-kept garden. And he had company. A stout black woman tending plants was staring up at him. She was only a few feet away. Almost exhausted, Haggerty gestured behind him.

'Please,' he said, 'I need help.'

The shouting was closer, the noise of scuffling feet louder.

The woman hardly hesitated. 'In there.' She pointed to the house door. He ran, reaching it and entered a dark passage. Pressed against the wall, he tried to control his breathlessness as he saw the door in the wall being pushed open and the burly Mel with the others enter the garden.

'What you people want?' he heard the woman shout. 'You get out of my garden or I call the cops. You hear! Right now!'

Without waiting to hear the outcome, Haggerty ran down the hall where flowers stood on a table under a religious picture. He opened the front door and found himself on a stoop facing a small street. Closing the door as quietly as possible, he ran north to the street where he had parked his car. No one followed. But he didn't slow. He found the car almost round the corner. He drew his keys, opened the door and jumped in.

He was just pulling away from the kerb when two of the white-coated attendants ran onto the street ahead of him. Haggerty sent the car into a squealing U-turn and accelerated away from them. He plunged into the first convenient side-street. Making random turns he kept going with his eyes on the rear mirror until he felt safe.

Slowing down, he began searching for a phone booth. It took three stops and more than five minutes before he found one that worked.

'I want to report what looks like a stabbing victim in the Mayburn Clinic on Risdon Avenue.' He told the police despatcher. He kept his eyes on the street as he spoke.

'Your name, sir?'

'Stephen Haggerty. Listen, you must hurry. I think the woman was dying.'

'Don't worry, sir. We're on our way. Your address, please?'

'I'm staying at the Miridiana motel.'

'Are you connected with the clinic, sir?'

'No. Look, this is really urgent.'

'I understand. Where can we contact you?'

'I'll be at the clinic,' Haggerty said and hung up.

When he found his way back to the Mayburn, a patrol car and an ambulance were already parked outside. Even he hadn't expected that response time. He got out of the car and approached the policeman who stood resting against his patrol car with arms folded.

'Hi, my name is Stephen Haggerty. I called you. Is the woman all right?'

The policeman straightened and dropped his arms. His dark Latin face was unfriendly, the expression hostile.

'So you're the son-of-a-bitch who made the call,' he said sourly. 'I ought to book you. Don't you know the penalty for bogus calls?'

Haggerty stared.

'What?'

'There's no injured woman in there.'

'Hey, hold on now, that's not true,' Haggerty said, recovering. 'I saw her myself.'

The policeman stared at him. 'Is that so?' He turned towards the ambulance. 'Hey, you back there!' he called. The white-coated attendant, Mel, who had held the scalpel to Haggerty's throat, came forward. The policeman pointed to Haggerty.

'Is this the creep?'

Mel nodded quickly. 'That's him, officer. We caught him sneaking into the back of the store-rooms.'

The policeman turned to Haggerty. 'He said you came in as a donor. Gave your name as Stephen Hayes. That correct, Mr Haggerty?' he emphasised the different name.

'Yes,' Haggerty said. 'I gave the name Hayes because I was looking for information that I wouldn't have gotten in any other way.'

'Sure,' the policeman said sceptically, looking at Haggerty's shabby clothes. 'Say you're a reporter, eh?'

'That's right.'

'So where's this crew you said you had with you? They take a powder or what?'

Haggerty pointed to Mel. 'That guy was holding a knife on me. What the hell would you expect me to do?'

The policeman's face flushed angrily. 'Listen, you prick. You made me search a building looking for a woman who doesn't exist.' He leaned forward close to Haggerty. 'I'd like to book you.

But these people here,' he gestured to Mel, 'have enough trouble from bastards like you. They don't need any more.'

'They're lying,' Haggerty said heatedly. 'I saw that woman. She was dying. I saw her with my own eyes.'

'You want to get booked?' the policeman asked menacingly.

'I tell you I am a reporter. I've been checking out the Mayburn Clinic.' He searched his mind for some proof. He had deliberately left his wallet behind. 'Look, I'm even doing research on it at the *Miami Sentinel*. You can prove that by asking. I've an appointment there tomorrow morning. You've got to believe me.'

'Get out of my sight!' the policeman roared in exasperation. 'If you turn up in this district again, I'll kick the shit out of you!' He dropped his hand to his nightstick. 'Move!'

Back at the car, Haggerty banged his fist in frustration on the steering wheel. The policeman stared coldly at him as he drove away.

Inside the clinic, the first rivulet of blood seeped out from beneath the piled cartons in the centre of the store-room.

4

'Hello?'

It was just past eleven o'clock in the morning and traffic was heavy at Miami Airport. But William Masters hardly noticed the throng passing the booth. His eyes had the glazed, tired look of someone totally immersed in an inner world. His restless fingers twirled and twisted the telephone cord as he waited.

He was remembering again the awful scene he witnessed on that first night at Dackman's villa. He couldn't get it out of his mind. If only it hadn't happened, he kept thinking. If only he had stayed in the clinic in Syracuse and refused Korner's request for help. If only now he could turn back the clock ... the mingled miseries ran like a ceaseless torrent through his head.

He couldn't get the affair out of his mind. Something like that had never happened to him before. He had never witnessed anything like it. Given his precarious mental state, it was a miracle he got through the night that followed. It had taken the mickey of rye he carried to survive. But on top of that was yesterday. With nothing to drink. That was the real nightmare. Dackman had disappeared early in the day. And, as the hours wore on, no boat turned up to take him back to the mainland. They had stranded him. High and dry was the best description. By last night, he had come to believe it was deliberate. It was almost as if they were manipulating him, orchestrating a new breakdown.

Well, it hadn't happened.

'Cal, is that you?' Finally, the familiar voice. For the first time in two days, William Masters felt a glimmer of relief from the preying torments. Cal was someone he could count on.

'William? Where the hell are you?'

'At Miami Airport,' William Masters said. Suddenly he was speaking in a rush. 'I'm just back from the islands, Cal. I've been there the last two days. Korner sent me to do that job he talked to you about. Listen, I've got to talk to you.'

'Wait a minute, slow down.' There was a hint of impatience in Cal's voice. 'What's this job you're talking about?'

'Korner sent me down here to assess someone.' He forced himself to take things more slowly. 'Listen, is this line secure?'

'Thanks for asking,' Cal said reproachfully. 'Yes.'

'Sorry,' he said. This was getting off on the wrong foot. 'Korner said he mentioned something about this job to you.'

'Korner?' Cal said. There was a pause as he thought about it. 'I remember he called a week or so ago. To ask if you might do some work for him. But he didn't say what it was.'

'Cal, something's happened. Something very unusual. I've got to talk with you.'

'Have you been drinking again?' Cal asked suddenly.

William Masters caught his breath. 'No,' he said. It would complicate things to say otherwise.

'Well, what's the problem?'

'Look, I saw my subject down here.' He wanted to stay in control now. It was important not to arouse doubts in Cal's mind, not to divert him from the issue. 'He was supposed to demonstrate that he could do a particular job for Korner.'

'What kind of job?'

William Masters paused.

'Take out,' he said.

There was silence on the line.

'My God,' Cal said.

'Listen, Cal, something happened I didn't count on when I was with this guy.' He paused. 'You're sure this line's secure?'

'I told you, yes,' Cal said harshly.

'Something terrible happened, Cal. A man was killed. Right in front of me. I'm implicated, Cal. And I'm not sure why. That's why we need to talk.'

'Do I know this guy you saw?'

'I don't think so. He's a medic. Who's worked in Central America.'

'The name, William.' Suddenly, Cal sounded different. It was as though he knew something that William Masters didn't.

'It's Dackman. Ernst Dackman.'

He heard the slow expelling of breath on the other end of the line.

'Cal?'

'Listen, William,' Cal said, 'what are your plans?'

'I need to come and see you.'

'When?'

'This afternoon.'

Cal seemed to hesitate. 'That's pushing it,' he said finally. 'What about later in the week?'

'No,' William Masters said stubbornly. This was not turning out right either. 'I'm coming up today.'

He left the phone booth, hiked the overnight bag on his shoulder and began to move through the crowds. Now even Cal was sounding strange. Or was he really? Maybe it was him. Getting paranoiac, even suffering from delusions. That hadn't happened to him before. Could it be a new stage?

He wandered along the busy walkways, aimless, hardly seeing anything in front of him. Suddenly, his vision cleared. He saw the dimly lit bar counter open to the busy hall on his right. He stopped, then finally shrugged and walked in. Slipping off the bag, he took a stool. The barman glanced towards him, eyebrows raised. William Masters rested both palms on the counter and offered a strained smile. 'Just a small glass of white wine, please,' he said.

The barman nodded and reached up for the Gallo.

Why did they always have to pretend, he wondered.

He missed two flights.

The working day was ending in the capital when he finally got to the Sam Rayburn building. The departing staff hurried by him as he walked down the long corridors. Although Masters's face had a darkish flush by now, the wine had brought him to an equilibrium. You had to be familiar with his type to know that he had been drinking. For himself, he felt almost normal, which was unusual given the stress he was under. He thought that if he was careful, Cal would not notice.

The door of the spacious corner suite was open. A young secretary whom he had never seen before, glanced up when he entered.

'I'm here to see Congressman Masters,' he said. 'I'm Cal's brother, William.'

'Oh,' she said. 'It's nice to meet you, Mr Masters. I'm afraid the Congressman isn't here.'

Masters was surprised. 'But he knew I was coming.'

She nodded. 'I know. But he had to leave. He left a message for you.' He took the envelope and opened the note.

William,
    I'm sorry, but something has come up. I couldn't wait to see you. Please don't make any moves until we talk. It's very important. Just take it easy and wait. I'll be in touch.

                                                    Cal

Masters looked at it, biting his lip. Aloud, he asked, 'Where's he gone? Do you know?'

'I'm afraid not. He left no indication.'

Alarm bells were going off in William Masters's mind. But the wine was now a safety harness, and the agitation did not show. He thanked the secretary and left.

Outside, he re-read the note. Make no moves, Cal said. Moves? Didn't Cal know the problems he was facing? Annoyed now and beginning to get more tense, Masters crossed the parkway beneath the huge dome of the Capitol. The yellowing winter sun glanced off it, throwing long curling shadows. But he didn't see that. He was immersed again in his thoughts. The more he considered the situation, the more he knew he needed help. Regardless of what Cal said. And he knew who the best man would be to talk with. He found a phone booth and called Vernon Railsback.

'Vern, you old scoundrel,' he said, hearing the clipped Boston accent. 'Say hello to your old Kwaegor room mate.'

55

'Bill? Billy Masters, is that you?'

'You got it,' Masters said. Hearing Railsback's voice warmed him again. It was almost fifteen years since the two of them worked at a remote listening station in Thailand compiling a study of Soviet/Chinese military preparedness. After their careers had gone different ways in the service, they met only rarely. But it had not spoiled their friendship.

'I heard you were in dry dock,' Vern Railsback said delicately. 'You okay now?'

'Fine,' Masters said. 'Listen, pal. I need help. I'm afraid I've got a new problem now.'

'My God, Billy, you know how to pile them up,' Railsback laughed, amused but sympathetic. 'What is it? Myra? Or one of the old girlfriends?' William Masters had had a number of affairs during his drinking years.

'I wish it was,' Masters said sincerely, 'but it's not. I'm afraid it's more serious.'

'I'm sorry to hear that, pal. What can I do to help?'

'I need some information. About a guy who's involved with the people in Western Hemisphere. You might even know him from your time there.'

'Who are we looking at?'

'Okay to give his name?' Masters asked.

'Yeah.'

'He's a doctor, an American, who's living down south. I understand he's well connected in Guatemala.'

'It's not Ern Dackman, is it?'

Jesus, everyone seemed to know this guy but him.

'How the hell did you know that?'

'Don't ask. But let me tell you this, Billy. If you're involved with that guy, you do have a problem.' He paused. 'We should talk.'

The black Corvette drew up by the Burlington Hotel on Washington's Massachusetts Avenue. William Masters, waiting under the awning, hurried across the sidewalk as Vern Railsback opened the door.

'Jesus, this town gets colder every year.' Masters slid into the front seat. 'Thank's for coming, pal.'

Railsback slapped his shoulder affectionately. He smiled, the dark eyes warm, the even, white teeth showing. He was small but his body was well proportioned and he took good care of it. He was dressed in a black leather jacket, flaming pink shirt with a dark woollen tie and grey pants. His thin blond hair was cut short over a pink scalp. 'Your goddamn blood must be thinning out, Billy,' he said. 'Getting old. Still, it's good to see you.'

They pulled away from the sidewalk. Traffic was light and there were few people about. 'Where do you want to go?' Vern asked.

'Makes no difference,' Masters said. 'How about Georgetown?'

'Can't,' Vern said. 'Andy's bringing home some students of his for dinner tonight. I've got some preparations to do.'

'Finally domesticated, eh?'

Vern grinned. 'I kinda like it.'

'Let's just drive about,' Masters suggested. He had to hope the smell of the wine wouldn't carry in the car.

'I really admire the way you threw over the booze, Billy,' Vern said as if he had picked up on his thought. That wasn't likely. Masters remembered he had always been easy to fool on that score. It used to trouble him afterwards because he really liked Vern. Now, it made him uncomfortable again. They stopped for a red light. 'I had doubts, you know,' Vern said, glancing across at him, 'but you did it. That took real guts.'

'Don't make me blush.' Masters kept his head away.

Vern shook his head. 'It was going to kill you, man. You did the right thing.' The lights changed and they moved forward again.

'It was tough, Vern, to tell the truth. Still is,' Masters said. Why was he saying this? He shook his head. 'I don't think I could go through it again,' he found himself saying.

'What the hell, you did it,' Vern said, 'and I'm really glad.'

They headed down Massachusetts Avenue.

'Well, what have you got for me?' Masters asked, glad now to drop the subject. 'Apart from that sermonising?'

57

Vern laughed, a soft laugh. He lit a cigarette, squinting to watch the traffic in the rising smoke.

'You've got a real bad one in this Ernst Dackman, Billy. That's a guy the world would never miss. You should watch out. Dackman's hung out a lot of people to dry in his time.' The buildings around them were grey and drab in the fading light. The leafless trees on the sidewalk waved in the wind.

'What's his background?'

'Surprisingly, he's a local boy,' Vern said. 'From Baltimore. Belongs to the time when the Agency was recruiting openly. Seems he was a medical corpsman in the Korean War. He was trying to get through Georgetown medical school on a vet's grant. But he was a hopeless student. I'm told he was on his last chance when they picked him up.' A spattering of rain struck the windscreen. Vern switched on the wipers.

'What did he do for them?'

'He was an informant. For the House Un-American Activities Committee. From reports I've seen, the little bastard turned everybody in. But Korner, who was running domestic spying at the time, liked his style. It seems he wasn't without balls. And he was streetwise. So they took him on full-time.' They turned off Massachusetts Avenue.

'They put him through medical school,' Vern said. 'Except his real job was spying on the student body. My guess is that they had to put the fix in to get him a degree. Not that that would worry Korner any.'

Masters nodded.

'His career took off when they made him a supplementary medical officer on the Bay of Pigs operation. That's how he learned his Spanish. Then they planted him in the World Health Organisation. Philip Agee actually named him as CIA when he served in Honduras. But nobody seemed to notice. That was just before he went into the commercial blood business.'

'Commercial blood?'

Railsback nodded. 'That's where he made his bucks. And big ones I hear. He opened up donor clinics in Columbia, Nicaragua and Guatemala. Then he sold the product in Europe. He ran tens of thousands of people through his plasma mills. He had them in the *barrios* down there, complete with barkers luring in clients. Or so they say. As for his safety standards, they were zip. He didn't have to maintain any – the fix was in with the health people. And I don't have to tell you how easy that is in the Americas.'

'What about the work you said he did for us?'

'I'm told there were questions about that. Some said it wasn't worth a shit. But he did have connections with the higher ups. Particularly in Guatemala. Of course, he could afford to buy his way in. I understand he became a millionaire very early on. Since then he's improved it a couple of times over.' They drove through a ghetto area where Washington's blacks were crowded into battered housing. Masters stared at the sagging buildings and the car wrecks.

'Vern, I've got to know,' he said finally. 'Is Dackman still working for the Agency?'

'Jesus, Billy, you of all people ought to know better. I have no idea. He could be. But it would have to be under very deep cover.'

They were returning in a circle to Massachusetts Avenue. Vern turned north heading for the hotel.

'Vern, I need your best opinion. Could Dackman be part of an assassination plan cooked up by the Agency?'

Railsback looked at him in surprise. 'You putting me on?'

Masters shook his head. 'I'm serious.'

Railsback shrugged. 'It's possible, I suppose. It really depends on who the target is.'

'Well, it was never said directly. But I understand it's Guatemala's top man. General Serena.'

Railsback snorted. 'Now you are putting me on.'

'It's true,' Masters insisted. 'I met Dackman only two days ago. And from my understanding that was the purpose of our meeting.'

'Jesus.' Railsback stared ahead. Finally, he shook his head. 'No way, Billy. Serena is the Agency's point man in Central America. It makes no sense to kill him. Korner would never go along.'

No, Masters thought, he wouldn't. But he didn't say anything.

'Does Cal know about this?' Vern asked.

'That's the next problem. I have a feeling he might, but he's not telling me.'

'Well, you've got to sling it to him, man. He's not vice-chairman of that fucking Intelligence Committee for show.'

'I can't. He's gone out of circulation.'

'You won't have any problem finding him, Billy. I liaised with those people at one time. He has to stay in contact with the Committee. Call the counsel, Wil Harper. He'll know where he is.'

They were nearing the hotel.

'Listen, Billy,' Vern said, 'I'm sorry about this. But I got to leave.'

Masters nodded.

'I'd bow out if I were you, pal,' Vern said, 'and I'd consider doing it pretty fast. What you're into sounds pretty hairy to me. And the days of surviving embarrassing connections in this town are over.'

They had reached the Burlington Hotel again. Vern pulled in to the kerb, the motor running.

'Vern, there are some important people in on this thing,' Masters said. 'But what you're saying worries me. Because if they're not going to snuff Serena as you suggest, then who the hell is the real target?'

'I can't help you there, pal.'

'Could you make a few more enquiries?'

Vern Railsback turned in his seat. 'Look, Billy. I love you like a brother. I mean that. You've been one of my really good friends over the years. You stuck by me during the times when very few people cared to sit in the same office with me. I've never forgotten that. I still appreciate it and I would dearly like to help you. But what you're talking about isn't on. I just don't want to buy a problem like that. I'm sorry, very sorry that you're in this situation. But I don't want the trouble that will come from what you're asking. You understand?'

'You're right. I'm sorry.'

'It's okay.' Vern smiled. He looked at his watch. 'Hey, I must go.' He held out his hand. 'Listen, old buddy. Don't leave it so long between visits, okay?'

'Sure,' William Masters said, opening the door. He leaned

across and chucked his friend on the arm. 'Don't forget to say hello to Andy for me.'

Vern smiled wryly. 'If the pot roast isn't on when he gets home, it will be more like goodbye. Take care, Billy. And have a strong talk with your brother.'

'I intend to. Where's Wil Harper living now?'

'Chevy Chase,' he said. 'You leaving or staying in town?'

'I think I'll overnight here.'

Vern grinned and winked.

'Say hello to Alva for me.'

But William had something else in mind.

He called Harper from the lobby of the Burlington. Cal's whereabouts turned out to be no problem. But it was a surprise. He was in the Hyatt Regency Hotel. In New Orleans.

Damn him, William Masters thought. What the hell is going on? Before he went to his room, he dropped by the liquor store. Later, he called the airline and booked an early morning flight to Louisiana.

5

It was a shame, going indoors on a warm, cloudless morning like this but Stephen Haggerty could take it. Along with blue skies and sunshine, newspaper libraries like the *Miami Sentinel's* stood high on his list of pleasures. He loved them. If you knew where to look, you could find embarrassing treasure trove in their packed files. Items like court cases that important men thought best forgotten; political promises that fell flat; deals that went sour and even relationships, once trumpeted, which could return to haunt the participants. Haggerty was prurient enough to enjoy them all.

A library put him in mind of a respectable, somewhat dowdy lady, who peered out quietly at the world but hid some terrible secrets beneath her skirts. 'Oh Lord! How could corruption lodge beneath so fair a form?' Boswell once cried in anguish after an encounter with a modest gentlewoman of his acquaintance. She would have fitted Haggerty's notion of a good library.

At 10 a.m. the *Sentinel's* library looked anything but scandalous. It filled a long, airy room with walls of pale yellow and wide, plant-filled windows. The librarian, Harold Leese, was a large, middle-aged man with grey hair and horn-rimmed glasses. The slim Dackman clippings that Haggerty had come to see were already on his desk.

'You'll have to wait a while before you can see the general blood files,' he said. 'There's a lady using them just now.'

He indicated a dark head bent over a file at one of the reading desks under the windows. Haggerty nodded and took his clippings to an adjoining desk. He saw at a glance that only one was important. It was a wire service story. And almost eight months old.

The Congressional Committee on Health, Education and Welfare rejected a request from Guatemalan exile groups yesterday for a US ban on imports of human blood plasma from that strife-torn Central American republic. The Committee said that Congress had no right to interfere with a legitimate trade that conformed with Federal regulations.

The exiles charged that the trade exploited Guatemala's poor and benefitted the country's dictator, General Antonio Serena, who is a major shareholder in the company exporting most of the plasma.

The exiles identified that company as the Purax Corporation of Guatemala. They said its two owners were Alessandro Cordillera, a nominee of General Serena, and a Miami medical practitioner and former WHO consultant, Dr Ernst Dackman, now domiciled in Guatemala City.

The Guatemalans' effort failed when Republican members of the Committee voiced strong opposition. Florida Congressman Caleb Masters said that cutting off trade could leave the US open to compensation claims under the Hickenlooper Amendment. He added that while he personally found the trade distasteful, he would consider it even more distasteful if the Government had to pay a company not to carry it out.

A picture of Congressman Masters appeared alongside the story. With sudden shock, Haggerty realised he had seen the man before. He was in the photograph with Ernst Dackman and Otto Lentz at the opening of Dackman's Bayview office. He made a note to find out more about the Congressman.

Even with that, it still looked like he had made a wasted journey. The *Sentinel's* library was not fulfilling the usual promise. His only hope now lay in the general files. Sometimes, newspaper cross-referencing wasn't what it should be. He glanced across and saw that the girl reading the files still had a way to go. There was nothing to do but wait.

With no reason to hurry, he put his hands behind his head and sat back in the chair. The subdued activity of people adding fresh clippings to the files in the well-oiled filing cabinets and the low toned conversations around the room, had a soothing effect. In this atmosphere, it was even harder to believe in the events of yesterday. The nightmarish encounter with the bleeding woman and the ugly scenes that followed were the stuff of bad dreams. It seemed an age now since they happened. And even more since Montreal.

Suddenly, bizarrely, he was thinking of Sheila Blais. They had spent time in Key West just after they met. She had been marvellous then. Young, driving, insatiably curious about life. And funny. They had some good times in that first year. Sensuous days. Making love, drinking, doing a little dope, all the time moving about. She never let him feel his age. Lulled by the memory, Haggerty began to forget his surroundings. But then a face suddenly swam into his vision. Soft dark eyes and creamy skin. With a shock, he realised that the girl with the blood files had raised her head. As his eyes focused on her, she looked down again.

Christ, she was lovely. He lowered his arms and watched her as she read. Finally, he rose and crossed the polished floor. He stopped by her desk.

'Hi,' he smiled when she looked up. 'You must have thought I was staring at you a moment ago.'

'No bother,' she said. 'They haven't made it an offence yet.' Her voice was soft, pleasant-sounding. The face was everything he had glimpsed at a distance. Haggerty guessed she was Hispanic and about twenty-eight years old. She had delicately tanned skin and almost almond eyes hinting Chinese ancestry. She wore a loose-fitting purple dress with a clipped silk scarf at the neck. He pulled himself away from the examination.

'I was daydreaming,' he said. 'About an ex-girl friend. She came in through that window of yours and ended up here.' He tapped his forehead.

She smiled, faintly showing perfect teeth. 'You sound like the *Sentinel's* lonely hearts man.'

He laughed and shook his head. 'No. I'm visiting. From Montreal.'

'You're a long way from home.' She raised a slender hand, the nails clear and unpainted, to push back her long hair. 'Escaping the weather up there, eh?'

'Right.' He gestured to the clippings on the desktop. 'I actually came here to see those files you're working on. Are you likely to be long?'

She looked at him. 'You came to Miami to see these?'

'Well, that weather you mentioned was an incentive,' he smiled. 'Do you suppose we could share?'

She shrugged, a mingle of grace and amiability.

'Don't see why not. I've finished with most of them.' She riffled through a pile. 'I can let you have everything up to 1978. That okay?'

'Sure.' He pulled out a chair. 'Why don't I sit here? There seems to be room.'

She looked at him, faintly amused. 'That's a bit pushy, don't you think?'

'No question about it.' He held out a hand. 'Stephen Haggerty. Canadian Broadcasting Corporation.'

'Oh?' She shook hands. Working on television broke a lot of ice, Haggerty found.

He nodded. 'And you?'

'Eva Valdes. I'm a researcher. Working for the medical department, University of Miami.'

'That's why you're looking at the files?'

'Yeah. I'm checking every promotional campaign run by the Red Cross since 1965. One of my professors is preparing another one of those papers that nobody reads.' She grimaced. 'On the whole, I'd rather be in Philadelphia.' She divided the bundle of clippings and pushed most of them across. 'There you go. I hope you get more out of them than I did.'

'Thanks.' Haggerty dropped his notebook and pen on the desk and began reading.

The earlier clippings from the sixties did deal mainly with blood donor drives and Red Cross appeals, as the girl said. And they were boring. It was only when he reached the seventies that Haggerty saw a new and more interesting pattern emerging. It was the kind of pattern you almost always missed in daily newspapers when the stories were small and widely scattered geographically. You only saw it when all the reports were gathered together in one file. Then the significance became apparent. In this case, it was a slowly developing drought in human blood which began in the United States and spread around the world.

In the first reports of shortages in the early seventies, the Vietnam war was blamed for taking millions of potential donors out of the US market. Then came sophisticated new operations for heart and cancer diseases which used up an increasing share of the existing supply. Following that came revolutionary new drug therapy which gave a higher life expectancy to haemophiliacs. There were up to 300,000 worldwide and all of them needed regular stocks of plasma to stay alive.

All of these technical advances came on stream so quickly that the blood gathering industry was caught unprepared. They could not cope with demand. By the early seventies, medical statisticians reckoned that operations, often requiring up to thirty pints of blood per patient, were taking place every six seconds in some part of the world. In very short order, the international health community woke up to find that there just wasn't enough blood to go round.

Reading about it, Stephen Haggerty suddenly understood why entrepreneurs like Otto Lentz had begun pumping blood out of the Third World. With the wild seller's market, these men were in on a bloody, even ghoulish equivalent of the Californian goldrush. And the clippings from the time outlined just how profitable the business was. Blood bought for $2 to $4 a pint from impoverished peasants and slum-dwellers in Latin America or Africa could be sold for $20 to $40 a pint on the European market where the giant drug companies turned them into blood-based drugs for use in the hospitals and pharmacies of the Western World. Few of those wealthy enough to buy them in the United States realised they were ingesting the blood of some Bogotá prostitute or a cave-dwelling Bolivian Indian.

'Red Gold' was what one enterprising reporter called the massive outflow from the underdeveloped countries which

66

American blood bankers admitted ran into hundreds of millions of dollars annually.

The *Sentinel* provided good coverage of the blood trade because – as Gedi Reubel told Haggerty in Montreal – Florida was the transhipment centre for blood moving between Latin America and Europe. And while the *Sentinel* monitored the trade, it also noted the scandals which erupted as brokers rushed to cater for the insatiable demand for blood from the developed countries. Some examples were horrifying. In Haiti, for instance, over-zealous Miami brokers set up dawn-to-dusk clinics. In little more than a year they bled over 180,000 Haitians who were herded through the clinics by club-wielding guards and paid as little as $2.50 for each litre of blood extracted.

The newspaper also pinpointed the activities of another Florida broker – an exiled Cuban – who was mercilessly exposed in a Nicaraguan daily for the primitive conditions under which he bled tens of thousands in the capital of Managua. The furious broker turned on his tormentor, newspaper publisher, Pedro Chamorro. With the aid of hired killers, Chamorro was assassinated. The broker, Pedro Ramos, was convicted of murder but he had already fled Nicaragua for Silver Springs, Florida, and never served his sentence.

All over Florida, there were cases of blood violations reported as the demand for plasma stayed high. In California, the *Sentinel* reported, blood was being extracted from corpses. In Maine, blood samples from hospitalised patients were being pooled by technicians and secretly sold. In New Jersey, it was underweight and undernourished donors who sold their blood. One woman cited weighed less than 100 pounds. Another had no colon.

While Haggerty noted the frequent raids by government agencies and closures of blood banks, this only gradually began to solve the problem within the United States itself. But the European transhipments from Central America, and increasingly from Guatemala, continued unabated.

However, there was no further mention of Ernst Dackman in any of the reports.

'I'm going for a coffee.'

Haggerty looked up.

'Can I get you one?' Eva Valdes asked.

'Thanks.' He guessed she would have felt embarrassed to drink one opposite him without making the offer.

Temporarily forgetting his work, he watched her cross the room to the coffee machine. She was taller than she appeared sitting down. Those long legs. Her purple dress, loose at the arms, showed off her shapely breasts. She moved like a gymnast. His eyes were still on her when she returned.

'You're staring again,' she said as she set down the styrofoam cups. 'I'd watch it. That could be habit-forming.'

He smiled, watching her slide behind the desk. She gestured to the clippings. 'Find anything useful?'

'Well, some of this stuff is really fascinating. But it's not exactly what I'm looking for.'

'Maybe these will help.' She pushed across the clippings she had been reading. 'I'm just about finished with them.'

He ran quickly through the bundle. Again no mention of Dackman. He tidied the stack. 'Nothing here either. I guess I'm out of luck.'

She raised her cup to her lips.

'Do you specialise in medical stories?'

He shook his head. 'No. I do just about anything that will get people to watch the box. Television is a barker's business.'

'Still, interesting,' she said. The dark glossy hair bounced softly on her shoulders as she shook her head in disgust. 'Not like the garbage I'm saddled with.'

The way she told it, as they drank their coffee, there wasn't a lot of satisfaction in what she did except that she made more money than when she was a secretary. Scholarly people were not great company, she explained.

That probably explained why they became scholarly in the first place, Haggerty said. She laughed at that.

They began to talk more as the morning sunlight filtered through the plant-filled window. In the background, faint metallic sounds floated up as filing cabinets were opened and shut. She moved the notebook around to make room for her coffee.

'I did think this job was going to be interesting when I took it.

68

You know, research, making big discoveries, that kind of stuff. And travel too. University people are always having conferences. But it hasn't turned out that way.' She smiled at him, the faintest crinkling around the dark eyes. 'You've done better than me just by coming to Miami. The farthest I ever got was Dearborn, Michigan.'

'That's tough. Being nailed to the same place.'

She nodded. 'I guess you spend a lot of time travelling.'

'Not as much as I used to.' He gave it a thought. 'Longest was two years in Asia. But that was a long time ago.'

'I've always wanted to see those places. Where were you?'

'Vietnam.'

'Oh.' She looked at him. 'Dangerous, eh?'

He began telling her a little about it. The talk came easy. Stories slipping into his consciousness now as smoothly as the nightmares did in his final months there before the breakdown. He told her the funny stories. About making the copper still that would only produce green booze; about Malvan's toilet seat that was specially made to burn the commanding general's ass; about all those odd intervals of fun and games that usually comprised the best part of war memories. He even told her how he once ran away from a battle, but that wasn't as successful as the other stories although she still laughed.

He noticed how soft her lips were, almost purple against the golden skin. She had a habit of rubbing her upper teeth against her lower lip as she listened. Occasionally, she would stir with sudden grace as she changed position or raised a hand to toss her black mane back. Since they seemed to be in tune, he asked her to lunch.

'Well,' she said, pretending a little shock. He waited as she pulled the clippings together. After a moment, she looked up. And grinned.

'What the hell,' she said. 'Why not?'

The lunch might have gone either way. If it hadn't been for the scar.

It lay at the lower end of her throat. A small webbed blemish about the size of a quarter. Someone must have worked on her trachea when she was young. The silk scarf had hidden it when they were in the library. But now as they sat in the beachside restaurant she took it off with a kind of defiant tug from her wrist. He knew she was watching him.

'Things like that worry some people,' he said, looking up. 'How about you?'

'No. It doesn't bother me,' she said, her head raised a little.

He nodded, remembering. 'I had an Aunt Rita with the same thing when I was a kid. Wild lady. She caught me peeking at it one morning when she was in bed. I felt really embarrassed at being caught but she roared with laughter. 'Stevie,' she said to me, 'marks like that come to a body that's been well lived in. Don't be ashamed to look. When you grow up and meet women, take my advice, child, and never trust any of 'em without a scar. If they're real, they have them.'

Haggerty looked at Eva Valdes and grinned. 'From what I've seen she was right, of course.' He nodded at the scar. 'You're lucky to be alive, aren't you?'

'It was very close,' she said. He saw that she was smiling. 'Diphtheria.' She touched her breast. 'Lucky, I had one of those hearts that wouldn't quit.'

She had needed it along with the rest of the family after they arrived from Puerto Rico. Her father had been offered a job in Tampa, that disappeared shortly after his arrival. From high hopes they were plunged into disaster.

'Being an out-of-work Hispanic with very little English and a large family to support was no picnic. Especially for my father. We went through some very bad times. Living on welfare, picking up all the diseases like diphtheria, just struggling to survive.'

'Did your father get work eventually?'

'No. Poor man, he died.' She grimaced. 'He never forgave himself for taking us out of Puerto Rico. I don't really recall that much about him. Just a tall, skinny man with big, sad eyes who sat by my bed during the time I was ill.' She touched the small scar on her neck. 'This always reminds me of him.'

As they ate, she told him more about that time. She spoke with a certain detachment but he knew it must have hurt like hell

70

when it was happening. There was the struggle to learn English and the school taunts. The Latin mother and her fierce insistence on Latin custom. She told him about her older brother getting into trouble when she was twelve and the endless shadowing day and night to save him. There were also the other miseries. The horrors of her sudden stretch in adolescence when she grew head and shoulders above her classmates and then tried to find ways to stunt her growth (she failed – she was now five feet ten inches); and of how she took up modelling after high school; then hated it when people used her like a clothes hanger.

'Why am I talking like this?' she asked suddenly as they neared the end of their second drink after the meal. He lowered his glass.

'I don't know,' he said, 'but I'm not complaining.'

She looked at her watch. 'Oh, oh,' she said. 'I have to go. Otherwise, I'll get into trouble.'

'Hell,' Haggerty said.

She nodded. 'That goes for me too. I've really enjoyed this.' She hesitated. 'I am glad I came,' she said lamely.

'Listen,' he said. 'I was worried about asking you out last time. Will I face the same trouble if I ask you again? Now?'

She looked at him. Suddenly, she smiled, the white teeth showing against the golden skin.

'No,' she said, 'you won't have any trouble. Because this time maybe I should ask you. How about dinner tonight?'

He looked at her and grinned.

'What the hell,' he said. 'Why not?'

After he got back to the Miridiana, Haggerty called Ned Williams, the VisionProbe editor in Montreal.

'Steve, where the hell are you?'

Haggerty grinned and lay back on the bed. 'You might say on top of the world. I've got a date with a beautiful woman and the temperature here in Miami is 83 degrees.'

'You're still in Miami? Good God, Steve, don't you know what's going on up here? You're in deep trouble, man. The cops are looking for you.'

Haggerty's smile faded. He sat up. 'How's that again, Ned?'

'That woman Gedi Reubel you saw. She was murdered here

71

two nights ago, that's what. And somebody is fingering you for it.'

'Jesus Christ.' Haggerty sucked in his breath.

'I got to tell you it doesn't look good, Steve. They found your calling card on the floor beside her bed. And a glass with your prints on the bedside table. The homicide guys have been swarming all over the office waving search warrants and tearing your old files apart. Everybody's tearing their hair out. What's this all about, fella?'

Haggerty sat on the bed, stunned, the shock stripping away his earlier euphoria.

'Steve? Are you there?'

'Yes.' Finally he stubbed out his cigarette. 'Tell me everything, Ned.'

'According to the cops, Reubel was killed at about 5.30 a.m. Tuesday morning,' Williams said. 'Her house was ransacked, everything personal gone. Some neighbourhood insomniac saw a camper leave the area around that time. But the cops really got interested in you when they found that card.'

'This is unbelievable.'

'I'll say. But at least you know now who your friends are. Just about everyone here, even Ben Brown' – the show's backbiter – 'has been in there fighting the cops, trying to protect you and your stuff. And Sheila's been marvellous.'

'Sheila?'

'Yeah. Look, Steve, I was worried about the cops getting into your apartment. I couldn't think of anybody who might help so I called Sheila. I hope you don't mind. Anyway, while the cops were in the office she went to the apartment and made sure there was nothing sensitive lying around. Not that there was any reason. Just safety first.'

'I didn't kill that woman, Ned,' Haggerty said.

'You think I don't know that?'

'I spent no more than two hours in her house. And she was fine when I left. I called you when I got back to my apartment, you remember. And that was about ten o'clock.'

'I told the cops already. But they're claiming you were trying to set up an alibi.'

72

'If I was, I'd be a lot fucking cleverer than that,' Haggerty said contemptuously. He was getting mad. 'Now listen, Ned. There is something. If that woman was murdered around 5.30 a.m. as they claim, that would let me out. I caught a 6 a.m. flight from Mirabel to New York. I couldn't possibly have made it in time if I was at her house when they say. There was a two-hour stopover at La Guardia and I was in Miami just before eleven. I couldn't have gotten here that early if I'd left Montreal any later.'

'That's something,' Williams said.

'It isn't the only thing, Ned,' Haggerty said. 'I think I came across another murder down here.'

'No shit!'

'I found a woman bleeding to death in this guy Dackman's clinic,' he said. 'And some guys tried to use a scalpel on my throat when they spotted me.'

'That's serious stuff, pal,' Williams said.

'Listen, I don't think that things are as bad as they appear. I'll get a declaration from a receptionist at the motel here,' Haggerty said. 'She'll remember me checking in. That should take care of the alibi. Did Sheila get my passport when she was in the apartment?'

'Why? You got something in mind?' Williams asked suspiciously.

'Just what I came here to do. Like going after this bastard Dackman, that's what. I believe he's down in Guatemala. And I'm going to need that passport to go down there.'

'Come on, Steve, that's really crazy,' Williams said. 'Don't you realise you could face a murder charge here, regardless of your alibi? Or is that not enough for you?'

'For Christ's sake, Ned, stop acting like an old woman. Not now. Somebody is trying to frame me and it can only be Dackman. Now listen. Go to Sheila and get my passport. She's sure to have taken it from the apartment. I want you to send it down here by courier straight away. I'll pay you later. Now here's the address. I'm in Room 237, Miridiana Motel, Benbow Avenue, Miami. Have you got that?'

'You're nuts, Steve. You're out of your mind.'

Haggerty ignored him. 'And while you're taking care of that,

I'll get the alibi statement from the receptionist and send it to the cops there. That should clear up the problem they've been giving everybody.'

'I don't believe it. You're treating this thing like it was nothing.'

'Just do what I ask, Ned. It's important. And remember, I'm counting on you. Don't let me down.'

———

The glass elevator climbed the inner wall of the Hyatt Regency Hotel in New Orleans. William Masters watched the tree-lined courtyard fall away below. He rubbed a hand across his warm forehead then lowered it to drum nervously on the white rail, wishing this visit was over. He realised his brother would not be pleased to see him. But he had made his decision. And after Cal's sudden disappearance from Washington, he was giving him no warning.

It had taken all his will-power to get this far. He knew that he was close to the end of the line. Last night in Washington, sitting on the bed in that boxy hotel room, he stopped fooling himself. He was sliding back to where he had been before the last collapse. If it wasn't for the need to see Cal, he would have gone back to Syracuse and checked himself in. Instead, he talked to Alva Martin, his former secretary in the Agency and the woman he was closest to. Their affair had lasted six years. But he couldn't meet her now, even though she was just across town. She would know he had been drinking. He felt guilty when he put down the phone. Afterwards he rang his wife Myra in New York although he no longer regarded her as his wife in the real sense. Only their son held them together now. Following that and for the rest of the evening, he drank as little as possible from the quart of wine he had bought to get him through the night. But it was almost empty when he left to catch his plane.

Now in the elevator, his nerves were jangling. His whole body was on edge. His skull ached, not only from the alcohol, but from trying to draw sense from the bizarre events of the past few days – that Korner invitation to work while he was still sick, Dackman's activities on the island, this sudden flight of Cal's. He kept trying, but he still couldn't figure out what it all meant.

74

This meeting with Cal could help. His brother had to know something to assist in unravelling the mystery. But why hadn't he spoken before this? It was very unlike Cal not to tell him.

Almost everybody who knew his brother, and the media who sometimes excoriated him, regarded Cal Masters as a calculating, cold, power-seeker, who never got involved with anyone or anything that didn't advance his career. William Masters was one of the very few who knew that the image was a mask which concealed a fragile inner being plagued by apprehension and doubts. How many times had he listened, drunk, across oceans and different time zones, to long rambling monologues as Cal sidled towards another of those ambitiously motivated decisions? If only people knew.

The capsule slowed to a stop on the tenth floor. Masters stepped onto the balcony corridor. He glanced at the room listings and headed down the long east wing to Room 1023. Outside, he paused to compose himself. He didn't want the drink issue to complicate this meeting. He took a deep breath and knocked on the door.

Time seemed to lengthen as he waited for an answer and no one came. He was about to try again when he suddenly heard the lock turn. The door swung open.

James Korner stood in the doorway.

William Masters stared, his heart pumping painfully.

'Hello, William,' Korner said, as if this was no surprise. A cold smile rose on his pale lips as he stepped to one side. 'Please come in.'

Obediently, Masters entered the short corridor. As Korner closed the door behind him, he hesitated momentarily but then went ahead into the living room.

Again he stopped. It seemed that there was no end to the shocks.

His brother Cal, who normally took great care of his appearance, sat dishevelled and haggard on one side of the room. Across from him with a drink in his hand sat Ernst Dackman.

As William Masters stood at the entrance, his mind whirling, Korner came in to join them. Suddenly, with all of them together, it hit him like a thunderbolt. Now he understood.

75

James Korner had not hired him out of the convalescent home for his ability. And Dackman had not killed that man in his presence on the island as an illustration of his power as a hit-man.

It was all part of a trap, laid with great care to ensnare him. But even with that, he realised he was not the ultimate victim.

He looked at his brother, shattered and broken, across the room.

Cal Masters, deputy chairman of the House Intelligence Committee, was.

6

She was late.

Haggerty stood on the steps of the Miami City Hall in the fading light. It was still warm and he was dressed for it in light beige trousers and cream sports shirt. He leaned against the balustrade, smoking.

Fifteen minutes went by. He began to lose hope. Then he saw her, hurrying towards him, her hair swaying loosely as she waved. She carried a bag on her shoulder and her moss green shirt was open at the neck. The loose khaki skirt clung to her legs as she came up the steps.

'Sorry I'm late,' she said, slightly breathless. The faintly dishevelled appearance made her seem even more attractive. 'I had some chores.'

They walked down the steps to get a cab.

'Listen,' he said as they waited, 'I've got to make a quick house call on the desk clerk from the hotel. It's fairly important. I have the address and it's not too far. Would you mind delaying dinner for an extra thirty minutes?'

She smiled.

'I owe you for being late.'

He hailed a cab and gave the cab driver the address which the manager of the Miridiana had given him. It turned out to be in a slightly run-down block not far from the motel itself. The door of the apartment was opened by a small, thin girl in a grey blouse and long skirt. Her hair was a slightly frizzled brown and her pale face accentuated the size of her eyes. Haggerty recalled her shy laugh when he joked with her at the reception desk two days earlier. Somehow she seemed a little sadder here.

'Hello, Miss Meadows.' He tried to break the ice with a smile.

77

'I'm sorry to disturb you at home but Norman, your manager at the Miridiana, said you wouldn't mind. I'm hoping you remember me. You took my registration when I checked in the day before yesterday.'

She nodded.

'Yes,' she said, 'I remember. Mr Haggerty, right?'

'That's it,' he said. 'Look, Miss Meadows, I have a problem. It seems that someone in Montreal where I come from was trying to impersonate me yesterday at exactly the time I checked in with you.'

'Oh?'

'Yes,' he said. 'Now, I've talked with the people up there in Canada and they've asked me to get a notarised statement to prove I was here when this person impersonated me. Could you help me? And testify that you saw me here?'

She looked a little taken aback. 'Gee,' she said, 'I don't know.'

'It's completely legal,' Haggerty said. 'The man who takes these statements is a court official. And we could do it very quickly at the Miridiana.'

The hesitation still showed on her face. Haggerty said nothing, knowing anything further might make her anxious. It took a few moments but finally, reassured by the presence of Eve Valdes, she invited them in.

When they left a half hour later, he had her agreement and a time set for the following day. Eva Valdes squeezed his arm as the door closed behind them.

'You must be very good at your job,' she said. 'I almost offered to sign myself.'

He grinned. 'I might have asked if she hadn't come through.'

The restaurant adjoining the Miridiana was warm, intimate and well filled. Candles flickered on the flower-topped tables, casting shadows across the room. On a tiny balcony above the diners, a small group played Latin music. Waiters moved between the tables with laden trays held high.

They moved to the small cocktail lounge to wait for a table. Haggerty ordered a dry martini for her and Scotch and water for himself. They sat up at the bar.

He took out his cigarettes. She looked at him.

'That's the only bad habit I've seen in you so far,' she said.

'Want me to put them away?' He held them up, hoping not.

'No,' she smiled. 'It's okay.'

'I would, you know,' he said. 'Anything to make a good impression.'

She leaned forward and touched his arm lightly. 'Listen, you may not realise it,' she said, 'but you already have.'

He grimaced, faintly disbelieving.

'Really it's true,' she said. 'You've got a nice disarming way. I can't explain it but maybe it has something to do with not pressing. Back with that girl in the apartment I saw it.'

The truth was he had felt sorry for the girl.

'You are nice, you know,' she repeated.

He looked at her, at the golden skin and the dark eyes. And remembered thinking about making a score earlier.

'Sometimes I wonder about that,' he said.

'There,' she said. 'Self-questioning. Another good sign.' She tapped his arm. 'Now, I know what you journalists are like, always probing, getting information. That's how you got me to talk at lunch today. To tell the truth, that's not normal for me. I'm much more comfortable listening than talking. I'd rather hear something about you. So how about it?'

He laughed. 'I don't know if it's very interesting.'

'Come on,' she said. 'I'd really like to hear.' She pulled herself a little closer on the stool.

'Where do I start?'

'At the beginning.'

'Well, let's see.' He thought for a moment. 'I was born in Queens, New York, where my mom and dad still live on a street called Grange Avenue. My eldest brother, Ray, lives there too. He's a public relations man. I did have a younger brother, Kevin, a reporter for the *New York Times*. But he was killed in Cambodia.' He drew on his cigarette. 'As you might guess, there's been a lot of journalism in our family. My grandfather was editor of a newspaper in the old country called the *Freeman's Journal*. After my dad emigrated to New York, he started a local paper in Queens called the *Irish Herald*. I started my own little rag when I was eleven or twelve in school. At seventeen, I started on the

Herald with my dad. And it really was a ball.' He grinned, remembering. 'We used to have a lot of fun covering the ethnic banquets. And getting canned afterwards. My dad was a great teacher. In more ways than one.'

'You seem close to your father.' She seemed wistful.

He felt that. 'I was,' he said. 'Not any more.' He put down his cigarette. 'At least not since Kevin died.'

'Oh, I'm sorry.' She knew she had made a mistake. 'Maybe you don't want to talk about it.'

He shrugged, then looked at her. 'You remember I joked about running away from a battle in Cambodia?'

She nodded.

'Kevin died in that battle.'

She bit her lip.

He shook his head and stared at his cigarette. 'It happened in 1974. When I was with ABC.' He stopped and turned to her. 'Are you sure you want to hear this? We could talk about something else.'

'No, I'd like to,' she said. 'If it doesn't upset you too much.'

'It was a long time ago,' he said. A little embarrassed, he raised his glass. 'I had a drinking problem at the time.' He lowered it. 'The results of too much tension and the wrong genes, I guess. Well, it all came to a head out there in Asia. During the invasion of Cambodia.' He gazed across the bar at the row of bottles stacked on the glass shelves. Then he began to talk.

'It was in a place called The Parrot's Beak, just over the Vietnam border. A pure hell of a place. Especially for the guys who did the fighting.' He shook his head. 'I was a little luckier than they were. My job was stay out of trouble, take the body count and broadcast the results every night. It was a strange time, that. I had done two years in Vietnam by then without a break. And like everybody, I was tired. But I wanted to stay until the finish. Or, as somebody said, until it finished me.' He drew on his cigarette. 'Well, it almost did.'

She was quiet. He hardly noticed.

'That advance into Cambodia I mentioned had been going on for about two weeks when this thing happened to me. I guess it was a kind of nervous collapse. I had been a heavy drinker before

80

arriving in Nam. Out there it got worse. Towards the end I was downing a bottle of scotch or vodka or whatever every day without noticing. It didn't seem to have any effect. Then one day, there in the Parrot's Beak, I ran out.' He shook his head, almost talking to himself. 'The most humiliating experience of my life. It was like a fever you couldn't control. And it wouldn't go away. The night it happened, I sat waiting for my broadcast deadline but when it came I couldn't broadcast.' He put down the cigarette. 'That was when I ran away. Just like I told you.'

Her hand reached across and touched his arm. He didn't notice. 'I remember only parts of what happened,' he went on. 'Like being in a decaying swamp. With all these pale rays filtering down through the mangroves. Even now, I'm not sure if it was a dream or not.

'Everything was dirty green with those long green tendrils clinging to your body. And all the time you couldn't stop the sweating and shaking. That, and the awful nausea were some of the last things I remember that day.'

She reached across and stubbed out the cigarette left burning in the ashtray. Pulling out a fresh one, she handed it to him.

'Some supply guys found me, I was told. Anyway, they took me to a field hospital. There was a doctor there, an older guy. He took one look at me and knew immediately.

'"You fucking reporters," he said. Then he went out and came back with a bottle of rubbing alcohol. "Here," he said. "Now get the hell out of here. We need you guys alive. Somebody's got to tell people what's happening out here." I went away. Just sat in the sun. And drank what I could hold down. It took a while but finally the shaking stopped and I drove back to the front.

'My wing and my brother Kevin's had just linked up. I was still bad by that time but I was serviceable. Then an information officer came by and told me about Kevin. And he handed me a tape.'

The *maitre d'* approached. Eva Valdes waved him away. He raised five fingers and faded into the gloom.

'Kevin had been standing on a rise above a small village called Sanh Khe. A combat team was clearing it and Kevin was describing the operation into his tape recorder. Then, in the

81

middle of a sentence, he just stopped. No dramatics, no screams, nothing. A single bullet had struck him on the side of the head. For a whole night, I listened over and over to that tape. Then I asked to see the village. It was just a cluster of huts in a clearing, that was about it.

'I stood looking at it for a while from the hill where Kevin had been hit. Then I walked down with the bottle of Scotch they gave me when they told me the news. At the first hut, I scattered some of the whisky on the roof, took out my lighter and set it on fire.'

He was lost in it now, reliving the time.

'A young officer came up and said, "Excuse me, sir. You're not supposed to do that." I just went ahead. When the second hut was burning, some soldiers pitched in as well. Between us, we burned that village to the ground. The advance went on soon after and I went with it. A few days later on my way back to the Vietnamese border, I passed the village again. It was just a blackened ruin.

'Kevin's body had reached the States by then. And so had the story of what I'd done. ABC tried to protect me. But when I refused to go stateside for treatment, they had to let me go. No other news organisation would touch me. As far as covering the war was concerned I was out in the cold. And that really shook me. But it also brought things to a head.

'I went to a place called Camh Ramh Bay where the military had a base. I stayed there on the beach in a makeshift hut. No drinking. Every day I swam, ran and chopped wood until my mind would let me sleep. For two, maybe three weeks, that went on. Then one morning I woke up and everything had changed. I heard birds and smelled the sea again and felt the sand under my feet. I never thought that would happen but when it did I knew it was over. The next day, I flew home to the States.

'My father didn't come to the airport to meet me although I had sent word that I was coming. When I did get home to Queens, he didn't even shake hands. Kevin's death and the publicity about what I'd done had shattered him. Later I found out there was more to it for him than just losing a son alone.

'During the Irish war of independence back in 1920, my father was a kid in a small village in Ireland called Balbriggan. During an ambush there, a British soldier was killed by some of the local guerrillas. The very next day, the British came back and burned down the village. My father witnessed the whole thing. But as a victim. It had a traumatic effect on him. That's why he could never forgive me. As far as he was concerned, I had done the same thing.'

Haggerty's voice was thickening.

'I had to leave. That's when I went to live in Canada. With a girl I knew.'

He fingered his glass.

'My father is one of the nicest old Irish gentlemen you could meet. But you know something, Eva?' He looked at her. 'I still can't go home.'

She shook her head slowly and reached for his arm.

'Come on,' she said. 'Let's go in.'

He rose with her, stubbing out his cigarette. She took his hand as they walked to their table.

They sat in a small alcove away back from the dance floor and the musicians. To him, the room still seemed warm even with air conditioning. He leaned towards her in the candle-light, the shadows playing across his face.

'I think I ought to tell you again that you're beautiful,' he said. He took her hand, holding it across the dark red cloth. The wavering light caught and magnified her smile.

'You don't stay down long, do you?' she said.

'It's your eyes,' he said. He gazed at her without speaking.

'That Irish charm,' she said. 'I've heard of it.' She looked back at him. 'I like it.'

The waitress came to take their order. When she left, Eva Valdes looked at him.

'Stephen, that business with Rita Meadows tonight. How serious is it?'

'Come on. You don't want to hear another monologue,' he said.

'It is serious, isn't it?'

'It could be.' He felt so easy with her after the Vietnam revelations, it was nothing to tell her some of the events of the past three days, ending with the Ned Williams phone call.

'My God,' she said, 'that is serious.'

83

'Well, I think it can still be sorted out,' he said, 'so it's a little early to say that.'

'Will you go back to Montreal after you get the statement from the Meadows girl? And leave Miami?'

He shook his head. 'I want to find this Dackman. There's a good chance he's in Guatemala. So that could be next.'

'You should be careful.'

He shrugged. 'Let's forget it for the moment. Come on, let's dance.'

As the evening passed, their personalities slowly blended under the influence of the wine, candle-light and the mood which had descended with his Vietnam story. Three hours fell away without either noticing. By the time she went to call her mother to tell her she would be home late, Haggerty knew Eva Valdes would not be going home at all – not that night.

It was still warm when they left the restaurant. The dark sky was flecked with stars. A slight breeze barely rippled the rose bushes on either side of the path by the pool. They stopped by the inner courtyard where the fountain sprayed water under the soft pink floodlights. They watched it for a moment and then Haggerty took her in his arms and kissed her.

As they drew apart, she looked up at him her eyes soft and moist in the darkness. 'Thank you. For a wonderful evening.'

Her lips were like moist petals, touching gently at first and then with growing strength. He felt her hands pressing into his back and her body against his. Then suddenly, she took her head away. Her face was inches from his as she rested against his shoulder.

'What is it?' he asked quietly.

She shook her head. He put his arms around her and they walked slowly to his room.

Inside, they kissed again, this time long and lingering. She drew away and went to the window where she pulled the curtains closed. He watched her unbuttoning her dark green blouse. She drew it off and reached behind to unfasten her bra. He looked at the light body with the firm breasts and the dark, almost brown nipples. Moving up, his eyes met hers and she came across to him.

As he took her in his arms, she put her hands behind his head and kissed him gently on the forehead.

'I'm glad, very glad I met you,' she whispered.

With unhurried movements, they undressed and got into the bed. They lay, arms around each other as they caressed and kissed. Slowly, the tenderness warmed into ardour as their lips and tongues blended. He moved above her, looking down on her face alive with emotion. She sighed, moving her head from side to side, as she felt him hard inside her. Her eyes were large and her lips glistened.

'Oh, Stephen,' she said, her breath coming fast, 'oh, God! Darling! Darling!'

7

It was late in Washington when the phone rang in Alva Martin's apartment. She switched off the National Geographic special she was watching and picked up the receiver.

'Yes?'

No one answered. In the background, she could hear a piano playing.

'Who is this?' she demanded impatiently.

For a moment, she heard just the piano. Then another sound came, slowly growing in strength. A man's deep sobbing, coming from far back in his throat. The skin crawled on the back of her neck. It was eerie, frightening. Her fist clenched around the receiver.

'Listen, whoever you are. Get off this line or I'll call the police.'

'Alva,' the voice said. Then more faintly, 'Alva.' It was so weak she could barely understand.

'Who is this?' she asked. 'What do you want?'

The man was weeping. Heartfelt, tugging sobs that went right through her.

'Oh, Alva, lovebaby.' The voice was still weak but it sounded more familiar.

'William?' she said uncertainly, 'William Masters? Is that you?' She waited, tense.

'My lost, love, Alva …' the voice whispered. And she knew.

'William!' she roared. 'Are you drunk?'

It was unimaginable. After months of treatment and a withdrawal agony that he told her would last a lifetime, he was back where he started. He had fallen off the wagon.

'Oh, William, you bastard,' she said. The thought brought her close to tears even though she really lost him when he stopped drinking. 'You didn't have to do this.'

But he kept on mumbling. He was making no sense. Words just came tumbling out chaotically.

'William! Stop it!' she cried. 'Don't say any more. Stop it right now.'

But he could not stop. Crying, babbling, then collapsing into breathlessness and more sobbing. It was horrifying.

'William, where are you? Tell me where you are. Please, William. I'll come and get you. Honest, lover. Just tell me.'

But he was past hearing. The babble flowed remorselessly, unchecked.

'Stop it!' she screamed. 'Stop, do you hear?'

Unable to bear it, she slammed down the phone. Clutching her body, she rocked, crying.

She had no idea of how long she sat there. But he did not call back as he used to in that state. She went to the bathroom to clean up. Still no call. Alarmed now, she called Vern Railsback's number.

'Hi, sweetheart,' he said warmly when he came to the phone. She explained about William.

'Oh, Christ. That's really a shame,' he said, knowing what it meant.

'What am I going to do, Vern?' she asked.

He sighed. 'I guess we'll have to track him down. Look, give me thirty minutes. I'll come over.'

'Thanks, Vern. You're a darling,' she said. She meant it.

He was true to his word. Alva, remembering the playing in the background, had taken a list of piano bars from the *Washington Post* diary. Soon, they were on their way.

'William's been doing a lot of worrying about this thing he's been involved in,' she said as they drove downtown. 'He called me last night. He told me he's been talking to you about it.'

'Alva,' Vern said gently, 'this isn't something we ought to discuss. You really should stay out of it. Late-night conversations like this have a habit of ending up in Congressional sub-committee testimony.'

'You and William,' she said. 'Doesn't twelve years in the Agency entitle me to some kind of respect?'

'You know it's not that, Alva,' Vern said as he entered the parkway, 'it's just not wise for someone in your job to get involved with tricky subjects. Particularly when you don't have to.' He looked at her. 'Alva, it's been over between you and William. It has been for a long time and you know it. You're not his keeper any more.'

She shrugged. 'He's still a friend,' she said defensively. 'He'll always be that.'

He smiled, glancing in the rearview mirror as he made a right, heading downtown. 'You love him, don't you?'

'I guess,' she said. 'He was always good to me. And stout ladies don't get a lot of that, you know.'

Vern laughed. 'Just you don't expect any sympathy from me. You're a fine woman, Alva. You're warm, funny, kind and honest. You have all the qualities.'

'Yes,' she said. 'Except I have them twice over.' She slapped her ample tummy.

'I told Billy I thought you two should have married,' Vern said, turning into Pennsylvania Avenue.

'Yeah? And what did he say?' She was more interested than she wanted to admit.

Vern watched the traffic but made a wry face. 'William Junior. You know, Myra really knows how to hold that kid over him.'

She nodded. 'Can't say I blame her. I'd fight for William too.'

'I always thought he made too much of that kid,' Vern said as they slowed for a light. 'If he worried about him less he might have a lot more fun as a father. The kid might too.' They pulled away from a stoplight and Vern made a quick turn by Blair House.

'I never met the little tyke,' Alva said. 'I think William was afraid it might burn into his memory. I wanted to, when he was younger but . . .'

'Shut up, Alva,' Vern said quietly.

'What?' Alva looked at him, astonished.

'Somebody's following us,' Vern said. She moved in her seat. 'Don't look back,' he said quickly.

88

'How do you know?'

'He's been there through three turns we didn't need to make,' Vern said. He glanced at her. 'Got any troubles that might cause this?' She shook her head. He looked back at the traffic. 'Neither do I,' he muttered. The car rode through the darkened street.

'William? Is that it?' her voice dropped.

'It might,' Vern said. 'Which means we could have a problem when we find him,' he checked the rear mirror constantly. 'Now, listen, Alva. I'm going to drop you at the Class Re-Union. No one will bother you there with Bosco McGuirk behind that bar.'

'Wait a minute, Vern ...' she protested.

He shook his head impatiently. 'Alva, I know what I'm doing. There's only two of them in the car. If they want to find William they'll have to split to watch both of us. And one-on-one will give me a better break.'

She shrugged. 'Okay.' As usual, Vern was a rock of sense.

'If I find William, I'll call you. If not, I'll pick you up anyway. But don't leave the bar until you hear from me. Okay?'

She nodded.

He smiled. 'Give yourself a break and have a few martinis. But no speaking to strange men.'

She leaned over and kissed him as they approached the Class Re-Union. 'Be careful, Vern.'

'Don't worry, sweetheart. I will.'

He waited until she had disappeared into the bar then gunned the motor and swept away down the empty street. In the mirror, he saw a man tumble from the car behind before it came in pursuit with hardly a loss in pace. Whoever was in the driving seat knew what he was doing.

The first bar on the list that Alva made up was O'Kanes on L Street. Cars lined both sides of the street. Vern found a space by a hydrant and parked. The tail double-parked a hundred yards back.

He entered O'Kanes but saw immediately it wasn't right. They had a piano but there were four other musicians on stage as well. It was too noisy. But just to make sure he did a quick tour before leaving.

After the raucous music and the bright lights, the dark, empty

89

street seemed full of menace. Vern wished he had brought his gun. He hurried to the car. Unlocking the door he glanced quickly down the street. No sign of the tail. Turning south, he headed for the second bar, the Oasis. He drove only three blocks before the familiar dim lights reappeared in his rear mirror. The shadow was back.

He drew a blank at the Oasis and moved on. By the fifth bar he had grown used to the tail but more worried about his failure to locate William Masters. He wondered if William had called home. At the sixth bar, the Abercorn, he put in a call to Myra Masters in New York.

He was mildly surprised when Myra, an avid party-goer, answered the phone herself. He told her he wanted to reach William urgently.

'You're not alone, darling,' she said. 'He said he was coming back here tonight. He still hasn't arrived.'

'When did you talk to him last?'

'Earlier today. He called me when he arrived in New Orleans.'

'How was he, Myra?'

There was a pause. 'Not so good,' she said finally. 'Between you and me, Vern, I think he's been hitting the bottle again.'

He drummed on the coinbox. 'Any reason for that?'

'God knows it isn't me. But I have a feeling. I think he's back with that bitch Martin again,' she hesitated. 'Is he, Vern?'

'If he is, he hasn't told me about it,' he said. 'Look, Myra, if he's drinking again we should find him before he does himself harm. Who was he seeing in New Orleans?'

'Cal,' she said. 'He was having trouble locating him in Washington. If that's the real reason why he went to Washington in the first place,' she said bitterly. 'There are a lot of things he doesn't care to discuss with me any more.'

'I've got to find him,' Vern said. 'Listen, if he contacts you get him to call me. Right away. Promise?'

'Will do,' she said. He rang off.

Standing in the alcove, he reflected on what Myra had said. There was no way William Masters could have made a long-distance call unaided to Alva. He must have flown to Washington. And probably drunk on the plane.

90

He called Washington National Airport and found the man he wanted in security, Ron McGrane. It took McGrane only a few minutes to check the passenger lists of incoming flights from New Orleans.

'William Masters. Arrived this evening on American Airlines flight 238 from New Orleans. he got in at 7.48 p.m.'

Railsback called the airport bar. Once he heard the pianist in the background, he knew he had located William Masters's last stop. The barman had no trouble remembering.

'Boy, he was stewed. He got really sick. We had to call an ambulance.'

'Know where they took him?'

'Sure. The National Orthopaedic Hospital. On Washington Ridge.'

Vern put down the phone. Time to collect Alva and give the tail the slip.

He crossed the half empty parking lot to his car, feet crunching on the gravel. There was no sign of the surveillance. He had his keys out before he reached the car and unlocked it without delaying. Sliding behind the wheel, he pulled the door closed.

Cologne.

He smelt it immediately. It was not strong but it was definite. Somebody was in his car. Very casually, Vern dropped a hand to the door handle as he turned the ignition. But before he could make his move, cold metal pressed into his neck.

'Not a sound, mother-fucker, or you're dead.'

'Oh, God, mister, don't do anything crazy.' Vern was at his most effete. 'You want money? Take my wallet.'

'Shut up!' The voice had an icy timbre and the muzzle pressed harder into Vern's neck. 'Don't play games. Where is William Masters?'

'I don't know what you mean.' Vern's left hand was slowly pushing down the door handle.

'Don't give me that.' The gun tapped suddenly against his skull. 'You've been in contact with him, haven't you?'

'Please, I don't want any trouble.'

The gunman was now very close. Vern could feel his breath on his neck.

91

'I'm going to ask you one last time,' the hidden voice said, 'and if you don't...'

Vern jerked his head back suddenly crashing against the gunman's forehead. A vicious whiplash sound exploded in the car as the windscreen shattered from a flying bullet. Vern hit the door handle and spun out onto the ground.

Scrambling low, he got round the car door and ran, knowing that the splintered windscreen would obscure the gunman's vision. Ahead, he saw a knee-high fence at the end of the parking lot. He got to it and threw himself over as a bullet tore into the metal. His body bounced off the grassy surface and he tumbled down a steep hill into a ravine. He somehow found a bush which stopped his slide.

With his head pressed against the soft earth, he lay still, breathing heavily. As the moments passed, he knew he was all right. Very slowly, he raised his eyes and looked up the slope.

The parking lot was backlit by a glow from the street lamps. As he watched, the light was split by a dark figure stepping up to the rail. He was no more than twenty yards away. The head was moving from side to side, sweeping the slopes below.

'Railsback?' the man called softly. 'Listen to me.' Vern didn't move. In the distance he could hear the hum of traffic. Around him, moisture fell from the trees and plopped to the soft earth.

'We have no argument with you, Railsback,' the man said. He peered down, waiting. Vern made no sound. 'Why don't you come up?' Vern saw him moving now, the light breaking and closing around his ghostly shape. He was heading towards a gap in the rail. Pressed against the damp earth, Railsback watched. But the man sensed the foolishness of the plan and stopped. He leaned forward into the gloom. 'Listen to me, Railsback. Think about your lady friend. We can still take her instead of you. You want that?'

Vern gritted his teeth.

'Which is it going to be?' the man called softly. He waited as the seconds ticked by. Finally he straightened up. 'Have it your own way.'

The figure receded and only a glow filled the skyline. But still Vern waited. The trees above swayed in a sudden whisper of wind. Raindrops pattered on the dead undergrowth around him. Very quietly, he looked below, eyes searching through darkness for some clue to the ground he would have to cover. Letting go of the bush, he began inching downwards, throwing quick glances up to the parking lot as he went.

No one appeared.

He reached the bottom almost fifty yards below the lot. His clothes and hands were caked with mud. He was on a small track which snaked through the ravine. He moved cautiously over the muddied path, heading east, eyes on the undergrowth around him. It took several minutes before he entered open parkland. It paralleled a wide street he knew to be Hastings Avenue. There were no parked cars around, no sign of anything suspicious. But he remained in the darkness of the park, moving cautiously, searching for a phone.

He almost passed one before he spotted it. Someone had taken time out from mugging activities to vandalise it. The light was broken. But the phone itself was working. Vern Railsback blessed the perpetrator. He pulled out his notebook, a relic of his cruising days and found the number of the Class Re-Union with a lighter.

Bosco McGuirk answered. 'Bosco, this is Vern Railsback. Listen, I haven't much time. Some guys are on their way there who might want to harm Alva Martin. Is she there?'

'Yeah.' McGuirk gave a surly laugh. 'Don't go splitting your pantyhose, Railsback. I can take care of her.'

'Fuck you,' Vern said. 'But I need her to come to me. I want you to get a cab out back and keep her out of sight until it comes. You got that?'

'Yeah.'

'Good. Now let me talk to her.' He heard a clatter as the phone was dropped on the bar. A moment later, Alva was on the line.

'Alva? Listen, I've found William.'

'Oh, thank God.'

'Look, there's a possibility that our friends may turn up over there so Bosco is going to take care of you until a cab comes. When it does, take it to the south-east corner of Hastings and Elland. I'll be waiting for you. You got that?'

'South-east corner of Hastings and Elland,' she repeated.

93

'That's it. Listen, I can't hang around. I'll explain when I see you. But be careful. Okay, sweetheart?'

'Okay. And you be careful too,' she said fervently.

Vern left the phone booth and slipped back into the darkness. Using the trees as cover, he moved carefully along the park until he reached the junction with Elland. Exhausted, he eased down against a tree and rested on the damp earth.

Fifteen minutes passed before Alva arrived. Vern rose, stiff with cold, and made his way to the sidewalk. Alva was horrified when she saw him. So was the cab driver.

'Hey, what's happening here? You gonna foul up my cab?' He displayed the kind of outrage only shown by a Washington resident who was carrying a concealed weapon.

'I was mugged,' Vern said wearily. 'Take us to the National Orthopaedic Hospital.'

'This job is getting to be a private ambulance service,' the driver muttered. But he was savvy. Cabbies who threw mugging victims back on the street ended up fleeing from TV cameras. You had to play the good samaritan – even when your cab ended up smelling like Dracula's living room. He opened the window discreetly as they went down Elland.

'I was really worried about you, Vern,' Alva whispered. 'You're sure you're okay?'

He nodded. 'It was close for a while. But it's William they want. He's at the hospital.'

'Thank God for that.' She helped him out of his muddy coat. 'Here, let's get some of that mud off your face.' Between them, they cleaned off some of the dirt with paper hankies. But Vern was hardly presentable when they reached the Emergency entrance at the hospital. Inside, where accident victims were common, no one showed any curiosity at his condition. He went to the washroom to clean up while Alva sought out William's room.

When he returned she was waiting. She stared at him critically. 'Feeling any better?'

He smiled. 'Yeah. You might say I'm bruised but a little exhilarated too,' he said. 'It's not every day you get to outrace a bullet.'

94

She shook her head and gripped his arm.

'Listen, I've found William,' she said. 'He's in the drying-out ward.'

'Let's go see him,' he said. Walking through the long corridors, he told her what had happened in the Abercorn's parking lot.

'What does it all mean, Vern?'

'I wish I knew. All we can hope is that William can tell us.'

The hospital room was standard but sparsely furnished. William Masters lay strapped in a railed bed under a soft nightlight. His face was grey and his sandy hair stuck in strands to his freckled forehead.

'Billy, can you hear me? It's Vern.'

Masters's eyes were closed but as Vern spoke his lips began moving restlessly.

Alva Martin's hand gripped Vern's arm as he leaned over the bed. William Masters's head moved towards the voice.

'It's Vern, Billy. I have Alva with me.'

The eyelids flickered faintly. A sob broke from Alva. Wordlessly, Vern reached for her hand and held it.

'Billy, listen. We've got to talk to you. Can you hear me?'

The eyes half opened.

'Vern.' William Masters's voice was barely a whisper.

Vern Railsback leaned down, close to the prone man's ear.

'Billy, there are people hunting you. Here in Washington. We've got to know why. You have to tell us, Billy. Why are they after you?'

William Masters's eyes opened fully, staring at the ceiling above them. It was clear that he was no longer aware they were there. Suddenly they saw his Adam's apple move as he swallowed.

'They're going to do it,' he whispered. A tremor shook his body. 'We've got to save him. Must stop them.' His body shivered.

'Save who, Billy?' Vern leaned closer, almost against Masters's ear. 'Who must we save? You've got to tell us, Billy?'

'Find Whitten.' Masters's voice was rising. 'San Antonio. Oh, be quick!' As they watched he began to thrash restlessly under the sheet. Vern put a hand on his shoulder to restrain him. It didn't help. He was getting more agitated.

In the background a buzzer went off.

95

'Whitten knows!' Masters's voice rose higher. 'He knows!' His head lashed from side to side. Sweat glistened on his forehead.

'Billy!' Vern said urgently, 'Who are you talking about? We've got to know. Who are these people?'

The door swung back. A nurse came running in.

'The Guatemalans!' Masters shouted. 'You've got to stop them. Or they'll do it!'

'Do what, Billy?' The nurse tried to push past Vern, elbowing him back. He moved sideways but held close.

William Masters's neck was rigid, the tendons standing out on the pale flesh. His eyes were bulging, staring at Vern but not knowing he was there.

'Blood!' he screamed. 'They want his blood!'

8

It was almost noon. The sun shone down on Miami as guaranteed by the Florida Tourist Council. In the heat-baked streets, the cars were bumper to bumper. Away on the beaches, the tourists basted themselves with suntan lotion and spread pale flesh on the sand. Over everything, the endless radio voices went on juggling news and music for an audience that knew little of the meaning of sound and nothing of silence. The bazaar was in full swing.

In Haggerty's room at the Miridiana, the curtains were closed, shutting out the daylight. The sound of traffic was muted and far-away. A bedside lamp cast a soft light across the tousled bed. It reached beyond to where Eva Valdes did press-ups on the floor.

'Twelve, thirteen, fourteen,' she panted.

'Grace under pressure.' Haggerty sat against the bedboard, watching her rise level with the breakfast trays on the coffee table at the end of the bed.

'Stop it.'

He reached and took a cigarette from the pack by his passport on the bedside table. It had arrived almost two hours earlier. At an embarrassing moment in post-breakfast activity. There was no note with it. He guessed that Ned Williams wanted to play safe in case the police intercepted it.

He drew on the cigarette contentedly. Eva came to a halt on the red carpet, her stomach flat on the floor and her head turned towards him. She gazed at him for a moment, her eyes softening. Then, with a quick sigh she jerked to her feet. Turning sideways, she began a series of toe-touching exercises, her body arching in a way that made Haggerty's stomach tighten. He threw off the sheet to show her.

97

'Come here,' he said.

She laughed, and straightened to come to the bed. He reached up to draw her in. The traffic noise had died away. Only the hum of the air conditioner broke the silence. He ran his fingers down her back, feeling the warm ridge of her spine. She laid her head against his shoulder. They were still for a moment, remembering the night before.

'You know something?' he said softly. 'I wish you were coming to Guatemala with me.'

'I wish it too.' She raised her head and kissed him.

He tightened his arms around her. She glanced at the clock radio by the bedside.

'Noon.'

They had just under half an hour before he was to meet Rita Meadows, the receptionist, in the lobby.

She nuzzled his chest.

He drew her over him, her falling hair enveloping their faces.

She smiled as she rose above him and then gave a slow heartfelt sigh as he drew her down.

'Oh, Stephen,' she whispered, her voice aching. 'Oh, my sweet.'

It was an hour later when they finally hurried down to the lobby. Haggerty fully expected to see an annoyed young receptionist when they turned the corner into the foyer. Instead, two police officers stood by the reception desk.

Without a word, Haggerty took Eva's arm and steered her to the main door. She saw the policemen but said nothing. They stepped out into the bright sunshine. He gestured towards the car.

'We'll have to get Rita Meadows out of there,' he said as they crossed the parking lot.

'Was she at the desk?'

'I didn't see her,' he said, 'but I wasn't about to ask.'

'Stephen, aren't you getting a little paranoid?' she asked as they hurried to the car. He looked at her but said nothing. They reached the car and got in. No one followed as they drove out of the parking lot.

Rita Meadows was not at the motel when he phoned.

'She hasn't turned up for work today,' the desk manager said. 'Did she call? Maybe she's not feeling well.'

'Maybe, maybe not. There's no answer from her apartment.'

Eva Valdes caught the look on his face as he returned to the car. 'What's the matter?'

'Rita Meadows. She's not at work. And she hasn't called in.' He pulled away from the kerb.

'You think something might have happened to her?'

'We'll see.'

'Stephen, why don't you go to the police?' Her face was full of concern. 'I'm certain they'll help you.'

'No,' he said. 'You don't understand. This thing in Montreal. Someone is trying to frame me.'

'But they'd never get away with it,' she said. 'I know you. I know you're innocent.' She reached across and touched his neck. He realised she was being affected now.

'Look,' he said, 'don't get so worried. It's going to be okay.'

When he glanced across he was surprised to see her lips tremble. She looked as if she might cry.

'Come on, Eva. Don't. Please.' He took her hand.

'Oh, Stephen,' she said. 'It's been so nice. I just don't want it to change.'

Neither did he. But he was getting a bad feeling. It was telling him that everything was about to change.

At Rita Meadows's apartment, he pulled in where the cab had parked only the night before. He leaned over and touched Eva's cheek.

'Listen,' he said, 'if anything happens while I'm gone, just take off. Don't wait for me, just do it. Okay?'

She nodded and leaned forward to kiss him. 'Be careful.'

'Don't worry. I will.'

The eighth floor with its slightly threadbare carpet and ivory-coloured walls, was silent as an undertaker's reception hall. He reached the chocolate-brown door with the number 834 in ornate black script. He raised a hand to knock, then stopped. The door was slightly ajar. He looked up and down the corridor. Nobody appeared. Very gently, he pushed the door in.

'Hello, anybody home?' His throat was dry as the door swung

slowly back into the empty hall. No one appeared. He moved into the apartment and paused to listen again, then quietly closed the door behind him. The place was deadly still.

'Rita?'

He moved down the hall.

'Rita, are you there?'

No one answered.

He kept going until he reached the living room. Strands of sunlight stretched across the empty room. The coffee cups of the night before were still on the low table by the sofa. He crossed to the bedroom door.

He stopped.

She lay on her side in the bed, head resting on a pillow. Even from the door, Haggerty could see that Rita Meadows was dead. He approached and dropped to one knee.

She had been shot at point blank range in the forehead. The powder burn was accentuated by the pallor of her skin. Her eyes were half open and her mouth was locked in a grimace like a small child. Haggerty took a deep breath. He had seen death often enough but rarely as pathetic as this. Slowly he rose to his feet. A half-full Jack Daniels bottle and a glass lay on the bedside table. Beside it was a small box of Valium. There had been no struggle. She probably never saw her killer.

There wasn't much else to see in the apartment. A few romantic novels on the dressing table, a *National Enquirer* opened at the headline 'Leaving Stress Behind' and some pantyhose drying in the bathroom. The story of a life. He shook his head, trying to kill the thought that she might have been alive now if it weren't for him.

At the door, he wiped the handle clean before leaving. He saw nobody on his way down to the street.

Eva Valdes watched him from the car as he came out of the building. From his face she knew something had happened but she was afraid to ask. Silently he got into the car. Turning the ignition he started the engine and they pulled away from the kerb.

'She's dead.'

'Oh, God.' She swayed a moment and he reached out to steady

her. Her face was pale. They drove by children playing in the sunshine.

'What are we going to do?' she asked finally.

'I'm going to find this man Dackman. Guatemala is the only place he can be. Somehow, I believe he's responsible for all this.' The cries of the playing children disappeared behind them. Haggerty turned to look at her. 'We should also think about you.'

'You know I'll do what you want,' she said. 'But there's still the police, Stephen. Won't you consider that?'

'No.' He shook his head, almost angry. 'My God, Eva, don't you see? Someone is setting me up. They want me to go to the police. I'll be charged with murder.'

'But you have an alibi.'

'Yes,' he said bitterly. 'A few words from a dead girl to say I couldn't have killed a woman in Montreal. And then a statement from you, to say I couldn't have killed the girl who told us that.' He looked at her. 'You're in danger now too, Eva. You're the only one who can say I didn't kill Rita Meadows.' He looked back at the road. 'You know what I'm thinking. What if they come for you while I'm away?'

They drove along the boulevard. Suddenly, the other traffic seemed distant, as if in another world. She gazed through the windscreen. They were both silent.

'You want me to go with you, don't you?'

He nodded. 'You won't get the protection you need here.' His free hand tightened on hers. 'Eva, I don't know who these people are. Or why they're doing this. But they're intelligent. And so far they've been effective. I'm afraid that if I leave you here, they'll kill you.'

'When do you want to go?'

'Now. Today.'

She thought for a moment. Finally, she nodded.

'I'll need my passport,' she said, 'and some clothes.'

'I just don't understand it,' Vern Railsback said to Alva, 'William must have gotten it wrong.'

They sat in her apartment after a day of discreet inquiries. While they had found a certain reserve in the intelligence

101

community when discussing the situation in Guatemala, neither discovered evidence of any kind of murder plot in their probing.

'As far as I can see,' Vern said, 'the only person in danger of being killed up to this point is me.'

Alva patted his hand sympathetically.

'Have you talked to Cal?'

'He's not around. The bastard's probably still skulking up the backstairs in Blair House.' A rumour had swept Washington months back linking Cal Masters to the Vice President's wife following a Jack Anderson column pinpointing his furtive visits to the VP's official residence. The Vice President himself had squashed the gossip by invoking that time-honoured pastime popular in the smoky backrooms of power. They had been playing poker.

'What a brother that Cal turns out to be,' Alva said. 'Driving William back on the booze. I'd like to strangle him.'

'You wouldn't have any trouble finding accomplices,' Vern said.

'What about going to Korner?' she asked. 'If anything happens down there, he knows.'

'Forget it,' Vern said. 'There's nothing he'd like better than to sink me on something like this.' Korner had already been responsible for Vern's reassignment to home duty after news of his extra-curricular activities in Thailand got out. Only a federal regulation banning discrimination on the grounds of sexual bias had saved Railsback from being cashiered. As it was, Vern now lived a precarious existence in the liaison section between the NSA and the Central Intelligence Agency. 'That bastard would love to see my head on a pole,' he said.

'Well, that brings us back again to William,' Alva said.

Vern nodded.

'I hope he's going to be all right,' she said after a while.

'He's lucky he didn't kill himself,' Vern said. 'The silly bastard. Christ, they warned him that he couldn't take it any more. His liver was already borderline.'

'And yet he went ahead anyway.'

'Right,' Vern said. He shook his head. 'God, Alva, it must have been something big to cause that.'

'Do you think he's ever going to tell us what it's all about?'

'He'd better. Speaking as a pal, I hope it's sooner rather than later. If I'm to be a shooting target, I'd like to know why.'

'Poor Vern.'

'You're absolutely sure there's nothing in what he said about San Antonio?' Vern asked.

'Yes,' she said. 'Not a single Whitten in the entire phone book. And just one unlisted. A shoe salesman. He must be harbouring delusions of grandeur.'

'Or trying to escape his past. Still, we should check him out.'

'It's in the works. Tony Considine is doing it. He owes me.'

'Look, something else occurred to me this morning. San Antonio is a pretty popular name in Spanish America. Maybe we should be looking in Guatemala instead of Texas?'

'Except that it seems unlikely that you would find someone with a name like Whitten living down there.'

'We should try it anyway. If we're going to find this guy Whitten, we're going to have to try every alley.'

She shrugged. 'Okay.'

Vern looked at his watch. 'I got to go if I'm to make the hospital by eight.'

'You'll let me know how he is? And what happens?'

'Sure.' Vern stood up. As he did so, the phone rang. Alva Martin pulled herself up off the sofa. 'Just a sec,' she said.

Vern wandered over to the window, a reflex of manners to keep out of earshot. He watched a plane rise from Washington National, appearing out of the jumbled skyline to the east. It climbed through the smoky evening air, caught in the rays of the setting sun.

'Oh, Jesus!' Alva Martin's voice was a half scream.

Vern turned quickly to see her sagging by the side table, the phone dropping from her hand.

'Alva? What's wrong?' He ran across the room to catch her. She was fainting. Awkwardly, he clutched her waist and lowered her to the sofa. In the background, he could hear a voice screaming from the fallen phone. He reached down and picked it up.

'Who is this?' He had to shout to make himself heard above the hysterical screaming coming from the receiver. He could tell it

103

was a woman. She was frantic, out of control. But now he could understand some of the words.

'Whore! Bitch! You did it! I'll kill you, do you hear?'

'Stop it, damn you!' Vern tried to make himself heard. 'Stop it now!'

The screaming began to fade.

'Vern?' The woman's voice was strung out, shaking with powerful emotion. 'Vern Railsback? Is that you?' Suddenly he recognised the voice.

'Myra? Myra Masters?' he said. 'Yes, it's Vern. What's the matter?'

'Oh, Vern,' she was sobbing, 'my poor William. She killed him. My poor, darling baby. She killed him. That bitch!'

'Myra, what are you talking about? What's happened?'

'He's dead, Vern. My William. The hospital just called. He had a haemorrhage. He's gone. What am I going to do, Vern?'

Vern Railsback's hand, still holding the phone, dropped to his side. The rumble of the plane passing overhead rolled across the silent room.

'Oh, Jesus,' he said. 'Oh, Jesus Christ.'

Eva Valdes and Stephen Haggerty stepped from the elevator on the fifth floor.

'Leave your door open while you check inside,' Haggerty said. She nodded.

He remained outside as she went in. She did not want to explain him to her mother. He waited, uneasy, until she reappeared.

'It's okay. Everything's quiet,' she whispered. 'I won't be long.' She blew him a kiss as she closed the door.

For the first time in twenty-four hours, Haggerty had time to think. About what had happened in the past two days and about what was coming up. He leaned back against the wall, drew out a cigarette and lit it. Maybe it was that move, or perhaps the waiting that sparked it but suddenly he was remembering the faded early days of reporting when he stalked scandal as if his life depended on it. A hint of the happy naïvety from that era floated back to him now. The prospect of tracking down Dackman to his lair roused a feeling of exultant anticipation. He hadn't felt that for a long time. It seemed to tell him, after all the alcohol and compromise, that there was still something there.

A few minutes later, Eva Valdes appeared. 'It's all clear,' she said. 'I told her I had a chance to go south for a few days.' She took his arm and squeezed it. 'If we hurry, we can make a 5 p.m. flight to Guatemala City.'

He smiled at her and took her suitcase. 'Let's go.'

For Stephen Haggerty, the first act in this drama that began with Gedi Reubel's phone call to VisionProbe, was finally over.

Now the real hunt was about to begin.

Guatemala

9

General Antonio Serena, just past fifty and growing fat, waited patiently as the cameraman changed rolls. With an elbow on the table and a hand propped under his chin, the President looked like a world-weary bartender. But years of authority had given him an aura that commanded respect. Even the hardened camera crew, in from New York, felt it.

'This won't take long, Mr President,' the producer said. Serena nodded, barely moving.

A scattering of aides and bodyguards lined the walls of the underground bunker which Serena favoured now that his war with the guerrillas had reached a critical phase. The rectangular room was ivory-coloured and dominated by a large mahogany table where Serena and his interviewer sat. Behind the President, an Indian tapestry of a flaring eagle covered the wall. In an alcove to the right, two white-coated servants laid out a small luncheon table.

The producer bent to the camera's viewfinder. Shifting the lens, he brought the talons of the eagle down until they seemed to hold the balding General's head like a giant, not quite hairless, egg. He beckoned to the cameraman who stood nearby, arms folded.

'This all right for you, Shocker?'

The cameraman grimaced at the nickname.

'If you say so.' Reluctantly he came forward.

The producer turned to the interviewer who sat to Serena's right. 'Let's do it, Ron.' The interviewer nodded and straightened his notes.

'Take it up on the Rias death, will you?' the producer called.

Serena prepared himself as he had done innumerable times in the past year.

'Action!'

The interviewer fixed the President with a steely stare. 'Mr President, it's almost three weeks now since your opponent, the late Adolpho Rias, was assassinated. And so far, not one suspect has been detained. Why is that, sir?'

The President shrugged. 'These things take time. Our police are still investigating.'

'The lack of action has given rise to talk, sir. About how convenient for you that the biggest constitutional threat to your government should be eliminated – in a hail of bullets.'

'Well it is true that Señor Rias offered an alternative – if a doubtful one – to my leadership of Guatemala. However, this administration was not responsible for his death. When his assassins are found they will be punished. Your viewers have my word on that.'

'The Rias murder, sir, is only one of the problems plaguing your country today. There are also the numerous disappearances. We hear about them regularly in the United States.'

'Ah, yes, the disappearances,' Serena nodded. 'I was expecting you to raise that. It is a favourite media topic. Every time a terrorist goes underground, we are accused of making him disappear. Even when one of these gentlemen is killed in a criminal confrontation with our security forces, the media cries murder.' The President showed some irritation. 'Either way, we end up being blamed. It is very frustrating.'

'Let me point out, sir,' the interviewer said, 'that your view might carry more weight if there were not lists prepared by Amnesty International and human rights groups which show cases of entire families disappearing. Including children as young as six months old. Surely you're not suggesting that they are engaged in criminal confrontation?'

'Of course not,' Serena said sharply. 'That would be a total misrepresentation of my position. But our so-called revolution-aries in Guatemala are skilled propagandists. They can, and often do, manufacture atrocity stories out of the thin air. Look at me, for instance. They say I have a private zoo where I personally

110

supervise the feeding of political prisoners to Bengal tigers. Bengal tigers? Can you imagine me doing a thing like that?'

The interviewer ignored the question and pressed on. 'It is still true, sir, that fifty to sixty dead bodies turn up in political murders around the country every week. The majority of these victims are liberals or social activists who oppose your regime. And most observers, including the Roman Catholic Church, blame your government for those deaths.'

'I wish you people would get the facts straight before you make statements like that,' Serena said. 'My government is not responsible for the banditry that is engulfing Guatemala. We are trying to get rid of it.'

'But you are not succeeding, General,' the interviewer said softly. 'From what we have seen ourselves, opposition to your government is growing. The violence is spreading. And the war gets more intense every day.'

The President sat back and waved a hand contemptuously.

'You journalists. You hear a few shots, see a few operations by our soldiers and listen to some rabble-rousers. Next thing you're talking revolution. What rubbish!'

He leaned forward and raised a finger, scolding. 'I sometimes think that the media is the Achilles' heel of our western societies. Sensationalising, distorting, often leading people to mistaken conclusions.'

'Like the President of the United States?' the interviewer cut in. 'With his decision to halt arms shipments to your country until civil rights improve here?'

Serena sat back.

'I do not propose to criticise my good friend, President Robson,' he said evenly, 'but the American people should understand that law and disorder are in conflict here in Guatemala. And if we do not stop the subversion here, it may one day explode on your own borders. Most of all, however, I want your people to understand that my government has only one aim. To uphold the law. We do not act illegally despite what our opponents say. Ever!'

When the film crew had left, Serena looked up at the aide who stood at the other end of the room.

111

'Well, Tomaso, how did I do?'

Tomaso Ordonez, who had taken notes during the interview, came away from the wall and approached his boss. Ordonez was in his mid-twenties and retained his youthful slimness. Like most Latin men he was not tall but his curling black hair, even features and brown eyes gave him a quiet handsomeness that made up for the lack of stature. He was wearing a well-cut two-piece grey suit that looked English-tailored. Now he smiled at Serena, his teeth showing white against the smooth olive skin.

'Superb, Excellency. You were superb. And in the face of so much hostility. I was amazed at how you kept your temper.'

The President waved a hand and smiled. 'You must not get angry in these television interviews. I learned many years ago that it is all theatre to them. They seek confrontation to build audiences. Otherwise, it has no value.'

Pushing both palms against the table, he stood up. 'If I had a choice, Tomaso, I would never talk to them. But we need to rally support from the American people. Otherwise, this embargo of Robson's will strangle us.'

They both looked up as Serena's secretary, a dark middle-aged woman, entered without knocking. Her three-quarter-length taffeta skirt swished as she neared them. Smiling at Tomaso, she handed Serena a phone message. Tomaso caught a glimpse of what it said before he discreetly averted his head.

The President looked sharply at his secretary. 'When did this come in?'

'Ten minutes ago,' she said undisturbed. 'I assumed you didn't want your interview disrupted.'

'Call him back,' Serena said. 'I'll take it in my study.' She nodded and left.

'Wait for me, Tomaso,' Serena said, extending his arm as he made his way to the door. 'We need to talk some more about this embargo business.'

Alone in the sombre room, Tomaso looked down to where the television crew had been only a short time before. On impulse, he dropped into the highbacked presidential chair. Staring across the table, he wondered what it felt like to take on the stony-faced foreign interviewers who were turning up on the presidential doorstep with greater frequency nowadays. But he soon gave up. It required special ability to survive the usually savage inquisitions which the media brought to the civil rights issue in Guatemala. Serena was one of the few people who could. By turn he was reasonable, guileful, sometimes even humorous. Whatever the tactic, he seldom failed to make the point for which he had granted the interview.

After eight months on the presidential staff, Tomaso had grown used to watching the President in action. It was easy to see why he reigned without challenge. Compared to him, his fellow generals were pygmies. The President towered over them. But then, Serena was an extraordinary man.

Even his background was unusual for a Latin dictator. His rise to power did not come from privilege. It was his father, a humble schoolteacher of Indian blood, who set him on the road. The elder Serena, an ambitious man long embittered by the limited destiny open to *mestizos* in Spanish America, had saved and then politicked to get his son into Guatemala's military academy. Even so, the young Antonio had to be more humble, and ultimately more intelligent than his peers to get the commission his father craved.

As a young officer, Serena was noted for his unquestioning obedience to his superiors and for his hard work. He also showed an unexpectedly ruthless streak in pacification campaigns which the army ran to crush discontent. Not least to suffer from these were the Indians from whom Serena's own forebears sprang. It was the young man's brutality against his own which gained him a reputation for iron-fisted impartiality.

This twisted image of impartiality was strengthened when a leftist officer, Jacobo Arbenz, who seized power in 1954, made Serena a battalion commander. Ironically, the appointment came because of his Indian blood. Under a reformist regime, it had become an asset. The radical Arbenz, taken with Serena's ability and imagining him a like soul, gave the young *mestizo* command of a vital suburban outpost which guarded the invasion route into Guatemala City. It was to be the first, but not the last time, a Guatemalan leader misjudged this hardworking, competent subordinate.

113

The Arbenz regime soon brought in a land reform scheme which threatened the holdings of powerful US conglomerates like the United Fruit Company which originally founded Guatemala. These companies and their allies in Washington began lobbying the Eisenhower administration for help. The temperature rose as diplomatic efforts to find a solution to the problem stalled. Fatefully, Eisenhower ordered the CIA to intervene. Using secret funds, the Agency began organising a counter coup by conservative officers. Crucial to their plans to seize Guatemala City was how to subvert Serena's garrison. Quiet talks with its commander began. The exact details of the talks never became known but when the ragged rebel units began their march on Guatemala City, Serena stood aside. His act sealed the fate of the regime. And brought the death of his benefactor, Jacobo Arbenz.

That move made Serena's reputation as a career officer who would work either side of the street. By the sixties, he became a familiar arbitrator in disputes between moderates and conservatives within the ranks of the military. He even became valued by the occasional civilian rulers of Guatemala. By the end of the decade, one such government finally appointed him army commander over the heads of fifteen senior colleagues.

Serena served that civilian administration efficiently for almost two years. But then, as party squabbles sapped the government's vigour, he finally stepped in and with a show of great reluctance took power. Antonio Serena was then just forty-three years old. Only his father – who had come in from his village school in the mountains to watch the inauguration – knew he had spent a lifetime preparing for that moment.

Within months of his accession, the new *caudillo* showed his colours. The deposed president who had appointed Serena his army commander was pulled from his bed one night and driven to the airport with the warning to get out of the country and stay out. He left in a suit pulled over his pyjamas and without his false teeth.

Four other ministers who resisted Serena were not so lucky. One was publicly executed. The rest were shot dead on the streets of the capital by armed gangs. Other opposition leaders began disappearing too as Serena consolidated his power. Soon, dissent became a memory. Even the generals who had backed his seizure of power hesitated to criticise their colleague. Those who did were soon ousted.

For almost two decades, Serena ruled Guatemala with considerable energy and without serious challenge. But the years took their toll. His grip began to loosen. The care he lavished on economic growth began to tail off. The bribery he once held in control became rampant. The countrywide tours, the constant hectoring in speeches and on television for greater national effort, all died away. Weeks came and went when Serena no longer left the Presidential Palace.

By the eighties, the situation had grown critical. Guatemala was in recession and dissent was growing. When student demonstrations and illegal strikes broke out, Serena responded predictably with political killings, disappearances and mass arrests. But now, the dissent would not go away. As the middle class turned against the regime, all that remained from earlier years was Serena's still uncanny talent for dividing the opposition and his ruthless determination to stay in power, whatever the price. Commentators agreed that it was he, single-handedly, who held the regime in place. But with the imposition of President Robson's embargo, it was becoming a life-or-death struggle. An increasingly powerful guerrilla movement was now operating in the mountains and in the *barrios* or city slums. It was clear to everyone that the battle for control of Guatemala was entering a crucial stage.

As Tomaso, sitting in the presidential chair, pondered this last challenge, the door opened. Tomaso glanced up to see Serena re-entering. He stifled a quick urge to rise, knowing the value of minor acts of independence in a staff of devoted yesmen. But Serena seemed not to notice. He appeared preoccupied. He stopped by the antique sideboard and for a moment fingered a box of cigars that lay on the table top.

Finally, he looked up, the cigars forgotten.

'Ah, Tomaso.'

'Excellency?' Tomaso rose.

Serena crossed to stop by the table. The ageing dictator, still not without charm, smiled at his aide.

'Tomaso, I have a problem,' he said. 'A serious and delicate problem. And I need your help.'

'I will be happy to do what I can, Excellency.'

Serena looked at the young man and nodded. He took his arm and they moved out from the table. 'As you know, Tomaso, I am very pleased with your work. But I'm afraid there is more to being a presidential aide than just simple effort. Occasionally, you must take on tasks that require intelligence and discretion. And even strong nerves. In that way, an aide proves his true value.' He paused. 'You understand what I am saying?'

'I think so, Excellency.' Tomaso's face was expressionless but his heart was quickening.

'Well, let me be more specific. I have a problem, Tomaso. And I want you to resolve it.'

'What is the nature of the problem, Excellency?'

Serena smiled. 'It is a journalist. An American. His name is Stephen Haggerty. He arrives from Miami at eight o'clock this evening.'

Tomaso hesitated. Serena saw it.

'Well, what is it?' There was a hint of sharpness in his voice.

'What am I to do with him, Excellency?'

Annoyance flitted across the President's face.

'Make him disappear,' he said coldly and walked past Tomaso to the luncheon table.

10

A stream of passengers left the Boeing 727 and crossed the weakly lit tarmac to the arrivals building. Heavily armed troops in camouflage stood by the terminal doors, now open to moderate the heat inside. The soldiers watched the arrivals, searching faces and eyeing hand luggage. Some of the passengers glanced back nervously at the grim-looking troops. They were an unpleasant reminder that Guatemala had lost its once-famed stability.

Tomaso, behind the wire mesh of the security office at the end of the big customs hall, could read the mixed emotions on the passengers' faces as they formed up on the other side of the passport desks. While he watched, a well-dressed group entered the terminal from the tarmac. Quickly, they brushed past the other passengers. Tomaso immediately recognised the silver-haired man leading the group as the deputy chief of the national broadcasting service and a member of one of Guatemala's leading families. His deeply tanned wife with two white-shirted boys followed him past the passport desk. Behind came an Indian maid carrying a young child. The group's disregard for the law was proof of their high position in the Serena hierarchy. Their baggage, Tomaso guessed, would be stuffed with contraband. No airport official would dare open it.

'Look, sir,' the plain-clothes security agent at his side spoke. Tomaso nodded. He had already seen the signal light set off by the passport officer. He looked closely at the man whom the President wanted eliminated.

He was trimly built, this Stephen Haggerty. Over six feet tall with curly greying hair. He wore brown cords and a short-sleeved shirt and carried a light grey windbreaker. The casual smile he offered as he handed over his passport revealed no sign of tension. Cool, Tomaso decided. He turned to his companions.

'Let's go. And remember, discretion. No trouble while we're in the terminal.'

The two men nodded. As they approached the door, the heavier agent, Peloquin, jerked his head back towards the wire mesh. 'What about the woman?' he asked.

Tomaso lifted his hand from the door knob.

'What woman?'

Peloquin pointed through the grille. 'That one.'

Tomaso walked quickly back. He saw Eva Valdes move to Haggerty's side and rest a hand on his arm. His lips tightened. Nobody said anything about a woman.

'One of you tell customs to detain her for a contraband search.' Peloquin's partner, Diaz, slipped out. Tomaso stayed by the grille, watching.

Haggerty and the woman passed through passport control. Beyond it he paused briefly to slip on his jacket and light a cigarette. Tomaso noticed that as the woman talked and Haggerty listened, his eyes still roamed the hall taking everything in. As his gaze came level with the security office, Tomaso stepped back even though he knew he could not be seen. Finally, the two moved on. When they reached the customs table, an officer stepped out and gestured to the woman. They spoke rapidly. Clearly she knew Spanish. After a brief argument, she followed the official into an office behind the baggage table.

'Let's go,' Tomaso said. Outside they were joined by Diaz.

Haggerty was standing by the table, watching the door through which they had taken Eva when the three men approached.

'Señor Haggerty?' Tomaso asked.

Haggerty turned, eyes alert. He nodded. Tomaso extended a limp hand.

'Tomaso Ordonez. Information Ministry,' he said smiling. 'Welcome to Guatemala.'

'Thank you.' Haggerty shook hands.

'I'm sure you are surprised to find a welcoming committee waiting.' Tomaso grinned. 'Every journalist is. Sadly, it is due to our security problems today. It can be dangerous here for reporters. So we try to keep a little control. For their own protection, of course.'

'How did you know I was a journalist?'

'There, you see? Already you seek restricted information.'

Haggerty smiled. 'What do you want from me?'

'We would like you to register with us. Then we can issue you with an official permit. Without it, we cannot allow you free movement around the country. The application process takes no more than twenty minutes. So if you would come this way, we can get it finished quickly.' He pointed to the exit.

'Hold on,' Haggerty said. 'My woman friend is still with your customs.'

'Oh, what's the problem?'

'I don't know,' Haggerty said.

'I'm sure it's not serious,' Tomaso said reassuringly. He thought for a moment. 'Look, I have a suggestion for you. Why don't we go down to my office and get the paperwork done. And if your friend is free before that, I'll have her brought down to us. Would that be agreeable to you?'

Haggerty nodded. 'I guess so.'

'Good.' Turning, Tomaso spoke rapidly to Diaz in Spanish. He said, 'Have them hold the woman for another thirty minutes. And follow us as quickly as you can.'

Diaz nodded and left. Tomaso turned to Haggerty, smiled, and extended a hand.

'This way, *señor*.'

Reassured by Tomaso's obvious authority, Haggerty went along. A soldier swung open the exit door and they passed into the terminal's main lobby. A small crowd outside pressed forward when the three men came through but quickly fell back again. Haggerty and Tomaso walked towards the main entrance with Peloquin following behind. Their footfalls echoed on the gleaming mosaic which two elderly cleaners were polishing by the door. Above the entrance a carved statue of some heroic but forgotten Guatemalan flier looked down.

They passed through the automatic doors and entered the humid night. A few yards away, a battered cab pulled away from

119

the kerb belching a cloud of blue exhaust smoke that hung in the air after the cab was gone. Tomaso gestured to their left. They walked down the narrow sidewalk leaving the smell of the exhaust smoke behind. It was replaced by the odour of decaying vegetation. The sweet, swamp-like odour was a reminder of how thin the civilised skin was in this Central American country.

The sidewalk was lined by a row of boarded-up, single-storey shops. Some showed signs of fire damage. The walkway was badly lit. The whole area was deserted. The only sound apart from their footsteps came from pigeons throating on the roof.

'Where is this office of yours?' Haggerty asked.

'Not far. Just down there.' Tomaso pointed vaguely towards the corner they were approaching. In what looked like an afterthought, he took hold of Haggerty's arm. 'By the way, I've been meaning to ask. Is this your first trip to Guatemala?'

Before Haggerty could reply, they heard the light sound of running feet. Tomaso stopped and Haggerty turned with him to look back. The second man they had left at the customs hall, Diaz, was approaching. As Tomaso's grip suddenly tightened on his arm Haggerty became suspicious. He shrugged it off.

'What's going on here?'

Tomaso raised a placating hand. 'Please, *señor* ...' Peloquin moved closer. Haggerty stepped back, looking from him to Tomaso.

'Who are you people?'

Tomaso sighed and dropped his hand. He nodded to Peloquin.

'Take him.'

The big man had his gun out almost instantly. He pointed the cold black nose of the Colt Commander at Haggerty's chest. Diaz reached them, panting, and fumbled for his gun.

'*Señor*, Tomaso said quietly, 'I think it would be better if you came quietly.'

Haggerty glared at him. He was angry at being fooled so easily.

'You son-of-a-bitch!'

Tomaso shrugged. 'Just keep walking,' he said and turned to speak quickly in Spanish to Peloquin. The security agent jabbed his pistol into Haggerty's chest with bruising force and pushed him on towards the corner.

'What the hell is this?' Haggerty staggered back. 'Where are you taking me?'

'National Security headquarters,' Tomaso said.

'You better have good reason.' Haggerty's voice was raised, hot and angry. 'This is kidnapping. Our Embassy will raise hell. I promise you that.'

'Please, there's no need for a scene. We just want to ask you a few questions.' The two agents hustled him on.

They turned the corner. A green Ford Falcon with parking lights on stood at the kerb. Peloquin moved ahead and opened the door.

'Inside, please,' Tomaso said.

Pressed forward by Diaz, Haggerty got into the back seat. The two security agents got in on either side. Tomaso took the driver's seat and peered back at Haggerty in the gloomy interior. 'Just relax, *señor*. Everything will be okay. So please, no trouble.'

The car pulled away from the sidewalk and did a U-turn on the empty plaza, headlights sweeping across the thick vegetation fringing the area. They left the airport trunk road and entered a bigger highway. The car picked up speed. There was no traffic about. The only light inside the car came from the instrument panel as the needle crept past 120 kilometres. Everything was happening very fast. In the back seat, wedged between his shadowy captors, Stephen Haggerty sat upright, his mouth dry.

Ahead, a faint glow in the sky showed they were headed towards Guatemala City.

'You may dress.'

Eva Valdes, naked and humiliated, snatched up her clothes from the table and started to put them on. The heavy-set woman in uniform, arms folded, watched impassively. 'You bitch!' Eva said hotly. 'Turn your back.'

The woman did not move.

'You have no right to do this to me.' Tears distorted Eva's vision as she struggled with her clothes.

'It's procedure, *señorita*,' the woman said suddenly. 'You have nothing to complain about.'

'Yes I have,' Eva said heatedly. 'You'll soon see.'

There was a long pause.

'You should not get upset at me,' the customs woman said. 'It is my orders.'

'Let me out of here,' Eva said as she finally buttoned her blouse.

'I don't wish to annoy you further, *señorita*,' the woman said, 'but I can't.'

'What are you saying?' Eva stared in disbelief. 'You can't hold me here. I've done nothing. Release me!'

The woman shook her head. 'My orders are to keep you here.'

The narrow beam from the Falcon's headlights swept over a copse of dead trees as the car suddenly swung off the highway and bounced onto a narrow dirt road. In the back seat, Stephen Haggerty swayed back and forward with his captors as the car slithered on the broken ground. The sudden change of direction sent an icy chill through him. This was a dangerous development.

'Look, I know you guys hate the media,' Haggerty said. He kept his voice calm, not reflecting his alarm. 'But if you're thinking of making me disappear, it won't help.'

'Don't be ridiculous,' Tomaso said shortly. 'This is not Argentina.'

The Falcon continued to rock up and down on the broken surface. The headlights flashed skyward off the rutted track. Nothing else showed in the darkness.

'We're taking a short-cut, that's all,' Tomaso said finally. 'A security precaution.'

'Don't give me that,' Haggerty said. He felt the weight of his big guards pressing in on either side. 'You're taking me away from the city.' It was true. The faint glow in the sky was passing to their right. Tomaso was silent.

The track ahead suddenly widened. It led into a broad earthen lot. Two big excavators lay abandoned at the far end. The Ford made a wide arc and came to a halt in the centre. The headlight

122

beams gleamed on the muddy earth. Tomaso switched off the engine.

In the sudden silence, he turned slowly to face the back seat. His face barely visible in the gloom, he spoke rapidly in Spanish. Quickly, the agents pinioned Haggerty. He gasped as they forced his body forward. Before he could resist, they clamped handcuffs on his wrists. Peloquin opened his door and started out backwards.

'Look now –' Haggerty began but Diaz cut him short, slamming the nose of his gun hard into his side. As he buckled in pain, Peloquin reached in and grabbed the neck of his jacket. With a quick jerk, he hauled him outside. Haggerty's knees banged on the ledge of the door and there was a sound of ripping material. The strong hands of Peloquin hauled him to his feet.

A face leaned close in the darkness. 'No more trouble, eh?' It was Tomaso.

'Fuck you!' Haggerty said. Behind him, Diaz understood the phrase. He sent Haggerty sprawling into the dirt with a sudden, savage blow in the back.

Silently, the three men stared down at him. Tomaso, the smaller, was in the middle. Haggerty with his hands cuffed behind his back, struggled to his knees. The humiliation of their gaze was too much for him. Fighting for balance, he got to his feet again.

'Damn you!' He spat at them, swaying and still panting from the effort. 'You won't get away with this!'

Peloquin stepped forward within inches of Haggerty. His face was expressionless. With the heel of his hand, he pushed Haggerty in the chest, sending him backwards. He toppled into the pool of light created by the headlights. His body hit the ground hard and for a moment he lay dazed and face down in the dirt. Slowly, breathing hard, he arched his body to stare up at them, his face marked with dried clay.

There were more words in Spanish. The three men stepped forward into the light, the lightbeams around them breaking into strange shapes. As Haggerty glared, Tomaso who stood behind the other two quietly raised his gun.

This was it. All the wonder, the heartache and pain, all those

123

foolish absorptions were over. Along with what hope there was. He would never know now.

'Bastards!' He spat it at them with all the strength he could muster. 'Bastards!'

*

In the airport terminal, Eva Valdes looked at the uniformed official standing by the empty customs table. 'I want to speak to someone in authority,' she said sharply.

The official, a small middle-aged man, took in the flowing dark hair around the oval face, now pale and set. He turned to look around the empty hall and then back to her. He lifted his hands and pulled a long face.

'I'm sorry, *señorita*,' he said, 'there is only me.'

'Don't be ridiculous!' she said. 'I need to talk to someone in command. Where is the office of the police?'

He pointed to the end of the hall. 'As you can see, they are closed. There are no more flights tonight. Everybody has gone home.'

She looked down the hall. The only people about were two cleaners, dragging brushes behind them. Eva's anger was replaced by bewilderment. And behind it was a growing dread. Something had gone terribly wrong.

The customs official cleared his throat.

'The *señorita*'s luggage,' he said timorously. 'Is that it, by any chance?' He pointed to the pair of bags resting by the wall. One was hers. The other was Stephen Haggerty's. So he had not picked it up.

'Yes, that's my luggage,' she said.

Encouraged, he pressed forward. 'Perhaps I can find a cab for the *señorita*?' he asked eagerly.

She looked at him without listening.

'I need to find a phone,' she said.

'Yes, certainly,' he said, nodding vigorously. 'There is one in the lobby, through that exit. Let me assist you.' He hurried over and picked up the two bags.

Eva Valdes was already walking towards the exit.

The night air was deadly still. The prone figure lay in the full glare of the headlight beams. The torn shirt showed a strip of exposed marked flesh. High above, the glittering stars hung suspended, almost breathless, in the black velvet sky.

Faintly, the figure moved. A faint shift of the shoulder, the body scraping against the earth. Slowly, very slowly, Stephen Haggerty lifted his head.

'Jesus Christ!' His voice was dry and cracked. He stared at the two bodies sprawled on the earth before him.

From the darkness, a low, relieved chuckle floated in. Haggerty lifted his eyes and strained to see through the glare.

Tomaso stepped out of the shadows. He still had a gun in his hand.

'Well,' he said, 'I'm glad that is over.' He dropped to one knee beside Haggerty. 'Forgive me. Are you okay?'

'Yes,' Haggery said, trying to sound more calm than he felt. 'Who are you anyway?'

'A soldier of the people, *señor*,' Tomaso said. He moved across to Peloquin's body which lay, arms outstretched, barely two feet from Haggerty. 'We do not have much time,' he said, searching quickly through the dead man's pockets. He pulled out a key. Moving behind Haggerty, he unlocked the handcuffs and helped him up. Still unsteady, Haggerty rubbed his numbed wrists and stared down at the bodies. That could have been him.

'Here, take this.' Tomaso handed him one of the dead man's guns. 'Put it away and help me get them into the trunk of the car.' Haggerty stuck the gun in his belt. Together they dragged the heavier Peloquin to the back of the Ford. Tomaso opened the trunk. Struggling with the dead weight, they got the body in. 'One more time,' Tomaso panted.

They picked up Diaz.

'Look, you want to tell me what the hell is going on?' Haggerty asked as they shuffled sideways towards the car.

'These men were police, *señor*. On personal orders from the President to kill you.'

'And your part?' They reached the side of the car.

Tomaso laughed. 'In a moment, *señor*. Come on, lift.'

Breathing hard, they pushed down the lid of the trunk on the bodies. 'That's it. Let's go,' Tomaso said. They hurried to the front and got in. Tomaso started the engine as Haggerty lit a crumpled cigarette. It was, he thought, one of the most beautiful tastes he had ever enjoyed. They headed back over the dirt track.

'Okay,' Haggerty said finally, 'let's hear your explanation.'

Tomaso laughed again but this time it was soft and without strain.

'I don't have one yet,' he said. He glanced across at Haggerty. 'But I do have a question.'

Haggerty drew on his cigarette. 'What is it?'

'I saw a phone message President Serena received before he ordered your death.' Tomaso wrestled briefly with the steering as the car struck a pothole. 'May I ask what you know about a Dr Ernst Dackman?'

It was almost midnight but life in the *barrio* where Tomaso took him on the outskirts of Guatemala City was still vibrant. Stephen Haggerty could hear the cries of playing children and the shouted talk of neighbours above the ghetto-blasting music. The earthen walls of the hut where he sat with Tomaso and a man named Hector helped dull the sound – but not by much.

The hut was guarded by armed men. But they too were relaxed. The army almost never came out after dark. The people felt safe then and so did the guerrillas. Like Tomaso and Hector who was now questioning him.

'Look,' Haggerty said, 'it must be clear to you by now that I know almost nothing about this Dr Dackman,' he stubbed out his cigarette, 'except that he wants me dead.'

Hector nodded.

'It is all very strange,' he said. His English, although highly accented, was good. From the way Tomaso deferred to him, Haggerty guessed that Hector was an important figure in their movement. He was a tall, dark man who was dressed in an open-necked shirt and a well-worn large grey cardigan. It was clear he did not give much thought to clothes. There were no lines around his mouth to show he spent much time on laughter either. He had a strikingly narrow skull that made his face seem long and very sharp. The small moustache on his upper lip did little to lighten the effect. His eyes were dark, almost black, even against the sallow skin but they showed a cool quickness that suggested a strong intelligence. To Haggerty, despite Hector's obvious authority over the armed men around them, he seemed more of an intellectual than a soldier.

It was clear he was using his mind now as he leaned forward and looked keenly at Haggerty. 'It seems to me, *señor*, that you must be close to discovering some damaging information about this man Dackman. Otherwise, he would not be trying so desperately to kill you.'

'I agree.'

'We know that Dackman is a close associate of the President. But that does not mean he could expect his help on a matter like this.' Now he tried a smile and Haggerty saw why the effort left no lines. 'Serena is not noted here for bailing out friends in trouble. Rather the opposite. So, I can only conclude that whatever is damaging in this case for Dackman must be damaging to Serena too. He would not take the risk in having an American killed otherwise. Because of that,' he looked at Haggerty, 'I believe we should help you.'

Haggerty caught Tomaso's smile and grinned back.

'Our knowledge of Dr Dackman is limited,' Hector continued, 'but you are welcome to what there is of it. Tomaso, if you would explain?'

'Before you do,' Haggerty broke in, 'I'm getting more worried about Miss Valdes. Isn't it taking a little long to get her here?'

'I wouldn't be too concerned,' Tomaso said. 'Our men are already at your hotel. Once she arrives there, they will bring her here. I suspect those customs people at the airport have been over-zealous. Don't worry. She should be here soon.'

'I hope so,' Haggerty said. 'Anyway, go ahead with what you wanted to say.'

'Tomaso nodded. 'What we know about Ernst Dackman is common knowledge here. He's lived in Guatemala for almost five years. As far as we know, his first two years here were entirely innocent. He came as a consultant for the World Health Organisation. That was when he started working for Dr Whitten.'

'Whitten?' Haggerty said. 'Who is Whitten?'

'He's a much revered man here,' Tomaso said. 'A medical missionary who gave up his work as a blood specialist twenty years ago in New York to come and work among the Indians. He lives outside the small mountain village of San Antonio. It's about two hundred miles north of here. That was where Dackman first went to work with him.'

'They were together for two years,' Tomaso went on, 'then Dackman left. No one knows why. But for the next three years, he ran a network of blood banks in the *barrios* around Guatemala City. It was a barbarous business. He bled the poorest and the most destitute. Mothers who had no bread-earner to support their families; children who had been abandoned and had no money; and drunks and drug addicts who needed to support their habits.

'For their blood, these people received less than $4 in your money. And sometimes a slice of bread or a soft drink. And it happened to many of them every week. Often there was no medical supervision because Dackman was not always there. And the orderlies were poor like everybody else. To keep their jobs, they had to donate their blood weekly too. It was tragic. Tens of thousands of people were used.'

'Where did all this blood go?'

'To the United States, to Europe, to Canada. It was given to wealthy people for operations and things like that.'

'I know of one broker,' Haggerty said, 'a former partner of Dackman called Otto Lentz. His secretary told me he bought blood here. Have you heard of him?'

Tomaso shook his head.

'I think Dackman murdered him,' Haggerty said grimly, 'although I still don't know why.'

'With this man, anything is possible,' Tomaso said. 'Here, his wretched business contributed to much sickness in our people. But that was not enough to halt his business. It was a death that finally brought his activities to an end. It happened last September. Two young girls – they were only thirteen and fourteen – gave blood so that they could buy party dresses for their annual feast-day celebration. The orderlies at Dackman's clinics were reusing infected needles. One of the girls died. The other was found to be paralysed.'

128

Haggerty shook his head in disgust. Tomaso nodded.

'A good many people had been trying to close the clinics before this happened. But with Serena's protection, it was hopeless. However, with the tragedy of those young girls, people took the law into their own hands. There was a demonstration that turned to rioting. The people burned down the clinics. And Dackman was forced to leave the country.'

'Do you know where he is now?' Haggerty asked.

Tomaso shook his head.

'No. But one man who might be able to help you is Dr Whitten. If anybody could unlock Dackman's secrets, it would be him.' Tomaso looked at Hector. 'I think he should go and see him, sir.'

'You really think so?' Hector sat back in his chair and rubbed his chin thoughtfully.

'Yes. Julio is from the area. He could take him.'

Hector looked at Haggerty. 'It's a hard journey. And dangerous. Are you interested?'

'If it brings me nearer to understanding why Dackman wants me killed, yes. I'd like to go,' Haggerty said.

'Very well. I'll make the arrangements,' Hector said. 'You may stay here tonight. Tomorrow you can travel.'

Tomaso looked at his watch. 'I must go. The President will be waiting.'

'Be careful,' Hector said. 'Serena is no fool.'

'What can he say? We took our friend out to kill him. He seized one of our guns and broke away. He tried to take the car. Diaz and Peloquin struggled with him. A gun went off and the gas tank exploded. Pouf!'

'How are you going to get a body to replace me?' Haggerty asked.

Tomaso smiled. 'It's already done. Corpses are not a scarce commodity in Guatemala, my friend.' As he rose to go, someone knocked on the door. 'Come in,' he said.

Two men led a frightened Eva Valdes into the room. She saw Haggerty.

'Stephen!'

She rushed across the room to embrace him. Hector watched,

somewhat cynically. Tomaso grinned. After some discreet moments he leaned forward to tap Haggerty's shoulder.

'I must go, my friend,' he whispered.

Haggerty disengaged to shake hands. He turned to Eva. 'This man,' he said, gesturing to Tomaso, 'saved my life.'

Eva looked at Tomaso and smiled as she clutched Haggerty.

'Thank you,' she said.

He bowed to her, smiled. Within moments he was gone. Haggerty turned to Hector.

'Would it be possible to take Miss Valdes with me tomorrow?'

Hector shook his head as he rose. 'No, I can't allow it. The route is anything but secure. You must go alone. After tonight, she can return to the hotel and wait for you to come back. Don't worry, she will be safe there.' He opened the door of the hut and gestured outside. 'This way please.'

It took another thirty minutes before they were finally alone. The room, above a small *cantina*, was tiny and the bed primitive.

'Stephen, I was frantic. I thought you were dead.'

He looked at her and saw that her eyes were still showing her disturbance at the experience. Still, he grinned and moved closer to take her in his arms. She was in the act of loosening her blouse but she twisted against his arms to face him.

'Come on,' she said, 'I'm serious. I really did think something terrible had happened to you.' She kissed him quickly. 'I don't know what I would have done if it had.'

He was moving his hands up under the blouse and along the soft golden flesh of her back. He unclipped her bra.

'Wait now,' she said, although her voice seemed a little weaker. 'You haven't told me what happened to you. You're all dirty and you've ...' he was working his hands down her back, 'got mixed up with some kind of subversives and there's this awful place ...' But she couldn't go on. He had her skirt opened and lowered and then the rest came down too. Her resistance was draining away.

'Stephen,' she said weakly, swaying, 'aren't you going to tell me what happened?'

He looked up from his knees. 'Later,' he said.

130

Much, much later, she turned to find him still awake. As she lay against his chest, he told her something of what had happened to him. But he could not bring himself to tell her everything. There were matters, he realised, that were better not talked about. No one could ever share them.

Like kneeling on an earthen lot, for instance. Or dying under lights.

11

The Washington sky was overcast and the temperature was below freezing when Vern Railsback joined the William Masters funeral procession at Arlington Cemetery. On the nearby hillside, patches of snow clung to the grass among the ordered rows of gravestones. Pulling his black coat closer around him, Railsback thought of a verse by one of his favourite poets, Wystan Auden – A memorial to W. B. Yeats.

> He disappeared in the dead of winter:
> The brooks were frozen, the airports almost deserted,
> And snow disfigured the public statues;
> The mercury sank in the mouth of the dying day.
> What instruments we have agree
> The day of his death was a dark cold day.

A dark cold day. It was that all right. Silently, Vern moved up to join the sombre group threading slowly up the narrow path. Most of them he already knew. Myra was there with her mother; and a dozen or so colleagues from the Agency. People who had worked with both William and himself. Cal was there, head bowed, looking terribly aged. With him was James Korner. William's former boss and now chief of Western Hemisphere Operations.

Korner? Vern stared. What was he doing here? He had no love for William Masters. If anything, it was people like Korner who likely contributed to his death. Vern watched the tall, gaunt figure gripping Cal Masters's arm and felt a wave of anger. But he stifled it and fell in behind the rest.

The procession moved up the hill after the hearse. At the

132

graveside up ahead, a small troop of Marines waited at attention. As the hearse drew in, the darkly dressed mourners moved awkwardly off the path and gathered in a circle around the grave. The attendants brought out the coffin. Myra Masters, holding on to her mother, was crying quietly. A marriage long dead in name, Vern thought, was now dead in fact. He kept to the rear, his head lowered. He was thinking again of his first meeting with William. It was easy to recall.

The two of them, sitting on their luggage beside the tarmac at Saigon Airport, waiting for a flight to their first posting in Thailand. Two skinny-faced kids they were then, thrilled at their first taste of espionage – even if they really didn't know what it was all about. William, already a heavy drinker but not yet an alcoholic. And Vern, acknowledging for the first time the shift in his sexual identity. They were truly the odd couple.

'Honour Guard! Tenshun!'

He heard the sound of heels crashing now and the metallic rattle of rifle bolts. He looked up to see the gun barrels rise skyward. The gathering was still as the bugler's lonely Last Post echoed through the drab winter air.

Oh, William, what a decent human being you were, Vern thought. He felt the tears welling and struggled to control them. This was not the time. He knew how the story would be told in the corridors at Langley if he cried. He stood, his face starting to freeze in the bitter weather, as the trumpeter sounded a rally then dropped to the slow final farewell. With the echoes dying in the gloomy air, the marine brought the bugle to his side. In the sudden stillness, the hum of morning traffic crossing Arlington Bridge could be heard.

'Fire!'

The volley crashed around the silent slopes. Bright shell cases spewed from the rifles. Another volley. Then a third. As the last shot died, a barked command brought the rifles banging to the frozen earth.

Vern swallowed and looked away. Turning towards the great memorial shrine where Jack Kennedy lay a few hundred yards away, he suddenly noticed a dark figure by the steps. Blinking, he stared again to make sure.

It was Alva Martin.

Oh, God. He shook his head and looked back at William Masters's coffin. It was all wrong. This wasn't the way it should be. Alva over there and people like Korner here. Particularly Korner, standing there with that white, bony face discreetly mournful and the eyes downcast. As Vern stared, some telepathy must have passed for those eyes lifted briefly and met his. Antagonism flared across the grave before Korner dropped his head again. But that was not enough for Vern. He held his stare, drilling the bowed grey head with hate.

He finally turned and slipped away. The murmur of the clergyman faded behind him as he walked.

Alva saw him approaching and came down the steps to meet him. He could see she was distraught. Silently, he put his arms around her as they met. They stood at the steps, her grief flowing.

'I miss him, Vern.' Her voice was muffled against him. 'So much.' He held her tightly, afraid to speak in case his voice would break.

'He was so gentle. Such a good man.'

Below them, the Marines were marching sharply away. The service was ending. Soon everybody would be gone. William Masters would be alone in the Arlington earth.

Alva suddenly pulled away. 'We can't let it end here, Vern.'

'It won't,' he said. 'I promise you.' There was an obligation to be honoured. And he would do it. He took her handkerchief and dabbed her tear-stained cheeks.

'Listen, Vern, I found our friend Whitten.'

He stopped. 'Where?'

'He's in Guatemala. A missionary. And that San Antonio? It's a tiny village he works in.' She tried to laugh. 'It wasn't Texas at all. No Neiman-Marcus there.'

He forced himself to grin. 'That's my girl. Where exactly is this place?'

'Tony Considine says it's almost two hundred miles north of the capital. In the mountains. It's guerrilla country. Tony says it's very dangerous for an American.'

'If that's where he is, there isn't much choice. I'll go.'

134

Alva looked at him, warmth growing again in her large tear-filled eyes.

'You're marvellous, Vern,' she hugged him. 'I love you.'

'Okay.' He smiled as he disengaged and held her arms. Turning, he looked down towards the funeral. It was breaking up. 'Listen, I'll have to get permission to take leave.'

'They'll want to know why you're going.'

He nodded. 'I guess we'll just have to keep our fingers crossed. If we're lucky it won't get beyond personnel.'

'When will you try for it?'

'As soon as I get to the office. Alva, I better go back down there.' He paused and looked at her. 'Before I go, remember one thing. That wasn't William's funeral down there with those people. This is it here. With us.'

'Thank you, Vern,' she whispered. She looked down, hesitant. 'I brought some roses for him.' She pointed to the bag on the steps.

'I understand,' he said.

Her large brown eyes looked helplessly at him. 'I wanted to wait until everybody left. You know what I mean?'

'Sure, I do,' his voice was choked. 'Listen, I gotta go, Alva.' Hurriedly, he kissed her and started back.

That afternoon, he got the message that James Korner wanted to see him. Right away. Walking down the long corridor to the Western Hemisphere Section, Vern knew it would be about his request to visit Guatemala.

Korner's secretary, a young blonde-haired girl who was reputed to be his mistress, smiled shyly at Vern as she showed him into her boss. The office was large but apart from a huge teak desk, it was sparsely furnished. Korner glanced up from some papers he was reading and gestured to a chair. Vern sat down.

With his grim, bony face and deep-set eyes, Korner could have stepped out of a horror movie, Vern thought. Some in the Agency made the mistake of treating him as if he did. Their careers soon stalled. Korner, Vern knew, was a brilliant and dedicated intelligence officer who had an intuitive talent for making the bureaucracy work in his favour. Since entering the service as a

135

Rhodes Scholar twenty-two years back, he had become adept at handling those who opposed him. But Vern Railsback was one of his few failures. And both of them knew it.

'I see you want to go to Guatemala.' Korner finally put down the papers. 'What's the purpose of the visit?'

'I've been interested in that part of the world for some time,' Vern said. 'I thought there might be room for an internal paper. A sort of minor contribution to the embargo debate.'

'I see,' Korner said. 'Have you a particular view you'd like to bring out?'

'Yes.' He had thought it out earlier. 'I think our policy is short-sighted, given the balance of forces in the area. There are other ways of forcing the Guatemalans to comply with our views. Monetary measures, for instance. Taking away their guns when the two sides are virtually split fifty-fifty is likely to bring down Serena. That would damage our standing with the other military regimes in the area. It might even hand a victory to the very people we're opposed to.'

'Well put,' Korner said. 'Railsback, we have disagreed on principle in the past. But on this one, we hold the same views. Although I would go a little farther than you on the conclusion. If Guatemala goes, and we agree that it's likely under present conditions, then Honduras and Salvador will tumble as well. With leftist governments in this area, the Soviets will have a thumb on our jugular.' He sat back in his chair. 'Having said that, and knowing we share some views, I still can't let you go. So I'm afraid your request is denied.'

'May I ask why?'

'There are two substantial reasons. Officially, I'll offer you one. Guatemala is extremely unstable at present. Aside from the numerous political murders down there, there have also been countless kidnappings. You are an analyst who has had access to highly classified information. You would be a godsend to any Marxist group who got their hands on you. It has always been Agency policy not to allow an employee of your classification to enter an area regarded as unstable.'

'You said there were two substantial reasons for the refusal. What's the second?'

'I don't think a person of your orientation is suitable for handling volatile situations as you would likely find in Guatemala.'

'So you're riding that hobby-horse again, are you?' Vern didn't bother to hide his contempt. But if Korner saw it he showed no sign.

'Homosexuals are a risk, statistically and factually,' he said. 'It's not a personal matter, Railsback. I would be derelict if I didn't oppose people like you in the service.'

'You're a rotten bastard, Korner,' Vern said. 'You pervert the regulations of this department and you defy the courts with those views. And all claimed as an upholder of American democracy. The hell you are. You're a death-watch beetle, that's what you are. But one of these days, you'll get stepped on.'

'The interview is over,' Korner said coldly.

In the corridor, Vern Railsback's anger had already drained away. Uppermost in his mind now was how to get to Guatemala. There had to be a way.

In his office Korner was already on the phone.

'He's going to try getting down there,' he said. 'I want him watched – around the clock.'

12

Someone was shaking him urgently.

Very unwillingly, Stephen Haggerty opened his eyes. The room looked even more appalling in the early light. The thin ray of sunlight falling from the broken skylight was filled with dust. Haggerty lay with his back to the mud caked wall. His skin felt prickly, like he was lying on straw. He looked down and saw he was.

'Stephen.' Eva was shaking him.

He stretched lazily, then suddenly remembered. 'Oh, God. What time is it?'

'I don't know.' She poked him. 'Your guide is here.'

He looked up. A young dark-haired man, grinning from ear to ear, stood in the doorway with a bag between his feet. Seeing Haggerty awake, he came forward.

'I am Julio, *señor*,' he said, extending his hand.

'Get him out!' Eva cried. Haggerty turned. She held part of the small blanket against her chest. He grinned, sat up and waved an arm.

'Okay, Julio. That's far enough. Come on, outside.'

Julio backed out, still smiling, eyes on Eva. The door closed.

'Cheeky bastard.' Haggerty threw off the blanket and swung his legs over the side of the bed. 'Oh, shit!' He caught himself at the sudden pain. He was aching in a dozen places.

'Still bad?' She dropped the blanket immediately and moved down to him, touching the dark weals gently. He straightened, the thought crossing his mind that he was in damned better shape than the poor bastards who did it to him.

Carefully he eased himself to his feet. Eva got off the rough bed with him, grimacing now at the touch of the dirty timber floor.

138

She crossed to the corner wash-basin. He marvelled again at the soft, easy grace of her unclothed body as she bent to turn the tap on. She waited impatiently. A thin flow of water emerged.

'Makes a change from Miami,' he said.

She looked up at the dirt-smeared walls. 'You know something? I wish to God we'd never come here.' He watched in silence as she bent to splash the trickling water on her face. She reached for the small grey-white towel alongside the sink.

'Eva, I'm sorry,' Haggerty said finally. 'I really wish I could take you out of here. And if there was any possible way, I'd do it. But I can't drop this thing. Not until I find Dackman.' He touched her shoulder. 'You know that, don't you?'

She lowered the towel and turned to face him. His hand fell away. He was struck by how upset she looked. 'Please, Stephen, couldn't we just go back to the States? And forget the whole thing?' She spoke in a rush. We don't have to go to Miami. We could go to New York. Or Canada even, if you want.'

He felt a glimmering of irritation. Didn't she understand? He took the towel she handed him and tossed it on his shoulder. He looked at her in the gathering silence. 'Come on, Eva, don't be like that. You know I can't leave. Not yet.'

She turned away.

'It's not turning out the way I thought,' she said suddenly. He stood there, looking at the delicate naked back etched against the mud-caked wall. It hit him that he was expecting too much of her. This was a girl whose daily grind passed in libraries with only the hum of a photocopier for company. He realised now that although she was both bright and beautiful, her life was played out in a very small area and with very few people – her mother, colleagues in the university and perhaps a few personal friends – she talked so little about them, he thought they must be few. And then he came along. Almost immediately, she was getting a crash course on murder, revolution, love-making (she needed no help there) and Third World squalor.

He looked at her, dressing now, awkward in her efforts to keep her clothes clear of the dirty floor. He knew she must be feeling revulsion at the spiky feeling the soiled clothes were giving her.

'Eva,' he said. She was working at the zip. 'I'm sorry. But I can't do it. Even though I know it's costing you.'

She didn't speak. He put a hand to her shoulder.

'I've got to see it through. I can't let that man go. Not after what he's done.' He leaned forward, trying again to see her face. But she kept it down, worrying the zip. He looked at the bowed crown of her glistening dark hair. 'Eva, you're very important to me. I want you to know that. And I don't want this thing to come between us. But you have to understand. Please.'

She raised her head. He saw her eyes were filled with tears.

'Oh, Stephen.' Her voice broke. He reached down and took her in his arms.

'It's going to be all right,' he said. He wanted her to believe that. More than anything, he wanted to believe it too.

Beyond the dirty skylight, the sky was blue. Outside, it was warming up slowly into a beautiful clear morning.

Throughout that day Haggerty and the driver Julio moved deeper into the mountains.

The journey by jeep from the capital had begun comfortably on the Pan American Highway. But eventually their route forced them onto the more primitive dirt roads which the Guatemalan highways department specialised in. (On one stretch, Haggerty thought he saw a group of workmen creating, rather than filling, holes in the road.) The trip was proving a bone-shaker.

Eva had recovered from her depression before they left. He arranged for her to get a room in the downtown Plaza Hotel and extracted her promise that she would not leave the hotel until he returned. He did not want to risk anything happening to her while he was away.

For her part, she insisted on double-checking the travel route to Dr Whitten's house with Julio; making sure his defective English would not create misunderstandings. She also bought their supplies and harried Julio to get enough gas for the return journey. Haggerty felt pleased, almost mothered, by the attention. But when he saw the depression returning as they prepared to go, he hurried the departure. Promising to return in three days, he gave her a last farewell kiss – her grip was so tight his bruises re-ignited in pain. His last sight of her was as she turned into the Plaza, her hand to her eyes.

For almost ten hours after that, he and Julio drove. All the time pressing deeper into the mountains. With darkness, they finally stopped in a clearing by the dirt road. They both slept after eating. But now Haggerty was awake again.

The dry air of the mountains should have been alive with sound. Instead, the blackness around them was cloaked in stillness. It was an eerie feeling. Lying on the hard earth in his sleeping bag, a chord echoed in Haggerty's memory. His mind returned to those nights on the beach at Cam Ramh Bay in Vietnam.

The question of why he was now suddenly thinking of it again was not hard to answer. Like in Vietnam, he had cut himself adrift from the world he was used to. And again, like Vietnam, he had known again the terror of facing death.

He pulled the sleeping bag tighter around his shoulders and shifted his head to a more comfortable position on the folded jacket, staring into the darkness.

He was thinking again of last night. Of that earthen lot outside Guatemala City. And that awful, ice-tingling sensation that spread like a cancer inside his gut when he saw the raised gun enter the lightbeam and realised he was about to die. The memory was still powerful, soul-shaking.

But yet, and this was strange, when he considered that feeling it was very different from the agony he had experienced in Vietnam. It brought to mind an inscription he came across while wandering through a Buddhist temple outside Saigon. The guide's translation moved him enough at the time to jot it down in his notebook. It was part of the Dhammaphada.

> Any man who hates
> Can harm another
> But one's own mind
> if badly used
> Can do the
> Greater harm.

141

He thought about that, staring up into the star-filled sky. Maybe that was the difference between the two. Here it was Dackman and his people who were doing the harm. In Vietnam, it had been himself.

In the silence, he brought a hand out to squint at his watch. It was just after 4 a.m. He sat up on an elbow and tapped the sleeping driver who lay across from him.

'Julio,' he said softly.

The driver shifted uneasily. 'Ay?' he mumbled.

'It's close to dawn,' Haggerty said. 'Time to move.'

By 9 a.m. that morning in Guatemala City, aides were arriving for work at the Presidential Palace. General Serena's secretary looked up and smiled as Tomaso entered her office.

'Well, what a nice beginning to the day,' she said. 'Good morning, Tomaso. You're looking very handsome.'

'Christina, don't say that,' Tomaso scolded as he took off his jacket. 'You'll create a scandal if anyone hears you.' But he grinned. Christina was at least twenty-five years older than he was.

'Oh, my pigeon, you are so sensitive,' she said. 'You must learn to accept compliments. Perhaps you might even let me teach you. A young boy with experience can go far.'

'Temptress,' Tomaso said. 'I'll forget my work next.'

Christina sighed. 'If only you would, Tomaso. This is no place for someone like you. You're not like the rest of this gang. But you watch. They'll drag you down too, if you're not careful. You should get out before that happens.'

'Come on, Christina, don't be so gloomy. I can see what goes on around here. And I am careful. Don't fret about me. I'm not dumb you know.'

She smiled, taken in by the boyishness. 'How sweet and innocent you are. And how I would love to spend just one night with you.' She leaned forward in her chair as though to grab him but he retreated hastily. Christina laughed and lay back.

'Well, my sweet, what is it you want?'

'The Boss wants me to prepare a report on our support in

142

Washington. This embargo business. He is trying to rally opposition.'

Christina shrugged. 'If you ask me, he's whistling in the wind.' She gestured to the filing cabinets. 'Take your choice. There are at least six drawers of political files in there. You can save time by going through the red-tagged files first. They're the people we're closest to. And don't expect me to cart the files back and forth for you. In this office, everybody looks after themselves.'

'Sure.' Tomaso grinned. Christina was not only highly sensual, she was also lazy. That would help since she was not likely to keep track of what he was doing. He cleared a desk in the corner and began carrying over files.

He was already pleased with the way things had turned out after the other night's affair. Serena had received him immediately and appeared to accept his explanation of what happened the night before. The President was even pleased that two potentially damaging witnesses to a politically sensitive murder had been eliminated. Afterwards, he had spent almost two hours with Tomaso talking about the embargo and working on ways to marshal support in Washington. To Tomaso, this was a golden opportunity to help the movement. If there was anything compromising in the American files, he would find it.

As it turned out, he was quickly disappointed. There were boring submissions from lobbyists, law firms, military consultants and right-wing windbags, but very few relationships with politicians of substance. One of those, he found, was with Cal Masters, the Florida Congressman. But Masters's file was puzzling. A number of the memoranda were cross-referenced to another file which was not among those in the group he had. It was coded black.

Puzzled, Tomaso continued through the files. A dozen notations later, he came across another file with similar cross-references to Masters's. This time the file belonged to James Korner, who appeared to be an important bureaucrat in the American intelligence community. It was also coded black.

He looked up at Christina, who was smoking a cigarette and reading a magazine.

'Christina, what are the black tags for?'

143

She stopped reading and slowly lowered the magazine to stare at him.

'What do you want to know for?'

He tapped the file in front of him. 'There are some references to it in these files. I just wondered if I was missing something useful.'

She shook her head. 'Well, you're not. Forget about them. They're not important.'

He nodded. 'Okay. Just thought I'd ask.'

He continued reading the files and making notes. Five minutes later, he heard her get up. With his head bent, he watched her go to a cabinet in the corner and lock it. She returned to her desk and threw the key into the drawer.

He had made numerous notes, none of great consequence, by the time Christina rose at 11.30 to leave for lunch. He looked up, smiling.

'Who is it today?' he asked. Christina was known around the Palace as an indefatigable luncheon partner.

She smiled back. 'General Guinoli. We are visiting Alfredo's.'

Guinoli, the air force commander, was a member of the junta.

'That will be nice,' Tomaso said. One day when his usefulness was ending, they would use information like that.

'See you later, my pigeon,' Christina said as she swept out of the door.

He gave her five minutes, then rose and crossed to the desk. It was typical of Christina that she had not bothered to lock it. He went through the drawers swiftly and took out all the keys he could find. Knowing how risky the enterprise was, he stopped to listen but there were no unusual sounds from outside.

He tried the keys one by one on the cabinet. It was almost the last that worked. Quickly, he pulled the drawer open. To his surprise there was just the single file. He took it out, closed the drawer and returned quickly to his desk. If anyone came now, he would appear to be working normally on his designated task. He placed the black-coded file on top and opened it.

For five minutes, he read the file in silence and with growing excitement. So this was what Dackman, Masters, Korner and

144

Serena himself were about. No wonder they wanted Stephen Haggerty dead. If he got even close it would ruin them all.

He had almost finished reading, when he heard a sudden noise at the door.

'Damn!' Silently, he shut the file and slid it under the others. He looked up as Christina entered.

'Christina!' he said in surprise. 'Back so early?'

She nodded shortly. He could see she was not in a good mood.

'The donkeys decided to hold a special meeting. Now I have to sit here and wait until it's over.'

'What a pity,' Tomaso said sympathetically. 'And you looking forward to Alfredo's.'

'Yes,' she said, 'I could kill that Guinoli.'

'Why not go yourself?'

'I can't. Guinoli tells me I may be needed.'

That was strange, Tomaso thought. Why hadn't Serena himself told her? But he was cautious and decided not to pursue it.

The important thing now was to stay cool and wait for the opportunity to return the file. He knew that Christina would leave the office again sometime in the afternoon on one of her regular visits to cronies in other parts of the building. All he needed was patience and a little luck that no one would call for the file before he returned it.

He returned to the job of taking notes from the open files on his desk. He even grew interested as the information from Washington offered a unique insight into how the underbelly of the American power system worked. For years, Serena had been spending hundreds of thousands of dollars on quietly influential campaigns to influence the Congress and the media. And, most of the time, it worked.

As Tomaso read on, the phone rang across the room. Christina picked it up. Tomaso heard her murmuring but paid no attention. Eventually, he became aware that the call was going on for a long time. He glanced up to catch her staring at him as she listened. A stab of alarm hit him. Was somebody going to ask for the file?

He lowered his head again. A few moments later, he heard her

145

put down the phone. Maybe this time she would have to leave the office.

'Tomaso?'

He looked up. 'Yes, Christina?' He looked as though he had paused in his work.

'The President needs you right away.' She seemed to be having trouble with a small addressograph on her desk. 'He says you are to go straight in.'

'What's it about?' Tomaso asked as he came around the desk.

'Don't know. You'll have to ask him.'

He shrugged and passed her desk to the big ornate door that led to the Presidential suite. He knocked and waited until the buzzer sounded. He would have to keep his fingers crossed that Christina would not go to the files.

Serena was waiting for him. He looked up from the table, an amiable smile on his face.

'Ah, Tomaso. Good of you to come so quickly.'

He rose and came halfway round the table to take the young man's arm. 'Listen, I have a surprise for you.'

He led him towards the opposite door from the one through which Tomaso entered.

'It's about this fellow Haggerty. The man you saw killed. It seems there's been some mistake. I've just learned he's very much alive.'

He saw the shock on Tomaso's face and nodded.

'It gave me quite a jolt too. But my informant is unimpeachable.' He reached down and pulled the door open. 'See for yourself.'

Tomaso stared, stunned.

Eva Valdes stood in the doorway.

13

It was past noon when they entered the valley. The gruelling journey in humid heat had exhausted Haggerty. His olive-green shirt was stained with sweat. But Julio, the driver, seemed unaffected. He turned to grin reassuringly as the jeep bounced and slithered on the rough track.

'Ten more minutes, *señor*, then we are there.'

On either side of the track, dark green hills jutted up against the blue sky. The primitive foliage which began just beyond the ditch soon thickened into an impenetrable curtain. It made the forest seem like a place of perpetual darkness. Yet, whenever the engine's tempo dropped, they could hear wild birds calling among the trees.

They reached a sharp bend where a large rock narrowed the track to a bare three foot width. Moving carefully, Julio sent the right wheel up along its sloping face. Haggerty gripped the overhead safety bar as the vehicle teetered at a 45 degree angle, but he said nothing. His earlier interjections had done no good.

They cleared the rock and bounced down in the mud. Turning the corner opened up a view of the remainder of the valley. Julio lifted a hand and pointed across the jungled ground. 'Look, *señor*. There it is.'

It was less than a mile away. Sitting in a clearing cut from the dark green slope at the end of the valley. A white two-storeyed house with a tiny cultivated field which ran down in front of the building for a bare two hundred feet. Alongside the house was a paddock where a lone mule grazed. All around, the jungle glowered down.

'From here, it is easy,' Julio said. He grinned at Haggerty. 'We have done it, *señor*.'

Haggerty smiled now and stared up at the house. Despite the rich grandeur of the scenery, it was clear that survival in this place would demand constant struggle. You had to wonder what kind of man would choose to endure it.

'It must be a daily battle just to keep that jungle off your doorstep here,' he said aloud. 'Whitten has to have some kind of balls.'

'The doctor is a man of God, *señor*.' There was a faint reproof in Julio's voice. 'He does not need the rest.'

Haggerty looked at the driver. It seemed his Marxism was barely skin deep. He wondered how intellectuals like Hector would deal with that when their time came to face it.

The last part of the trail, although muddy and strewn with pools of smelly water, was rock-free and easy to traverse. As they entered the clearing below the house, a dog barked in greeting. The jeep crossed the rough field and came to a stop in front of the verandah. An old man came out as Julio switched off the engine. In the silence, Haggerty gripped the top of the windshield and pulled himself upright.

'Dr Whitten?'

The old man nodded, smiling as he came forward. Haggerty jumped down from the jeep. They met at the foot of the steps and shook hands.

Whitten looked in his early seventies although with people who had his kind of spare frame it was often hard to tell. His face was lined but the skin was clear and tanned under the cropped white hair. Haggerty felt the serenity. He had seen it before in those who spent their years in the service of others. But Whitten's grasp was strong and businesslike too. He was probably a very practical man. He wore a faded blue short-sleeved shirt and khaki pants with sandals on his bare feet. Haggerty noticed a faint clouding on the faded blue eyes. But they still showed lively sympathy for what he knew his visitors must have endured on the journey up from San Antonio.

'Those machines are marvellously efficient, no doubt about it,' he said, nodding back at the jeep as they climbed the steps, 'but they can be very punishing in terrain like this.' He looked critically at their sweat-stained shirts. 'I think you could do with something to drink.'

Opening the old wooden-frame door, he ushered them inside. They entered a large room which was shadowed and cool after the muggy heat outside. The walls were lined with books and piled papers. A battered sofa leaned against one of the grained timber walls. The window to their left looked out on the valley they had just crossed. It was wide but broken into four sections so that the green panorama outside looked like panels from a Matisse painting.

Whitten smiled as they looked around. 'After so many years, you forget how it must look to a visitor. But it's comfortable. This way.' He led them across the long polished wooden floor and through a narrow hall decorated with faded family photographs. From there they entered the kitchen.

'I can offer you fruit juice. Or coffee freshly ground.' He pointed to the pitcher resting in a basin of water on the worn table. 'The juice is papaya. I think you'll like it after that heat outside.' Haggerty nodded and he poured.

'Thank you.' Haggerty took the mug. He found the liquid delicious and cool after the heat they had endured. Whitten watched smiling as they drank. He refilled the mugs as the two men finished. Julio took some water to refill the jeep's radiator and Whitten and Haggerty sat down at the table.

'You must excuse me for offering so little,' he said, as he pushed the pitcher closer to Haggerty, 'but I haven't had a visitor from outside in a long time. Nobody uses that little road any more because of our troubles here. It can be dangerous.'

Haggerty smiled. 'After the jeep ride, I'm not surprised to hear you say that. It's been one of the toughest trips I've made in years,' he said. 'I didn't realise how tough it would be to visit you.'

Whitten looked surprised. 'You came especially to see me?'

Haggerty nodded. 'I'm a reporter, Dr Whitten. I came to talk with you about a man who used to work with you. Ernst Dackman.'

'Ernst? Well, that is a surprise.' Whitten shook his head. 'I'd given up hope of hearing from him long ago.'

'He did work with you then?'

'Oh, yes. But it must be, let me see, almost three years since he left. How is he, anyway?'

'I haven't actually talked to him, but I imagine he's doing all right. Tell me, why did he come to leave you?' They settled back in their chairs.

'Well, he wasn't really supposed to leave when he went down to Guatemala City. At least, that was how I understood it.'

'You had an arrangement?'

Whitten nodded. 'Of sorts. You see, we had both been working on a prototype of a new vaccine for treating heart disease. It was designed to dissolve blood clots and ease the blood flow in potential victims. We had reached a clinical stage and Ernst suggested taking it to one of the bigger drug houses for evaluation. But he never came back.'

'Can you tell me a little more about this vaccine?' Haggerty asked. 'You say it removed clots?'

'That's a simple outline. To be accurate, it could do a lot more than that,' Whitten said. 'It could remove every clotting factor in the blood. All we were attempting to do was to moderate its effect so that the patient wouldn't bleed to death after we had dissolved the clots. The extraordinary thing about this haemophiliatre is that it was a natural substance. I stumbled on it by accident here in these mountains many years ago. Actually, it's a very strange story. Reminds me of Rider Haggard.' He smiled at Haggerty. 'Would you like to hear about it?'

'Please.'

The old doctor reached for the pitcher and without asking, refilled Haggerty's glass.

'When I first came here about twenty-five years ago,' he said, 'I went to work with a small Indian tribe called the Sequaintil who lived in a very isolated mountain range about a day's hike north of here. The Sequaintil were very primitive people but they were also fairly healthy which meant that my job as a medical missionary wasn't burdensome. There was no doubt that their lives were hard but they had enough to eat and the climate was good. And they were far enough removed from what we call civilisation to avoid the usual social epidemics. My biggest problem lay in earning their trust so that I could tell them

150

something of the Christianity which had brought me to their land. But they were very superstitious. They had all kinds of primitive gods and their folklore was chockful of fearful legends.

'Most of their legends were predictable,' Whitten went on, 'but at the time there was one that kept recurring. And it fascinated me.

'It concerned an extinct volcano within their territory. Over the centuries, it had become known as – and I translate roughly – The Basin of the Blood God. It was a very eerie place even for those mountains. The walls of the crater were almost seven thousand feet high. And at the bottom the rich volcanic dust and the hothouse effect had created a spectacular plant and insect life which must have survived in isolation for hundreds of thousands of years.

'To the Sequaintil, the Basin was a sacred place. According to legend, it housed the unhappy son of the Earth God who had been cast forth to bring misery to the world. The tribe believed that their mission in life was to stay by the Basin and placate the Blood God with regular sacrifices. Otherwise, the world would be destroyed.'

Haggerty held up his cigarette pack. 'Would you mind if I smoked?' Whitten smiled and shook his head.

'Please go on,' Haggerty said.

'The Indians had some justification for their belief in the Blood God's malevolence. They had learned that anybody who strayed into the crater died in there or very soon after they came out. Some of these victims were criminals fleeing tribal justice. Others were innocent children who had gotten lost. The Indians assumed that only a god with a grudge would kill so indiscriminately. So their shamans developed a response to placate the Blood God. Every five years they would send in a young healthy member of the tribe as a sacrifice. When the young person did return after the prescribed week in the crater – and that didn't always happen – he would soon bleed to death from some trivial injury. It was tragic but the Indians felt it was necessary. They had done something for the world and thus fulfilled their obligations.

'I had been ministering to the tribe for four or five years when

151

a convert told me about it. Well, I was younger and arrogant enough then to try stopping the whole business on the spot.' He shook his head, 'It almost cost me my life. The Sequaintil believed halting the ritual would bring world-wide disaster. Only a very spirited defence by some of my converts saved me. However, I did manage to wring a concession from the tribal leaders. They agreed to let me try my powerful medicine on the next young man who went through the ordeal.'

Remembering, Whitten's eyes clouded for a moment. 'It was a disaster. When the young man came out he seemed all right. That seemed proof to me that the whole business was another example of primitive superstition. But after only a few hours, he picked up a minor cut somewhere. What made it extraordinary was that the bleeding wouldn't stop. When the villagers sent for me it was just about too late. I tried to do what I could but it was impossible to staunch the flow of blood. Within a couple of hours the young man was dead.

'I carried out an autopsy. To my astonishment, I discovered that the young man, who had never shown symptoms, died of acute haemophilia. It was unique in my experience but there was no doubt about it. He had absolutely no clotting factor in his blood.'

Haggerty's thoughts flashed back to the morgue in Montreal and the pallid corpse of Otto Lentz. Whiter than the first snowfall in Westmount, Zossy Gingras had said.

'I went over the young man's body very carefully,' Whitten said. 'There were a number of tiny punctures on the torso which were consistent with mosquito bites. When I taxed the Indians with this, they just pointed to the crater and left it at that.

'Well, I was a pretty determined fellow in those days. I guessed that the bites had something to do with what happened.' Whitten rose and filled a coffee pot on the counter top. He put it on the propane stove and turned it on. 'And I was determined to find out why.

'I made a very rough beekeeper's outfit. And early one morning without telling anyone, I went into the crater.' He came back to the table and sat down again opposite Haggerty. He shook his head in wonder. 'You would not believe what I saw.

'It was like a lost paradise that a Hollywood film-maker might have dreamed up. As I went over the lip of the crater and down the slope – and it was no easy job – the plant life got larger and more strange. By the time I reached the volcano floor, there were species and insects that must have come from an earlier age. And, of course, there were the mosquitoes. They were murderous little devils, much larger and more vicious than their modern counterparts. But luckily, my outfit was effective.

'It took some hard work because of my clothes, but I managed to catch a few specimens. After that, it took all my strength and over a day's climbing to get out again.'

The water in the percolator was boiling and Whitten rose to make the coffee.

'I had some reasonable lab equipment even back then,' he said over his shoulder, 'and I used some mice for the experiments. Are you familiar with how mosquitoes work, by the way?'

Haggerty shook his head. 'I picked up malaria from them in Asia some years back but that's about it.'

Whitten nodded. 'When mosquitoes puncture the skin to get at your blood, they release an anti-clotting factor into the blood at the same time. If they didn't do that their prod would get stuck when the blood hardened. The anti-coagulant keeps the blood liquified around the punctured area and allows them to withdraw without difficulty.'

He carried two cups to the table. 'Sugar?'

Haggerty nodded. Whitten pushed the small bowl of brown sugar across.

'This species I brought out of the crater carried a much stronger weapon in their armoury. When these mosquitoes punctured the skin of a victim, the anti-coagulant they carried did not just keep the blood liquified around the wound. It actually travelled down the blood stream until it ate up the entire clotting factor in the body. I can only assume that in the primitive world they came from, the tough skin of the animals that they lived off must have made it very difficult to survive. So they developed this special quality to stay alive.'

Haggerty sipped the coffee. It was as good as he had ever tasted.

'Why only in the crater?' he asked. 'Why didn't they spread elsewhere?'

Whitten smiled. 'Very simple when you think about it. The bottom of the crater is like a hothouse. The sun beats directly down and it's also well protected from the elements. But the temperature changes dramatically as you ascend. It is much, much colder on the slopes. If the mosquitoes attempted to reach the top, they would quickly freeze to death.'

'So they remained trapped in there?'

Whitten nodded. 'You could almost say they're caught in a biological time warp.'

Haggarty raised his cup. 'This coffee is very good, by the way.'

Whitten smiled. 'Thank you. I must bring some to your driver.' He went outside.

Haggerty rested his elbows on the table. Outside the screen door he could hear the remote sound of birdcalls echoing from the forest behind the house. He knew now that this journey had been worth the effort. He was one step nearer to understanding the mystery of Otto Lentz's death.

Whitten returned. He showed some signs of age as he bent to sit down again at the table.

'You mentioned a vaccine?' Haggerty asked.

'Yes,' Whitten said. 'I have a passion, Mr Haggerty, for research and experimentation. This mosquito business allowed me to indulge it. For a start, if this virus could dissolve clotted blood, and it clearly could, then it might prove a boon to heart attack victims. The challenge was to develop a means of using it without killing off the recipients who could easily haemorrhage without coagulant. On my first tests, I tried injecting coagulant into animals immediately after they received the virus. But I found the virus quickly ate it up along with the victim's original supply. It took a good many trials but finally I hit on the solution.

'The virus, I discovered, was much like you or I. To survive, it had to eat after it left the mosquito's body. If it got no sustenance in the form of clotting factor for a period of ten to twelve hours, it would die of starvation. Once I learned that, I had the key to controlling it. Although it meant reversing the conventional treatment.

154

'Normally, if a person has no clotting factor in his blood, you renew his defences with transfusions of clotting factor from a compatible donor. As you can see, that's fairly straightforward, eh?'

Haggerty nodded.

'Now, in the case of our victims, I decided on the opposite approach. My treatment called for no clotting factor for a period of ten to twelve hours. If one managed to keep the patient alive through that time, then the virus would die from starvation.'

Haggerty lit another cigarette. 'But wouldn't your patient be bleeding through the period you're talking about?'

Whitten nodded. 'That could prove the most difficult part of the treatment. You have to check the bleeding with bindings while you recycle fresh blood without any clotting factor in it through the victim's system. If you can do that the virus will starve to death. Then you can safely put back coagulant from another donor. And the patient is cured.

'That's what I was working on when Ernst Dackman arrived here. He was a contractual physician with the World Health Organisation at the time. His job was to survey public health in the area but he took a keen interest in what I was doing and helped with my experiments.'

'From what I've learned about Ernst Dackman,' Haggerty said, 'I find it hard to visualise him working in the job you describe. It seems totally out of character.'

'I'm afraid that a good many people around here felt that too. He was suspected of being an intelligence agent who was here to monitor the activities of guerrillas in the area. When he agreed to take my vaccine out for testing, his life had already been threatened.'

'What arrangements did you make with him?'

'There wasn't much to it. I just didn't have the facilities for fine-tuning here. Ernst said he would get that done. But it seems he didn't. I'm sorry to say I haven't heard from him since.'

'Let me tell you something about this Dackman,' Haggerty said. 'From what I've seen and heard, he seems to be the last person you should have trusted. He may have used your vaccine for murder.'

155

Whitten looked at him, shocked. 'Oh, no.'

Haggerty nodded grimly.

'I've seen a former associate of his,' Haggerty said. 'He was dead in a Canadian morgue. And he had all the symptoms you described. Where else could he have gotten them?'

'That's unbelievable. Ernst was helpful in my work. It is true that he spent much of his time away from here and the local people did suspect him as I said. But murder? It just doesn't seem possible.'

'I'm afraid it's very probable,' Haggerty said.

Suddenly, they heard Julio shout. They both looked up at the sudden sound of his running feet coming from the verandah. The screen door rattled and they heard him cross the living room. He appeared in the door, his face alarmed.

'*Señor*! Come quickly!'

The two men rose from the table and hurried after him as he ran back to the verandah outside.

'What is it?' Haggerty asked.

Julio pointed towards the far end of the valley facing the house.

'Helicopters.'

They listened.

'I don't hear anything,' Haggerty said.

Whitten lifted a hand to his ear. 'He's right,' he said.

Haggerty strained. Very faintly, he heard the rumble.

'There are no other houses in this valley,' Whitten said suddenly in the silence. 'If they enter at all, this is where they'll come.'

'*Señor*,' Julio said anxiously. 'We must go. Quickly.'

'Start the jeep,' Haggerty said. He turned to Whitten. 'There's no time to explain but I believe Dackman is behind this. You must come with us for your own safety.'

'You have no chance with that jeep,' Whitten said calmly. 'Leave it. You can use the bush behind the house. They'll never find you in there. Driver!' he called, starting down from the verandah towards the jeep.

'Doctor, you must come too.' Haggerty stood on the steps. Whitten gestured to Julio to get out of the jeep.

156

Whitten shook his head. 'You musn't worry about me.' He reached to take Julio's arm and brought him up on the verandah.

'Doctor, please,' Haggerty said urgently. 'You'll be in danger once they find out we've been here. You must come with us.'

'Look, *señor*!' Julio shouted. 'There they are!' They turned.

Like two dark predators, now gliding into a wide turn, the gunships entered the far end of the valley. Squat and dark with their snouts lowered, they came abreast and headed towards the house.

'Back inside,' Whitten said sharply. 'Quickly now!'

'Doctor …!' Haggerty tried a last time.

'Don't argue.' Whitten pushed them into the house. 'This way.' He pushed past and led them across the living room with the noise growing outside, and then into the kitchen.

Whitten hurried to the screen door at the back and held it open.

'Listen carefully,' he said quickly. 'There's a large teak tree two hundred yards into the bush. Keep to its left until you strike a trail. That will take you to San Jaoquin. You'll find help there. Now go!' He pushed Julio who spilled out onto the roughly cleared back and started running up towards the bush. The noise of the gunships grew thunderous.

'For Christ's sake, Doctor,' Haggerty shouted above the roar, 'you can't stay now!'

'Don't worry about me.' Whitten smiled an almost youthful smile. 'Just go!' With sudden strength, he pushed Haggerty out the door.

The rattle of the rotor blades reverberated around the valley. Haggerty ran, zigzagging between the uprooted tree stumps and piled stones. He reached the first outcrop of bush. The shadow of one of the gunships rolled over the house like a great vulture as he entered the thickening forest. Julio rose from the undergrowth and pulled him down.

Together they scrabbled higher into cover. Hidden in the smothering vegetation, they turned to look back. From their higher vantage point, they had a clear view of the house.

Thirty feet above its roof now, clattering menacingly, the two helicopters hovered in the air, tails swaying slowly from side to side. As Haggerty watched, Dr Whitten appeared in the clearing

157

at the front of the house where the abandoned jeep stood. The dust whipped up by the rotor blades billowed around him like a windstorm as he raised a hand in greeting.

In the sky, the gunships rocked as they manoeuvred above him, the engines chattering at fever pitch.

For a long moment nothing happened. Then slowly one of the gunships began to back up, its nose lowered like an animal stalking its prey. Haggerty knowing, his nails pressed into his palms, found himself beseeching. Whitten slowly lowered his hand, watching the helicopter.

It was clear what was going to happen.

'No!' Haggerty shouted.

A white stream hissed back from under the gunship.

Julio was hanging like grim death onto Haggerty.

With an ear-splitting roar, a rocket shot straight down at the small figure on the ground. The earth around him suddenly exploded in fire and smoke.

'Oh, Jesus!' Haggerty's throat was tight. Julio beside him was babbling in Spanish, his fingers digging like vices into Haggerty's arms.

The gunships began circling slowly, covering the ground around the house foot by foot. There was no sign of Whitten. Just blistered, smoking earth and the burning carcass of the jeep. Now the second helicopter began backing up. Suddenly, with a searing crack, it fired straight into the centre of the house. The timber frame blew apart in a blast of fire.

'Bastards ...!' Haggerty half rose. A frightened Julio pulled him down again.

'*Señor*, we must get back.' Almost unwillingly, Haggerty allowed himself to be dragged further into the forest. The sky was lost to sight under the heavy tropical vegetation as they put more distance between themselves and the house. But the rattle of the engines was still thunderous as the helicopters circled above them now.

They were over a hundred yards in when the ground halfway back exploded in a shower of debris which fell all round them. Panic stricken, their anger forgotten, they scrabbled farther into the darkness through the undergrowth.

'The tree,' Haggerty panted, 'there it is.' He pointed into the gloom. Before them, like a ghostly vision from a fairy tale, it stood out from the surrounding trees. As they pushed towards it, orange explosions lit up the jungle behind them. They hurried on, bearing to the left, moving deeper into the brush. Soon the explosions began dying away. For the first time they felt safe.

They found the trail, a bare imprint, shortly after. It took almost four hours to reach San Jaoquin. By then, the villagers already knew about what the army had done to Randolph Whitten. They offered mules for the first part of the journey back to Guatemala City.

By that time, it seemed to Stephen Haggerty that there was no end to the disasters wrought by Ernst Dackman. And he was still no closer to catching up with him than he was before.

14

'Please extinguish all cigarettes and fasten your safety belts. We are about to make our descent into Guatemala City. Thank you.'

Vern Railsback watched as the aeroplane skimmed across the top of white, billowing cloud and then plunged into the grey mist. Soon they were rocked by turbulence. The elderly woman next to him gripped her seat rests tightly. Vern smiled encouragingly at her, tucked his elbows in and lay back, closing his eyes.

He didn't know what he was going to find on the ground in Guatemala or even if he would track down the mysterious Dr Whitten. But he knew his career would be finished back in Washington. Korner would have him cashiered for disobeying his directive not to leave the country. And there would be no case to answer.

But there wasn't any other way, Vern thought. He couldn't drop the obligation he felt to William Masters because of an arbitrary order from a bureaucrat who had his own reasons for stopping the journey. He had to go through with it. Besides, he was getting tired of the Agency. His career had stalled ever since he came out of the closet. Now the gossip never stopped. The more he thought about it, the more he realised it was time for a change.

But he was worried about Alva Martin. She was going to suffer for this. If Korner couldn't get him, he would make Alva pay. They could depend on that.

It was Alva who first learned he was being watched. One of Korner's anonymous enemies, someone who obviously liked Vern, passed the message. That was what decided him. If they believed it was important enough to stop him, then it was important enough to go. Alva got his passport from the pool and they used a visit to her apartment to spike the surveillance team. He wanted to avoid involving her but she would not hear of it. He realised she wanted to be identified with his flight and gave in.

He was still thinking about it when a sudden brightness pierced his eyelids. He sat up and looked out the window at the first sight of Guatemala streaming by below. It was a rich, brilliantly green countryside. Huge cultivated fields mingled with pastures where cattle gathered in large herds that he could see clearly from the sky. A river, reflecting the white clouds above, meandered across the landscape.

The first suburbs of the capital appeared in the distance. To the right of the plane's flight path, Vern saw what looked like a large refinery. At first sight it seemed to be split into black and silver patterns. Then he saw that at least half of the storage tanks were burned out ruins.

'Excuse me.' He raised a hand to the passing flight attendant. 'What happened down there?' He pointed down at the refinery.

The girl, dark-haired and elegant in her pearl-grey uniform, glanced past him, coffee cups in hand. 'That was the MRN, señor. It happened maybe two weeks ago.'

'They operate that close to the capital?'

She nodded. 'Everyone says it's getting worse. There's hardly a day now without an incident.'

He turned back to the window, straining to watch the refinery as the aircraft banked on its approach to the airport. It must have been a well-mounted attack to cause such damage. If the guerrillas had that kind of strength, he wondered how safe it would be to travel up country.

It was almost noon by the time he checked into his hotel. He unpacked and selected a flowered shirt and white pants to suit the climate. Fastidious, he showered again and pasted down the wet, thinning hair before a critical mirror. He dressed and thirty minutes later, he called a cab and headed for the Embassy. He had considered ducking it but decided that would compound his troubles. Fighting a command of Korner's which he considered capricious was one thing. To bypass the Embassy as an Agency employee would be a serious breach of duty.

Security around the building was tight as he arrived. He had to

161

leave the cab some distance away, pass a Guatemalan army roadblock and walk the rest of the way to the entrance through concrete barriers. A husky Marine in combat fatigues with a carbine resting on his hip examined his government identification pass and let him through.

After a series of calls at the reception desk, a security man took him to the office of public safety which doubled as the Agency headquarters in Guatemala. The person who greeted him there was an affable, middle-aged man. He was bald, with grey-streaked thatches of hair on the side and kind-looking brown eyes. His desk was decorated with family photographs and an array of pipes. He looked like a high-school teacher rather than an intelligence agent. His name was Daniel Winter. Vern liked him immediately but wondered how he came into the job.

'It's a temporary thing,' Winter confessed as they chatted about affairs back in Langley. 'I'm really the analyst here. Bob Carter is the boss but he's been called back to your neck of the woods for consultations. To tell the truth, I'll be glad when he returns. I'm not very good at administration.' He gestured rather helplessly with a large hand. Hairs sprouted along the back. 'But I guess that's my problem. Now, you'll need some help, I'm told.'

Vern masked his surprise. 'You knew I was coming?' Winter nodded. 'Telex arrived a short while ago. Said you were to receive assistance in your travel plans.'

'And who am I indebted to for that?'

'Who else but Korner?' Winter smiled. 'Nice to know the boss is looking after your interests, eh? Now what do you want us to do?'

Jesus, Korner? He wondered what the hell was going on but decided not to ask.

Instead, he described his plan to go north to San Antonio to see Randolph Whitten. He was careful to make it appear that he was on Agency business – without saying so directly. Winter accepted his story without question.

'San Antonio.' He swivelled in his chair and pulled down a book of maps. 'That's a pretty remote spot. I've heard of this man Whitten, as a matter of fact. He's something of a legend down here. I believe he's spent most of his life helping the Indians and

162

that kind of thing. Strikes me as the type of quiet American we could do with a lot more of in this part of the world.'

'What's the situation like on the ground here?'

Winter shook his head. The slow deliberate move strengthened the school teacher impression.

'Really bad, I'm afraid. We have a bunch of people running this country who are little better than gangsters. They've spent the past two decades feathering their own nests and terrorising anyone who opposes them. And now the chickens are coming home to roost.'

'That grim, huh?'

Winter nodded. He laid down the map and reached for a pipe from the desk. He started filling it.

'I know there's something of a split in Washington over this embargo business but I have to come down on President Robson's side on this one. We just have to put our foot down. We can't let them continue brutalising the people the way they've done in the past. I mean, it's just not the American way, is it?'

'Well, we've got to be realists,' Vern said. The wider implications had to be considered. 'A sudden change could easily destabilise the country. And that could open up the place to Marxist rule. I don't have to tell you that they could be a lot worse.'

Winter had his pipe going. He nodded. 'I guess there's a certain amount of truth in that too,' he said, 'and I suppose we're not paid to be moralists.' He took up the map book again. 'Anyway, let's have a look at this San Antonio of yours.'

As soon as he located it, Winter shook his head.

'I'm sorry, Railsback,' he said, 'but I can't let you travel to that area without an escort. The place is alive with guerrillas. You wouldn't survive a day in there without them catching you or worse.'

'So what do I do?'

'You'll have to wait until we arrange something with the military. That's going to take a few days.' Winter drew on his pipe. 'They've got their hands full at present and they're not too pleasant to us. But we still have army personnel working with them. We'll work out something.'

163

'You said a couple of days. How many exactly?'

Winter sighed. 'Let's say three,' he said finally. 'In the meantime, go out and enjoy yourself locally. See the sights. But don't stray too far from your hotel phone.'

It was early afternoon when Haggerty and Julio reached the city of Antigua. Julio led the way to a *cantina* near the bus station. It was just off the main square where the weekly market was in full swing. Stalls and wandering pedlars filled the cobble-stoned area. Stoic top-hatted Indians sat with coloured blankets and intricate metal work which they had brought into the town to sell. Armed militia in pairs strolled among the crowds.

With memories of what the military had done still fresh, the two men were glad of the refuge the *cantina* offered. After a beer, Julio left Haggerty sitting in a darkened corner while he went to check with the local contact on how secure the bus route was that day. Although there was still danger, Haggerty felt more at ease than he had since the murder of Randolph Whitten. He sipped his beer and gazed around the darkened interior at the animated customers. This was not the cocktail hour on Madison Avenue. But there was something familiar and even comforting about it. Particularly after the tension of travelling down the mountains on a hard-backed mule when you knew a pair of gunships might appear any moment to put you away for good.

His mind drifted now to making plans. As soon as he got back to the capital, he would link up with Eva and they could both return to the States. There was no point in staying now he knew that Ernst Dackman wasn't there any longer. In Miami, they would go to the FBI and tell them what had happened. He wasn't quite sure what they could do with the information but it would be out of his hands. After that, he would go back to Montreal to clear his name.

He wondered if Eva would go to Canada with him. He thought she would. That would be a pleasant prospect. But it would be even more enjoyable to see her again in the capital. He wanted to phone but Julio explained how they monitored the telephone system and he decided to wait. Still it did no harm to dream.

He was still thinking about it when he saw Julio reappear at

164

the door. He had another man in tow. His face was grim as he came through the tables. Something was wrong. He stopped by Haggerty who gestured across the table.

'Sit down,' he said.

Julio shook his head.

'What's wrong?' Haggerty asked, his voice low.

'We've got to go, *señor*. At once.'

Haggerty glanced up at the man standing behind Julio.

'He's all right,' Julio said. 'He's one of us. But we must leave now.'

'What's the problem?'

'There's no time to explain. Please, *señor*.'

Haggerty took a final swig from the beer and rose.

They left the *cantina* with the other man guiding. For several blocks, they followed through a series of narrow streets that led away from the main square. Suddenly, the guide turned into an alley. It was deserted and lined with reeking garbage cans. The guide paused halfway down, pointed out a door and hurried on. As they reached it, Julio glanced about then quickly opened it. He ushered Haggerty inside.

The interior was dark. When Haggerty's eyes adjusted to the gloom, he saw they were in an old stockroom. A man standing at the other end had watched them enter and now beckoned silently. They followed him down a corridor to a small office. The man pointed and withdrew. Haggerty entered.

The guerrilla leader Hector, the man he had met two days earlier with Tomaso, sat at a table. An oil lamp hung overhead. The place reeked of fish.

'Good afternoon, *señor*,' Hector said. 'Please sit down.'

Haggerty took the offered chair.

'I have unpleasant news,' Hector said. 'Tomaso has been arrested.'

'Oh, Christ!' Haggerty said. He knew Serena's people would give him a bad time.

'Julio told me of your narrow escape and of Dr Whitten's death. You are a lucky man, *señor*.'

'I realise that,' Haggerty said. 'What happened to Tomaso?'

165

'We don't know yet.' Hector paused. 'But we have some suspicions.' It hung in the air.

Haggerty watched him. The room was cold after the heat outside. But it wasn't refreshing.

'You think somebody betrayed him?'

Hector shrugged. His hand brushed against the paper-weight and he moved it carefully aside.

'We can't be absolutely certain. But it appears that way. Now we are trying to uncover how it happened. So we need to ask questions. Of everybody.'

Haggerty nodded.

'I understand.'

'*Señor*, what do you know of this woman you had with you when we last met?'

'Miss Valdes?' Haggerty looked at him in astonishment.

'Yes.'

'You suspect Eva?'

'As I said, we don't know the full circumstances. But, yes, we think she could have been involved.'

Haggerty was more surprised than shocked. 'You must be mistaken.'

'*Señor*, outside a very trusted group, you and this woman Valdes are the only people who could identify Tomaso. And knew he worked for us. We are satisfied that you were not the informant. Julio has been with you since you met Tomaso. And besides, you were almost killed by the army. We are satisfied that you are a genuine person. But this woman? After you left, she was free in the city to do as she wished.'

'Wait a minute,' Haggerty said. 'There's no question of her being free to do what she wished, as you put it. We already agreed before I left that she would stay put in the Plaza Hotel until I returned. It was a safety measure. She would not have wandered around the city as you suggest.'

Hector looked at him.

'She is not at the Plaza, *señor*.'

Haggerty stared.

'She checked out the day Tomaso was arrested. The day you left.'

Haggerty's face paled at the implication. In the awkward silence that followed, Hector drew a packet of cigarettes from his pocket and tossed them across the table. Haggerty drew one out.

'Is there a possibility,' Hector asked quietly as he reached across with a lighter, 'that this woman might also have betrayed you? Somebody must have told the military that you were seeking information from Dr Whitten.'

'I can't believe that,' Haggerty said. He lit the cigarette and shook his head. 'You must be wrong.'

'Tell me,' Hector said. 'How long have you known her?'

Haggerty looked at him with a hint of irritation. 'Look, I know Eva well. I'm certain she wouldn't do a thing like this.'

Hector stared evenly at him for a moment. 'You didn't answer me, *señor*,' he said. 'So let me ask again. How long have you known this woman?'

Haggerty felt like a fool. 'A week,' he said.

Hector's eyes widened. 'You can't be serious.'

'Listen, I've had no problems about trusting Eva since I met her,' Haggerty said. 'I think I'll continue trusting her until you show me otherwise.'

'Well, we may be about to settle this matter very quickly.' Hector looked directly at him. 'But we will need your help.'

Haggerty met his gaze. 'You have that.'

Hector leaned against the table. 'We have a plan in mind. To get to Tomaso. You would be involved. But I must warn you. It will be dangerous. Very dangerous.'

'Whatever,' Haggerty said. 'I couldn't do any more for Tomaso than he did for me. Whatever you want from me is okay.' He meant it.

Hector straightened, relieved. He smiled. 'Good.' He looked now at Julio who had been standing at the back of the room, fascinated. 'Julio, go outside and make sure we are not interrupted.'

They could feel the driver's disappointment but he nodded and left.

Hector rested his elbows on the table. His long gloomy face pressed forward. 'I'm going to be frank with you, *señor*, because your life will be at stake in what has to be done. And you will not be allowed to leave until the task is completed. You understand?'

'Yes,' Haggerty said.

'Good.' Hector sat back. 'First, let me explain the background to this affair. What has happened with Tomaso has created a very serious crisis for our movement. You see, Tomaso was not just a simple informer in Serena's entourage. He was much more. For the past eight months, he has compiled information on troop strengths at every major military installation in the country. We have been matching those forces against our own units in each of these areas in preparation for a final offensive. The work is now complete. And so are our plans for attack. Unfortunately, Tomaso is one of the few people who knows the precise military units we intend to attack. And when. If they force him to talk, our offensive will be destroyed.

'We have already put a year of work into our preparations. There is no guarantee that we can attain the same level in twelve months' time. Therefore, it is imperative that our offensive take place as planned. And that Tomaso does not talk.' Hector leaned over to take a cigarette from the pack. 'We have to rescue him. Or kill him if we can't do that.'

The building was quiet.

'Where is he?' Haggerty asked finally.

'In a holding prison called Las Grisas fourteen miles outside the capital. We had already planned an attack there during the final offensive. Now we must move it forward.'

'To when?'

'Prepare yourself, *señor*,' Hector said. 'It must be done tonight.'

15

The *barrio* square bustled with activity. The guerrillas had slung up temporary lights but not enough to dispel the gloom. Shadows and people blended and broke until the square offered an eerie kaleidoscope of light and shade. Yet the work was getting done. When Haggerty emerged with the guerrilla commander, Medinos, the *guerrilleros* were marshalling by platoons. With faces blackened, dressed and helmeted as soldiers of the Guatemalan Army, they looked sinister enough to be just that. Except they remained boisterous, joking and laughing with each other. Haggerty, remembering South East Asia and other young men like them, shook his head.

Medinos glanced at him. 'Something wrong?'

'No. I just hope they come through okay.'

Along the edges of the square, the *barrio* dwellers watched the spectacle with fascination. But their absorption was tinged with fear. They were finding it difficult to distinguish between the real Army with its terrifying raids and this one which was made up of young men they actually knew.

Haggerty moved through the guerrillas, looking at the faces, trying to judge their abilities. In turn he was stared at. It wasn't every day they had a Special Forces major in full US Army combat gear fighting on their side.

Hector's plan, when he outlined it that afternoon, was as daring as it was desperate. Haggerty was to be the Trojan horse who would get them into Las Grisas. He would be a US Special Forces adviser leading trainees from the army's crack Ranger battalion. For almost three years, United States Special Forces personnel had been training counter-subversion units in the Guatemalan Army. There were usually around a hundred in the

169

country. They held a privileged position in the armed forces. Serena had given them high immunity. Hector believed – and Haggerty hoped – that no Guatemalan soldier would fire on one when they turned up at the prison gates.

Standing under the lights, watching the *guerrilleros* and their attitude to him, he saw there might be some basis for that opinion. Seeing his tall figure and smart olive green uniform, some found it hard to believe he was not a real gringo officer. Haggerty almost believed it himself. At least the uniform was genuine. The guerrillas had seized it with other equipment at an abandoned mountain post. Soon, he would have to be worthy of the image he portrayed. His life depended on a convincing performance.

While he watched, the platoon commanders marched their men alongside three of the four military trucks which the insurgents had captured in earlier encounters with the military. There were twenty men to each truck. The last truck remained empty. At a shouted command, the men began piling aboard. The *barrio* dwellers raised a ragged cheer. To Haggerty, it appeared to come as much from relief as from any feeling of support.

'Major?' A grinning Medinos approached and saluted. Behind him was Julio who would drive their jeep. 'We are ready to move out.'

Haggerty smiled and returned the salute. Together they walked to the jeep that stood at the head of the convoy and climbed in. Julio started the engine. One by one, the trucks chattered to life behind them. Slowly, they began moving off the square. Almost immediately men moved in to disconnect the hanging lamps. Soon the area would return to darkness.

Now it was all for real, although the speed of transition from journalist to aiding the guerrillas was making it difficult to accept that. Stephen Haggerty had to keep what he was doing at the simplest level – that of rescuing the man who saved his life – to believe it at all. That was why he was there. It was an obligation that he could not refuse. If only Tomaso could hold out, he thought. It would make this involvement and everything associated with it worthwhile if he could save the life of a man who

170

had already risked his own for him. But even as he thought about that, he brushed it from his mind. He knew the outcome of this affair would be dictated, not by sentiment, but by nerve and a lot of luck. All he could hope now was that he had both.

The convoy rumbled through the mean streets of the *barrio* under hooded lights. People stood in the open doors to watch, their shapes silhouetted against the oil lamps that hung inside. They rolled by like magic shadows in the dark.

Medinos looked at the luminous dial on his watch. '8.02.' he said. 'Seventeen minutes to rendezvous. Feeling okay?'

Haggerty smiled. 'Don't worry about me. I'm fine.'

'Good.'

He thought of the other thing wrapped up in this. If he could snatch Tomaso from Serena's clutches, he was sure it would lead to clearing Eva's name.

Medinos leaned across in the darkness as the convoy rumbled through the narrow streets. 'Do you need to go over it again?'

Haggerty shook his head.

They left the *barrio* and entered the darkened highway that led into the countryside. Slowly picking up speed, they headed for the rendezvous, one mile from Las Grisas prison.

The journey through the warm starry night was almost pleasant because of the breeze that swept over them en route. They arrived at the roadside meeting point without incident. The second group of guerrillas was waiting for them. They used a small signal lamp to show their location in the darkness. The trucks slowed and came to a halt in line. They were under the brow of the hill. From his earlier briefing, Haggerty knew Las Grisas prison was on the other side. Medinos jumped down from the jeep and waved for Haggerty to follow. The guerrillas waiting at the roadside were about fifteen strong. Two men in civilian clothes stood awkwardly apart from the rest with rope halters around their necks and their hands apparently bound. Although they seemed like prisoners, one held up his bindings as they approached and laughed. They were part of the group. The commander Medinos silenced the noisy man sharply. Increasingly, Haggerty felt good about his professionalism.

Apart from the civilians, the rest were dressed in army

171

uniforms. They were all liberally bloodstained and bandaged like wounded combatants. Some sat on a pile of empty stretchers.

'Julio,' Medinos called softly, 'get that empty truck up here.'

As they waited for the truck to come into place, Medinos inspected each of the supposedly wounded men on the roadside carefully, altering a binding here or a bandage there. When the truck came up, Julio and the driver rolled back the tarpaulin. Piled rifles and grenades lay in a corner of the lighted interior. The bandaged soldiers, each with a stretcher, climbed aboard and arranged the stretchers on the floor. Each took a share of the grenades and a single rifle from the corner store and concealed them under ponchos which they draped over themselves. The driver of the truck moved around, spreading more of what looked like blood on their bandages. The interior began to reek and Haggerty moved back from the tailboard. After a final inspection, Medinos was satisfied. He moved along the trucks with last instructions.

Returning to the jeep, Haggerty took a final cigarette.

'*Senor.*' It was Julio who held out a hand. Smiling, Haggerty passed the cigarette. They smoked without words. Medinos appeared.

'Well, amigo, this is it.' He leaned forward to embrace Haggerty, then stepped back and slapped his shoulder. 'It's in your hands now.'

Haggerty nodded and tossed away his cigarette. 'Don't worry,' he said. 'It will go well.' Turning, he climbed into the jeep and stood upright, gripping the rollbar. Medinos and the two supposed prisoners got in after him and sat below. Julio started the engine. At a wave from Medinos, the trucks chattered to life. Everybody waited, engines idling.

'Ready?' Haggerty looked down.

Medinos nodded. 'Good luck.' he said.

Haggerty took the US Army issue pistol from his holster and raised it. 'Go, Julio.' he said. He waited until the jeep was on the move and then fired the signal shot into the air.

The first ragged burst of returning rifle fire echoed from the trucks behind. The convoy began to gather speed in its ascent up the hill. The firing increased as they approached the top. This is

172

it, Haggerty thought as they roared towards the crest. Medinos raised himself and waved back to the following truck. Almost immediately its headlights came on.

The upright Haggerty and the jeep were bathed in a dazzling glare. Simultaneously from the rear of the convoy, tracer fire shot off into the sky. Gathering speed, the line of vehicles zoomed over the top of the hill. They were touching fifty miles an hour. The blackness around them was now ablaze with the flash of gunfire. Grenades hurled from the trucks exploded in the nearby ditches. From a distance, it must have looked as if the convoy was involved in a spectacular battle.

With the wind howling around him, Haggerty could see the brightly lit compound of Las Grisas on the plain below. The prison stood out like a silver palace in the darkness with arc lights glittering along its wire fence.

The convoy tore down the hill towards it, the jeep bouncing heavily on the rough surface of the road, the distance closing rapidly. The crash of gunfire mixed with the roar of engines. Haggerty, the forage cap jammed down over his eyes, stood stiffly erect, fully exposed in the lights of the truck behind him. He had no quarrel with the posture. If that was what it took to get Tomaso out, then that was how it was going to be. Anyway, he told himself, there was no stopping now, even if he wanted to. They had passed the point of no return.

As they neared the prison, he could see the first hurried signs of activity inside the fence. Men were running across the prison square towards the guardhouse which faced the road they were coming down. Below Haggerty in the jeep, Medinos was on the radio, repeating the call sign of the Rangers Battalion and shouting that they had been ambushed. He repeated it over and over on the Las Grisas frequency without allowing time for anyone to reply.

Haggerty squinted into the wind. The buildings were exactly as described. The guardhouse and entrance were in the centre of the fence. To the left was the headquarters complex which housed the radio building. On the right were the guards quarters from which half dressed men were now spilling onto the square. At the rear of the square, lay the two-storeyed cell blocks.

173

As he took it all in, the jeep suddenly left the road and bounced across the rough parking lot. Julio swerved and brought it to a skidding halt close to the entrance gate. The journey downhill had taken less than a minute. Already the truck with the wounded soldiers roared up alongside.

Bathed in light from the prison arc lamps, Haggerty jumped to the ground. He turned and grabbed the loose halters of the two now cowering prisoners and pulled them from the jeep. Medinos kicked brutally at them as they stumbled out. He clambered down after them, shouting to add to the din and confusion. Behind him, the men in the trucks continued to fire back towards the darkened hill at the mysterious enemy who was supposed to be pursuing them.

Haggerty waved sharply now at the truck with the wounded.

'Get those men out of there!' he shouted above the turmoil. Medinos screamed at the men in one of the trucks and they jumped down and ran to pull the stretchered soldiers off.

Turning his back on the scene and with his two prisoners in tow, Haggerty strode towards the barbed wire gate with the smaller Medinos running to keep up.

The two guards at the entrance stiffened as he approached, uncertain of what to do. Before Haggerty reached them, an officer came running out of the gate, buckling on his revolver.

'You there!' Haggerty roared, stopping by the guards and pointing to the officer. Turning to Medinos, he snapped. 'Tell him we need assistance.' Viciously he flung the two prisoners to the ground. 'And let him find room for this swine!' One of the prisoners screamed and held up a bloody arm. Medinos aimed a kick at him.

The officer, a young man, slowed in bewilderment at the sight. He stared at the glowering Haggerty. 'Tell that son of a bitch to move!' Haggerty barked. Medinos began to speak but Haggerty, as if he could not wait, moved forward and got to the officer first. Reaching out, as Medinos spouted rapid fire Spanish, he grabbed his shirt front. 'Medico! Medico!' he bawled. Behind him, soldiers were already streaming forward with the wounded.

The officer stood, his mouth working. '*Si, Commandante.*' he finally stammered.

'Come on.' Haggerty grabbed his arm and pulled him towards the gate. By the time they reached it, the officer was convinced. He gestured angrily at the sentries to open it.

'Bring those wounded through!' Haggerty shouted back to where Julio was supervising the flow from the truck. He led the way through the gate with Medinos at his side. They passed the guardhouse and reached the prison square as the first of the wounded was being carried through. Haggerty knew that this was the crucial moment. If someone took it into their heads to close the gate now, they were all finished.

Turning to his left, he strode towards the headquarters building. They needed to destroy the prison's communications with the outside world before they could fight their way into the cells where Tomaso would be held. Behind him, Medinos was shouting a voluble description of the ambush. The young officer nodded, taken in by the wild urgency surrounding the visitors. They crossed the square. As the ragged group approached the door of the headquarters building, an elderly officer appeared in the doorway, gaping at the sight.

Haggerty reached him before he could gather himself, and shouting about the wounded, pushed past him into the hallway. 'Come on, bring them in,' he waved the stretcher bearers through. The hall was crowding up. Haggerty kept going, making for where he knew the radio room was. Medinos was ushering more and more stretchers in. The young officer tried to protest. They were in the wrong building. Medinos stood sideways in the door, pushing more men through. He was watching until the last stretcher was inside the prison compound. When he saw that happen he tore the starting pistol from under his jacket. Pushing it out of the door, he fired the flare across the square.

At the signal, the man on the last stretcher by the guardhouse slipped off. In one quick movement, he hurled a grenade through the door. The bearers who had dropped his stretcher had already unleashed their submachine guns. Now they dropped to the ground and opened fire on the guards at the gate. The man who had hurled the grenade waved them down just as the guardroom exploded. A fiery blast lit the night sky.

In the parking lot, men in the trucks who had been firing away

175

from the prison at their supposed ambushers suddenly turned and opened up on the watch towers. Others opened up on the half dressed guards outside the living quarters who were now standing thunderstruck at the violence before them. In the glare of the white flare, they began falling in the hail of bullets. From the end of the trucks two men now jumped down, lugging a rocket launcher. Everywhere, guns were chattering.

Inside the headquarters building, the bearers had already dumped their stretchers and taken care of the two protesting officers. Mixing with the supposed wounded, they fanned out behind Haggerty who reached the radio room. In one movement, he kicked in the door and rushed through. A young man in earphones looked up in horror. He started to shout but Haggerty downed him with a blow from his pistol. Across the room, another operator was shouting into a microphone. Haggerty was starting towards him when a blast exploded by his ear. The operator tumbled to the ground. Stunned, Haggerty turned. One of the bloodied guerrillas raised a thumb in salute. Haggerty blanched. More men burst into the room. Haggerty grabbed a carbine from one. Outside, gunfire echoed from the hall.

'Get back!' Haggerty shouted, waving those around him away. Raising the rifle, he sent a stream of automatic fire into the radio equipment.

'Okay,' he shouted, turning from the smoking shattered remains, 'Out you go. Move it!' He began pushing them back into the hall. Scattered shots echoed around the building. Medinos appeared out of nowhere. 'So far, everything is good.' He called to Haggerty as he tossed a fresh magazine across. 'The corridor to the cells is this way. Come on.' They turned down the passage to the left.

Suddenly, a massive blast shook the building and everything was plunged into darkness. Through the window, they saw a fireball bloom.

'The generator.' Medinos shouted. The men with the rocket launcher had done their work. 'Julio! Where's Julio?' he shouted again.

A flare fizzed alive. Julio, grinning, advanced through the turmoil.

176

Medinos, his face smudged but smiling, slapped Haggerty's arm. 'Let's get to those cells. Tomaso's got to be in there somewhere.' They advanced down the corridor, hugging the walls.

'We need to wrap this up quickly,' Medinos said as they neared the corner. 'Serena is not going to let this go by without a response.'

Serena was having dinner with his chief secretary, Alessandro Cordillera, when they both heard the dull rumble of the explosion.

Serena put down his napkin.

'See what that is, will you, Alex?'

He went back to his meal as Cordillera rose and hurried to the phone.

'Excellency.'

Serena looked up. 'Well, what is it?'

'Las Grisas. It's under attack.'

Serena put down his knife and fork.

'How bad?'

'They can't say. Radio contact is lost.'

'Damn! Who's in charge out there?'

'Brigadier Crusas should have been. But he's on leave. Colonel Feydeau has taken over.'

'That idiot.' Serena pushed back his plate and got to his feet. 'Come on.' They crossed the room and entered the wide hall lined by busts of Guatemala's nineteenth-century liberators.

'Get me Guinoli. And Robles.' They were the Air Force and Army commanders. 'Those swine picked the right time for their dirty work. They know we can't use the roads. We'll have to send in the Cobras.'

'Excellency, we have only four that are operational. The other two haven't come back from that mission to San Antonio. They're still up north.' The secretary had stopped by one of the phones in the hallway.

'That bastard in Washington,' Serena said angrily, 'He leaves me a handful of helicopters to fight a full scale war.' He stopped and turned. 'We should be prepared to scramble them anyway. Tell Guinoli to meet me on the roof.'

16

At Las Grisas, they were pinned down by gunfire from the last door before the cell-block area. It was only twenty feet from where Haggerty and the guerrilla leader Medinos lay but it appeared impregnable to frontal assault. The steel plating was too thick for a successful grenade attack. And already the shattered corridor was littered with dead and wounded.

Medinos and Haggerty squatted around the corner. Every few minutes they would duck as a hail of bullets ripped into the wall opposite. Each time, more dust would billow into the thickened air. It was becoming harder to see.

Finally, Medinos leaned close to Haggerty. Sweat ran down his powdered face. The particle-filled atmosphere was making it difficult to breathe.

'We're wasting time,' he panted. His voice was hoarse. 'Their defences are too strong. We'll have to use the rocket-launcher.'

For Stephen Haggerty, it was infuriating to have come this far and still find another barrier between Tomaso and rescue. The tension and fury of the battle had already swamped his earlier reservations about getting involved in other people's revolutions. Now all he wanted was to get the thing over with.

'Where do you want to do it? Here?'

Medinos shook his head. 'Too dangerous. We should try from the outside. Blast the wall down. Where they're dug in.' Gunfire exploded again in the corridor. They both pressed back. The firing died away.

'I'll get the crew.' Haggerty's throat was raw. He peered at Medinos. 'Okay?'

The guerrilla commander managed a grin, his face crinkling under the dust. 'I was hoping you would say that, *amigo*.' He leaned on his carbine. 'Just make sure they hit that wall at least twenty feet from the corner. We'll keep them busy here while you set it up.' He stuck the point of his automatic around the corner and fired off a fusillade. 'But, for God's sake, hurry it up.'

Haggerty nodded. He crawled away, down the corridor to the main hall. The smell of cordite was everywhere. At the door, a handful of guerrillas were exchanging fire with some of the prison guards who were still entrenched in the living quarters across the square. He found Julio.

'We need the rocket-launcher!' he shouted above fresh gunfire. 'Where is it?'

'Outside the gate. They've just destroyed the far watch-tower.'

'Give me cover.'

He pulled the body of the young officer who had let them into the prison from across the doorway. Moving well back into the corridor, he paused, counted to five and began a sudden dash towards the door. He entered the square at full speed. The sharp crackle of gunfire from behind him rose to a crescendo as Julio gave him cover. He sprinted. Around him, the darkness was rent by flashes of fire. Ahead, he could see the guard-house burning, with smoke billowing from the wreck of the generator behind it. As he reached the guard-house, the window panes were slowly cracking in the heat. At the gate, two dead soldiers lay in the dust. He leaped over them and kept going.

Some guerrillas were still in the truck, firing at the living quarters. Haggerty ran towards them, gesturing.

'Rocket-launcher!' He mimed the action of firing from the shoulder.

'Si.' One of the men vaulted over the end of the truck. He pulled Haggerty's arm. Together, they ran to the far end of the fence.

The rocket crew were crouched below the fence. A burning watch tower hung at a crazy angle nearby. Haggerty got them up and led them back at a run through the main gate. Hugging the inside of the fence, they went round the back of the headquarters building. They found themselves on a wide well cut lawn with the Guatemalan flag hanging from a white pole in the centre. To their right was the wall of the long prison corridor where resistance was located. Haggerty led the rocket

179

crew to a position facing a part of the corridor where the defenders were likely to be.

He raised a hand. The two men knelt, watching as Haggerty went over to the wall only twenty yards away and pointed at the spot to be hit. When he saw they understood he came back behind them and watched as the gunner adjusted his sight and brought the long cylinder up on his shoulder. His companion slipped the missile in and gestured to Haggerty to cover his ears.

When he had done so, the assistant tapped the gunner on the shoulder. Instantly he pressed the trigger. There was an ear-splitting roar and the rocket streaked forward in a sheet of flame. Almost simultaneously, it struck the wall. The masonry shattered in a huge blast of fire and smoke. Haggerty threw his arms over his head as debris rained down.

A mushroom of pulverised dust blossomed and rose skywards. The loader pointed and clapped his hands. A huge gaping hole was taking shape in the wall. The gunner looked up at Haggerty. His black, grimed face split into a grin.

A rattle of gunfire echoed from inside the corridor. Haggerty quickly raised his carbine.

'Don't shoot, *amigo*!' Medinos emerged from the smoke still billowing from the gaping hole. Haggerty rose and hurried forward. Medinos helped him through the rubble and the ghostly dust.

'It is what you call a bull's-eye. A perfect shot.' Medinos pointed to the whitened remains of bodies thrown against the far wall in the battered corridor. Haggerty glanced down but when he saw what the rocket had done, he turned away.

Medinos shrugged. 'They should have surrendered. Come on, it's all over. We must find Tomaso.'

With a guerrilla holding a flare high, they picked their way down the shattered corridor. It was littered with broken masonry, hanging wires and glass and filled with fog. All resistance seemed to have died, but they still clutched their carbines against their sides. They heard their first human sounds as they entered the dustladen prison corridor. It came from prisoners coughing in their cells. They caught glimpses of pale, starved faces in the flickering light of the flare. Medinos reached the first cell and peered in.

'Comrade, it's the MRN. We've come to release you.' As Haggerty watched, a thin hand with long nails emerged from between the bars and squeezed Medinos's arm. For a moment there was no sound in the white smoky passage. Medinos turned. Haggerty saw his dark eyes were angry. 'That swine Serena! To treat human beings like this. The poor devils. I only wish we could have got here sooner.' He reached up to touch the hand still gripping him and nodded to the man behind the bars. 'We'll have you out soon, my friend. Be patient.'

He turned to Haggerty. 'We'll have to split up if we're to find Tomaso in this light. Maybe you could find Julio back there. He can help too.'

Haggerty nodded. He was about to turn back when they heard someone running towards them.

'*Commandante*!' A guerrilla was stumbling through the wreckage. Medinos eased the prisoner's hand off his arm and called the man to him. They held a rapid conversation in Spanish. As Haggerty watched, Medinos suddenly clenched his fist.

'What is it?'

Medinos drew him away from the cells.

'The power system,' he said in a low voice. 'When we destroyed the generator, we took away the current. The cell locks are electronically controlled. The men can't open them.'

'Oh, Christ!'

'There's over two hundred prisoners in here.' He looked at Haggerty. 'Apart from Tomaso, I have those to think about as well. It could take hours to break them out.'

Haggerty knew the question uppermost in Medinos's mind.

Would Serena give them time?

The President stood on the observation deck of the National Palace. His binoculars raised, he was scanning the horizon in the direction of Las Grisas. Guinoli, the air force general, hurried in. He looked as if he had been sleeping.

'Ah, Guinoli.' Serena dropped the binoculars on his chest and sat back on the stool he was resting against. 'I've got a job for you.'

'Yes, sir?' The elderly, rather stout Guinoli was being formal rather than deferential. He had risen with Serena through the officer corps and his small air force had helped cement Serena's position as President after the coup. So he saw himself as a partner rather than as a subordinate. But years of habit ensured that he maintained the military code.

'We're going to need your helicopters,' Serena said. 'I take it you've heard the swine have broken into Las Grisas?'

Guinoli nodded. 'I'm not surprised. I'm told that old Feydeau was in charge.'

Serena nodded.

'Robles will have somebody's head for that,' Guinoli said. There was a certain satisfaction in seeing the army embarrassed.

'Yes, yes,' Serena said impatiently. 'That can come later. What we need now is a quick response. I can't use ground troops because there is the possibility that they may be using the prison attack as a diversion.' He looked at the rumpled air force general. 'So it all comes down to your boys.'

'We're not well placed to handle a substantial operation just now,' Guinoli said, suddenly cautious.

'It won't be substantial,' Serena said shortly. 'How many Cobras have you got in this area?'

'Three.'

'Three? Alex said four.'

'We had to take parts from one of them for the ships you sent north. Without the Americans, we have to cannibalise all the time.'

'You don't have to tell me that,' Serena said bitterly. 'Well, what do you advise?'

Guinoli shrugged. 'Manpower is the only area where we can afford losses. I say send in a strong armoured unit by road.'

Serena snorted. 'Didn't I tell you already that's out? Listen, I know you want to save your units, Guinoli. But it can't be helped. We're going to have to use those helicopters.'

Guinoli flushed. 'We'll be dangerously weakened if we lose any of them.'

182

'It'll be a lot worse for us if they overrun Las Grisas and free those prisoners,' Serena snapped. 'I want those choppers airborne, Guinoli. Immediately.'

'All three?' Guinoli protested. 'We risk everything if you do that.'

'All right, two then,' Serena said. 'And to ease your mind, they won't be taking much risk. I don't want them in direct combat.'

Guinoli looked at the President, surprised.

'Look at this.' Serena rose and led him over to a plan of Las Grisas which an aide had placed on an easel. 'I'm told there are two hundred and thirty prisoners in the prison. In these cells along here.' He pointed to the E-shaped blocks. 'As far as I'm concerned these people are all subversives. Imprisoned or free, they're a permanent danger to the state and a damned nuisance. So why don't we carve an opportunity from this problem the MRN has given us?' He rested an elbow on the map board and smiled at Guinoli. 'Let me put it this way. Why can't your boys ignore the fighting? And just blow up the cell-blocks? That way, we'll rid ourselves of a lot of trouble-makers. And deprive those bastards of their victory.'

Medinos and Haggerty surveyed the rescue work. Haggerty had given up the search for Tomaso. Without Spanish, it was too confusing at first. Then it became dangerous as the prisoners grew overwrought at the delay in getting them out of the cells. Medinos had found his command problems too demanding to continue. Finally, by consent, they left it to Julio who was now scouring the interior.

With resistance over, Medinos had brought in trucks behind the cell-blocks to tear out the bars of the cell windows. But they were hampered by the limited room between the cell-block and the fence. Progress was slow. Even with other men using acetylene torches from the maintenance sheds inside the prison building, he had still freed only twenty-one prisoners.

Inside the cell-blocks, hysteria was spreading among the prisoners. They knew if they were not freed quickly, Serena's troops would return. Then all hope would vanish. The torture and brutality they had suffered during their imprisonment had already taken its toll. This fresh tension was making their incarceration unbearable. Only the strongest managed to remain silent. The rest were creating bedlam.

To Haggerty, who was drawn into working with the truck teams as he waited for news of Tomaso, the screaming and tearful begging sounded as if they were coming from the gates of hell. It was like nothing he had heard before. As Medinos left, Haggerty moved back to work.

'Come on, in closer!' he shouted as he guided a truck back to another cell window. 'That's it!' He beat on the back with his bare fists as the truck continued to back up. 'Hold it, damn you!' The truck stopped.

One of the men shackled one end of the chain to the tow bar while a second held up the other end to the prisoner waiting at the cell window. The prisoner passed it around two bars and pushed it out again. Quickly, the men re-attached that end to the tow bar.

After all that work, the first attempt failed. The chain spun off viciously and cracked into the wall. The second time, the bars came away. The men cheered and ran forward to help pull out the prisoner.

'Get back to the truck!' Haggerty tore them away, pointing to the next window. Pushing and shouting, he got them organised for the next attempt.

'Señor Haggerty! Señor Haggerty!'

He looked up. Julio came towards him. His face was excited.

'We found him. We found Tomaso.'

Leaving the men to carry on, Haggerty ran to follow Julio through the smashed-down entrance of the cell-block. Inside, torches whirled like ghostly beams in the white-dusted air. Prisoners cried out and hands reached out between the bars trying to grasp them as they passed. Pale, thin faces were caught by the torch as they stared out, beseeching, and then screaming as they hurried by. It was stuff from the very worst kind of nightmare.

At the end of the corridor, Haggerty stepped on something soft and quickly drew back.

'Careful,' Julio said. He flashed the beam. A dead soldier lay face up, his hands clutching his chest. Julio pushed back the door which the soldier had been guarding and led the way down a metal staircase into an underground section. Brief flashes of light illuminated the stairwell. They could hear an acetylene torch working.

The lower level passage was narrow and crudely built. The floor was earthen and the smell of damp and human decay was overwhelming. Desperately, Haggerty fought an urge to retch.

'Down here,' Julio said. 'They're still working on his cell.'

The torch cutter moved to the side but kept working as they approached. Wordlessly, Julio handed Haggerty the torch and stepped back. Leaning forward, Haggerty shone the light through the bars. He gasped.

Tomaso was unrecognisable. He was lying on rough straw with a torn blanket over his naked body. His face was battered and his jaw was twisted out of shape. There were burn marks on his chest. His hands, lying by his side, were grotesquely swollen. It was almost impossible to believe he was the same man Haggerty had met a few days earlier.

Haggerty drew back. 'How long before we get him out?'

Julio muttered to the torch cutter. He turned to Haggerty.

'Five minutes.'

The steady blue flame cut slowly into the lock.

'Tomaso,' Haggerty called, 'it's Stephen Haggerty.'

Tomaso's eyes flickered in the light. He seemed suddenly aware that someone was there. With a choking cry, he tried to draw back across the straw. The pain of the movement brought a scream to his lips. He lay, legs contorted, his lips working.

The torch cutter looked up, sympathy on his face.

'For Christ's sake, hurry.'

The man nodded as if he understood and went back to working. It felt an age before the lock cracked and the door finally parted.

As the cutter gathered his equipment to move to the next cell, Haggerty pulled the door open and entered the cell. He kept the torch beam away from Tomaso's face as he knelt beside the injured man.

'Tomaso, we've come to take you out of here,' he said softly, touching the battered face. Tomaso's eyes opened a little as he turned his head in Haggerty's direction.

185

'It's true, my friend believe me.' Turning, Haggerty beckoned to Julio who stood outside the bars. Hesitantly, Julio entered.

'Look, Tomaso, it's Julio. Can you see him?' Julio leaned closer. Tomaso's eyes raised to his face. They both saw the spark of recognition and then tears well in his eyes.

'We've taken over the prison,' Haggerty said.

'It's true, my friend,' Julio said. He reached down to touch.

'Careful,' Haggerty hissed.

Julio nodded, barely caressing the injured man's shoulder. 'Soon, Tomaso, you will be well again,' he said, his voice breaking.

Tomaso groaned and they heard a choking sound in his chest. He closed his eyes.

'He looks bad,' Julio whispered in Haggerty's ear. 'I hope we are in time.'

Haggerty nodded. 'You better get Medinos down here. And a stretcher. Hurry.'

Julio slipped away. There were beads of sweat on Tomaso's forehead. Haggerty slipped off his khaki scarf and began patting his forehead dry.

Tomaso's eyes opened again. Hesitantly, he raised a hand to touch Haggerty's arm. It dropped again.

'You're going to be all right, Tomaso,' Haggerty whispered. But Tomaso was lost again in pain. Carefully, Haggerty patted his forehead again with the scarf.

Minutes later, he heard boots clattering in the stairwell. He flashed his torch at the passageway giving light.

Medinos appeared, followed by a second man. They reached Haggerty's side and knelt.

'How is he?' Medinos asked in a low voice.

'Bad. I think it might be a problem to move him.'

'Let Jiminez look at him. He's an intern.' Haggerty moved back as the young man moved in. He pulled a stethoscope from inside his shirt. Medinos drew Haggerty aside.

'Has he said anything?'

'No. Listen, Juan, he looks to me as if he's dying.'

Medinos bit his lip. 'We have to know if he's told them anything.'

186

The young intern heard them and looked up. His face was grim.

'He won't be able to tell you if he has. They've mutilated him. He'll never be able to talk again.'

'Oh, Christ!' Haggerty felt a wave of nausea.

'The bastards!' Medinos gritted his teeth.

The intern stood up, the stethoscope dangling loose.

'He may get back his health, but I'm not certain,' he said. 'He has pneumonia and some of his ribs are broken. And his spleen may be ruptured. It's risky but I think we should move him right away.'

'Can you give him something to ease that pain?'

'No. It is better that he stays conscious.'

'Okay,' Medinos said. 'Let's get him out of here.'

The intern turned and waved to the men waiting outside with a stretcher.

'*Commandante*! *Commandante*!' Someone shouted from the stairs.

Medinos swore. 'What is it now?' he called, peering down the passage at a man bending over the rails.

'Helicopters!'

'Oh, Mother!'

Medinos scrambled along the passage. Haggerty shot a last look at Tomaso and hurried after him.

At the top of the stairs, they could hear the hum of the gunships in the distance. The sound was almost drowned by the rising crescendo of panicked shrieking from the cells. The two men ran down the passageway, dodging the grasping hands thrusting out from the cells.

'We'll get you out!' Medinos shouted. 'Don't worry. Be patient!'

He and Haggerty ran through the hallway and out into the prison square. One of the men waiting outside pointed into the inky sky towards the city as Julio came to join them.

'Get the rocket crew over here!' Medinos snapped. He pointed to the men still standing on the square. 'And tell those people to take cover behind the cell-block. Hurry!'

187

They watched Julio double across the square, shouting. Men began scattering to shelter.

'It looks like we're for it, my friend,' Medinos said. 'Just pray our boys can stop them. Otherwise, the people in there are as good as dead.'

'How many have you freed?'

'Thirty-four by the last count.'

Haggerty was silent.

Medinos scanned the sky. 'Can you see them?'

'No, but it sounds like there's more than one.'

'I can believe that. Just hope they're not troop-ships.'

The men with the rocket-launcher arrived, panting and dishevelled. Medinos chose the hallway of the headquarters building as the best cover. He sent Haggerty and Julio with them while he went to organise a defence against a possible ground attack.

Haggerty and Julio cleared the debris from around the door of the headquarters building as the rocket crew peered into the dark sky for some sign of the gunships. Although the noise of the helicopters was now a loud thunder it was still impossible to see them. They would have to attack to give away their location.

Just as Haggerty was wondering where that attack would come, it happened. A searchlight beam suddenly shot down from the sky, tracking quickly across the prison compound. The gunner holding the launcher realised he could not get in a shot from inside the building. He called to his companion. Hiking the launcher on his shoulder, the two of them ran out into the square. To Haggerty, watching, it was an incredibly brave act.

The two men were standing with the launcher raised when the chopper's searchlight suddenly flashed on again and located the wall of the cell-block. In seconds, the men on the ground got in their shot first. But it was wide.

The pilot threw his craft sideways as the rocket streaked by. In doing so, he missed his target too. But his shot was spectacular. The shell glanced off the side of the building and sent a ball of fire careering across the square. As Haggerty watched in horror, the men with the launcher were hurled to the ground in the ensuing explosion.

The helicopter took fright and soared skyward, the sound of the motor rising to a scream.

Haggerty peered into the square, suddenly plunged into darkness when the flaming explosion went out. He grabbed Julio who crouched beside him.

'Can you see what's happened out there?' The air was filled with the smell of the explosion. The noises from the cell-block across the square could be heard in frightful chorus.

'I can't see them,' Julio said. 'I think they must have been hit.'

Haggerty got to his feet. 'I'm going out.'

'Let me go with you, *señor*.'

'Okay, come on.' They ran, bent double onto the darkened square, searching for the missing men.

'Look, there they are.' Julio pointed. Lying by the launcher was the gunner, his head bent at an awkward angle. Nearby, the loader was groaning, clutching his leg. As Haggerty approached, he could see the gunner was unconscious.

'Fuck!' Kneeling, he pulled the man away and hauled out the launcher. Although he wasn't sure it seemed undamaged. He hefted it up, feeling for the trigger, remembering how they had fired it at the cell-block wall earlier.

'Julio, get the missiles.' The launcher was comfortable, but heavy, on his shoulder. There was no time for a replacement. Julio came forward, fumbling in the bag.

The long interval without returning fire must have reassured the helicopters. They heard the noise of the engines coming closer again.

'Hurry up, for Christ's sake!'

With gut-wrenching suddenness, they were suddenly bathed in a brilliant white light. Julio, in the process of loading the missile into the launcher, froze.

'Get it in, man!' Haggerty screamed. Julio recovered and rammed it home. Haggerty shot a glance skyward and shoved the launcher's sight up guessing at two hundred feet. Turning, he bumped into Julio and almost fell. 'Get the hell out of here!' he barked. Grabbing the injured loader, Julio dragged him away.

Across the square Medinos was returning from dispersing his

189

men behind the cell-blocks. He turned the corner and stopped, appalled.

One of the helicopters, its shape faintly visible behind the glare of its searchlight, was circling with its nose down, trying to hold the beam on Haggerty who kept backing out of the light as he tried to take aim. The frustrated pilot was manoeuvring his machine in a tighter and tighter circle as he lined up for a shot. To Medinos, the sight of the lonely man on the sandy square and the huge black shape stalking him, could only be compared to a bullfight.

As though fulfilling that fantasy, the matador acted.

Stephen Haggerty, moving with eyes glued to the white beam, and turning as it turned, suddenly stopped. Launcher raised, he stood frozen in the centre of the beam. For a fraction of a second everything was still. Then Haggerty sighted and squeezed the trigger.

The rocket streaked skywards, swirling like a Roman candle. Medinos and his men held their breaths. For an instant the beam in the sky flickered. Suddenly it went out. In the space of a single breath, the sky was ripped by a dazzling flash of light and a fierce explosion.

Medinos stood transfixed as a slow stream of burning debris fell to the ground. Then, like everybody else, he was screaming.

Hands waving wildly, he raced across the square to where Haggerty had fallen from the recoil. 'You did it!' he shouted. Breathless, he hauled Haggerty to his feet. 'You did it!' Julio rushed in to help.

'Goddamn it, let go.' Haggerty struggled to free himself. 'There's another one up there.'

Medinos stopped.

'Here, Julio!' Haggerty shouted, 'Get me another shell!' Julio grabbed one from the bag. He started to shove it into the launcher as Haggerty was raising it to his shoulder again. 'Easy, man,' Haggerty snapped. 'It's not a fucking toy.'

'Come on,' Medinos gripped his arm. 'Let's get to cover while we can. Oh, *amigo*, you were beautiful!'

Haggerty found time to grin as he trotted awkwardly across the square. 'I thought I was dead meat,' he panted.

They reached the edge of the cell-block and crouched down to look back. The remains of the gunship were burning outside the perimeter fence. They stared upwards into the black sky. It took them a few moments to realise that the noise of the other craft was growing fainter. It was moving away. They waited, scarcely daring to hope. But it was true, the sound was fading.

'He's gone,' Medinos said, his voice brimming with delight, 'the bastard is gone!'

'Jesus Christ.' Haggerty was laughing now with relief. He lowered the launcher. 'Shit, I never want to go through that again.' Men were coming out of hiding, edging down to them, pointing to Haggerty and clapping with joy.

Medinos, recovering his poise, shouted at them. Reluctantly they moved away.

'What happens now?' Haggerty asked. 'Think they'll try again?'

'If they do, it will be by road. My guess is they can't afford to lose another helicopter,' Medinos said.

'Can you handle a ground assault?'

'I think so. There's only two roads they can use. My boys can hold both, while the freed prisoners get their comrades out.' Medinos rose and helped up Haggerty. 'As for you, my friend, I want you to take Tomaso back in the jeep. Julio can go with you and pass the word that we need transport to get these people out of here. Julio, go get Tomaso.'

Taking Haggerty's arm, Medinos and he crossed the blackened square moving through the broken and scattered dead. They passed the still smouldering guard-house and the twisted wreckage of the watch-towers. They stopped by the dust-covered jeep from which Haggerty had jumped down as an outraged Special Forces officer less than thirty minutes earlier. It seemed like an age ago now. They stood for a moment in silence, slowly realising it was over.

'Time to say farewell, my friend,' Medinos said, finally. 'You know, I almost wish you could stay with us. You've shown a real talent for this kind of work.'

'No thanks,' Haggerty said. He learned the price of war a long time before and it was too high.

'I'm sorry you say that. We could have done great things together.'

He stepped aside as they brought Tomaso up. All of them helped strap the stretcher onto the rear of the jeep. Julio, Haggerty and the young intern, Jiminez, who was going with them, climbed in.

'We will meet soon, Tomaso,' Medinos whispered to the barely conscious man. He straightened and shook hands with Haggerty. 'As for you, *amigo*. Anytime you need help, call on me.'

'I'll remember that,' Haggerty said. '*Adios*, my friend.'

17

'This has been a major defeat. There is no other way to describe it.'

Serena knew he was in trouble. The speaker was his former protégé, the army chief General Robles. Robles rarely intervened in cabinet discussions and then only to back Serena. Taking an initiative like this was a bad sign.

'It is a setback, no doubt about that.' Serena moved to take control of the debate with his minor admission. 'But we must remember the underlying reasons. Our equipment problems are growing more severe every day. And that's placing limits on what we can respond to.'

'Excuse me, Excellency,' Robles said. 'If we cannot protect our prisons from destruction, how can we be expected to survive?'

'Don't try to turn this into something more than it is, Robles,' Serena snapped. 'Guinoli could easily have taken out those attackers if he had had enough gunships. But he's starved for parts. Right, Roberto?'

Guinoli nodded. 'If you ask me, the operation last night should have been handled by the army. Except now, they can't even secure our main highways after nightfall. That's the state we've fallen into.'

'And what would you expect?' Robles shot back. 'I can't control the countryside without adequate logistical support. Have you any idea of what it would take just to secure the roads to Las Grisas from ambush?'

Serena sat back, temporarily relieved. Robles had been side-tracked. But that did not solve the real issue. If the country was to be saved from falling into the hands of the Marxists, they had to get resupplied. The Americans didn't know it yet but his flirtation with the Russians had failed.

The Soviets had demanded cabinet seats, not for the rebels, but for their own tiny Communist Party in exchange for minor military aid. Serena knew he would never sell that to his generals. He had to refuse. Now, all he had left was the Dackman operation. But Dackman wanted a postponement. Time, he said, to bring Cal Masters, who was having second thoughts, around again.

Serena drummed his fingers on the table quietly as the generals argued bitterly over the supply problem. There could be no delay, he thought. Dackman will have to carry out the scheme at the first opportunity.

As for the situation around the table, there was a quick cure for the dissension. He leaned forward.

'Gentlemen, gentlemen,' he said. 'If you ask me, most of our troubles come from the support the *guerrilleros* are getting in the *barrios*. I think we should make a move to blunt that support.' He looked at them and smiled. 'It's time we brought that rabble back under the jurisdiction of this government. What I'm proposing is that we drop our soft-hearted policies and go in there with everything we can throw at them. I think the time has come to give it to them good and hard.'

Later he met his private secretary, Alessandro Cordillera, in his study.

'Alex, I want you to arrange a rendezvous with Ernst Dackman. Set it up immediately. I want you to impress on him that we can't wait any longer for action. These donkeys are ready to turn on me. The *barrio* raids will divert them but it's only a matter of time before they start grumbling again. If we don't get a sympathetic listener in the White House very soon, we're finished, Alex. All of us.'

Cordillera shook his head, troubled.

'There are serious risks in moving it up, Excellency. Masters is very unstable after his brother's death. He could collapse if he's pushed.'

'We'll all collapse if he's not pushed,' Serena said impatiently.

194

'Guatemala is at stake, Alex. We can't wait. We have to take the risk.'

Cordillera shrugged. 'If you wish, Excellency. I'll catch a flight tonight. Incidentally, there's something else. I hate to burden you but it's important.'

'What is it?' Serena asked wearily.

'There was a survivor from Las Grisas, a corporal. He hid beneath the bodies when they shot the other guards who surrendered.'

'The swine. What about him?'

'He said the attack was led by an American.'

Serena stared, astonished.

'What?'

His secretary nodded. 'It was the same man who shot down the Cobra.' He slid a sheet across the table. 'From the description, there seems little doubt. It was Stephen Haggerty.'

Serena sank back in his chair as the magnitude of what he heard sank in. Haggerty was the one man who could already know enough to destroy the Dackman operation.

'Pass the word to Robles. If that fellow is in Guatemala City, he'll be in the *barrios*. We've got to find him. Do anything you have to do. But make sure he doesn't leave the country.'

'I'm sorry,' the telephone operator told Stephen Haggerty, 'but Miss Valdes is not registered here any more. Her room has been taken.'

'You're absolutely sure?'

'Yes, sir.' There was a hint of sharpness in the operator's voice.

Haggerty put down the phone. He had deliberately put Eva out of his mind during the Las Grisas business. But now her disappearance filled his mind.

Where had she gone? There had to be an answer. He didn't want to believe she would betray him. Not after that time they spent together. He just didn't want to believe it was possible.

He stepped out of the tiny booth into the brilliant morning sunshine. The long, waiting line edged forward. This was the only phone in the *barrio* serving a population of thousands. It had taken Julio's clout to get him to the head of the queue.

Julio said, 'Gone, eh?'

Haggerty nodded.

'Maybe she moved. Our hotels do not always suit foreigners.'

'How many are there?'

Julio shrugged. 'Five or six.'

'Get your truck,' Haggerty said.

In bright sunshine, they drove through the crude alleys of the *barrio*. Everywhere, there were people; cooking, gossiping, bargaining or just sitting in the sun. On the few vacant lots, gangs of young teenagers played football. Julio drove on his brakes and the horn.

The *barrio* slowly gave way to a broken, hilly area. They reached a paved road. Almost immediately, they were in a prosperous residential area with well-kept, tree-lined streets and spacious, ranch-type bungalows. It was a jolting contrast but Julio seemed not to notice.

They moved onto the Avenida Bolivar, Guatemala City's main artery, feeding in traffic from the Inter American Highway and the Pacific region. As they drove down in brilliant sunshine towards the city centre, Julio suddenly gripped his arm.

'*Señor*.'

A long line of military trucks was rolling down the opposite lane towards them. Cars moved in hurriedly to let them pass. You did not hold up the military in Guatemala.

'Trouble for someone,' Julio said grimly as the camouflaged convoy came level. Inside, armed stone-faced soldiers sat back to back in rows. Haggerty began counting as they went by. Over thirty trucks in all.

Julio watched in the rearview mirror. 'Oh, no.'

Haggerty twisted around to look. The trucks were turning into the intersection they had just left.

'They're going to San Isidro,' Julio said.

'Jesus! Can we warn them?'

Julio shook his head. 'That phone in there is never idle.' He blessed himself quickly. 'All we can do is pray that they're ready.'

'They knew this was coming?'

'They guessed. After last night, Serena was bound to do

something. There will be broken heads today that's for sure. But they should be okay.' As quickly as he worried, it was gone. 'Let us try your hotels.'

One by one, Haggerty checked them, the Maya Excelsior, the Pan American, the Palace, the Biltmore and again the Hotel Plaza. Eva Valdes was not in any of them.

By then, he was desperately searching for other possibilities than betrayal. She might have been kidnapped by the people he was after. Or injured. Or even worse. From the Plaza he called the place most likely to know. The American Embassy.

'Hello, I need to talk with someone in connection with a missing American citizen,' he told the Embassy operator who answered.

'Hold the line.'

He waited.

'Office of Public Safety. Daniel Winter speaking.'

'Mr Winter, my name is Stephen Haggerty. I'm a journalist and a US citizen. I came to Guatemala several days ago with a woman called Eva Valdes who is also an American citizen. I had to go away for two days and she was supposed to wait for me at the Hotel Plaza. When I returned she was gone. The operator at the hotel told me she checked out and left no message.'

'Well, Mr Haggerty, that needn't be alarming. She may have decided to go back home. These things happen, you know.'

'Not in this case,' Haggerty said. 'Listen, there is something else I've come across that you should know. It happened up country in a place called San Antonio.'

'San Antonio?'

'Yes. I went up there to see a man called Whitten, an American medical missionary who lives there.'

'Hold on a moment. Are you saying you met this Dr Whitten? In San Antonio?'

'I not only met him,' Haggerty said grimly, 'I saw him killed. By government soldiers.'

'Good God!' There was a long pause. 'Mr Haggerty, there's an American government security official who's just arrived here with the express task of seeing Dr Whitten.'

'Well, you can tell him he's too late.'

There was a pause.

'Maybe you better tell him that yourself. His name is Vern Railsback. He's staying at the Biltmore Hotel.'

18

Haggerty entered the Biltmore bar and sat down to wait. The lounge was small and panelled in natural wood. The alcoves and ceiling were festooned with lush plants, giving the impression of an overgrown forest clearing. From his corner seat by the balcony, Haggerty had a clear view of the lobby. When the waiter approached, he ordered a margharita.

A few minutes passed and the elevator doors opened across the lobby. A man in a flowered blue shirt and white trousers emerged. He glanced about, then started towards the bar. He was in his mid-thirties with a pale but firm-skinned oval face and blond, thin hair over a pink scalp. Although he was not tall, Haggerty could see he was nicely muscled under the gaudy shirt. As he came to the bar steps he saw Haggerty and gave an odd, loose-wristed wave.

Jesus, Haggerty thought, he's gay.

Vern Railsback climbed the steps and came to the table. 'Stephen Haggerty?'

They shook hands. Railsback stood aside as the waiter put down the margharita. 'I think I'll have the same,' he said pulling out a chair.

'You didn't waste time getting down here.' Haggerty tapped his watch. 'Right on the button.'

'Yes. Sort of thing that makes our government proud.' Railsback grinned and sat back. 'You wouldn't believe the sacrifices we make to keep Uncle Sam happy.'

'Well, you do get to travel,' Haggerty said. 'Although I wouldn't recommend going where you planned. To San Antonio, I mean.'

'It doesn't look as if I will after hearing your news. It's true, is it? Dr Whitten is dead?'

Haggerty nodded.

'They shot a rocket into him from a helicopter. I was close by.' The horror was still fresh in Haggerty's mind. He shook his head grimly. 'There wasn't much to see afterwards.'

'The bastards,' Railsback said bitterly. 'And to think it was our weapons they used. There has to be a message in that.' He paused as the waiter placed his drink and left. 'Any idea why it happened?'

'A few theories.' Haggerty tasted the margharita. 'But nothing solid.'

'Care to try them on me?'

'Mr Railsback ...'

'Vern.'

'Vern, I'm in a difficult position on this one. I didn't plan it that way but that's how it worked out.' He tapped some ash into the tray.' I don't know if you were told by the Embassy but I'm a journalist. Barely a week ago I took up what looked like a half-promising story in Montreal. Since I started working on it, and this might seem unbelievable but it's true, two of my contacts have been murdered and somebody has been doing their damnedest to kill me.' He saw Railsback's astonishment and grinned. 'And that's apart from the non life-threatening stuff. I've been tailed, had the hell chased out of me, been threatened by everybody from medical attendants to policemen. I've even been framed for murder.'

'Jesus!' Vern looked at Haggerty with new respect. 'And I thought I was having a tough time.'

'How's that?'

'Well, I know this won't rate with your troubles,' a slow grin crossed his face, 'but somebody has tried to kill me too.'

'Really?'

Vern nodded and raised a thumb and forefinger. 'I was that much away from it.'

'You better explain,' Haggerty said, 'because I still don't get it. You're a government official. Why would people be trying to kill you?' He smiled as the thought struck him. 'Apart from the normal reasons, I mean.'

Railsback grinned back. 'At this moment, I don't know. All I'm certain of is that a friend of mine who died this week was probably murdered. And his last words to me were to find this Dr Whitten. I've been looking ever since. That's what brought me here.'

'What exactly happened to your friend?'

'Haemorrhage. He bled to death.'

Haggerty sighed.

'Here we go again,' he said.

Vern Railsback looked at him, puzzled.

'I don't suppose,' Haggarty said, 'you know a guy called Ernst Dackman?'

They parted an hour later on the steps of the Biltmore.

After sharing stories, Railsback was now concerned for Haggerty's safety. The only secure refuge in Guatemala City was the US Embassy. But the compound was guarded by Guatemalan army security patrols who would arrest him once he showed his face. Railsback thought he might be able to work out some form of safe conduct with the Embassy. In the meantime, Haggerty would have to lie low.

'Be careful, Stephen,' Vern said as they parted. 'We both need to stay healthy if we're going to bring Dackman to heel.'

After the meeting, it was all becoming clearer to Haggerty. His innocent acceptance of Gedi Reubel's proposal had drawn him into a plot which now seemed to involve some very sinister aspect of United States policy in Central America.

Whatever slim doubts he might have retained about Dackman were gone now. The man was a killer, and a powerfully effective one. Both Railsback and he agreed that when they returned to the States, they would go straight to the FBI. So far as they could tell, Dackman was responsible for the murders of at least five people – Otto Lentz, Gedi Reubel, William Masters, Dr Whitten and Rita Meadows. It seemed that Vern and Haggerty were his only two failures so far – and Haggerty's case was far from closed.

From what they could gather, the killings were connected to a mysterious assassination plot designed to keep Guatemala in the hands of the Serena regime.

Haggerty and Railsback had growing suspicions about who the potential victim might be. But to press accusations of a murder plot, without proof, against men like Dackman and Serena, would make them a laughing stock. They agreed that all they could do would be to pursue charges on the known killings against Ernst Dackman in the hope he would be put off his plans by the ensuing investigation. The most serious problem they had now was getting back to the United States to present their evidence to the authorities. For the moment, it was a matter of waiting for Vern Railsback to do his stuff.

In the parking lot, Haggerty found Julio standing by his truck with a transistor to his ear. When Julio saw him he shook his head.

'The news is bad, *señor*,' he said, taking the radio down. 'They've cut off San Isidro. There's much fighting. And many arrests.'

'Damn. Are they likely to catch our friends?'

'I think not. There are ways of leaving the *barrio* that the army does not know about. But you and I, we can't go back there now.'

'Well, what do we do? We can't stay here.'

'Don't worry. There is a safe house. Hector and the *Commandante* use it. I will take you there.'

They left the lot and drove east and then north passing the main post office and the capital's downtown park. Beyond, to their left, Haggerty saw a massive stone building with the flag of Guatemala fluttering overhead.

Julio spat.

'The National Palace, *señor*. Home of the pig Serena and his gang.' Making a right, they passed the Cathedral. A block beyond, a huge market loomed up. Julio slowed and made a left into a narrow street opposite. It was flanked by high walls with recessed grilled windows looking down on the street. At the far end, Julio turned sharply into a small square and pulled up by the narrow sidewalk. He pointed to a pair of tall timbered doors just beyond the truck. 'That's it.'

Haggerty climbed out onto the cobblestones and followed

202

Julio. The door was opened by someone in the darkened hallway and they went in. The man who closed the door behind them was a pallid but heavy middle-aged man in a sleeveless shirt. Julio burst into a torrent of Spanish. The man looked sourly at Haggerty and grunted some kind of grudging consent. He pointed up the stairs.

'This way, *señor*.' They climbed the stone slabbed stairs where a single light burned to hold off the gloom. The air smelled of a sweet disinfectant that was not unpleasant. They reached a landing with a wrought-iron rail. Julio turned down along a corridor with Haggerty following. Halfway down, an Indian girl with black hair slicked down looked out from a door and smiled invitingly. Julio grinned and shook his head.

'What is this, a bordello?' Haggerty asked as she closed the door again.

Julio nodded, amused. 'The air force own it,' he said, 'but we control it.'

They reached the last door at the end of the corridor. Inside, the small room contained a brass-framed bed, a single chair and a small table by the tall French windows.

'In here,' Julio said going to the window, 'no one wishes to be seen. So they are not curious. And it has many exits.' He pulled back the thin muslin curtain. A narrow metal stairway led from the window to the court-yard below. A small door in the court-yard wall led to the street they had just driven up.

'The women here are all with us.' He winked. 'So if you wish to pass the time, you know, with any of them, that's okay.'

'I think I'll pass,' Haggerty said. 'But I appreciate the thought.'

Julio shrugged. 'That's up to you, *señor*. Me, sometimes I do, sometimes I don't. It is not something I worry about.' He grinned at Haggerty.

'You're a cheeky young bastard, Julio,' Haggerty said, as he sat on the bed. 'Anyway, what's next?'

'I will make enquiries about our people in San Isidro. As soon as I find out what's happening, I will come back. For you, there is just the wait.'

At the door, he paused. 'Are you hungry?'

'I could handle a coffee.'

'I'll have them send some up.' He slipped out.

Vern Railsback went through the Embassy security check and took the elevator to the third floor. Daniel Winter looked up as he entered.

'Hi, Vern.' He put down the paper he had been reading and sat forward at the desk. 'Well, did you get to see our friend?'

Vern nodded. 'That information about Dr Whitten,' he said, 'I'm afraid it turned out to be true. He's dead. Mr Haggerty witnessed it.'

'Gosh, I'm sorry to hear that,' Winter said. 'Was it the army?'

'Yes.'

Winter shook his head in disgust. 'Savages. They disgust me.'

'Daniel,' Vern leaned forward in the chair. 'I'm worried about Mr Haggerty's safety. He tells me the security forces have been looking for him since he arrived in the capital. I'm afraid they might kill him.'

'That's very likely now he knows about Whitten's murder.' Winter looked at Vern. 'Why don't you arrange to get him in here to the Embassy? Then we can work out a plan for getting him back to the States.'

'That's a good idea. But how do we get him past those roadblocks outside? They'll arrest him as soon as they find out his identity.'

Winter nodded. 'You're right. It's damnable.' He paused. 'Why don't I make out some coverage for him? Something temporary just to get him in here?'

'Could you do that?'

'Sure. We could give him some diplomatic coverage. The only snag is that I'm going to need the First Sec's signature. And he's at the Ministry. He's not expected back before four. But we could certainly get it done then.'

'I guess we'll just have to wait.' Vern looked at his watch. 'Mr Haggerty promised to call later. When he does, I'll tell him to hold on until five. That okay?'

'Should be fine,' Winter said. He rose from the desk. 'By the way, when you talk to him there's something he should know.' He grinned at Vern. 'I was over in the Annexe arranging for a shipment bag to Langley on the next flight out. Know who I ran into there?'

'Who?'

'That lady friend of Haggerty's. Eva Valdes. She's been here at the Embassy all the time. Out in the Annexe. She's just got clearance for a military flight back to the States.'

19

Haggerty was half dozing on the bed, with Eva on his mind, when he heard the soft tap on the door. He rose as a young Indian girl, slenderly shaped in a black dressing-gown, brought a coffee pot and a few tired cookies. She looked no older than sixteen. Her small lips parted to show white teeth in a shy smile as she laid down the tray before leaving. Haggerty wondered how she would look when the air force finished with her in a few years.

His thoughts soon returned to Eva. Staring into the white light from the window, he drank his coffee. The longer she was gone, the more damning it became. Although he still wanted to fight against it, the evidence against her now seemed overwhelming. He felt a seething anger at her betrayal. But he was baffled too. The intensity of passion she showed in their love-making and those intimate and very real gestures of attachment seemed too authentic to be faked. Eva Valdes had behaved in every way like a woman in love. Even now, recalling how it was brought an involuntary craving, a knotting in the pit of Haggerty's stomach. His mind, caught between emotion and reason, churned in confusion. Memory and emotion made him long for her. Yet reason kept insisting that the Eva he wanted was not the Eva he would get – if the evidence was to be believed.

Determined to put the inner wrangling behind him, he finished off the coffee and looked at his watch. It was just past two. Almost time to call Vern Railsback. Where the hell was Julio, he wondered irritably. He went to the window to look down into the court-yard below. In one corner below the whitewashed walls, an elderly woman sat by a table washing vegetables from a bucket at her feet. The scene was serenely peaceful and still with only the faint hum of traffic in the distance. He watched for a few moments then went to the wash-basin where he dashed some water on his face. As he straightened, he caught sight of his face in the small, square mirror. It brought a certain shock. The crinkled hair at his temples was greyer than he remembered. His cheek-bones were still burned from the journey to see Dr Whitten but now there was a hollowness beneath. His chin seemed to jut out more and there were deepening lines about his mouth. For the first time Haggerty saw a resemblance to his father in his own worn face.

Shrugging, he drew out a paper towel and dried himself. There were other things to think about. He wondered if he should call Vern or wait until Julio returned. He looked at his watch again. It was getting late. The prospect of more ruminations on Eva did not please him. To hell with it, he thought. He crossed to the door and let himself out.

On the landing, two women were leaning on the rail, chatting. They looked up.

'*Telephono?*'

One leaned over the railing to point underneath.

'*Gratias.*' He went down the stairs pulling the number Railsback had given him from his back pocket. The phone was hidden in a semi-dark alcove at the bottom. He had difficulty seeing the dial but he finally got the Embassy. Vern Railsback came on the line after a few moments.

'Stephen Haggerty here, Vern. How are we doing?'

'Good, pal. Better than you hoped.' Vern paused. 'Listen, we found your lady friend.'

'Eva?' Haggerty's heart gave a sudden thump. His breath caught. He felt a sudden ambivalence as his previous resentment mixed with hope. So she hadn't fled after all. The evidence which seemed overwhelming ten minutes earlier now looked weak. Maybe they were wrong. 'Is she okay?' he asked, keeping his voice steady.

'Yeah. You don't have to worry about her. She's here in the Embassy.'

'Vern, that's great.' He let his head touch the cool stone wall and rest there for a moment. It had suddenly hit him. He should have been thinking only of whether she was guilty or innocent.

207

But he was not. His predominant feeling was gladness that she was safe. He knew then that could mean only one thing. He had fallen in love with Eva Valdes.

'Steve, are you there?'

Haggerty lifted his head. 'Yeah. Listen, Vern, can I talk to her?'

'Sorry, pal, that's out. She's in another part of the building. But she wants to come with me to pick you up later. Is that okay?'

'Maybe that wouldn't be a good idea,' Haggerty said. Not with the suspicions that had been raised about her among the guerrillas. 'Better if she stayed where she is.'

'I'll have a hard job convincing her. She's primed to go.'

'Try, Vern. It's important.'

'Okay. Now let me give you the situation. Dan Winter, the public safety man, is going to put together some papers that will get you into the Embassy. But they won't be ready until after five. Can you wait?'

'If I have to.'

'Best if you do. Now tell me where I can find you.'

Haggerty described how to reach him. 'And, by the way, it's a bordello.'

Vern Railsback chuckled. 'That should keep you occupied for the afternoon. See you at five.'

Haggerty put down the phone and started back upstairs. The women were gone and the corridor was empty. With the news about Eva, there was a new lightness in his step. The fact that she wanted to come and see him said everything. She had to be innocent. There was no way she would do that if she had betrayed him. Right now, all he wanted was to see her. Four days had been a long time.

That mood preoccupied him as he reached his door. He opened it and slipped inside.

'Hallo, *amigo*.'

Haggerty stopped, startled.

The *Commandante*, Medinos, stood by the window.

'Jesus, Juan. You gave me a start,' Haggerty said and closed the door behind him. 'Where in hell did you come from?'

Medinos grinned and pointed to the window. He came forward

208

to take Haggerty's outstretched hand. 'Good to see you again, my friend.'

'You too. What brings you here?'

'We just got away from San Isidro.'

'Bad?'

Medinos nodded. 'They're tearing the place apart.' He looked at Haggerty. 'Listen, *amigo*, we brought out Tomaso.'

'Tomaso?' Haggerty looked at him in surprise.

Medinos nodded. 'At this moment, he's downstairs. With Hector.'

Is he all right?'

'Physically, he's still in bad shape. But he can move around. Stephen, he wants to see you.'

There was something in his voice that made Haggerty uneasy. 'Oh?'

Medinos nodded. 'But you should talk to him yourself.'

Together, they went through the window down into the courtyard. The earlier quandary, briefly allayed, was back for Haggerty. He knew this was going to be about Eva. And yet she wanted to come and see him. What the hell was going on?

The old woman washing the vegetables was gone. Two men, obviously bodyguards, lounged by the table. Medinos and Haggerty entered an old kitchen with white walls and crockery on the shelves. Medinos led the way around a large scarred table. At the far end, he opened a door and ushered Haggerty through.

They entered a heavily furnished drawing room that might have come from the turn of the century. A single large window, draped with transparent curtain, opened onto the square outside. Tomaso sat with his back to it, on a heavy sofa. Beside him was Hector.

'Tomaso.' Haggerty immediately crossed the room. 'It's good to see you up, my friend.' He tried to mask his revulsion at the sight of the grotesquely swollen face, which looked even worse than in last night's darkness. Leaning over, he looked into the battered features. 'Are you feeling any better?'

Tomoso nodded. There might have been a faint trace of a smile although it was hard to tell.

'Please sit down, *señor*.'

Haggerty turned as Hector spoke. The older man looked tired and strained. The events in San Isidro must have taken their toll. Haggerty pulled a chair out and sat down opposite the two men. There was a mood now, an atmosphere in the room, that felt bad.

'Something's wrong?'

Hector nodded. 'Yes,' he said. He straightened and spoke briskly. 'It's this woman friend of yours, Eva Valdes.' Leaning forward, he handed Haggerty a sheet of paper. 'Tomaso says she betrayed him. He's written it all out for you.'

Haggerty stared at him then silently took the paper. It was in English. Tomaso had taken some trouble, given his injuries. He began reading. It took an effort to remain calm. But it was all there. The whole story of how she had stood before Tomaso in the office of the President, within two hours of leaving Haggerty, and exposed Tomaso to Serena as a spy and a traitor.

Haggerty continued staring at the paper even after he finished. His face had grown pale. Just a few minutes ago he was prepared to believe Eva was innocent. Now that choice was gone. Finally he looked up at Tomaso. 'You're sure, Tomaso?' It was a question that had to be asked despite the hopelessness that was in him. 'There's no possibility of a mistake?' His throat was dry, making the words difficult to say.

Tomaso, compassionate, shook his head.

Haggerty looked down again at the paper. There was no disbelieving Tomaso. He closed his eyes. Medinos, standing alongside him, bit his lip and touched Haggerty's shoulder.

Hector looked at Haggerty. 'Do you know where she is, *señor*?'

Haggerty nodded. 'The American Embassy.'

'You must know we want her, *señor*.' Hector's voice was sharp now, and cold. 'She must be brought to account.'

Haggerty looked up. He felt sick at the thought of what had happened. To be raised and dashed in so short a space was cruel. 'I need time to think,' he said.

'Time to think?' Hector looked momentarily puzzled as if he could not believe it. Then he leaned forward angrily on the sofa. 'What is there to think about? Everything we've gone through these past days has been due to this woman. She must be punished.'

'I understand that,' Haggerty said. He felt drained. He gestured to Tomaso. 'And I know what Tomaso has suffered. But Eva was very close to me. I cannot give her up without thinking about it. You must give me a little time.' He knew what would happen if he handed her over: execution, probably preceded by torture. Even his despair could not excuse the terrible images that evoked.

Hector stared at him, silent. Haggerty saw for the first time that this was a man who did not like to be flouted. Somehow that strengthened his resolve. They stared at each other.

'Please, *Commandante*.' Medinos stepped forward now. 'Let him have a little time. This is not easy.' From the sofa, Tomaso nodded.

The room was quiet as Hector continued to stare at Haggerty. Now they were eye to eye. You can't get her without me, Haggerty thought, and you know it. His dislike at being forced into a corner and at Hector for doing it was growing. It gave him new strength. He was prepared to sit there all day. Finally Hector, who knew he was beaten, nodded. 'All right,' he said sourly. Haggerty could see the suppressed rage. 'You can take some time. We will wait.'

Outside, Medinos gripped his arm.

'That was bad, Stephen,' he said. 'You've angered Hector. He does not forgive that easily.'

'He's another Serena, Juan,' Haggerty said. 'To hell with him. Listen, will you let me talk with Eva? To see if there is any explanation for all this?' He knew it was grasping at straws. But he had to. Those earlier nights brought an obligation.

Medinos dropped his hand. 'No,' he said. 'Come on, let's go to your room.' He gestured to the stairs.

In the room, Haggerty sat on the bed as Medinos crossed to lock the door. 'Sorry I have to do this,' he said.

Haggerty was silent.

Medinos sighed.

'Like some coffee?'

'Okay.'

Medinos hesitated then slapped him softly on the shoulder. He crossed to the French windows and let himself out. Before he reached the court-yard below, Haggerty had left the bed and

211

moved fast and quietly to the curtains to watch. The two bodyguards below had found chairs. Medinos spoke briefly to them and pointed up at the window before he went into the kitchen. It was clear to Haggerty that he wasn't going to get out that way. He returned to the bed and lay against the brass head.

He had two hours before Vern turned up. He had to warn him against bringing Eva. No matter what, he couldn't turn her over to an execution or torture squad. Even though his fists tightened at the thought of what she had done. She might deserve it. But it was too barbaric. He couldn't do it.

Just thinking about Florida now filled him with terrible bitterness. How could she have behaved the way she did, with all that gentleness and love and still betray him? Was she that powerful an actress, that skilled in deceit? Had she really planned it as it now seemed?

He lit a cigarette and pulled deeply on it.

He could see obvious connections between her and what had happened to him in this affair. It was all clear once the matter of trust was taken away. He had been thinking of that. For instance, she had turned up at the Miami *Sentinel* apparently by chance. But he had blurted out that he would be there to that patrolman outside the Mayburn Clinic. And one of Dackman's henchmen was listening. She was also the only one who knew that Rita Meadows could give him an alibi before she was murdered. And then there was her hurried visit home before they left for Guatemala. She could have used it to set him up for the abduction. Luckily for him, Tomaso was there. Unluckily for Tomaso, she found out.

When you considered it coldly like that, it was impossible to dismiss the evidence. It was all so well done, so smoothly executed. He felt such an idiot for being taken in.

He walked back to the bed and punched at the worn pillow as he sat down. Damn her, he thought. And yet he still couldn't turn her in.

He heard Medinos coming up the fire escape and swung off the bed to open the window.

'Thanks, *amigo*.' Medinos was carrying two cups. He handed one to Haggerty.

'Listen,' Haggerty said as he went back to sit on the bed again. 'I've been going over the whole thing and there's not much doubt that Eva did what Tomaso claimed. I realise that. But I need to know what would happen to her if I persuaded her to come here?'

Medinos sipped his coffee. 'She would be tried. As for the verdict ...' He shrugged.

'You think she'll be shot, right?'

'I would think that likely.'

'Would you agree?'

'Sure,' Medinos said. 'You saw what happened to Tomaso. And the damage it's done to us. Who would think of clemency in a case like that?'

'Will she get a hearing? In case she has an answer to the charges?' Haggerty insisted. 'I must know before I do anything.'

'Of course, my friend. We are not savages.'

Haggerty took some time. Then he stubbed out his cigarette. 'All right,' he said. 'There is an official at the US Embassy who located Valdes for me when I reported her missing. His name is Vern Railsback. He can bring her here to meet me. But, listen, if it's at all possible, I would like to get her back to the United States. I'm facing charges there too for something she had a hand in. It would go a lot easier for me if you would let me take her back.' It was a last try but he decided to make it anyway.

Medinos shook his head. 'That's impossible, knowing Hector's views. But I'm sure he'll co-operate in getting a true statement from her on your case if you're worried about that.'

Yes, Haggerty thought. A death-bed confession. Probably taken under torture.

'Okay,' he said. 'Tell Hector I'll make the call.'

20

Medinos wanted to squeeze into the narrow alcove with him but when Haggerty demonstrated how uncomfortable that was, he moved back. Haggerty, phone raised, hoped it would be far enough.

'Mr Railsback, please,' he said when the Embassy came on.

Medinos nodded encouragingly. But he still stood close.

'Hello?' Vern was on the line.

Haggerty took a quiet breath. This was it.

'Mr Railsback, this is Stephen Haggerty. We had a conversation earlier on the matter of bringing Miss Eva Valdes to see me. Do you recall it, sir? You wanted the address.'

'What the hell ...?' There was a longish pause. 'I'm sorry, Mr Haggerty, I was talking to someone else.' Van Railsback's voice was slow now, deliberate. 'Say, this connection sounds strange. Is there someone on the line?'

'No, Mr Railsback.'

'What is it then? Are you in trouble?'

'Yes, that's right.'

'Someone with you?'

'Yes. If you hold on, I'll get him to pass you the address.'

The phone close to his mouth, he turned to Medinos who showed no alarm. 'He wants the address. You better give it to him.' He handed him the phone.

'Hello, sir,' Medinos said. 'You want the address?'

'Yes, please,' Vern said.

'It's 21 Plaza del Mercedo. Just off Calle 6A.'

'Just let me write that down,' Vern said. 'Okay. Put me back to Mr Haggerty. I'm not sure about when I can get Miss Valdes down there.'

214

'Hello?' Haggerty said.

'Steve, what floor are you on? Is it the first?'

'No.'

'The second?'

'Yes, that seems okay.'

'I need to know the room. Just answer yes or no. Is the room on the left-hand side?'

'Yes.'

'Tell me when I get to the right room. Is it the first – the second – the third – the fourth – the fifth?'

'Yes, that's right.'

'The fifth,' Vern said. 'Okay, let's make sure we're right. You're on the second floor, in the fifth room on the left-hand side.'

'That's fine, Mr Railsback.'

'Listen, I'll be there at four-thirty,' Vern said, 'but you can tell them it's going to take till 5.30.'

Haggerty turned to Medinos.

'Will 5.30 be okay?'

Medinos nodded.

'He says that's okay,' Haggerty said. 'I look forward to seeing you and Miss Valdes. And Mr Railsback? Thanks for the help.'

'Stay cool, Steve. We'll do our best to get you out of there. So hang in. Okay?'

'Sure. And thanks a lot, Mr Railsback.' Haggerty hung up and turned to Medinos. 'What happens now?' For the first time, he noticed two men were now guarding the front door. It was not going to be easy for Vern.

'We wait,' Medinos said. The concern must have shown on Haggerty's face because Medinos took his arm and smiled. 'Come on, it's not so bad. You did the right thing.'

They walked up the stairs. A woman passed and Medinos stopped her. 'You could do with a drink, maybe?' he asked Haggerty.

He nodded, forcing a smile. With a drink coming maybe the waiting would be a little easier. Medinos spoke rapidly and they continued along the corridor.

Back in the room, Medinos locked the door behind them. He drew his chair across to the window, cutting off that possibility of

215

escape. Haggerty sat on the bed, deliberately casual, but now starting to size up Medinos as an opponent. Despite the Guatemalan's courage of the previous night, Haggerty could see he would not be difficult to take in a fight. He was several inches shorter and at least twenty pounds lighter. That was encouraging.

Medinos leaned forward in his chair. 'You are still feeling something for this Valdes woman, right *amigo*?' He had misinterpreted Haggerty's silence.

'Yes,' Haggerty said. Suddenly, he was aware of a fresh problem. And it was not good. Medinos was armed. His revolver was stuck in the belt under his jacket. Haggerty rolled his cigarette between his fingers. He looked up at Medinos. 'It bothers me, this thought of her being executed.' He looked up and shook his head. 'I still find it hard to believe she would do such a thing.'

'If it was a man,' Medinos asked, his eyes glinting with amusement, 'would that bother you so much?'

Haggerty shrugged. 'I guess not.'

There was a knock at the door and Medinos went to unlock it. The young Indian girl who came earlier appeared. On the tray were two glasses and a bottle of brandy. She laid them on the small table and poured two portions of the liquor. 'Thank you,' Haggerty said as she brought him a glass. She gathered the used coffee tray and smiled with childishly warm innocence as she left.

Haggerty gestured to the door after her. 'How old would that kid be, Juan?'

Medinos shrugged as he went to lock the door. 'Fourteen, fifteen maybe.'

Haggerty shook his head. 'I find it sickening that people accept it so easily. Don't you feel a little ashamed of belonging to a people who would turn a nice kid like that into a prostitute?'

Medinos looked at him sharply for a moment then shook his head. 'I'm afraid that kind of morality is a luxury that a lot of people can't afford. We have no room in this part of the world for fine feelings.' He came back and sat down. 'They were beaten out of us a long time ago.'

'That's the trouble with the fucking Guatemalans, if you ask me,' Haggerty said. 'As far as I can see, you're either wallowing in

216

self-pity or slaughtering each other.' His voice was impatient. He had to arouse Medinos, divert him. And find a way to move him from the window where he could call for help in any confrontation. Of course, there was also the matter of his gun. Last night they might have risked their lives for each other. Now it was one man against the other. Keeping Medinos's mind off that fact might tip the scale.

Medinos, for his part, needed no urging to talk about politics. He began to defend his movement and to describe the effects of the Serena regime as well as the seemingly endless exploitation which Guatemala had suffered from successive military regimes. All that was done, he said, with American backing. Haggerty argued back but mostly with Vern Railsback's impending arrival on his mind. The room grew thick with smoke as they talked.

They had reached the point of arguing about the Marxist ideology which fuelled the guerrillas, when the first sounds of disturbance came from downstairs. Medinos, deep in his argument, didn't notice immediately. Haggerty heard feet clattering up the stairs. He raised his voice.

From outside in the corridor, there was a sudden rush of whooping laughter. People were moving down the hall. Medinos broke off and glanced towards the door. He did not seem alarmed. The noise sounded like drunken revelry, not unusual in a brothel.

'Where's dem whores!' a deep American voice shouted suddenly in the corridor. Medinos alert now, rose. His eyes were on the door. To his side, Haggerty began quietly easing his legs off the bed. Outside the noise grew louder. Medinos faced the door, his hand moving inside his jacket. Haggerty was just rising from the bed when Medinos caught it from the corner of his eye. He turned, his face darkening with anger and drew out the gun.

Just as he did so, the door smashed. The Guatemalan was briefly distracted. Haggerty dived just as two husky crew-cutted men burst into the room, with pistols raised. As Haggerty and Medinos crashed against the wall, Vern Railsback appeared behind them.

'The window!' Haggerty shouted as he grappled with the Guatemalan. One of the men ran to the curtain while Railsback

217

took two strides and very deliberately sideswiped Medinos with his gun. He tumbled to the floor. Haggerty pulled himself free.

'Thanks, Vern.' Haggerty prised Medinos's gun away.

The man at the window pushed the curtains closed. 'They're coming up,' he shouted.

'Get the hell out!' Vern shouted. Pushing Haggerty ahead, they rushed through the door with the burly escorts behind them. They both ran down the corridor as one of the men pulled the door closed and sprinted after them. On the landing by the stairs, two more big men in T-shirts stood. Both were armed and one held the fat proprietor with the gun barrel to his head. They waved Vern and Haggerty forward.

'Go through,' Vern shouted to Haggerty. They passed the men and clattered down the stone steps. Seeing they were well down, the man holding the proprietor pushed him headlong into the corridor and they all scrambled down after Vern and Haggerty, the sharp sounds echoing around the walls.

Leaping over the unconscious guards who lay across the doorway, Vern led the way into the blinding sunlight of the small square.

'Over here!' he shouted, pointing. Haggerty ran with him to where a truck stood with its engine running. The door opened and he threw himself in. Eva Valdes was at the wheel.

'Get going! Vern barked. She accelerated and the truck skidded in a wide circle on the cobblestones. The second car with the others in it was already turning tightly. Both cars bounded into the side street with the others leading. Haggerty saw the grinning faces looking back from inside.

'Thanks, Marines!' Vern shouted, and slapped his hand on the dashboard. 'We did it. We fucking did it!'

Haggerty's jangled emotions didn't allow him to smile. He stared at Eva who was driving like a woman possessed. The truck bounded down the street with Vern looking back. But there was no pursuit. Eva shot a glance across at him. 'You all right, Stephen?'

Haggerty said nothing. She bit her lip.

'Slow down,' Vern said, 'we're going to be okay.'

They entered the main avenue by the markets. The car with the

Marines was pulling ahead in the traffic. One of the men in the back seat turned and waved a farewell.

'Jesus, those boys were something, eh?' Vern said. He waved back.

'How did you manage to rope them in?'

'Said one of the Agency's men was in trouble. They jumped to help.' Vern tapped Eva's shoulder. 'Just like this girl. All great people.'

Haggerty stared ahead.

'What do we do now?'

'There's been a slight change of plan. We have to wait until morning before going into the Embassy. Winter's got us a safe house to stay in tonight. He'll come and collect us then and take us through the roadblocks. All sweet and simple.'

He took out the small rough map which Daniel Winter had drawn and began giving Eva directions.

In silence, Haggerty lit a cigarette. It tasted like ashes.

'Okay,' he said. 'Tell me what happened.'

They were alone in the court-yard of the house Daniel Winter arranged.

She looked at him, silent and pale, seeing his rage.

'They mutilated Tomaso,' he said brutally. 'He'll never talk again. They killed Randolph Whitten, a harmless missionary. And they've been trying to kill me ever since you talked.'

His face looked worn. The mouth was hard and his voice was filled with bitterness. 'And to think I believed everything you said to me before. I thought you loved me.'

'Oh, Stephen.' Suddenly she was crying. She couldn't control it. Her body shook. She tried to turn the flood away by putting her palms to her face but the tears rolled through and fell staining her dress.

He reached forward and grabbed her wrists.

'Why?' he shouted. 'Why did you do it?'

She put her head down, her black hair spilling around her face. She didn't want him to see her. Her chest heaved with sobs.

'Why?' he demanded again, twisting her wrists, trying to turn her towards him. But she struggled to keep her face averted. 'Don't Stephen. Please.'

The pent-up despair flooded through him. He shook her wrists, hardly aware of the roughness of his grip.

'Why?' He was beside himself with agony. 'Damn you! Why did you do it?'

She could feel the waves of pain emanating from him. It seared her to know he was suffering because of her. She began to struggle. 'I had to!' she shouted. 'I had to!' She stared wildly at him, wanting to do anything rather than have this go on. But her face collapsed when she saw the fresh agony in his eyes. She slumped as he released her wrists. 'Oh, God...' she sobbed, unable to stop the flood of grief.

He stood up. His face was white now, drawn. He looked old.

'Stephen...' She had slipped to her knees. Her tear-stained face looked up at him, beseeching.

'Stay away from me.' His voice swept over her like an icy wind. It was like a judgement. Final, impartial, merciless. 'I can't look at you. Go away. I can't bear the sight of you near me.'

She slumped, her face in her hands, locked in the misery of someone who felt justly damned.

Haggerty rose and left the court-yard. Vern Railsback, who had been standing by the door during the whole encounter watched him go in silence.

That evening, in a narrow room upstairs with the blinds drawn, Haggerty tried to sleep. But his mind would give him no rest. Finally he sat up against the rough headboard and chain-smoked. Fragments of feelings, hate, love, anger, and pity, collided with each other, creating a maelstrom of emotion that swept away reason. He knew now that whoever said that the one in love got the better deal was a liar. Nobody had ever hurt him like this.

Later, as fatigue finally triumphed over the pain, he drifted into an uneasy sleep. When he awoke the room was in darkness. As his eyes adjusted to the gloom, he saw the outline of someone sitting by the bed. He stared. It was Vern Railsback.

'Awake?' Railsback asked.

Haggerty nodded. Lying back, he stared at the ceiling. The room was quiet.

'She has a case,' Railsback said suddenly.

Haggerty was silent. The pause lengthened.

'I said she has a case,' Railsback repeated.

'I heard you,' Haggerty said. Somewhere, far away, a radio was playing.

A match flared in the darkness and came forward with a cigarette. Haggerty took the cigarette and lit it. Railsback blew the match out.

They sat in silence.

'Want to hear it?'

'No.'

'I didn't either. But I heard it eventually. And I know it's true.'

Haggerty turned on the pillow to look at him.

'What could possibly excuse what she did?'

'What she told me doesn't excuse it. But it does show why she did it.'

Haggerty turned away. 'I don't want to hear it.'

The cigarette flared as he pulled on it.

'You really want to understand, don't you?' Vern Railsback said. 'But you feel so betrayed, you don't want to let her off the hook.'

'Why don't you fuck off, Railsback?' The voice was rough in the darkness. 'That would make it easier for both of us.'

'She's got a case, Haggerty,' Vern said firmly. 'Now do you want to hear it or not?'

Haggerty did not reply.

'Okay, if you don't want to hear it, I can leave. And maybe take her with me. And you'll never be able to forget that you didn't listen when you had the chance. Because you're going to learn one day that you should have listened.'

The moments passed, then lengthened into silence. Finally Vern Railsback started to rise. Just as he did so, Haggerty spoke.

'Say what you have to say.' His voice was low.

Vern Railsback nodded and sat down. He held back any sign of relief. 'Before I tell you about Eva, it's important you know something I didn't tell you before. I know you've heard lots of

221

stories about guys like me. People who turn up at our embassies around the world with nobody quite sure who we are or what we're doing. The media tend to lump us all together as CIA. Almost always, they're wrong. But in my case they'd be right. I am CIA.' He paused for a long moment. 'And so is Eva Valdes.'

The bed creaked as Haggerty stiffened.

Vern nodded. 'I don't have the official word, it's true, but personally I have no doubt. Her postings, her classification, even her salary checks out. The people she works for are known to me.' He shook his head grimly. 'Although what they've done to her is beyond belief.'

Haggerty sat up to crush out the cigarette Vern had given him and drew another from the pack.

'This comes much better in the dark,' Vern said as the match flared.

'Tell me.' The match went out.

'Valdes is her real name. She was recruited at the University of Tampa five years ago. She's been involved since then in the selection of Hispanic agents for work in Central America. Her position wasn't too important but from the responsibilities she was given, I could tell she did a good job. I knew her boss and she knew of Dackman, William Masters and me. We all once worked in the same department – Western Hemisphere.

'Last week, on the day you arrived in Miami, she received a visit from a man called James Korner. Korner is the head of the Western Hemisphere section and a very important man in Washington. Eva was overawed by the visit. It was as if the Head of ABC News, or whatever, had taken time out to call on you in Miami.

'Korner told her that Ernst Dackman – whom she already knew – had gotten his hands on a biological warfare secret that the Russians were desperate to recover. He told her that the Russians were sending in an agent from Canada to hunt down Dackman.'

Haggerty's breath hissed.

Vern nodded. 'Right. It was you. Naturally, Eva asked why not arrest you and have done with it. But Korner said they wanted to watch you in an effort to uncover your contacts.'

'I'll be damned.'

'She took the job.' Vern chuckled softly. 'But what she didn't count on was your charm. The poor girl started falling in love with you.'

'But I told her everything. About who I was, what I did.'

'Yeah. To her, it sounded like a great cover.'

'Give me another cigarette,' Haggerty said.

'Think about it,' Vern said, passing the pack. 'You say you're a journalist from Montreal. Hunting down Dackman because he might be involved in a murder. What a crock! It was as clear as daylight to her that you were an agent. Your contact even sent in a fresh passport to you at the Miridiana when you had to change plans and come down here to Guatemala.'

'Ned Williams's package,' Haggerty murmured.

'I tell you, pal, I would have believed Korner in her place,' Vern said. 'Wouldn't you?'

Haggerty said nothing.

'Anyway, by the time you were leaving Miami her emotional problems were getting too much for her. Before you left, she called Korner and asked to be relieved. He refused and ordered her to go with you to Guatemala. After that, she found the story rounded out by your meeting with those Communist guerrillas in the *barrio*. You told her a wild story about being kidnapped at the airport. She thought that was an excuse for giving her the slip so you could get on with your business. After that, she decided that she had to finish her job and leave – even though she knew then that she loved you.

'She called Korner. He told her to go and see Serena. After you left to visit Whitten, she went to the President. From her story, Serena immediately realised that Tomaso had lied to him. Without telling her, he brought them together. Well, you've got to remember her job. She had to do the patriotic thing. And she did. She exposed Tomaso as a Communist agent.' He rubbed away some of the perspiration gathering on his forehead. 'The rest you know.'

Haggerty smoked in silence.

'Look, Steve,' Vern said earnestly. 'I know this business. And don't doubt it. It happened the way she said it did.'

'She could have gotten me killed,' Haggerty said.

Vern waved that away. 'She never imagined that would happen. She thought you would have been caught all right. But then there would have been the traditional swop. In her mind, she pictured you going back to Moscow to a patient wife and maybe a couple of babushkas or whatever they call them, and a big promotion in the KGB. The way she pictured it everybody would have been happy – except her. But that would have been all right too, once she knew you were safe.'

Haggerty sent a stream of smoke across the darkened room.

'Listen, Steve,' Vern said quietly, 'I didn't tell you this story because it's my natural art. That girl is suicidal. God knows what she'll do if you don't back off. I'm serious.'

The music in the distance had faded away. The room was quiet.

Haggerty stubbed out his cigarette.

'Where is she?'

'Next door.'

He swung his feet off the bed. He paused, looked at Vern Railsback, then held out his hand. Vern took it.

'Thanks.'

He turned and walked to the door.

Vern Railsback watched him go. At that moment he was glad he didn't have to talk.

Like Haggerty's room, hers was in darkness. She sat on the bed, with her knees raised, staring in front of her, no longer able to think. She was only vaguely aware of footsteps in the corridor and then the door opening. She didn't move out of the unfocused nothingness in which she sat.

'Eva.'

It was his voice. Stephen's. The realisation that he was there sank in. Slowly she turned her head.

His silhouette was framed in the doorway.

'Vern told me everything,' he said. 'It's all right.'

She stared.

'It's all right,' he said again.

Thousands of tiny chains fell from her. Her spirit, freed, rose upwards. Oh, God.

'It's all right,' he repeated.

Everything was bursting forth. She scrambled, her long legs ungainly, her dress riding up but she didn't know or care. She came off the bed and ran across the floor towards the figure standing in the door, throwing herself into his arms.

He held her as shivering waves swept over her body.

They slept late.

It took three knocks from Railsback to rouse them. 'Hey, wake up in there. Come on, open up.'

Eva stirred and opened her eyes. She saw Haggerty beside her and for a moment she found herself trembling with sudden fear. Slowly as it passed she reached over to touch him softly. He awoke, still sleepy. He turned awkwardly. She waited, watching as comprehension came. He looked at her. And then he smiled. It was all right. She hugged him.

'Are you going to open this damned door?' Vern demanded. 'Or do I break it down?'

'All right, all right,' Haggerty said as he pulled on a pair of underpants. 'I'm coming.'

He opened the door and went back to the bed.

Vern entered with a large tray.

'Breakfast. Eggs, sunnyside up, bacon, toast and coffee.' He grinned down at them. 'I trust all had a good night?'

Eva laughed delightedly and sat up, the sheet around her. Haggerty smiled lazily at the food.

'What time is it, anyway?' he asked. He took the tray.

'Nine forty-five,' Vern said.

Haggerty offered some food to Eva. 'Isn't it a little late?' he asked. 'I thought your Mr Winter would have called by now.'

'Give him time. On foreign postings, they keep gentlemen's hours. Something we learned from the British.'

'Well, the sooner we get into that Embassy, the happier I'll be,' Haggerty said. Eva ate, saying nothing.

'I'll give it another thirty minutes,' Vern said. 'If he doesn't call by then, I'll call him.'

But they finished breakfast and he still hadn't called. As Haggerty rose to shower, Vern took the dishes downstairs. He hadn't said it but he was mildly worried at Daniel Winter's silence.

He wondered if the First Secretary was proving difficult about providing papers. He thought it unlikely. The Agency habitually used diplomatic coverage in emergencies and even sometimes when it was simply convenient. If there was a problem that wasn't likely to be it.

He was washing the dishes when the phone rang. At last, he thought, wiping his hands and hurrying to the living room.

'Vern, that you? Daniel Winter here.'

'Geez, Dan, I was getting worried. You guys working on Washington time or what?'

'Vern,' Winter's voice was low and strained, 'there's a problem.'

'Problem? What are you talking about?'

'That man Haggerty. We can't help him.'

'What the hell are you talking about, Daniel? Can't help him? The man's an American citizen. His life is threatened. We have to help him.'

'Vern, you know how I feel about this matter. But I can't. The Guatemalans want Haggerty for questioning. And Washington agrees they have the right.'

'Washington? Who in Washington are you talking about?'

'Korner.'

'Korner? What fucking right has he to say who should or shouldn't be helped by our Embassy?'

'Look, Vern ...'

'Since when does that Boris Karloff imitation set the standards for our diplomacy?'

'For crying out loud, Vern, listen. He's not setting standards. He's simply saying that the Agency does not want the normal practices bypassed in this case. Meaning Haggerty has to find his own way in to the Embassy, if he can.'

'And if he can't? He could get killed. Is that how it's to be?'

'Good God, Vern, don't be like that.' Railsback could feel him squirming with embarrassment. 'You make it sound like it's a death sentence.'

'Who told Korner, anyway?' Vern bored in. 'Was it you?'

'I had to, Vern. It's required. You know that.'

226

'Mother-fucker!' Vern spat in venom. 'If I could get my hands on you.'

Stephen Haggerty was coming down the stairs drying his hair. He stopped in astonishment.

'Have you told them he's here?' Vern demanded. Haggerty came over, tapping his chest questioningly. Vern nodded. Haggerty lowered the towel.

'Well, don't even think of it, do you hear?' Vern slammed down the phone.

'The Embassy backing off?' Haggerty asked.

Vern nodded. 'Korner's orders.'

Haggerty sat down on the sofa. 'So what do we do?'

'I don't know, Steve. But I'm betting there's no way you're going to get near the Embassy now that Winter's passed the word. They'll ring that place with troops.' He looked at Haggerty. 'If it's any consolation, you're not alone. Eva and I are on the bad guys list too, for helping you.' It wasn't true but it was the best he could think of. There was no way he was going to abandon Haggerty now. And he knew Eva wouldn't.

'Shit.'

'Shit, right.' Vern looked at Eva as she came down the stairs. 'But at least we're three shits now instead of one.'

They discussed the options quickly, spurred on by fears about Daniel Winter's trustworthiness. He could betray them at any time and bring troops crashing through the door. There was no time for delay.

But even if they had that luxury, it was clear that the choices were limited. The Embassy was out. If they tried to hide out, the army or the guerrillas were bound to find them. The obvious option left was to leave the country. But that brought up the question of how. With the airport under surveillance and their ignorance of the ports, it would have to be by road. They finally agreed that the best solution would be to take the Embassy truck and try to make it to the Mexican border. But it would have to be through the mountains. Serena would have his troops out on the Pan American Highway and at all border crossings.

The unspoken knowledge they all shared now was that the guerrillas ruled the mountains.

21

At the Embassy, Daniel Winter finally gave in and told them of the safe house. But they were forced to use Korner in a long-distance call from Washington, to do it. The delay in arranging the call made the crucial difference. By the time army commandos reached the safe house, it was empty. When they questioned the terrified neighbours, they found that they had missed Haggerty, Railsback and Valdes by an hour.

Serena, linked directly by radio to the command post at the scene, smashed his fist on the desk when he heard. Robles, the army commander, who had never seen the President so upset, flushed under his furious glare.

'Idiots! That's what you command! Idiots!' Serena rose from his desk and pushed his chair angrily aside. 'I am served by incompetents!' He went to the door and pulled it open. 'Christina!' he shouted. He came back into the room where Robles and Guinoli still sat in embarrassed silence.

'The descriptions,' Serena demanded, 'are they out?'

Robles nodded.

'Add this truck they took. And make sure they get to every town and village in the country. I want every policeman, every soldier on watch. Everyone, you understand?'

'Yes, sir,' Robles said. Guinoli nodded.

'We must find them. They cannot be allowed to leave the country. No matter what. The fate of this government depends on it. I don't care how you do it. But find them!'

He looked up at his secretary Christina who had appeared in the doorway. 'Get me Korner again.' She nodded and disappeared quickly.

Serena glared at his two commanders.

228

'Well, what are you waiting for? Get out and get to work!'

The two men rose hastily.

'This is a national emergency, you understand!' he shouted as they left. He banged the desk. 'I want those people. Dead or alive!'

By the time Korner came on the line, he had regained some of his composure.

'Everything possible is being done to find them,' he told the American. 'We are leaving no stone unturned.' His voice was calmer now, more confident. 'I realise our plans are at risk while these people remain at large. But I have no doubt they will be caught. Now leaving that aside, I must insist that we go ahead with the operation. It is absolutely essential. Events are already overtaking us here. I cannot guarantee our survival beyond weeks. You must understand that after the Las Grisas business. Anyway, I have spoken with Dackman about carrying out his part. He expressed reservations, naturally. But if you agree he is prepared to go ahead. I must insist that you approve.'

Korner, with no more faith than Serena in the efficiency of his military, reluctantly acceded. Given the deterioration in the Guatemalan situation, he had little option but to agree.

After six months of plotting, the die was finally cast. Only Haggerty, Railsback and Valdes could stop what was now set to happen.

They had begun their journey north in high spirits. It did not last. Two hours of travelling on the Pan American Highway, with police and military patrols racing back and forth, brought home the danger they were in. Once they realised that, the jokes faded.

They barely spoke after Haggerty turned off the main highway onto a crude dirt road that Vern recommended. The extra security this lonely route bought was more than paid for by the constant jostling as the truck bounced along the crude trail. The pervading heat added to the tension. The cab was filled with unspoken friction.

They were crossing a barren stretch of highlands that unrolled like a faded brown carpet up to the snow-capped mountains on the horizon. The tiny road ran like a narrow thread across the lifeless landscape. Overhead, the sun glinted flint-like from a metal-blue sky. The emptiness around them heightened their sense of isolation.

Haggerty, concentrating on the battered road in front was the least preoccupied with their situation. Vern masked his feelings. But Eva was getting more tense. She shifted irritably when Vern unfolded the map once again and raised a hand to push the sheet out of her face.

'Sorry,' Vern said. He bent to another fruitless examination.

'Stephen, can we stop a minute?' she asked suddenly.

Haggerty nodded, content to rest his tired shoulders. He turned off the motor and the truck shivered to a halt.

The sudden silence was an assault on their ears. Haggerty pulled out his cigarettes.

'How far do you think we've come on this stretch?' he asked as Vern slid aside to let Eva out.

'Thirty miles, maybe?'

Haggerty winced. He leaned towards the open window seeking relief from the heat. Vern flushed an insect off the windscreen and gazed out at the empty landscape.

'Jesus, it's forsaken.'

'It might be keeping us alive.' Haggerty drew on his cigarette. 'Serena's not likely to waste troops on chasing us in here.'

Vern nodded. 'I guess it's really the border we've got to worry about.'

Haggerty rubbed his back against the seat. 'I might be prepared to give up by then.'

'Stephen.'

Eva stood at his window. 'Look. Up there.' Haggerty leaned out the window. She was pointing to where they could see the last trace of the track entering the steepening hills.

'I think it's a village,' she said.

He stared. A cluster of small white shapes clung to the edge of the hillside. They could have been houses but he was not sure. Vern got out onto the footboard to look in the same direction. He nodded to Eva.

'You're right. It is a village.' He reached into the cab and pulled out the map to pore over it. 'It must be Quepaco. That means we've made better mileage than I thought. It's supposed to be fifty miles in from the Pan American.'

Haggerty stared at the glimmering image. 'I wonder if it's big enough to hold a garrison.'

They were silent.

'Well, we can't get around it,' Vern said finally. 'We have to go forward and through it. Or back the route we came. There's no other way.'

'What if we wait for nightfall?' Eva asked.

'I don't know what good that will do,' Haggerty said. 'They'll hear us long before we get to the village. And they don't get a lot of traffic around here. So they're going to be interested.' He tossed away his cigarette. 'No use torturing ourselves out here when we can do it just as well on the move. Let's go.'

Behind the wheel he glanced across at Vern and gestured to the black Walther sticking out of his belt.

'Figure out some way to hide that thing, eh?'

It took almost two hours and they were bone-tired when they reached the foothills where the village lay. They could easily identify the adobe houses now, nestling along the broken heights. Only a part of the settlement was visible. The rest curled around the back of the hill. They had no way of knowing what size it was. Or even if it was inhabited. There was no sign of life among the houses.

It was mid-afternoon by then and the sun was high in the sky. Beyond the village, the range of snow-capped mountains glittered against the blue sky. The frozen picture held a stark, timeless beauty. Deadened by its constant presence, that beauty was lost on all three of them.

The truck, engine revving, moved up the hill. The rough trail resembled a dried river-bed with deep scorings made by earlier torrents. On either side, scattered among the slopes were small flocks of grazing sheep. A closer look showed small children guarding the herds.

As they neared the top of the hill, Haggerty saw now that the houses were less imposing than first sighting suggested. Faint wisps of smoke were now visible among them. But still no one appeared.

231

'It's an Indian settlement,' Eva said.

'Not very curious, are they?' Vern said as they stared up at the rough houses.

'Indians can't afford to be,' Eva said, 'not in Guatemala.'

The buildings lay inside an old stone wall that looked like part of a fortification. The only opening was for the road. As they entered the gap, the road surface turned to a level grounded stone. After the brutally hard dirt road, the sudden smoothness felt eerie.

They watched the closed houses pass. Vern dropped a hand to his knee where he could reach the gun taped under the dashboard. Haggerty lowered the truck's speed to a crawl. Then came a bend. Turning into it they entered a shadowed street less than fifty yards long. Beyond, they could see what appeared to be a square. Still, there were no people about.

'So far, so good,' Vern muttered.

The truck crawled along the shaded street. Suddenly it left the shadow of the buildings and entered the bright sunlight of the town square. It was like passing from night to day. In more ways than one. They stared, astonished.

There were people all around the square. Sitting at café tables or on the ground by the old buildings facing the white, baked centre area. Quickly all three looked for soldiers or police. There were none.

Haggerty slowly braked and the truck came to a halt. They were almost in the centre of the square. He turned the motor off.

The sudden stillness blanketed the square. As they stared, nobody moved to break it or to come near. But everyone was looking at the truck now. Inside the cabin, the three stared back. They got more puzzled as the silence lengthened.

'What do you think?' Haggerty asked softly.

The heat lay oppressive on the still bright square.

'Straight out of a spaghetti western,' Vern said.

Eva gripped Haggerty's arm. 'Stephen, they're all old.'

She was right. Nobody looked less than fifty. Although the sunlight was brilliant and it was still hot, most wore heavy clothing and antique bowler hats. They could have been the mountain poor of any Latin American country. But although they appeared apathetic, they were watching closely.

232

Vern Railsback pointed. 'What about trying for some information over there? Looks like a hotel.' The squat building he gestured to was whitewashed like the rest of the square but it was made from heavy stone blocks and its windows were larger than the other buildings. Three men sat at a table on its large verandah.

'We should be careful. It could be the administration,' Eva said.

As they sat momentarily undecided, they heard a faint rustle rising. It sounded like a wind running through a grove of trees. But there were no trees on the dusty square. And there was no wind.

'What the hell is that?' Vern leaned through the window to hear better.

'It's the people. They're whispering,' Eva said.

'Look.' Haggerty pointed.

Everybody was slowly beginning to stand up. For some it was a struggle. They used canes or sought help. Others came upright from the pavement. Within a minute, everyone was standing. Like a long wave, they began moving towards the truck.

'I'll be damned.' Vern reached forward and began untaping the gun.

'Easy, Vern,' Haggerty said.

The slow advance continued from all sides until the crowd joined and became a circle closing on the truck. Inside, the three watched tensely. Then, just twenty feet off, everybody stopped. Haggerty could see the burned and darkened faces clearly now, careworn and expressionless, as they stood silently before him. The slitted eyes stared without blinking. The seconds ticked by in the bright sunlight.

'What the hell is going on?' Vern muttered.

On the verandah of the building they looked at earlier, a man got to his feet. He was stocky but not as dark-skinned as the others. The heavy sweater he wore was more expensive. So were the high-heeled boots.

He called out in Spanish from where he stood.

Slowly, like an audience at a political meeting the crowd began to clap. It was slow and done without rhythm. It was impossible

233

to tell if they were being enthusiastic or sarcastic. Even those with sticks rested them against their stomachs so they could clap too.

'What did he say?' Haggerty asked, keeping his eyes on the staring faces.

'He just said clap,' Eva said.

'I'll be damned,' Vern said.

Silently they watched as the man on the verandah turned and went inside the building. The crowd continued to clap. Haggerty felt Eva's hand tight on his arm. More people were appearing in the doorways. The noise, slow and unforced, filled the square. The man on the verandah returned. This time, he was carrying a bale of papers. As the three of them watched, he slashed the binding and let the loosened bundle fall to the ground. He bent and picked one up and then kicked the rest viciously so that they spilled across the verandah. With the single sheet he came down the steps of the verandah and walked across the square towards them.

''Allo,' he called.

'I got that,' Vern whispered.

The crowd, obedient as a choir, repeated it. From his window Haggerty smiled and raised a hand. '*Gratias*,' he said. On the other side, Vern did the same. The man advanced through the crowd and stopped at Haggerty's window. He spoke, then smiled and bowed.

'He said welcome to Quepaco,' Eva said. She spoke rapidly. The man listened, still nodding and smiling. Finally, he spoke again, raising a thumb contemptously to gesture at what looked like the outside world. Then he held up the printed sheet he held by his side.

'Sweet Jesus,' Vern said.

It was a wanted poster. Artistically arranged within the red borders were images of all three of them.

'That bastard Winter. He really laid it on us,' Vern muttered.

'What does it say, Eva?' Haggerty asked. She leaned across them.

She read it and laughed.

'It says we're hired assassins who have attempted to kill the President. Now that the attempt has failed we are fleeing justice.

234

Anyone who sees us and fails to report the sighting to the authorities will face the most serious penalties.' She finished reading. 'It says we're in the pay of the *Communistas.*'

'How did it get here?' Haggerty asked. 'Are there soldiers about?'

As Eva questioned him, the man shook his head vigorously and pointed to the sky. They talked further and he gestured to the people around him who stood silent. Eva nodded and turned to Haggerty.

'He says there are no soldiers here. They dropped these by helicopter. He warns they will be in all the villages ahead up to the Mexican border. He said we must be careful.'

The man began speaking again, more fiercely, as he pointed to the now quiet villagers. Eva watched and began speaking over him.

'The army is hated here. He says that six months ago, they came to the village and took away all the young men and women. More than sixty. Now fathers cannot find their sons and the children cannot find their parents. They have been to Guatemala City but the government has no answer for them.'

'The swine must have killed them,' Vern muttered. Haggerty nodded.

'They have offered their goods, their animals, anything to bring back their children, but no one can help. Now it is said in the newspapers that their children are *guerrilleros* who have taken to the hills. All here say that is not so. But the children do not return.' She listened to the end of his statement. As he finished others in the crowd began nodding. There were scattered cries of approval. Eva looked at Haggerty.

'They believe we are guerrillas. They are asking that we get their children back.' She paused. 'What do I say?'

Haggerty looked out the window at the rows of faces, all waiting for his reply. Tragedy in Latin America seemed like part of the fabric when you watched television at home or read about it in the newspapers. But here, with the barren, helpless faces, it was real. Vietnam all over again.

'Their children are likely dead,' he said.

'Stephen ...'

'Come on, Eva. What else can you tell them?' He looked at her. 'You know as well as I do that people like Serena don't jail Indians. They shoot them. They're almost certainly dead and these people might as well learn it now as later.'

'Wait a minute, hold on there,' Vern broke in. 'I don't think it's up to us to say that kind of thing to them. Jesus, they could be alive for all we know.' He leaned over. 'Listen, Eva, you tell them that although we're not guerrillas, we know them and we'll ask about their children. Come on, Steve, don't act like a bastard in this. Look at those people. They're really feeling it right now.'

Haggerty looked down through the open window at the throng. The anger began to fade when he thought of the feelings palpitating behind the racial masks.

'I'm sorry,' he said finally. He looked across at Vern. 'You're right, pal. Let's just excuse me for that. Okay?'

Eva began speaking and although neither Haggerty or Vern could understand, they sensed the feeling in her voice. When she finished, the people began clapping. This time it was spontaneous. She sat back and breathed deeply.

The man from the verandah now came to the window of the truck. He rested both hands on it as he spoke to Eva. She sat forward again to listen.

'We can't use the truck,' Eva said. 'The helicopter patrols the road every second day or so. If they come, he says we will be seen because there is nowhere we can hide the truck.'

'What if we travel by night?' Haggerty said.

The man listened to the translation and shrugged doubtfully.

'It is possible.' Eva watched as the man gestured off to the north-east and began speaking again. 'But he has a better suggestion.' She turned to them.

'They promise a mule if we will ask the guerrillas to find their children. He says there is a route away from the road which the military know little of. It is very hard and cold to go that way but he says it will take us to the Mexican's land. It is the old gold route used by the first Spanish.' Her translation slowed as she watched him. 'He says it's haunted.'

'Tell him we will pay for the mule,' Haggerty said.

The man shook his head vigorously when Eva made the offer.

236

'No,' she said over his voice. 'He says an Indian with money in Guatemala signs his own death warrant. They offer the mule as a gift.'

'And the truck?'

'They will take it down and hide the pieces.' The man finished with some smiling words. Eva turned to them. 'He says that when our people win, perhaps we will return to claim the truck. They will keep it until then.'

Haggerty nodded. 'Tell them that we are very grateful for their kindness, Eva. But they should know that the worst may have happened to their children. They should be prepared for that – although we hope it will be otherwise.'

She nodded.

Haggerty watched the man and those behind him as she spoke. Their faces barely changed but he fancied that he saw some softening. The man nodded as Eva finished. He answered in few words.

'He said he understands. And he asks if we would take some food and rest to recover from our journey.'

'Marvellous people,' Vern said as they drove the truck off the square and left it with some of the less elderly men. They were led into the main house. Inside the cool stone kitchen a woman hurried to prepare some bread and fruits and poured white wine from an earthen jug.

They ate and drank as the host talked and Eva translated between bites. He turned out to be a lively man, more worldly than the rest. But not worldly enough to save his son and his daughter-in-law. The two grandchildren playing in the back were all that was left of the family.

The disaster which hit Quepaco was all the more shattering in that the Indians there had avoided such trouble for more than two generations.

Before that, Quepaco had an ill-starred history. When the Spanish chose it as one of a string of outposts to guard the gold convoys, they seized the surrounding Indians to act as porters. The mules lived better than the Indians who died from disease, malnutrition and brutality. Within a generation, the Indian population was practically wiped out. Then, as the gold died out, the Spanish moved away. Gradually, the Indians moved back in and their numbers grew. True, their lives were primitive. They had no education worth speaking of, no modern industries or health services. But for several generations they managed to live in relative peace around Quepaco.

Now, as Haggerty and the others heard, the Indians were facing a new crisis. The guerrillas had been operating out of the nearby mountains. Although no Indians were involved, the rebels forced them to supply food. A captured leftist, under torture, finally implicated them. And General Serena – perhaps because of his part-Indian background – decided to make an example of Quepaco. Once again, the Indians were reduced to pleading with both sides as they died in the middle.

They had finished eating as the story ended and it left them in a sombre mood. Haggerty looked at Eva who sat across the table from him. Suddenly he realised the toll she had been paying, not only today but in the past week. She looked dead on her feet. Her face was deeply sallow and the skin was drawn tight across her cheek-bones. She hardly seemed to listen now as she translated.

The Indian woman who had stood at the back of the room as they talked must have noticed too. She came forward and whispered to the man at the table. He nodded and leaned forward to touch Eva's hand softly as he spoke.

'He says we should rest.' She rubbed her cheek and turned to smile wryly at Haggerty. 'I think he's right. It's beginning to hit me. I'm finding it harder to understand what he's saying.'

In the small loft above the kitchen, they lay close together. Vern had stayed downstairs on a cot. Eva's head rested on Haggerty's shoulder. He was too tired and ached too much now to lay more than an arm across her.

'Stephen?' It was their first chance to talk. Her skin felt hot under him.

'Yeah?' He was barely listening to what she was saying.

'About those things that happened. About what I did.' She shifted. The rough timber boards creaked. 'I can't get it all out of my mind.'

'You're tired, Eva,' he said. 'It'll be better when you're rested.' He wanted to sleep, not to talk.

'Stephen, everything keeps running through my mind. It won't stop. About what could have happened to you. And what they did to that man Tomaso.'

'Not now, Eva. You've got to get some sleep.'

'I can't.' Her whisper had an awkward pitch as though she might suddenly break into tears. But his fatigue blinded him.

'Jesus.' He turned to put an arm around her. 'We've got to get some sleep, Eva. Otherwise we're not going to make it. Then it won't matter what's on any of our minds.'

She was silent. Wearily he tightened his arm on her and kissed her forehead.

'Come on,' he said, 'don't worry about it. It's going to be all right.'

It was long after him when she finally slept.

22

'*Señor! Señor!*'

Haggerty woke to rough shaking. He looked up to see Eva already awake and sitting up. Their host stood by the bed.

'What is it?'

'A convoy of military is headed this way,' Eva said.

'Shit!' Haggerty reached down the bed for his clothes. The Indian waved them off, offering dark native garments instead. 'Thank you,' Haggerty said. Smiling quietly, the Indian withdrew.

'We've got some time,' Eva said. 'The trucks have just entered that dirt road we came in on.'

'How long?'

'He says two hours.'

'Good.'

The evening was cold as the Indians had warned. But now they were dressed for it in the woollen ponchos and heavy trousers they had been given. Vern who had been woken earlier was already dressed. His smaller figure almost disappeared under the thick clothes and the broad straw hat.

Haggerty grinned. 'If your friends could see you now.'

Vern nodded. He was eyeing the mule doubtfully. 'Do these things bite?'

They were in the cobbled lane behind the house. Quickly they swallowed some hastily prepared coffee and tortillas and met the guide who was to take them up the mountain to the gold trail. Their host explained the route very clearly, taking his time, showing no alarm about the approaching troops. The way seemed uncomplicated. But it was potentially hazardous. To avoid ambush in earlier times, the Spaniards had set the old trail

240

on the bare terrain above the treeline. Which meant they would now be exposed to patrolling aircraft. It would also be tough going. The high slopes were rocky, very uneven and often frigid at night. The big advantage was that it would take them straight to the Panara River which made up the border with Mexico. And that was what they wanted.

Their host told them that the army usually ignored the trail because the guerrillas avoided it due to its exposure. With a little luck they could traverse it without being detected. The Indians had supplied food for four days. The trip, they were told, would take only three.

The mule clopped about on the stones as they tied on the supplies and blankets. Haggerty listened as Eva translated the Indian's last warnings about the journey. They were not to eat any of the fruit found along the way. And if they met anyone on the route, they must treat that person as an enemy. Their host reassured them that if they were driven off the trail in the first two days, for any reason, they could rejoin it simply by walking uphill again. At the end of the second day, however, he warned them to be careful. They would have crossed the main range by then and would be heading downhill to the border. After a few minutes of repeating the instructions they had received, he was satisfied that they knew what they were doing. With that, he handed Haggerty a sheet of paper. The lettered script was incomprehensible to him.

'It's a list of their children,' Eva said. 'He asks that we present it to the guerrillas in the hope that they can save their children.' She turned and spoke softly to the Indian and then embraced him. It was spontaneous and touched Haggerty.

'The weight of this stuff,' Vern said from his side, 'I don't know if I'll make it but if I do happen to go down, for Chrissakes, don't put me on that mule.'

Haggerty grinned. 'Don't give me that, Railsback. You're going to outlast Eva and me. Maybe even the mule.'

'The hell I will,' Vern muttered.

The first hours proved a nightmare. The guide, who was thin and bent, proved to be tough rather than decrepit. He knew his way but to the three of them – and sometimes to the mule – it

241

seemed to be by the roughest route. He muttered and shifted impatiently when Haggerty enforced a brief rest. But Haggerty had to because of the pace. On their third rest, with the air thinning at the higher altitude, a panting Vern tugged on his arm.

'Look. Down there,' he said. Haggerty and Eva stared back into the darkness past Quepaco. It took a few moments but then they saw them. Like miniature fireflies, a long row of tiny lights glinting in the night. It was clear that they would take some time even to reach Quepaco, but the knowledge that they were coming at all made the three of them uneasy. They needed no urging from their guide to resume the journey. By that time, the guide was piling on the effort as if to make up for the time lost in rest. They slipped and stumbled, taking turns to lead the mule, immersed in the task of staying upright among the broken treacherous rocks and still keeping up with the Indian. Each time Haggerty glanced back the lights were there, winking in the sea of blackness. And always a little closer.

As the sky began to grey, the lights behind them gradually disappeared. They carried on, each now in a private agony. When it seemed that they could go no further and the first rays of dawn brightened the edge of the horizon, the guide suddenly gestured at the grey gloom ahead and began muttering. They stopped, squinting ahead. But no one could see anything.

'What the hell did he say, Eva?' Vern asked, slumping down.

'I don't know.' Eva had dropped to one knee, a hand out to rest her body. 'It's dialect.'

Haggerty squatted down against a rock. The Indian began a louder muttering. Eva stirred.

'He said trail.' She looked towards Haggerty in the gloom, 'It's the trail. We're there.'

'Thank Christ for that,' Vern said. He lay back against a rock.

'Stephen, our friend wants to go,' Eva said. They looked up. The Indian was miming his return down the trail, nodding to them.

'I guess he's done his job,' Haggerty said. With an effort, he pulled himself to his feet and bowed to the Indian. '*Gratias, señor.*' The Indian nodded unsmiling. Then he turned to Eva.

Muttering something, he produced a transistor radio from inside his poncho. Before she could say anything he placed it into her hands. They stared in silence as he disappeared down the trail.

She looked up at the others, embarrassed.

'A gift.' She touched the cheap plastic covering. 'It could be all he had.' Chastened by the guide's generosity, they took only a short rest this time. In the growing light, they moved uphill through the thinning tree belt. The landscape above them was taking shape in the morning mist. The escarpment they could see was rocky and bare. It looked like the side of a volcano. Finally, and almost reluctantly, they left the treeline. Soon after, Vern spotted the trail. It was like a winding ledge running along the side of the mountain about halfway from the top.

With the mule in tow, they scrambled towards it over the broken rocks. The trail, they found when they got there, was superior to the track they used earlier. But to people used to city pavements, it was still a nightmare. As the day brightened, the view became spectacular. Mile after mile of mountain and valley emerged from the mist below.

But they were conscious now of exposure, of being well above the treeline. As the Indians had warned they had no chance of concealment from any observer in the sky. But there were other things to occupy them too. Like their clothes. The air was cold at that altitude and they were forced to keep on the heavy ponchos for warmth. The extra weight was a brutal handicap. Pulling the mule around some of the bigger stones was energy draining too. It was becoming very clear that this journey would stretch all of them to the limit.

On the first halt, they agreed on rules. They would pit stop at ninety minute intervals. Meals would be at noon and sunset. And Vern and Haggerty would take turns pulling the mule. With that settled, they pushed on.

In the bright mountain air, as the mist burned away and the sun took on a hard glitter, they could see, without enjoyment, the endless green vistas below. From the wooded area farther down the slope, they could hear birdcalls rising from the trees. The echoing musical notes floated up over the scrambling footfalls of the mule who now showed a total absorption in his work and a complete indifference to the troubles of his new masters.

'He's been dehumanised,' Vern panted once, watching the animal pick its way through the rocks without complaint. 'You'd never get his brothers up north to do that. They've crushed his spirit.'

That proved one of the few humorous remarks of the morning. The brutal necessity of putting one foot in front of the other and clearing the obstacles in between left little time for diversion. At least, Haggerty thought, it will be over when we get to the other end. Not like the Indians who trekked back and forward here with the Spaniards' gold until they died. In the smallest way, he sensed what it must have been like.

In the early afternoon, with all of them struggling to stay upright, they heard an aircraft. The sound induced panic at the thought of their vulnerability. They looked about quickly for somewhere to hide as the sound deepened and grew in strength. But the rocks about them were too small – most hardly a foot wide – and the forest was at least five hundred yards away. Feeling utterly naked, they crouched down and stared into the sky.

'There it is!' Eva pointed far to their right. It was a small speck in the magnificent blue sky. They watched as it crawled slowly across their front.

'Looks like a fixed wing,' Haggerty said.

'Thank God for that,' Vern said. The thought that it might be a helicopter had filled them with dread. But still they remained uneasy until it finally disappeared to the north, the sound fading away. Now they knew what it meant to be exposed.

When they finally stopped in late afternoon, it was on all their minds. They chose a small gully which would hide them from below and lit a tiny fire. Soon they were eating their tortillas and washing them down with steaming coffee.

'Jesus,' Vern said as he put down his mug to knead his feet, 'this is murder. But you know something? I think that plane took more out of me.'

'I know what you mean,' Haggerty said. He was chewing slowly on the tortilla, trying to absorb himself in it. The agony in

244

his feet might disappear if he could do it. He looked across at Eva who had said little through the day. 'Are you okay?'

She nodded. 'The plane, it scared me more than anything. It means they could get us anytime.' She was sitting with her feet stretched out on a rock. 'Is there anything we can do to prevent it?'

Haggerty shrugged. 'We could camouflage ourselves, I suppose, with mud and that. But I don't know that it would do much good.'

'I feel like I'm walking across a lion's den,' Vern said. 'I just keep hoping the lion won't turn his head.'

'Any ideas?' Haggerty asked.

'Don't think I haven't been working on it, but no. This trail is bad. But going lower without any trail at all would make it impossible. Then again we can't move at night without slowing ourselves and possible injury in the dark. And if we travel only at dawn and dusk, our supplies would run out before we got halfway to the border. All I can suggest is that we pray for rain. At least that would keep the bastards away.'

Haggerty drew on his cigarette, the firelight flickering across his face. He pulled his poncho tighter. The first wisps of mist were closing in around them.

'Want to try the radio?' Eva inquired. 'There could be something useful about what the army is doing.'

Awkwardly, Haggerty rose and found the radio in the baggage. Pushing its little aerial high, they tried to raise Guatemala City. But the small depression they had chosen for the night affected reception. They could only find music on what appeared to be a local station. If Serena was pulling out the stops to find them, it seemed he was keeping it from his own people in the mountains. They listened to ten minutes of erratic bossa novas before Haggerty gave up and went to put the radio away. Even that short move from the fire was chilling.

The cold mist swirled in around them as they lay down by the small fire under their ponchos. Eva huddled in with Haggerty and this time, he held her tight until he knew she slept.

It was past dawn and growing light when Haggerty woke. He

245

stared out from the poncho, uncomprehending for a moment. Then he remembered and sat up quickly.

'Christ!' He looked at the sky. They must have lost at least an hour. 'Hey, come on, wake up!'

None was exactly sure how much sleep they got. All thought it was too little.

Cramped and aching from the damp chill now, they shared part of the bread from the satchel and took turns with a mug of the thin milk which the Indians provided in a goat-skin bag. They could not light a fire for fear the smoke would be seen. The small portions of food did little to ease their sense of misery.

As Haggerty piled their tiny bundles on the patient mule, Vern scraped dewy mud from between the rocks and spread it across the animal's torso. Afterwards, he plastered it on their ponchos and tentatively rubbed some into their faces. At another time, it might have spurred some jokes. Now, even Vern was silent.

They began again as the sky grew brighter and the countryside below took on its familiar green hue. After yesterday's experience, they were adapting to the trail. Silent, eyes down, stepping over and sometimes between the rocks. It wasn't possible to think of reaching the border, of getting back to the States, or of anything else. The next step was all that mattered.

The hours merged as they stumbled on across the sierra with the sun offering light but little heat and the scenery offering great beauty but little consolation. The trail spun out over the barren heights winding above the rich valleys where there was heat, food and most probably soldiers. At noon they stopped to eat a little but hardly spoke. The journey had become an endurance test. There was nothing to spare.

They were sitting, resting after the food, when they heard the sounds of explosions in the distance. Haggerty dragged himself to his feet.

'Where the hell is it?' He stared as the others joined him.

'It's somewhere ahead,' Eva said. As they stared at the panorama, Haggerty saw a white plume of smoke slowly rise from the horizon. It was down in one of the valleys. He pointed.

'Listen,' Vern said.

In the stillness, they heard a faint rattling sound. It could only be gunfire.

'Oh boy!' Vern said. 'Someone's having a firefight.'

Haggerty grinned. 'They're beating up on one and other.'

'Thank you, Jesus,' Vern said. He looked at the other two and grinned. 'Well, what are we waiting for? Let's move it.'

For the next hour, they moved to the accompaniment of the distant battle. But as their route led them away, the sounds died away. Under the bitter slogging, the elation faded. Eva, who had seemed least fitted to the trek, was now proving as determined as the others, accepting the pain and making no sound as the rough boots chafed and cut her feet. Haggerty would take her arm when the trail got especially rough. She accepted the help but she never asked for it or complained when it was withdrawn.

By the late afternoon they hardly noticed when the colours in the landscape began fading and dusk crept in. They kept moving seeking the extra distance in the darkness. Panting, slipping, dragging on the mule, the nightmare continued. Suddenly Vern shouted.

'Hey!' He was behind with the mule. Haggerty and Eva stopped, swaying at the sudden loss of effort.

'What's wrong?' Haggerty's mouth was dry.

'The trail. It's going downhill.' Pulling the mule, Vern scrambled towards them.

Haggerty looked down. He could see nothing in the darkness. He waited for Vern to catch up.

'You sure?'

'Yeah.' Vern drew alongside. 'Charlie here, he goddamn near crushed me. He's been slipping forward the last five minutes or so.' So they were across the main range. And ahead of schedule.

'Thank God,' Eva said, holding onto Haggerty's arm. He held her as she swayed.

'Great. Let's break for the night.' Slowly, he eased Eva down.

'If I'd known you were going to say that, I'd have said it half an hour ago.' Vern dropped gratefully onto a rock.

Using wood scraps they had gathered on the way they lit the evening fire. A mound of rocks hid it from the valley below. As soon as the flames took, Haggerty laid the coffee pot on top.

247

'Care for toast?' Vern asked. The prospect of warm bread was alluring in the mountain cold and they nodded. Using sticks, they held the pieces of bread to the flames watching it blacken as much as it browned. With some warmed up beans and the scalding coffee, it might have been a banquet for the way it tasted.

'That battle today. What do you think?' Vern asked, chewing the last of his beans.

'Has to help us.' Haggerty said, his mouth full. 'I'm assuming Serena was sending those troops to the border when they got hit. The less that get through, the better it is for us.'

'Maybe we'll get something on the radio about it,' Vern said.

'Good idea.'

Vern rose, then stopped to clutch his thighs. 'Jesus!' He almost fell as his muscles cramped. Eva rose quickly to steady him. 'I'll get it,' she said and went to the hobbled mule who was searching for roots among the rocks just away from the camp-fire. Vern watched her from the ground. 'She's turning into one tough lady.'

Haggerty gazed at her in the gloom and nodded.

Eva returned with the transistor and crouched down by the fire where Vern was pulling himself up, kneading his calves. 'Want me to do that?' she asked, raising a smile.

Vern chuckled. 'I'd prefer him,' he gestured to Haggerty.

Haggerty laughed. 'Screw you, Railsback.'

'Stephen!'

Vern laid a hand on her arm. 'It's all right, sweetheart. We'll just ignore him. Here, give me that thing.'

She passed him the radio. He turned it on to a crackle of static. 'From where we are, I wouldn't be surprised if we raised Buffalo,' he said. Almost immediately, he picked up a strong Spanish station. 'Here, let's have a translation,' he said, handing it back to Eva.

The voice of the announcer was strong and authoritative. 'It's Mexican,' she said.

'That's got to be good news,' Haggerty said. He caught the words, *'El Presidente* Robson!' then stared in surprise as Eva suddenly let the radio fall to her lap.

248

'Oh God!' She looked up at Haggerty, her face horrified. He reached across to her.

'What's the matter?'

'The President. He's ill. He's haemorrhaging.'

'Jesus!'

They sat frozen, their suspicions coinciding.

Haggerty took the radio, still broadcasting, from Eva's lap and put it gently back in her hands. 'Eva, you need to listen.'

Slowly she sat up, her face looking worn now in the glitter of the fire. With the radio in her hands, she stared, listening intently. She began to translate.

'Washington and the whole of the free world is in turmoil tonight, is what he's saying.' She listened. 'It was completely unexpected – symptoms of acute haemophilia – soon after attending Democratic Chairmen's convention – now in Walter Reed Hospital – Vice President Schofield in attendance – life and death crisis.' She stopped to beat a hand on her knee. 'Oh, God! They must have been planning it all along.'

Haggerty's face was grim. 'Just keep listening,' he said. He turned to Vern. 'So we were right. Dackman, Serena, Korner, Masters, the whole bunch of them, they're all in on it.'

Vern nodded, the light of the fire playing over his face. 'That's really why they wanted to stop us so badly. If you ask me, Steve, we're going to have a hell of a time getting out of this country.'

Haggerty nodded. He leaned over to touch Eva's arm as she listened. 'How long ago did it happen?'

'Around 6 pm. That would be about 4 pm our time.'

Haggerty looked at his watch.

'Three hours ago.' He squatted on his heels over the fire. 'There's a chance we could help. If I can pass on what Whitten told me.'

'They say that doctors are trying remedial treatment,' Eva broke in, 'but soon after each transfusion, he starts to bleed again.'

'That's it,' Haggerty said. 'It's Dackman all right. And they're handling it wrong.'

Vern nodded.

'We've got to get word to Washington. Somehow.'

'That means getting over the border even quicker than we planned,' Vern said.

'Right,' Haggerty said. 'Listen, one of us is going to have to try for it straight away – on the mule. The others can follow as quickly as possible.'

'I agree,' Vern said. He looked at Haggerty. 'I'm at least forty pounds lighter than you, Stephen. I'll go.'

'What?'

'Makes more sense that way.' Vern rose, without showing cramps now. 'I won't wear Charlie down as much. I'm less likely to fall on my ass.' He looked down at them, 'And I've got a US government passport.'

'Listen ...' Haggerty protested.

'Listen, nothing,' Vern said. 'I even look more like a Guatemalan than you do.' Without waiting for a reply, he began gathering up his poncho.

'He's right, Stephen,' Eva said. 'Except I'd be better than either of you.'

They both refused to consider that. But it helped Vern win as a compromise. They stood by the lightly-loaded mule as Haggerty explained what Whitten had told him. The doctors must recycle uncoagulated blood through the President until the virus died. Only then could they give him the coagulating Factor V111 which would cure him.

'The first Mexican village ...' Haggerty began.

'Is El Ecatol,' Vern said patiently, 'but I must cross the Rio Selegua first. When I get to El Ecatol, I order, buy, beg or steal a ride to Comitan where there is an honorary US consul. And that's where I pass the word and wait to team up with you.'

'Vern,' Eva said, 'it might help if you tell them there that we're coming through. Just in case.'

Vern grinned. 'Will do.' He looked at Haggerty and hesitated. 'Listen, pal, if I don't make it, I'm counting on you guys. So be careful how you go.'

'You take care yourself,' Haggerty said roughly. 'Eva and I are going to need an escort when we get to Washington.' Leaning forward, he suddenly embraced the smaller man. Eva watched, her eyes brimming.

'Don't worry,' Vern said. 'It's not every day I get the chance to save the Commander-in-Chief. I'm not going to spoil this one.'

'Oh, Vern.' Eva moved in as Haggerty stepped back. She was in tears now. 'Don't let anything happen to you.'

'Hey, now.' He patted her back. 'You're forgetting, I get to ride down. You guys have to walk.' He held her away from him and looked into her face. 'Sweetheart, we're going to get these animals. Just count on it.' She cried. He looked up at Haggerty who took her away. Vern shook his head and turned to the mule.

'Come on, Charlie,' he said, swinging himself up. 'We got a date with the White House.'

Standing by the glimmering flames, they watched him disappear into the darkness with a last jaunty wave.

23

The journey downhill had taken almost four hours.

In the darkness, Vern Railsback did not see the hut until he was almost on top of it. Luckily, the thunder of the river masked the noise of his approach. He had dismounted earlier – wary that the mule might take them both over what he suspected was a waterfall. Now, as he came on the hut, he dropped Charlie's rein and pulled out his gun.

The door was partly open, shedding a faint glow. Vern crept forward, his aches forgotten. Beyond the hut he glimpsed the dim outline of the bridge and understood why the hut was there. A guard post. He halted in the darkness for a moment then inched forward again. Staying outside the pall of light shed from the lamp inside the hut, he peered through the gap in the door.

An arm, clad in a jungle-green shirt, lay in his vision. It was stiff and outstretched with an ashtray on the floor beneath it. Vern moved nearer. Now, he could see the man's head on a simple camp-bed. He was asleep. Closing in quietly, Vern reached the door, gun raised. He could smell kerosene fumes and the stuffy, warm air inside. He leaned forward and looked around the crude timber door. Then froze. He was staring straight into the eyes of a second soldier whose head had lifted from a magazine.

It was hard to say who was more surprised. But the soldier reacted first. Before Vern could move, his mouth opened and he uttered a sudden ear-splitting scream. For a second, it chilled Vern's blood. Then it also brought him to life. He kicked in the door and pointed his revolver.

'Get your hands up!' he shouted. But the soldier continued screaming. Jesus, what a wake-up call, Vern thought as the sleeping soldier below him shot upright. He stared in shock at his opposite number and then he saw Vern. His eyes bulged. Suddenly, he started to scream too. Vern instantly realised he was going to have an easy time of it.

'*Silencio!*' he shouted, trying for the commanding tone he always despised in others. But it was too shrill. The soldiers went on screaming. It was bedlam.

Decisively, Vern jabbed the barrel of his gun into the soldier on the cot, hard. The soldier jumped at the physical contact but it seemed to bring him down to earth. He stopped screaming. His companion's voice died away. They both stared at Vern now in embarrassed silence.

'You ought to be ashamed of yourselves!' Vern said sternly. 'Call yourselves soldiers!'

The one on the bed was staring up at him with big Buster Keaton eyes. Neither could have been more than eighteen years old. Vern quelled his sympathetic feelings. This was not the place. He moved into the hut.

'Up!' He gestured to the man on the bed who came off it and stood beside his companion. Watching them, Vern reached down and tossed a belt from the chair to the first soldier. Miming the signs, he showed he wanted the other man tied up.

The binding operation, when it began, generated an irritated crosstalk. It was clear that the man from the bed was not displeased with the task. The other man had a stripe on his sleeve and seemed to be his superior. Vern watched, somewhat amused, but he knew the problem wasn't over yet.

He thought of Haggerty and Eva still to come through. They might be a couple of hours behind. Leaving this pair could endanger them. But what could he do?

As he finished tying the second man, the soldiers' shock seemed to subside. They were trying to tell him something. But he couldn't make out what it was. He took their rifles and went outside briefly to toss them into the gorge. He had decided he would take them part of the way into Mexico and dump them, still tied up, where they wouldn't cause any harm. Gesturing to the door, he moved them out into the darkness and led them over to where Charlie, the mule, was patiently feeding on some scrub. The soldiers stood quietly as he tethered them to the mule with a length of rope from the hut. Satisfied that it was as escape-proof as he could make it, he led them forward.

At the bridge, he suddenly realised he had a problem. The plaited floor was unstable and swayed as he stepped on it. It might cause trouble for the animal although he had proved utterly docile so far.

Gingerly, pulling gently on the halter, Vern brought him forward. 'Come on, Charlie,' he said encouragingly, backing deeper onto the bridge. The mule stepped on without hesitation but as he moved forward the bridge began wobbling under him. His movements became less assured. Crooning, Vern pulled him forward with the soldiers tethered behind. The mule stumbled on uneasily, but his head was beginning to jerk upwards and he was snorting in distress.

Vern cursed himself for committing the mule before he knew if he could do it. Now they were about twenty feet in and there was no way he could back him out. He had to go forward. He held firmly onto the halter and eased him further. But the legendary stubbornness was beginning to show..

'Come on, baby,' he repeated, making whatever sympathetic noise he could think of. But Charlie would have none of it. He was stopped for good. 'Jesus,' Vern muttered in exasperation. He pulled hard on the rope. The mule jerked his head back and began to bray. It was loud and frenzied. Vern held onto the bridge's now swaying side rope and stared up at him.

He couldn't leave the beast blocking the goddamn bridge. And besides the two soldiers were on the other side. He couldn't leave them there either. They could break free later and endanger Stephen and Eva. He looked along the side of the animal, judging the gap. With care, he thought he could get them through. He came forward and reached along Charlie for the rope tethering the men. They watched silently as he beckoned them forward. Neither moved. Irritated, Vern pulled sharply on the rope. Very reluctantly, they began to inch forward.

The mule barely stirred as they approached its left side. It was going to be a tight squeeze.

'Careful!' Vern said before he remembered the language barrier. Lamely, he tried to gesture caution. The first man edged past the animal's haunches sideways, his tied hands against the bridge's support rope and his face to the mule. For a few moments, it seemed to work. But what Vern hadn't counted on was the change in balance that the extra weight brought to the left-hand side of the fragile bridge. As the soldier came level with the mule's belly, the slanted angle of his body began to push the matted floor away from him. For the mule, the matting was shifting under his feet. Uneasy now, he began moving restlessly. The bridge began to rock.

'Whoa!' Vern said, holding tight on the halter.

But the sudden rocking was now frightening the soldier. He tried to move along faster, pushing against the bridge rope as he did so. The bridge rocked again. This new motion upset the mule even further. He began to panic. As Vern pulled desperately on the halter, he started to buck. Suddenly, he kicked back with his hindlegs, entangling himself with the rope holding the second soldier. The young boy, guessing what was likely to happen, screamed. Startled at the sound, the mule reared, ripping the halter from Vern's hands. His front legs came down on the first soldier who had almost squeezed through when it happened. Beast and man, tangled together, toppled sideways against the guide rope.

It snapped like thread. The bridge swung up from under the wildly kicking mule. Realising what was about to happen, Vern threw himself at the nearest guide-rope. He caught a glimpse of tangled bulk as the mule and the first soldier and then the second soldier, scrabbling wildly, plummeted down into the gorge.

The screams ringing in his ears, Vern held on to the wildly swinging bridge as it see-sawed back and forth. He felt the mist drenching his sweating face. His legs hung loose over the edge. He clung like a limpet to the thin guide-rope, his mind frozen with fear.

It must have taken an age but slowly the crazy motion subsided. The bridge began to level off. Vern lay across the floor with his two hands still gripping the guide-rope above his head and his legs hanging over the side. He had no idea of how long he lay there above the torrent roaring and gushing a hundred feet below.

As the panic passed he began shivering uncontrollably. He tightened his grip. The bridge started to roll again.

'Oh, Jesus.' He fought for control. A few feet away, he could see bloodstains on the matting where the mule had struck the young soldier. Like a warning about the price to be paid for panic, it helped bring him to his senses.

Slowly, he moved one leg up onto the floor, willing himself to ignore the rocking motion of the bridge his movement caused. He paused before continuing. The misted water was dripping from his face now. With great caution, he brought up the second leg. He lay on the slender matting with his hands gripping the guide-rope at right angles to his body. It took time to summon up the reserves but eventually he steeled himself to lower a hand to grip the edge of the floor. Seconds later, he brought up the other hand.

He lay stretched out on the floor, his cheek pressed against the rough surface. His heart was still pounding but now the crisis was lessening. He was still alive. And that was everything. Very gently he raised his head. In the darkness, he could make out the upward slope of the bridge to the other bank. He tried breathing very slowly and deliberately, calming himself. Then he stretched out both hands to their full length and started to pull himself forward. As he slid onwards, he felt a sharp snagging against his groin. He stopped. Lowering his hand, he felt down over his stomach.

The butt of his gun had gone through the matting. The barrel, inside his belt, was firmly stuck into his testicles. It was a bizarre fix with the fibre inextricably tangled around the gun's trigger guard. The more he tried to free it, the more the danger grew that it might go off.

'Damn!'

He was trapped.

Haggerty and Eva left two hours after Vern. The journey was worse than either had foreseen. The cold mountain air and the cumulative fatigue drained their limbs of strength. Many times during the descent they tripped or sprawled among the rocks. After each fall, the upright one would stumble over to help pull the other up. It went on, hour after hour, until their feet were worn and bleeding and they lost all track of time.

It was Eva who first heard the river. It came on as a dull rumble in the distance. The more they advanced, the more thunderous it became. The sky was greying by that time but the noise filled them with dread. It sounded like a powerful barrier to reaching Mexico. Forced to wakefulness by the thought, they continued downwards.

When they were close to the bottom, the grey light was already creeping across the landscape. Above, the rocky slope remained obscured in mist. Suddenly ahead, they saw a turn in the trail. The noise told them the river was just beyond. They slowed as they approached.

'Stay close,' Haggerty said. Eva fell in behind him as he inched up to the corner and took a look.

He had a clear view of the trail as it ran down to the gorge about eighty yards away where a narrow rope-bridge hung between its two sides. On the near bank, he saw the small hut beside the entrance to the bridge. The area between the trail and the hut had been cleared of vegetation. Although there was no sign of life, Haggerty realised they would have to expose themselves to get to the bridge. He bit his lip. Eva moved to his shoulder to look. They peered at the scene in silence.

'At least it's possible to cross,' she whispered finally. He nodded. But now the problem was the hut.

'Think it's empty?' she asked, drawing back with him.

'We'll know pretty soon.' He stood with his back to the rock-face and glanced back along the trail. A patch of jungle began about forty yards away. He pointed to it.

'You wait back there while I take a look,' he said, 'just in case.'

She looked at him, then shook her head.

'No. I'm going with you.'

'Eva,' he said patiently, 'it's too dangerous. If there are soldiers in that hut, they could cut us both down. It's foolish to take that risk.'

'I'm not leaving you,' she said, stubborn now. 'Anyway, it would make more sense for me to go instead of you. Nobody's going to shoot a woman without investigating first. Not in this part of the world.'

'To hell with it,' he said. 'We'll go together.' Briefly he embraced her. Letting go, he took her hand.

'Ready?'

She looked up at him. Smiling, she nodded.

Slowly, they came out from behind the bend and started towards the hut. A curious stillness hung over it. Behind it, they could see the mist rising from the river. The bridge was swaying gently in the updraft. One side of the rigging appeared to be broken.

She squeezed his arm hard. 'I love you,' she whispered.

Haggerty smiled briefly. He was assessing the distance. Barely forty yards. The noise of the river was rising in volume. He paused. 'We'll make a run at that door. Okay?' She nodded.

'Now!' he said.

They dashed forward, Haggerty in front blocking her from anyone who might take a shot. They were within twenty feet of the hut when he realised it was empty. He slowed as he reached it. Eva came level with him as he stopped. He pushed in the half open door.

Inside, there were two small camp-beds and some magazines on a shelf. Otherwise nothing. Haggerty exhaled heavily and leaned for a moment against the door. Eva rested her hand against the wall and shook her head.

'I don't know how many more of these goodbyes I can take,' she panted.

'Me neither,' Haggerty said. He reached to take her arm. 'Come on,' he said, 'let's get over that bridge while there's still time.'

They went quickly to the edge of the gorge and surveyed the bridge. They could see now that the guide-rope on one side had been broken. Far below, the river crashed and foamed between the sheer rock walls of the gorge.

'Be careful,' he said, helping her onto the matted floor. It was a bare two feet wide. Carefully, he stepped on behind her. The structure swayed under their weight as they held on to the remaining right-hand guide-rope. Slowly, they began edging forward.

258

'Try not to look down,' he shouted above the roar. The mist rose around them, quickly drenching their clothes. Underfoot, the matted floor dipped precariously. They reached the middle and edged on.

'Stephen!' Eva turned, her hair matted around her face. Horrified, she was pointing to the floor.

He looked down and saw the matting was smeared with blood. Stuck between the heavy fibres was a gleaming black gun. He leaned down to look.

'Vern's!' he shouted. He tried to free it but the bridge swayed dangerously and he let it go.

He looked at her and shook his head. They stared into the foaming river, the same thought on both their minds, fear forgotten. Something must have happened to Vern.

'Let's go!' Haggerty shouted above the roar of the river. They edged onwards, clutching the right-hand rope and finally reached the Mexican side. With so much to preoccupy them, they had no thought to rest. From the bridge, the small trail to El Ecatol led away to the left. Still soaking wet, they hurried across the low scrubland.

24

They need not have worried. Vern had lost time but he had managed to disengage himself from the trapped gun by temporarily removing his trousers. It had been tricky, very dangerous and finally embarrassing, having to crawl across a rope bridge in briefs but Vern comforted himself with the thought that in this case even President Robson would have approved.

The first grey streaks of a new day were breaking over El Ecatol village when he reached the main street. It was wide, dusty and the crude tarmac needed repair. A line of trucks stood parked by the customs station, a single-storey building flying the Mexican flag. Some of the drivers sat on the verandah waiting for the offices to open. A policeman sat on a rickety chair outside the door. He watched Vern approach without interest.

Vern had been worried about this kind of encounter. Despite a wash in rainwater, it would have been easy to take him for a bum. But when he glanced at the waiting men on the verandah and saw what local style was like, he realised he was only mildly shabby in comparison. Encouraged, he mounted the steps and stopped before the policeman.

'*Buenos Dias, Señor. Hables Ingles?*' It was the best he could do. The policeman's flat Indian features hardly changed expression. He shook his head.

Vern pointed to himself. '*Americano,*' he said.

The policeman stared, unmoved by the declaration.

'*El chef, por favor.*'

Slowly, the policeman raised a leg to rest it across the other. He said something in Spanish. It meant nothing to Vern.

Jesus, he thought, what do I do now? He turned to the men sitting farther down the verandah.

'Anybody speak English?'

A small man, in a stained shirt and a battered fedora, rose from the group. 'I speak a little,' he called, coming forward. 'What you want?'

'I need to get to Comitan. It's urgent.' The man looked at him sceptically. The margin of cleanliness between them was small. But it was enough to give the Mexican the edge.

'I'm an official of the United States government,' Vern said. 'My car broke down. I had some trouble getting here.'

The Mexican turned, grinning, to the group of men watching and said something in Spanish. They laughed.

'Can you help me get to Comitan?' Vern said. 'I'm prepared to pay.'

The Mexican stopped smiling. He looked at Vern with new interest.

'How much?'

Vern thought carefully. Flaunting money could get you in trouble in a place like this.

'Twenty-five dollars.'

The Mexican considered. Then he smiled again.

'Forty dollars. I take you for forty.'

'Thirty and it's a deal,' Vern said.

The Mexican looked back at the others and drew Vern down the steps away from the verandah.

'Look, *señor*. I do it for thirty dollars. But you pay me now.'

'No dice,' Vern said sharply. 'You take me to Comitan, then I'll pay.'

The Mexican looked at him, rubbing his chin.

'Half now. Half in Comitan. What you say?'

'Half when I'm sitting in your truck,' Vern said. 'The rest in Comitan.' The man sighed.

'You hard man, *señor*. But okay. For thirty-five.' He took Vern's arm. 'Come on.'

'Thirty,' Vern said. 'You get an extra five if you get me there in under an hour.'

The Mexican looked at him and smiled. 'Okay, my friend. You have a deal.'

261

They walked down the line of trucks. One of the men in the group called after them but Vern's companion waved it off.

'We make it fast,' he said. 'I must reach Guatemala City by tonight.'

The refrigerated truck they climbed into had seen better days. It clanked and rattled as the Mexican forced it into a U-turn. By the time they left El Ecatol, he had forced its speed up to twenty-five miles an hour.

Before he saw the truck, Vern had been concerned about what might happen if he fell asleep on the journey. After a few minutes of bouncing up and down on his broken horse-hair seat, he knew that was a pipedream.

The trip took an hour and a half. Much of it was filled with the driver's reminiscences of his youth as an illegal immigrant in Los Angeles. He turned out to be a pleasant, much put-upon man who traded in ambition for the sake of his large family. When he finally dropped Vern off on the outskirts of Comitan, his face flushed with pleasure at the forty dollars which Vern handed him.

'Say hi to Barbara Stanwyck!' he shouted through the window as he trundled away down the road back to El Ecatol.

Glory days, Vern thought. He turned away to hike down the road to Comitan. It was close to 8 am.

Comitan turned out to be a fair-sized town. The climate was cool from its location on a high mesa and the population was already astir. Although Vern was now deadly tired after more than twenty-four hours on the move, he was buoyed by the thought that he was close to the end of his mission. He stopped at a battered phone booth on the edge of the down town area and found the address of the US consul. The office was on the Plaza Benito Juarez.

It was past eight-thirty when he climbed the stairs in the old Spanish-style building to the office on the third floor. His sense of accomplishment was momentarily dashed when he tried the glass plated door with the eagle insignia and found it locked. The hours of opening were listed from 9.30 am to 5 pm. Weighed down with exhaustion, he slumped to the stone floor alongside the door and lay back with his eyes closed.

He must have slipped into a doze. For he suddenly felt a vigorous shaking. He opened his eyes. A man in his thirties, dressed in a grey business suit, with short cropped blond hair was shaking him. Vern stared up, still dazed with tiredness. The man said something in Spanish and pointed to the stairs.

Vern struggled to his feet.

'Hold on,' he said, 'I'm waiting for the consulate to open.'

The man looked at him in surprise.

'You American?' he asked in disbelief, taking in Vern's ragged appearance. He had a faint Mid-West accent.

'Damn right,' Vern said. 'Are you the consul?'

The man stared at him then nodded. Reluctantly, he held out his hand. 'The name is Guidest. Ron Guidest.'

'Vern Railsback.'

'Jesus, you're in some state,' Guidest said as he unlocked the door. 'What have you been doing? Hunting for the treasure of the Sierra Madre or what?'

'I've been having a hard time,' Vern said testily. He followed into the modest suite. 'Anyway, that's not important.' Guidest led him into his office which overlooked the plaza and gestured to a chair. Vern sat down.

'Well, what can I do for you?'

Vern looked at him, conscious again of his shabbiness. 'Listen, I know this is going to sound unbelievable,' he paused, 'but I work for the Central Intelligence Agency and right now, I've got to call Washington.'

Guidest looked at him sceptically. 'What do you take me for, Mr Railsback? The tooth fairy?'

Vern drew out his wallet and tossed his government identification card across the desk.

'Read it.'

Guidest examined it and looked up in astonishment. 'Good Christ,' he said.

'Spare me,' Vern said shortly. 'Now listen. We need to get on to Washington. This is an emergency.'

Guidest raised a hand. 'Okay, okay. You want to tell me what the problem is?'

263

'President Robson is the problem,' Vern said. 'What's the latest on his condition?'

'He's still critical. Look, what's this all about?'

'I need to talk with the Secret Service,' Vern said. 'Have you got the Federal telephone directory for Washington here?'

'Should do.' Guidest started looking through the desk drawers. 'I gotta say this is a new one for me.'

'Look, just find the phone book. Okay?'

'I'm trying, I'm trying.' He continued fumbling through the drawers. They both heard the outer door opening. 'That will be my secretary, Rosa. Maybe she has it.'

Guidest rose and came out from behind the desk. As he crossed the office, there was a light tap on the door and a middle-aged woman looked in.

'Good morning, sir.' Her voice was heavily accented.

'Morning, Rosa. We were just looking for the Government Services directory for Washington. Any idea where it is?'

'In that cabinet, sir.' She pointed to the cabinet inside the door. 'Mr Guidest usually keeps it on the top shelf.'

Vern stood up slowly. 'Hey, now,' he said.

'Thank you, Rosa.' The man who had been calling himself Guidest moved forward quickly and shut the door on the surprised secretary. He turned.

Vern Railsback found himself staring into the barrel of a gun.

25

'What the fuck is going on?'

'Sorry, Mr Railsback.' The smile was genial, even friendly. 'We've been waiting for you. Our mutual boss, James Korner, will be glad to know you've come in from the cold.'

'Who the hell are you?'

'Just call me Sidney.' The eyes crinkled with enjoyment. 'Looks like I drew the winning ticket. The odds makers thought you guys would come out at Tapachula.'

'Listen,' Vern said urgently. 'Korner is a traitor. They're trying to kill the President. We've got to stop them.'

'In a pig's eye,' Sidney said. 'Where's Haggerty and the girl?'

'Are you crazy? Don't you know the President is dying?'

'Sure,' Sidney said. 'In case you haven't heard, it comes to us all.'

'You bastard!'

'Come on, Railsback, don't be a pain.' Sidney gestured with a hint of sharpness, at the chair. 'Sit down.'

Slowly Vern sat down.

'You know, for a bright man, you're making a very common error,' Sidney said as he sat down behind the desk. He raised a foot on the edge but made sure he kept Vern Railsback in the line of fire. 'You're confusing the man with the office. Presidents die. But the Presidency lives on.'

'I'll ask you again,' Vern said, 'who the hell are you?'

'I told you. My name is Sidney and like you, I work for James Korner. My heart just doesn't bleed as much.'

Vern stared hard at him, remembering. 'You're Evan Reese.'

A much-admired operative, Evan Reese had played a vital role in what was James Korner's only scandal in the service. The

265

murder of Uruguayan dissident, Oscar Ledera. Reese had disappeared after the killing and the uproar that followed. Everybody in the Agency knew he was involved. But Korner stonewalled until the issue died in one of the minor House sub-committees.

The other man nodded slowly. 'Not only smart. Good memory too. Anyway, let's stick with the new leaf. I'm Sidney now. And I've got a gun.' He stared at Vern. 'Where's Haggerty and this woman Valdes?'

'I don't know.'

Sidney shook his head. 'I think you're giving me shit, Vern.'

'Look, I told you. I don't know what you're talking about.'

'I see.' Sidney took his leg down from the desk and straightened in the chair. The gun never wavered. 'Well, since you're sticking with that line, let's just consider the possibilities. One, Haggerty and Valdes are dead. Two, they got out ahead of you and they're already on their way north. Three, they're headed into Tapa-chula. And four, they're coming here after you decided to split up in the hope that one would make it.' He smiled at Vern. 'That's the baby I'm counting on. My hunch is they're coming through here.'

'You're in for a long wait,' Vern said.

'I'll bet,' Sidney said.

'What did you do with the consul?' The options seemed limited now to delaying, in the hope that something – anything – might turn up to change the situation.

'He's in Mexico City. Called out for consultations.' Sidney nodded to the window. 'Not a bad deal when you've been in this burg for a while. The night-life here is worse than Detroit.'

'For Christ's sake, cut the funny stuff.' Vern made to rise. The gun went up and he stopped.

'That's a no-no, Vern. I bat a thousand at this distance.'

Vern sank back in the chair.

'That's better.' Sidney wagged the gun at him. 'I'm trying to cut down, you know.'

'I can't believe this,' Vern said. 'You sit here, making casual conversation and bad jokes, while the President – your President – is dying in Washington. While the means are here to prevent it.'

266

'Like what?'

'Like understanding that I have information that will save his life. All you have to do is let me call Washington.'

'Vern, Vern. I try to be nice. And you treat me like a jerk. There is no way you're going to call Washington. Or anywhere else. Can't you understand that?' Sidney's face was warm, almost friendly.

'What if I make a move?' Vern asked suddenly. 'You might shoot me but Rosa gets to hear it and maybe other people too. Remember, they still hang the guilty party down here for murder.'

'Oh, I'm dealing with a Patrick Henry, am I?' Sidney said. He thought about it and shrugged. 'Well, it might work out the way you say. On the other hand, it might not. But you wouldn't be around to find out. You'd be dead, Vern. Now, you think it's worth the risk?'

Vern looked at him bitterly. 'That's already decided, isn't it? You're planning to kill me anyway.'

'Well, I won't say that's definite – but if you don't co-operate, it is very likely.' Sidney leaned forward. 'I understand from Korner that you're gay. Is that right?'

'What's it to you?'

'Just trying to make conversation, that's all. Who knows, it might even be helpful to you. They say it's harder for the killer when the victim is friendly to him. Assuming he's not psychotic.'

'You sound psychotic to me.'

'You think so? Maybe I am. Although I never lost a day's work over it.' He looked down at the gun and then up at Vern. 'And I've had lots.'

'How many people have you killed?'

'I hope you don't think my talking about it is going to raise regrets about the departed,' Sidney said. He smiled. For the first time Vern detected a slight edge of craziness hovering about him. 'It's not something I think about too much. But, since you asked, we could say around twenty-five.'

Crazy he might be, Vern thought. But he was obviously a professional. 'Why are you doing this?' he asked aloud.

267

Sidney laughed. 'I told you. I work for Korner. He pays, so he calls the shots. And I deliver.'

'So he sent you and your buddies down here to wait for us?'

'Right,' Sidney said. 'You might call us the second line of defence. Just in case the Guatemalans missed you – which they did.'

'You know,' Vern said carefully, 'if you were to switch sides, you could wipe the slate clean on that Ledera business. You'd be helping save the President's life.'

Sidney nodded. 'Right.'

'Well, why don't you do it?'

'Because I don't want to. It's as simple as that.'

'What is it, ideology?'

'No, I don't care for that stuff at all. It's just that I like my job. And my boss, to some extent. It's what is called loyalty. There's not much of it around, in case you hadn't noticed.'

'I don't believe this.'

'That's your problem, my friend.' Sidney suddenly sat up and raised his gun. 'Quiet!' he said, his voice low.

Outside, Vern heard a door close. Someone was talking in the reception area with Rosa, the secretary.

'Don't make a move, Railsback.' Sidney was suddenly as cold as ice. He rose softly, like a spring uncoiling.

The intercom crackled.

'Excuse me, sir,' Rosa's voice came on. 'There are people here to see you. A Stephen Haggerty and ...' Sidney cut in.

'Thank you, Rosa. I'll be right there.'

Smiling, his eyes on Vern, Sidney circled the desk. With the gun pointed, he backed over to the door. He looked at Vern.

'Remember, Railsback, one whisper and you're a dead man. Is that clear?'

Vern, sick at heart at this new development, nodded.

Half-turning, Sidney quietly unlocked the door. Raising the gun, he pulled it wide open, grinning.

'Come in, Mr Haggerty ...' He stopped, the grin fading.

Stephen Haggerty, handcuffed, stood before him. Between two policemen.

26

At the beginning, Haggerty and Eva had a lucky break. Two miles outside El Ecatol, they met a boundary worker travelling the road in a GM truck. A dark, moustached man, he listened in silence to their request for a drive to Comitan. Fifty dollars, he said finally. Haggerty felt it was a rip-off but he had to agree.

Eva tried to make conversation on the ride. But apart from monosyllabic grunts and a few side glances, the journey passed in almost total silence. Aching with exhaustion, neither Haggerty nor Eva were too displeased with the lack of conversation. In Comitan, as they drove past the outskirts, the driver finally spoke again.

'He has to find the consul's address,' Eva said, 'then he'll drop us off.'

Haggerty nodded.

They stopped close to a cross-street. The driver got out to enquire. They watched him disappear around the corner.

'Not much of a talker,' Haggerty said.

'Gringos can have that effect down here,' Eva said. She rested her head against Haggerty's shoulder. 'Oh, Lord, I'm tired.'

'I just hope to hell Vern made it.'

'I've been praying since we left that bridge.' He could feel the hotness of her body. He lay back against the seat, his eyes closing. He felt himself slipping away.

'Stephen.' Her hand was on his arm.

He opened his eyes. Eva gestured. The driver stood at the side of the truck. With two policemen.

'Oh, shit!' Haggerty sat up.

One of the policemen pulled open the door and gestured for

269

them to get out. Haggerty slid down and Eva followed. Haggerty glared at the driver who was watching impassively.

Eva began talking with the policeman who pushed the door shut. After a few sentences she turned to Haggerty.

'He thinks we're drug smugglers. He wants us to come to the station.'

Haggerty shot a last bitter glance at the driver. 'Bastard,' he muttered. The driver shrugged and got back into the truck.

The policeman stood to one side and his partner to the other. They waved them forward.

'Fifty bucks and this is how he repays us.' The truck pulled away.

'Stephen, they wanted to know our point of entry into the country.'

'What did you tell them?' Passers-by glanced curiously at them as the policemen pressed close on either side, gripping their arms.

'I explained we had an emergency. There was no time to go through the normal process.'

'How did he respond? Give you a raspberry?'

'Just about.'

They turned the corner.

'Think we can buy them off?' Haggerty muttered.

'I don't know. Depends on their boss, I guess.'

Their boss was a short greasy man in khaki shirt and trousers. His office was piled high with files. He sat at a small desk in front of a tall, ornate window. The dirty glass seemed designed to keep the sun off his back. He was smoking the morning end of a fresh cigar when they entered. He didn't ask them to sit down.

At his first question, Eva launched into an explanation. Haggerty felt at a loss as he watched them swop words that seemed to grow a little more heated as they went along.

Eva turned.

'We need your passport. And some other piece of ID.'

Haggerty pulled the passport from his inside pocket and took out his wallet. The police chief's eyes widened as he saw what was inside.

'He likes the green,' Haggerty said softly. He handed over his press card and passport. 'We might be able to do business.'

270

Eva nodded. She handed them over with her own passport and US government card. The police chief began examining them.

She began again. Haggerty heard the words CIA and watched the little man's eyes grow even wider and then narrow in disbelief. But he shouted for an aide to bring chairs. As they sat down, he went over and closed the door.

Eva smiled some quick encouragement at Haggerty. 'Now for the haggling,' she said.

Ten minutes, and three hundred dollars later, they had an agreement. Haggerty, under strict escort, would be taken to the US consul for verification of their story. Eva would stay. As he made the last point, he launched a greasy smile that looked like it illuminated many a whore's bedroom in its time.

'Watch the little scumbag, Eva,' Haggerty warned as he left.

'Don't worry. I can take care of him.' She leaned forward and they kissed briefly before he was ushered out. In the day room, over his protests, he was handcuffed by his dour escorts. They were not about to lose a prisoner of the chief.

He was still feeling angry fifteen minutes later when the consul's door opened and a smiling crew-cutted stranger in a summer suit pointed a gun at him and the two policemen.

He saw the smile fade and the gun lower. Then all hell broke loose as one of the policemen charged, catching the still surprised Sidney in the midriff and sending him careering back into the office.

The astonished Haggerty saw Vern Railsback appear from behind the door to leap on the fallen Sidney who still retained his gun.

The plucky Mexican cop was making frantic efforts to get on top. All three wrestled until Sidney was disarmed and finally raised to his feet.

As Vern got off the floor, he grinned at Haggerty. It faded when he saw the cuffs.

'Jesus, what's going on?'

Haggerty could barely hear him with the secretary babbling hysterically in Spanish at his ear.

'Misunderstanding,' he said finally. 'We'll sort it out later.'

The policeman, who nodded curtly at Vern, began dragging

Sidney towards the door. The other policeman took Haggerty's arm. Haggerty looked over his shoulder.

'They think you're the consul,' he said quickly to Vern. 'Stay free.'

The secretary, Rosa, standing with her hands to her cheeks, heard him. She burst into a torrent of Spanish, pointing at Sidney. The policeman stopped.

'It's not going to work,' Vern said quickly, 'and he's one of Korner's boys. What do we do?'

'Accuse him of something!' Haggerty said desperately. 'Drugs!'

The brave cop was speaking in Spanish to Vern. He held Sidney in an arm hold.

Vern pointed at Sidney, nodding excitedly. '*El Chef.* Marijuana, cocaine, *el hombre peligro.*'

Still holding Sidney, the policeman raised a finger for Vern too. Rosa came forward protesting but the policeman pushed her away.

'Nice touch of Spanish back there,' Haggerty said as they settled into the patrol car, 'I didn't know you spoke the language.'

'Just a little,' Vern said modestly.

'What does that *peligro* mean?'

'I'm not really sure but I think dangerous. I picked it up off a street sign.'

'Christ!'

At the police station, hustling and shouting, the two policemen pushed them through the day room, picking on the still dazed Sidney especially. They stopped outside the chief's office to straighten their uniforms. But when they opened the door, the office was empty.

'Hell,' Haggerty said, 'I just hope that sly bastard hasn't done anything to Eva.'

He explained what had happened to Vern as they waited in the day room. One of the policemen went to the desk sergeant for instructions.

He came back a few moments later and gestured for them to follow him downstairs. They were lodged in an evil-smelling holding cell. The plastered walls were crumbling with damp and covered with graffiti. Two wooden camp-beds stood on either side with a slop bucket in the middle.

'We must have got the luxury suite,' Vern said, looking around. The cell was about eight by ten.

'Who's this?' Haggerty gestured at Sidney, who had not spoken in some time. He sat on one of the camp-beds.

'His name is Evan Reese. But he likes to call himself Sidney.'

'Hi, Sidney!' Haggerty said.

Sidney nodded, glum now.

'Sidney's a big hitman,' Vern said. 'But he doesn't like to boast about it. Right, Sidney?'

Sidney was not looking well.

'He's also hot on social psychology,' Vern said. 'He promised not to feel happy when he killed me.'

'No kidding?' Haggerty said. He turned to stare at Sidney.

Vern nodded. 'He's also very industrious. After he killed you, Eva and me, it would have brought his score to twenty-eight.'

'Well, well,' Haggerty said, rising to his feet. The two of them gazed down thoughtfully at Sidney. He now looked unhappy as well as sick.

'He's very, very cool,' Vern said. He glanced at Haggerty. 'Have you noticed that?'

'Can't say I have.'

'Yes, sir,' Vern said. 'And tough as bejesus. Am I right, Sidney?'

'Look, guys ...' Sidney said miserably.

'Hey, he talks!' Vern said. He turned to Haggerty. 'Listen, Steve, I don't want to be a greedy wart on this, but would you mind if I had first shot?'

'Be my guest.'

He turned away as Vern dragged the unresisting Sidney to his feet. There was the rustling sound of movement and the sudden fierce impact of a fist on flesh. Haggerty gripped the bars of the cell door as a second blow landed and was followed by a sickening retching sound. He turned. Sidney, white-faced, was on all fours on the filthy floor.

'Vern,' Haggerty said.

'It's all right.' Vern's chest was heaving. 'It's done.'

He looked down at the helpless figure on the floor. 'He made me feel bad back there. Very bad.'

Haggerty put an arm around his shoulder. 'I understand.'

'He was working for Korner. And he didn't care if the President died. The swine!'

Oblivious, Sidney had dragged himself up onto a camp-bed. He lay foetal-like, breathing heavily.

'It's the President that worries me now,' Haggerty said. 'Who knows how long he can hang on. We can only hope Eva has some luck. Come on,' he guided Vern towards the vacant bed. 'Get yourself some rest.'

Almost half an hour passed. Only the sounds of people moving about in the day room overhead broke the silence.

Haggerty, holding the bars, was swaying with fatigue. Vern was dozing. Sidney, with his summer suit stained with grime, was quiet. They heard the massive door at the far end of the corridor rattle as a key went into the lock. Then it swung open.

'Stephen, Stephen!' It was Eva.

'Down here!' he shouted. Vern opened his eyes and sat up.

They heard her running.

'It's okay!' Her voice was high, excited. 'Everything's fixed.'

'Thank Christ!' Haggerty felt a sudden overwhelming relief. He swayed against the bars. Vern was swinging off his bed.

'Oh, Stephen!' Her face was beautiful when he caught sight of it coming down the corridor. She ran to him, alight with happiness. 'We've done it! Oh, Stephen, we've done it!' Impulsively, she put her hands through the bars to take his head to kiss him. He felt the metal against the side of his face as he met her lips. As a celebration it wasn't the best. But it would do.

'Whoa!' Vern said. 'Don't I get any?'

'Oh, Vern,' she said, moving along the bars to him. 'Come here.'

Haggerty looked at the police chief who stood back in the corridor, looking embarrassed. He had a bright red mark under one eye. Shifting uneasily as he saw Haggerty looking at him, he muttered to the gaoler who came forward to open the cell door.

The key turned and the door swung back. Haggerty stepped forward to Eva and they embraced. Gently Vern eased them

274

forward so that he could get out. Sidney made as if to rise, but the police chief waved a negative finger.

The steel-barred door rang closed. Vern looked back at the crushed man sitting on the bed alone. Reaching to the jacket of the hugging Haggerty, he drew out his cigarettes.

'Here.' He tossed them to the sitting man behind the bars. Sidney caught them. He flashed a small, woebegone smile and nodded acknowledgement.

'Thanks a lot,' Haggerty said, looking back.

'Just helping you to quit,' Vern said brightly as he followed them down the corridor.

The station upstairs now seemed a warmer, friendlier place. Haggerty tightened an arm around Eva's shoulder. It was all due to her. Standing by the duty sergeant's desk, waiting for a cab, she told them what happened.

27

Unlike Haggerty, Eva Valdes knew how bureaucracy worked – from the inside. When she saw Haggerty leave in those handcuffs, she thought he would have a hard time persuading any self-respecting consul to believe he had come to save the life of the President of the United States. More likely, he would be taken as a lunatic. But even if the consul did accept what he said, it would still be difficult to persuade anyone higher up the ladder that his story was true.

Sizing up the police chief, she decided to try an independent route. Laying a hand on his sagging bicep, she offered him five hundred US dollars – and a later intimate *tête à tête* – if he would let her call the American Embassy in Mexico City. The chief, a man of limited intelligence but superior passion, acceded with grace to the lady's offer. His eyes sparkling – his good friend Maria told him they were his best points – he almost danced across the office as he brought her upstairs to the private room where he did his interrogations.

Opening the door, he passed her through with an ample hand caressing the lower part of her back. She moved forward a little faster than he could keep up. He closed the door, slightly discomfited but still gamey. The room had no windows, but there was a phone in the corner as well as a sofa and a table which held a carafe and two glasses. 'Now, *señorita*,' he said, the fat cheeks parting in a smile, 'which shall it be first?'

He stood waiting, the Cheshire Cat, not knowing which he would enjoy most. But he thought it would be the sex. Getting paid always helped ease the sadness afterwards. That was usually the way it was with Maria, when he visited her whorehouse.

'I want you to place the phone call first,' Eva said. 'Then I pay you.' She took out her wallet and drew the money from it. Holding it, she looked at him deliberately. 'Afterwards, we fuck.'

'Oh,' he said, clasping his hands. 'Oh, *señorita*. You Americans, you are so, so direct.' He couldn't take his eyes off the beautiful breasts. And that tantalising belly!

'The phone,' Eva said harshly. If this call doesn't work, she thought, I'm dead.

'Right here, *senõrita*.' He tripped lightly across the room. Picking up the phone, he growled. 'Get me a long distance connection. The American Embassy in Mexico City.' He put down the phone.

'Deal one,' Eva said. She was trying to stay hardboiled. Otherwise he would swarm all over her. 'You get paid, right?'

He nodded. 'But if you wish, it can wait,' he smiled. 'Until later.'

'No, no,' Eva said. 'That's not the American way. We made a deal and I'm not going to welsh on it. We said five hundred dollars and that's what I'm going to pay you.'

He came closer. She moved to the table ostensibly to count it.

He followed again.

'Lot of twenties here,' she said, beginning to move the wad. He was breathing against her shoulder. She was afraid if she moved again, he would get fractious. Steeling herself, she began to count.

'Twenty, forty, sixty, eighty . . .' His hand was creeping around her waist. Please let him go up, she prayed, not down. She didn't know if she could take that. His hand was playing with the flesh under her rib cage. Slowly, it glided down her stomach, slipping lower.

'One hundred, one twenty . . .' She reached down, took his hairy hand, raised it and slapped it to her breast. 'Don't distract me while I'm counting,' she said sharply. He hung his head like a small boy caught with his hand in the cookie jar. Good God, she thought, maybe that's his bag. But she didn't want to risk it. She went on counting. Emboldened, he began to massage the breast; not hurting, so soft it was almost pleasant. She tried to keep her mind on the money. His head moved in, the dark crown against her shoulder as his hand opened the blouse. She tried to control her trembling.

'Hey!' she said roughly. 'Don't you want your money?' The head nodded without moving away. She felt the lips trace a moist path to the nipple. Her chest was heaving. Oh, God.

The caress was feathery light, the soft breath wavering around the curve. She stopped counting and closed her eyes.

The telephone rang.

She jumped and he staggered against the table, his hand slipping on the money.

'The phone,' she said quickly, 'the phone.'

The chief straightened up, nodding sourly. He swept his dark hair back and went over to pick up the phone. She pushed her naked breast back inside her blouse.

'*Si,*' he growled into the phone and waited. Turning, he held out the receiver. 'Your Embassy.'

She hurried across to take it, cradling the receiver tightly to her ear. The chief began to gather up some of the money which had fallen to the floor.

'First Secretary Walters, please.' She said it in Spanish so the chief would know where she was coming from. He stared and straightened up, a certain astonishment creeping over his face.

Pray he's there, she thought.

'Hello. John? Thank goodness! Look, I don't know if you remember. But it's Eva Valdes. We dined at the same table at the WHS seminar in Washington last year.'

'Eva? That you? Of course, I remember. We had strange duck soup. Right?'

'Turtle. And it was terrible.' Her relief was tangible.

He laughed. 'The soup I can forget. The dress you wore I remember. Long, pale green. And you had an extraordinary flower, I remember.' He paused. 'So what's the call for? You going again this year?'

'No, John. Listen, it's something more serious. It's about the President.'

'You heard, eh? It's devastating.' He realised what she'd said. 'What do you mean, Eva?'

'John, it's his illness. I know something that can help.'

'What on earth are you talking about?'

Very carefully, for fear she might scare him off, she began to explain the symptoms Robson had as Stephen Haggerty outlined them. Then she began to describe the treatment needed to save his life.

'Where did you get this, Eva?' Walters interrupted.

'It came from a man working in the outback in Guatemala. A medical missionary. An American named Whitten.'

'Randolph Whitten?'

'That's him,' she said excitedly. 'You know him?'

'Sure. He's been a fixture in Central America for years. He was known as a great blood spec...' He stopped. 'Blood specialist,' he said slowly.

'John, he's been murdered.'

'Good God!'

'Listen, this is the difficult part. Somebody gave that virus to the President.'

'Come on, Eva.'

'I don't care if you doubt me,' she said impatiently, 'but at least listen.'

'Go on.'

'Two people besides Whitten knew what was going on. One was a man named Otto Lentz. He died in Montreal eight days ago. From the same virus that the President has. It was reported in Montreal papers. The Canadian Embassy will verify it for you. The other man who knew was one of our own people, William Masters. He died in the National Orthopaedic Hospital. Again of the same disease.'

'I'm staggered,' Walters said. 'I don't know what to say.'

'Well, that's not all. I've got another of our people down here who can back up what I'm saying.'

'Down where? Where are you calling from, Eva?'

'From Comitan. We just got out of Guatemala. Listen, the person I'm talking about is from Langley. His name is Vern Railsback.'

'Vern? Vernon Railsback?'

'That's the man.'

'Vern worked for me. He's a good man.'

279

'John, this thing goes very deep. It involves people in the Agency itself. Guatemala became the catalyst.' She heard him catch his breath.

'The arms embargo?'

'You've got it.'

There was silence on the line.

'Korner?'

'Yes.'

'Christ almighty!' Another silence followed. 'Listen, Eva, I'm going to have to get back to you. Let me get this stuff you told me to the President's doctors.'

'John, before you go I've got a problem here. I had to bribe the local police chief to get through to you. He's in the room with me.' Her voice trembled at the admission. 'He's been playing with me.'

'Put him on the phone.'

Eva looked across the room at the police chief who stood by the table where he had put back the money. He was watching her nervously.

'For you.' She held out the receiver.

He put the phone to his ear. '*Si?*'

She watched his face turn a sallow grey as he listened.

'*Si, señor,*' he said unhappily as he put down the phone. Hesitantly, he looked at Eva.

'Well?' she asked.

'He said,' his voice shaking, 'that he will personally inform the Minister for Justice of my behaviour,' he fumbled, 'unless I treat you with the greatest courtesy from here on.'

'Good.'

'And,' his voice trembled, 'to make amends, I am to allow you,' he was almost crying, 'to punch me on the nose.'

Eva laughed.

She came forward and put both hands on his shoulders. Leaning forward, she planted a large kiss on his broad forehead.

He looked up, beaming.

Then she hit him.

280

28

Haggerty's ribs ached from laughter.

They were sitting on the bed in the suite the Embassy had provided in the International Hotel. He rolled against her as she raised her slender hand with a dark bruise on the knuckle.

'It still hurts,' she said.

He got up, gripping his side.

'Oh, God. Don't say any more.' He staggered to the bathroom. She fell back on the bed, closing her eyes, not caring about the dirt, the torn clothes or anything else. Her cup was running over.

She heard him moving about, chuckling. The shower came on. Then something fell by the bed. She opened her eyes and raised herself on her elbows. His shirt was on the floor. His trousers followed through the bathroom door. He leaned out and beckoned.

Her face glowing, she came off the bed. He watched her unbutton the blouse and drop it on the floor. She unbuckled the rough trousers and took them off. Quietly, her slender body golden in the room's soft light, she reached back to unhook the bra. It came away and her taut breasts, the nipples rose-tinted, stood out. She looked up at him and smiled. The tiny white panties, hooked on her hips, sloped across the soft pouting belly. Haggerty, his throat dry, moved from the bathroom door as she put her fingers into the clinging sides and let the tiny garment fall down her smooth legs to the floor. She looked up at him, her red lips moist and open, her eyes soft and darkly lustrous. As he neared her, he dropped the towel he was holding and she opened her arms to receive him.

She drew him back to the bed and down on the slowly yielding surface. They lay side by side, her lips and tongue moving across his roughened face. He held her in his arms and let his fingers stroke the softness of her body. It was a rediscovery that was fresh now for him as well as her. She moved over him, questing, seeking, then offering in an act that seemed to flow from her every pore. When he took her finally, among the crumpled linen, it seemed almost a dream, the passion was so far raised above reality. The only sound, apart from the symphony of breaths, was her choking cry of love as they came in union.

For Eva Valdes, this was the most beautiful moment of her life. Nothing, not anything in all her experience, had ever been like it.

Stephen Haggerty, as he lay there, could not find words either.

Afterwards in the shower, they made love again. But it was an experience of a different kind. As if the earlier mysteries could not be repeated. But that rush of pleasure had happiness built into it too, serving like an affirmation of their joy at being together after what they had passed through together.

They emerged at last, tingling, dried. Again Haggerty held her in his arms. As they stood, locked together, someone knocked at the door. They hardly heard it.

It persisted.

'Come on, open up!' It was Vern's voice. 'I got news!'

They stood, bodies joined, hardly breathing.

'What do you think?' Haggerty whispered. The knocking was approaching a crescendo.

Her lips moved off his neck. Reluctantly they drew apart. 'Better let him in.'

She moved quickly to the bed as he went to the door. Gathering the rustling sheet around her, she inched up against the pillows, watching his lean back, feeling her stomach flutter.

Haggerty slipped the lock off.

'Give me ten seconds,' he called and ran back to the bed. She grabbed him as he threw himself under the sheet. Then he was wriggling again under her soft hand.

'Here I come, ready or not.' Vern Railsback poked his head in and then entered. They both stared, astonished. He was dressed in a bilious green shirt and very wide trousers. He grinned at them, closing the door, and approached the bed. He was carrying a parcel.

'Where did you get the outfit, Vern?' Haggerty asked, grinning, as he sat down at the end.

'Bellboy.'

'You rascal,' Haggerty said, 'we'll have to keep our eye on you.'

'Come on, spare me the Victorian morality,' Vern said. 'Now listen. I just talked with John Walters. Wait 'til you hear this. The President's condition has stabilised. He's stopped bleeding.'

'Thank God!' Eva bounced on the bed, a flash of breast showing. She grabbed the fallen sheet quickly and pulled it up.

'Fabulous,' Haggerty said.

'It's not over yet,' Vern said. But he was grinning too. 'There's a few complications. But he's through the worst.' He leaned forward to tap Eva's knee. 'All thanks to your phone call, sweetheart.'

Her face was alight with happiness. 'It was all of us. Oh God, I feel so good.' She threw an arm around Stephen Haggerty's neck. He drew her to his shoulder and looked at Vern, smiling.

'How about some champagne?'

'You bet.' Vern went to the house phone. Haggerty moved his head across the side of Eva's face. 'I love you,' he whispered.

He felt her breath on his cheek as she turned, her lips raised to him.

'Hey, cut that out!' Vern said, putting down the phone. 'You're turning this into soap opera.' He looked towards the bathroom. 'It even smells like one. What the hell were you doing in there?'

They grinned.

He sat on the bed again and brought up the parcel he had carried in.

'What's that?' Haggerty asked.

'Clothes,' Vern said, passing it over. 'We'll be leaving this burg in a couple of hours.'

'How come?' Haggerty began opening it.

'They're sending down a plane. They want us back in the States, pronto.'

'Great.' He let Eva dip in with him. 'Jesus, what's this?' Haggerty drew up a black garter belt and lace panties. Eva snatched them away, giggling.

283

'Just trying to help,' Vern said defensively. 'Isn't that the kind of thing you guys love?'

'Christ, I'm afraid to look at mine,' Haggerty said. He did and laughed uproariously. Beside the blue shirt and pale grey trousers, there was a pair of boxer shorts with hearts on them.

'Hope I got the right size,' Vern said grinning.

Haggerty held them up for Eva who was wriggling into her panties under the bedsheet.

'What do you say? Turn you on?'

'Absolutely,' she said, finishing. 'Don't take them out in the launderette. They'll cause a riot.'

'You guys are making fun of me,' Vern said.

'There, there.' Haggerty reached down to pat his hand. 'We're just small-town primitives. We're not used to your Washington ways.'

The champagne arrived. They drank it sitting on the bed. Eva had put on the burgundy shirt Vern got her with the panties. Haggerty wore his boxer shorts.

'I feel overdressed,' Vern said, regarding them.

They raised their glasses.

'To friendship, like it's seldom been before,' Haggerty said, 'and to the two friends who will live in here,' he tapped his chest, 'for the rest of my life.'

They drank, not saying anything for a moment.

'My turn,' Vern said finally. He filled the glasses. Looking across the bed at them, he raised his glass. 'To Stephen and Eva. Two very beautiful people who don't know the meaning of the word quit. You are a couple for whom I'd go to hell and back. You have more guts, grace and humour than anyone I know.'

Haggerty, moved, tapped his glass with the others. 'Thanks, Vern.' He and Eva drank.

They waited for her.

'I don't know what to say.' Her voice trembled, then it came out in a rush. 'I love you both.'

'It's the fucking champagne,' Haggerty said to Vern. Underneath the sheet, he squeezed her thigh.

Vern shook his head as they ended their drink.

'All very heavy stuff. Makes me feel a bit queasy inside.' He shook his head. 'After all we've been through, I can think of just one final word that's appropriate.' He hauled up the magnum. 'Refills?'

For those curious
about the aftermath

29

Miami, Florida
The blue sky hung serene but remote from the shabby Florida street. The small group was already gathered, waiting for the clinic to open.

Stephen Haggerty, a worn baseball hat low over his eyes, stood first in line. Under his coat, the gun felt hard against his belly. Somebody was in for a surprise.

At eight-fifty, just like clockwork, he saw the white Chevette of the nurse, Dorothy Kreise, enter the street. Shortly after, Eva appeared on her tail. So far, so good. Kreise's car came by the clinic and turned right into the alley alongside. Eva turned in, following. The front door-lock rattled as it was withdrawn. Haggerty remained slouched, eyes on the ground where the door would open. It swung back. He saw white shoes and white trousers appear.

'Morning.'

Haggerty looked up, smiling, his hand inside his jacket. It was Mel, the man who had held the knife to his throat at their last meeting. It seemed an age ago.

'Good morning to you,' Haggerty said cheerfully. Mel's jaw dropped. He saw the gun which Haggerty had drawn up under the jacket. He looked up into Haggerty's eyes and was scared. Haggerty pushed him back into the reception room.

'Down to the back,' Haggerty hissed. 'Move!' Leaving the other customers to shuffle in, Mel walked hesitantly to the door at the rear of the room. Haggerty pushed him through.

'Nice seeing you again, pal,' he said as he closed the door behind them. 'Now take me to Kreise's office. Let's go.' They walked up the green corridor.

289

Dorothy Kreise, platinum hair piled high in intricate design, sat white-faced in her chair behind the desk. Eva Valdes sat opposite with a gun in her hand. Haggerty motioned Mel to the back of the desk with Kreise.

'Nice work,' Haggerty said to Eva. 'Any problems?'

'No.' She didn't take her eyes off Kreise. 'She's been the perfect lady.'

'Good.' Haggerty looked at the two. 'Now, I'm not going to waste time. As you've probably guessed I'm looking for your friend, Ernst Dackman. Where is he?'

'We don't know,' Mel said. 'We haven't seen him in weeks.'

Haggerty stared at Mel. 'Let me make one thing clear. You're going to tell me where Dackman is. Because if you don't, I'm going to hand you over to the FBI as a major suspect in a conspiracy to murder President Robson.' He looked at Dorothy Kreise. 'And the same goes for you.'

'Conspiracy? What the hell are you talking about?' Mel looked genuinely puzzled.

'Ernst Dackman has just tried to kill the President.'

'You're crazy,' Mel said.

Dorothy Kreise was silent. Haggerty looked at her.

'You knew, didn't you?'

She looked at him, scared. 'I had nothing to do with it.'

'Hey now.' Mel had forgotten Haggerty. He leaned over Kreise. 'Are you saying the doctor was involved in that?'

'I don't know! Leave me alone!' She was agitated.

'Dackman had the means to do it all right. You knew, didn't you?' Haggerty said.

Finally, she nodded.

'Listen,' Mel raised a hand, 'you can count me out on something like that. I ain't about to get tangled in no assassination.'

'Where is Dackman?'

'He's in the islands.'

'The Bahamas?'

'Yeah.'

'We want him.'

Mel was silent.

'You help me nail Dackman,' Haggerty said, 'and I'll try to make it easier for both of you. Otherwise, you can expect the worst.'

'He's in the out-islands,' Dorothy Kreise burst out. She looked at Mel. 'He takes the boat there all the time.'

Mel said nothing. Haggerty stared at him.

'Well?'

After a long pause, Mel finally shrugged. 'I didn't know nothing about killing the President. I don't go for that kind of stuff.' He looked at Haggerty. 'What are you planning on doing with him?'

'We're going to bring him in,' Haggerty said. 'But bear this in mind. If he gets away, the rest of you will swing.'

Mel made up his mind. Quickly.

'I'll take you.'

Langley, Virginia

At the Agency headquarters in Langley, they walked the long corridor to the Western Hemisphere section. Four agents of the Secret Service, with Vern in the middle. Outside the passing windows, the garden looked dull in the bleak Washington weather. No one spoke.

There were few people in the corridor but those that were there moved aside to let them pass. They reached the door of James Korner's office and paused. One of the agents unbuttoned his jacket.

'Ready?' The small barrel-chested man in charge looked at Vern. He nodded.

The agent opened the door and they walked in. The blonde secretary looked up from her desk in surprise at their sudden appearance.

'Can I help you?' she asked as the last man in closed the door.

'We're Secret Service, miss. Here to see Mr Korner. You just remain where you are, please.' The supervising agent nodded to one of his men. 'Lowe, you stay here.' The agent moved behind the desk to stand by the secretary who looked at him, her lips trembling.

'Through there,' Vern said, pointing. They moved up to the

solid teak door. The man in charge took the handle and suddenly pushed it open.

James Korner was writing at his desk. He looked up as the four men came quickly into the room, fanning out. Korner saw Vern and his big raw-boned face drained of colour. He sat perfectly still, the pen gripped in his hand.

'James Korner?'

Korner lowered the pen.

'I'm Agent William Kelly, Secret Service. We're here to take you into custody, sir, for questioning in connection with the attempted assassination of the President of the United States. You have the right to ...'

Korner raised a hand. 'Please,' he said. His voice was icy calm. 'I've been a public servant for too long not to know my rights. Would you care to sit down and tell me what this is all about?'

'No, sir,' Kelly said, 'I'm afraid you'll have to come with us.'

They stood waiting.

Korner nodded. He looked at Vern. 'I suppose this is your doing, Railsback?'

'You mean my duty,' Vern said. Once, a scene like this would have warmed his thoughts after all the humiliations Korner had put him through. Now he felt like an observer in what could have been a condemned cell.

Korner nodded at his words.

'Duty, acts, what's the difference?' he said slowly. 'Doing what you think is right is all that matters.' He looked at them, his gaze growing remote. 'I knew there was a possibility it would end like this. Anything worthwhile always carries the risk of sacrifice. There's no shame in that.' He looked up, more businesslike. 'Now that our plans have failed, I think it would be better for the country if the whole matter was brought to a quick conclusion. You know who was involved?'

'I think it would be better if you told us, sir.'

Korner nodded. 'I agree. The participants were President Antonio Serena of Guatemala, his secretary Alessandro Cordillera, Congressman Caleb Masters, Dr Ernst Dackman and myself.

'There were no other primary participants. Our aim, as you have likely gathered, was to ensure that Guatemala and ultimately Central America did not fall into the Soviet camp as seems certain now with the continuation of President Robson's embargo. I had no animus, then or now, against the President as a person or against any other unfortunate casualty in this affair. I regret that the violence we contemplated was necessary to achieve our aims. But those aims, we believed, were vital to the best interests of the United States.

'Now that we have failed, we have no further responsibility in this matter. It will be up to others to undo the harm that I believe the President has foolishly brought on this country.' He rose and looked around the room. 'I'm ready to go now.'

Agent Kelly nodded. Korner came out from behind the massive desk and stopped to look at Vern.

'You know, Railsback,' he said, 'you've shown such impressive qualities in this business that I'm almost prepared to accept your homosexuality.'

Vern felt the other men in the room glancing at him and his face reddened slightly. Korner, apparently not noticing, smiled and held out his hand. 'Let me shake hands.'

Mutely, Vern took it.

Nodding to himself, Korner went to the coatrack to get his raincoat. They watched as he began taking it down, his back to them. They saw his hand fumble.

'What are you doing, sir?' Kelly shouted suddenly and started forward.

A shot rang out, echoing around the room.

'Jesus!'

Korner, like a great aged oak, toppled to the ground, the coatrack tumbling over him. They stared, shocked. Then Vern pushed forward.

It was hopeless. He had shot himself through the roof of the mouth. The eyes were already glazed and the jaw had fallen slack.

'Out of the way!' Kelly knelt beside him and began pumping the chest. 'Somebody call an ambulance.'

Vern rose slowly to his feet.

It was all so stupid, he thought. People killing each other and themselves for the sake of a world that never got any better. It was like a disease that seemed to invade even the most rational people.

Korner had a brilliant mind, the envy of many in Langley. But it had self-destructed, deluded by images of flag and country.

'Oh, God!'

Vern turned to the agonised cry. Korner's secretary, the young, blonde girl reputed to be his mistress, was standing in the doorway. The agent beside her caught her as she fell.

'Ambulance on its way, Bill,' the agent on the phone said.

Kelly, still pumping away at Korner's chest, nodded.

The agent crossed to stand beside Vern, watching.

'At least, we got Cal Masters,' he muttered. 'That gives us a trial.'

Vern nodded. Serena and Cordillera were out of reach and probably would remain so. Only Dackman was left.

He wondered how Stephen Haggerty was doing.

Off the Florida Coast

At sea, the day was near flawless. The majestic blue of the sea with its spattering of white-capped waves was matched in the pale eggshell blue of the sky. Barely a shred of white cloud marred its infinity.

Mel guided the powerful thirty-six-foot cruiser. Dorothy Kreise and Eva sat in the cabin. Haggerty remained outside, at peace with the beauty of the surroundings, his mind on the problem of what he would do when he found Dackman. He didn't want to kill the man, or even injure him. But bringing him to justice, as he told Mel, had an odd ring to it. It sounded like he was performing a selfless act. And that wasn't quite right.

'The coast is coming up.'

He looked up as Mel pointed to a smudge on the horizon. 'That's it,' he said. The cruiser ploughed on, leaving a long churning white trail in its wake. 'Ten minutes,' he said.

They had already decided on what to do when they reached the island. Mel would land at a small inlet. From there Haggerty could reach the tiny road. Dackman's villa was less than a mile away on a narrow peninsula. While Haggerty was gone, Eva would guard Mel and Dorothy Kreise. Afterwards, they would all return to Miami. Eva wanted to go with him but it was so obviously impractical, she soon gave up. Haggerty himself was

294

not afraid of what was coming up. But he knew he would need his luck to get by.

The island gathered shape as they closed on it. The coastal plateau was lined with holiday homes which lay below the rising interior. The dark green vegetation gave it a sombre appearance even in the bright sunlight. They could see long beaches barely occupied and lonely breakers crashing on the empty strands.

The cruiser went into a long curve parallelling the coast.

'Stephen.'

Eva had come back. He slipped an arm around her hip as she stood over him. He could feel her slender flank. 'You won't do anything crazy, will you? I don't want anything to happen to you.'

'Don't worry. I'll be careful.' He rested his head against her breast, his eyes still on the shore. It was eerie but he could feel her heart beating. She ran her fingers through his hair.

'I just hope for a time when there'll be no risk, no danger,' she said softly. 'When we can wake up without worrying that someone is going to kill us.'

'I know what you mean,' Haggerty said. 'It's been a tough time.' He gazed out at the rushing waves as they whipped by, trying to think of comparisons for all the things that happened. But none matched. 'It's strange,' he said, 'I don't feel anything like I did in Vietnam. The danger and all the fear – it seemed to gather like layers on me then. Now, it fades as quickly as it happens.' He looked up at her. 'I don't even dream much any more.'

She shook her head. 'I do,' she said. 'I still shake for you when I think of what could have happened. And it would all have been my fault.'

He looked up at her beautiful face and the dark head, silhouetted against the blue sky and shook his head. 'No,' he said. 'Nothing was your fault.'

She tightened her hand on him and kissed the top of his head. 'You are such a fine man.' She leaned down to his face. 'I love you.' She kissed him.

'Eva,' Haggerty said gently after a few moments, 'we're getting close. I think you should get back there.' He squeezed her waist as she straightened up reluctantly. 'There'll be other times.'

Her hand trailed across his shoulder as she returned to the cabin. Fleetingly, he worried at the depth of her intensity. It was so powerful, so all-giving. The thought made him feel disloyal and he gave it up.

They were within three hundred yards of the shore. The sound of the breaking waves could be heard above the engines. Haggerty moved down to the cabin under the canvas. Mel pointed.

'That's the place in there.' It was part of a ragged promontory. The rock face seemed unbroken but as they came nearer, the shapes started to take on perspective. Mel was steadily reducing power and the boat began to drift under the weakened drive, the water slapping heavily against the sides. Mel swung the wheel back and forward as they closed slowly on the rocks. Now Haggerty saw the gap, opening into a still backwater where a few small boats lay at anchor.

'It ain't as dangerous as it looks,' Mel said, as the cruiser took a forty-five degree angle and edged towards the entrance. Large grey rocks with seaweed lapping about them drifted by only ten feet away. As they closed on the opening, Mel eased the throttle forward and the renewed power shook the cruiser as it moved through the gap. A rough stone causeway loomed up. Mel, skilfully and with small adjustments, brought the boat alongside. He cut the engine and Haggerty backed to let him by as he tossed ropes to the jetty. With a foot on the side of the cruiser, he paused to look back at Haggerty.

'Go ahead,' Haggerty said.

Jumping ashore, Mel quickly tied the cruiser. Slowly, he came back.

'What happens now?'

'You wait with Miss Valdes until I come back,' Haggerty said. With his hand on the gun in his belt, he pointed to the small cabin that lay below decks. 'In there.'

He saw merit in Mel's protest – it was getting very warm – but he was not prepared to increase the risk to Eva just for their comfort.

By midday, the heat had spread its shimmering veil across the landscape.

Stephen Haggerty's shirt clung to his back as he lay among the tall cane plants in the field opposite the villa. For twenty minutes he had been watching the grounds. Nothing stirred among the well-kept shrubbery. It had all the stillness of a painting. And quietness too. Only the occasional cry of a faraway bird broke the silence.

Satisfied, Haggerty rose and stuck the Walther pistol deeper in his belt. Leaving the canefield, he ran softly across the narrow road and dropped down by the ornamental wall fringing the property. He paused to wipe away the sweat gathering on his temples. Raising his head cautiously, he surveyed the sprawling pink-dashed façade of the villa now less than thirty yards away. Still nothing moved.

Maybe it was siesta time.

The heavy-timber front door with its black metal cross-frames looked too tough to force if it were locked. But there were several windows. One, a french window, looked easiest. Satisfied that he was not observed, he vaulted the wall and sprinted quickly across the closely-mown lawn. He reached the window and stopped alongside it. With his back to the wall he drew his gun. Holding it shoulder high, he leaned forward to peer through the glass.

He was looking into a large room filled with traditional furniture. It was unoccupied. He reached across to the grip on the glass door and pushed. Locked. He moved on to try the other two windows. Both were sealed. Retracing his steps, he rounded the side of the villa. Passing an outcrop of bougainvillaea he found a side door. This time it was open. He slipped inside.

He was in a white-walled hall with a polished pine floor. At the far end two doors faced each other. He could see that one was ajar. Softly, gun ready, he moved down the hall and stopped by the open door. Gently, he eased his head around.

A black man, his hair spiked with grey, sat on a table with his back to the door. He was reading a newspaper.

Very quietly, Haggerty entered the room. Holding the gun on the unsuspecting man, he reached over with his free hand and pushed the door closed. The man heard the faint sound and looked around.

'Lord Almighty!' The newspaper dropped to the table.

'Don't be alarmed,' Haggerty said quickly. He approached the table. 'I'm not going to harm you.'

The man stared at him. He was about sixty years old and his heavily pouched eyes were very white in the black face. He looked frightened to death. Haggerty stopped by the table.

'I'm looking for the man who owns this villa. Ernst Dackman. Is he here?'

The man didn't answer. He stared at Haggerty in shock. The air conditioning hummed in the background.

Haggerty lowered the gun a little. 'Look,' he said soothingly, 'I can understand that you might be a little frightened. But you don't have to be. I'm not going to rob you. All I want is to find Ernst Dackman. It's very important.'

The man said nothing.

Haggerty was wondering about how to break the stalemate when his eye caught the huge headline on the newspaper over a picture of President Robson. He gestured. 'Have you been reading that?'

The man looked down and nodded.

'That's why I'm here,' Haggerty said. 'Your Dr Dackman helped cause the President's sickness. I want to bring him back to the United States to face justice.'

The man stared at him in awe. 'The doctor?' His voice was back. 'You saying the doctor do that?'

Haggerty nodded. 'Right. We arrested the people who were partners with him.'

'Oh, Lord!'

'It's the truth.'

The fright seemed to be disappearing. The man gestured to the paper. 'You know something? I was just thinking about what happened there. Before you came in. That very same thing ... it happened here too.'

'Oh?' Haggerty suddenly remembered how Vern said that William Masters witnessed a murder by Dackman down here.

The black man nodded. 'Happened to one of the people working here. Name of Oscar. He died.'

'The President almost did. But we stopped that.' Haggerty began putting the gun back in his belt, letting the man see him do it. 'What's your name, anyway?'

'Andrew. Andrew Stoeckle. But folks call me Andy.'

'Listen, Andy. Ernst Dackman has murdered a whole mess of people.'

Andy looked at him. 'That thing with Oscar. Lots of people say that the doctor do it. Me, I couldn't say that.'

'Well, you can now.'

The black man shook his head. 'That's terrible. Oscar, he weren't no bad man. He liked to take things, sure, but he didn't deserve what came to him. Bleeding 'til he died like that.'

'You know where Dr Dackman is, Andy?'

Andy nodded. 'He's in his bedroom. At the other end of the house. Packing to go away.'

Haggerty rose. 'I want you to take me to him.' He held the Walther at his side.

Andy looked down at it. Then up. 'You fixing to kill him?'

Haggerty shook his head. 'No. I told you. I want to take him back alive.'

Andy got up slowly. 'Killing Oscar. That was a wicked thing to do.' He looked at Haggerty again. 'Okay,' he said. 'Come on. I'll take you.'

They left the kitchen, crossed through the door on the other side of the hall and entered a heavily-carpeted corridor. The two picture windows on one side showed the wide spreading garden. On the other were a line of doors. Haggerty glimpsed a bedroom through one.

The black man, Andy, pointed to a door at the end of the corridor. 'That's where the doctor is,' he whispered. Haggerty nodded and moved ahead. He stopped at the door with Andy behind him. Raising a knuckle he tapped gently. Just like a servant.

'Who is it?'

The voice, American, had an element of annoyance in it.

299

Haggerty looked at Andy quickly and nodded. The black man cleared his throat.

'It's Andy, sir.'

'Dammit, I told you not to bother me.' They heard him walking to the door. The lock unlatched. Haggerty raised his gun. The door opened.

'What the hell...' Ernst Dackman stopped and stared at Stephen Haggerty.

'Hello, Dackman.' Haggerty held the gun levelled at his chest. Dackman stepped back.

'Who are you?' His face had gone a dirty grey.

'Stephen Haggerty.' He came forward and pushed the gun none too gently into Dackman's chest. 'You may not remember me. I'm just another poor sucker you tried to kill. Like the President of the United States.'

Dackman backed to the bed where a pile of clothes and a suitcase lay.

'I don't know what you're talking about,' he said, eyes on the gun.

'The hell you don't.' Haggerty was watching him carefully. Dackman looked powerful, like a trapped bull. 'You're coming back to the States with me. You and Cal Masters are going to face trial.'

'You're crazy.' Dackman's shoulder muscles were bunched.

Haggerty raised the gun higher. 'I wouldn't.'

Dackman saw it was hopeless and shrugged. 'As far as I'm concerned, you're talking crap. I've never killed anybody.'

'Don't give me that. I talked to Randolph Whitten. You used his virus to kill. The President was lucky, that's all.'

'Virus?' Dackman stared coolly at him. 'You're talking moonshine. I don't know anything about a virus.'

'Moonshine? I'll give you moonshine,' Haggerty said. 'You extracted the virus from those mosquitoes that Whitten found in the Basin of the Blood God. And you used it to bleed away the people you didn't like.'

Dackman folded his arms across his chest.

'Horse shit. I have no virus. And I don't know anything about these mosquitoes you're talking about.'

300

'Hey now! You got mosquitoes.' Andy, the black servant, suddenly shouted loudly. Haggerty had almost forgotten him.

Dackman glared, malevolent. 'Shut up!'

Haggerty raised the gun.

'Where does he keep them?' he asked over his shoulder.

'They down in the basement,' Andy said. 'He got a lab down there.'

'Well, now,' Haggerty said. 'Isn't that interesting?'

Dackman's face was dark with anger as he glared past Haggerty.

'Get your goddamn stuff and get out of here, you bastard!' he shouted. 'You're fired!'

'The folks is right!' Andy shouted back. 'You killed Oscar! You devil!'

Haggerty raised his free hand.

'Back off, Andy. I want to see this lab he's got. You,' he gestured with the gun at Dackman. 'Downstairs.'

Reluctantly, Dackman led the way. Staying well back, Haggerty followed along the corridor to the basement stairs. Andy trailed behind, unwilling now to give up his part in the drama.

The lab door was locked.

'Open it.'

Dackman shrugged. 'I don't have a key.'

'He do too,' Andy said excitedly. 'He don't let nobody go in there except hisself.'

'Goddamn you, I told you to get out of here,' Dackman shouted up the stairs. 'Get out now, d'you hear!'

'I go!' Andy spat across the banister, 'but I come back. After I tell Oscar's people they right. Die, you devil!'

'Open that door.' Haggerty pushed Dackman forward. 'And be quick.'

They heard Andy stamping away upstairs. A door slammed. Dackman stood by the door.

'Are you going to open it?' Haggerty asked coldly. 'Or do I give you a pistol whipping first?'

Dackman grimaced and drew keys from his pocket. He turned one in the lock and stepped back.

'You first,' Haggerty said. 'And turn on the lights.'

They entered the laboratory. It was a square white room with a tiled floor, almost dazzling under the fluorescent lights. Two walls were lined with benches and scientific equipment.

'Listen,' Dackman said before Haggerty could complete his inspection, 'we can talk about this.'

'Yeah?'

Dackman nodded. 'Right.' The anger had disappeared. There might have been a hint of worry in his eyes. But he controlled it. Nothing showed in his voice.

'You don't have to tell me I'm in a jam,' he said, standing against one of the benches. 'I know that. But what you have is not the full story. You've got to understand that. I did not put this together. I was under orders from the Central Intelligence Agency. My boss, James Korner, set this whole thing up. None of it was my doing.'

'Is that so?'

Dackman nodded. 'Ask Korner,' he said earnestly. 'He'll tell you that himself. Everything we did was in the interests of national security. That's what he said.'

'Like killing the President of the United States? That was in the interests of national security?'

Dackman sighed. 'It's what I said. Because that's what I was told.'

'Who are you trying to fool?'

'It's true, I tell you. All this,' he waved around him, 'comes from the Agency.'

'Including the virus?'

'Including the virus. Agency couriers brought in the mosquitoes I got the virus from. Over there.' He gestured across the laboratory.

Haggerty glanced aside. He had barely time to glimpse a rectangular glass container.

Then Dackman was upon him.

He couldn't shoot. The force of the attack carried him back across a table laden with magazines and files. Papers flew everywhere as the table collapsed and they toppled to the floor. Locked together, scrabbling over the tiled floor, they fought for control.

302

Haggerty was underneath, struggling to keep the gun out of Dackman's reach. Dackman had one arm around his neck. The other stretched out seeking the gun. As the fingers neared, Haggerty butted his head into Dackman's face. The shorter man gasped in pain but brought his fist back in a blow at Haggerty's head. Haggerty moved his head just in time and the knuckles skidded off his temple.

They fought across the floor, limbs thrashing madly, each desperate for control. Dackman was stronger but Haggerty's longer arm gave him an advantage and kept the gun out of reach. Yet he could not turn it to fire. Suddenly, Dackman brought a loose elbow hard into Haggerty's neck. He gasped in choking pain as Dackman's hand closed around the gun. Struggling but still locked together, they came up off the floor. Dackman's hand was like a vice, crushing Haggerty's against the gun. Haggerty swung a wild blow which sent the shorter man reeling for an instant but he came back with a fist to the stomach that sent Haggerty crashing into the bench. Equipment scattered and glass smashed around them. They closed, flailing wildly, their shirts shredded, the area around them turning to a shambles.

Grimly, Dackman pounded away with the heavier blows, slowly getting the advantage. Losing strength, Haggerty was being forced back against the bench, his gun hand still stretched out of reach. Desperately, he dodged another blow. Head sideways, he glimpsed the glass container with the mosquitoes a few feet away. Turning the gun, with Dackman grasping his wrist, he pointed it and fired.

The room rocked with a deafening explosion and the container shattered and collapsed. Dackman, stunned, loosened his grip. Haggerty powered him backwards and broke free. They were less than a foot apart when Dackman saw the first mosquito emerge from the smashed container. Haggerty, knowing what would happen, broke by him as he hesitated and hurtled for the door. Almost instantly, Dackman came after him. But he was too late. Haggerty reached the open door first, grabbing the knob and slamming it closed behind him. Outside, he scrabbled at the key and turned the lock.

The door shook with a thunderous banging. Haggerty slumped against the wall opposite, exhausted.

'For Christ's sake, open the door!' Dackman was shouting inside.

'Let me out!' The pounding reached a new intensity. It filled the hallway. 'Oh, Jesus!' Dackman's voice rose to a scream. 'Oh, God, no.'

Haggerty slumped to the ground.

He stared at the white-painted door as Dackman's voice fell to a whimper on the other side. 'Please,' he was sobbing, 'oh, please, let me out.' Suddenly there was a flurry of activity inside. Then it died away. Haggerty waited.

'Dackman?'

There was silence.

'You want to come out?'

'Yes.' The voice now was shaking, weak.

'Okay,' Haggerty said. 'But no tricks. Understand?'

'Please. Just let me out.'

'And nothing comes out with you. You got that?'

'Yes.'

Haggerty raised his gun as he unlocked the door.

'Okay, you can come out now. But don't open that door wide. And don't let any of those mosquitoes out. I'll kill you if you try that.'

Slowly, the door came ajar. Dackman slipped through and closed it behind him.

Haggerty stared, stunned.

The tanned face was dotted with bites. Already the swelling was starting to distort his features. His body shivered under the tattered clothes as he stood against the door.

Haggerty waved the gun. 'Upstairs.'

Dackman had no more fight in him. Unsteadily, he mounted the stairs. Haggerty could see more marks on his back. 'I need to get to a hospital,' he said, his voice quaking, as they reached the top of the stairs. He was breathing heavily.

'Keep going,' Haggerty said.

They turned into the corridor leading to the front of the house. Suddenly they heard the noise of trucks outside.

'Hold it,' Haggerty said and they stopped. He moved up to a window and looked out.

Two old trucks had stopped by the gate. A mob of men with cudgels and sticks were jumping down to gather alongside. Haggerty saw the older man Andy in the centre of the group.

'Shit!' He glanced at Dackman. 'Is there another way out of here?'

Dackman looked out the window. He began to shake again. 'Oh, Jesus.' He tried to take Haggerty's arm but Haggerty pulled away. 'Don't let them find me. Please.'

'Where can we go?'

'The beach. There's a Zodiac.'

'Come on.' They hurried back through the house. They could hear the shouting start outside. They reached the patio when the first banging started on the door.

'Over there.' Dackman pointed to the steps leading down to the sea. They began to run. The noise behind them was growing more shrill. They could hear glass breaking.

They reached the wide steps. The beach was forty yards below. Away to the left, the rubber Zodiac was moored by a small jetty on the waterline. Farther off, people were playing beachball.

They scrambled down the steps as the turmoil grew behind them.

'There he is!' a voice screamed.

Haggerty glanced back. A mob of black faces, filled with hatred, stared down from behind raised cudgels. He turned to see Dackman's sweating face, now puffed with red, looking back in terror. 'Hurry!' he shouted.

They scrambled down the steps. With an ugly roar, the crowd came after them. Seeing the distance to be covered, Haggerty knew they were not going to make it. But he had to try. He stopped, letting Dackman go, and turned to face the descending mob.

'Wait!' he shouted as the crowd spilled down towards him. He held the gun high over his head. 'Hold it a minute!' Before he could say more they were on him. Somebody aimed a blow and he fell sideways against the stone balustrade. More people pressed around him and he felt more blows.

305

'Stop!' It was Andy hemmed around. 'He good man. Leave him alone, I tell you.'

The crowd surrounding Haggerty hesitated.

'It's the doctor we want,' Andy shouted. 'Don't let him get away!'

With a roar, the people swept away from Haggerty and down the steps in pursuit of the fleeing Dackman. Andy moved in and helped him to his feet.

'Thanks, Andy.'

They both looked down at the beach.

Dackman had reached the sand but he was tiring. His feet ploughed into the heavy sand as he stumbled forward. The mob, full of energy and excitement, came off the steps in full cry. Dackman, his face bloated with fear, looked back over his shoulder. He saw that he could not reach the Zodiac in time. Panicking, he turned towards the water only thirty yards away. The mob, less than a hundred yards behind, streamed after him in full cry. Reaching the hardened sand, Dackman ran faster and reached the water.

The sea splashed up around him and then swirled as he went in deeper. It was clear he had no plan. He just wanted to get away. Haggerty watched in horror. There was no way he could.

The water had reached his chest when the crowd arrived at the edge. They stood, screaming in impotence, as he went in deeper.

Someone threw a stick. Others did too. But they all fell short. Then somebody hurled a stone. Haggerty saw the splash as it hit the water beyond Dackman. With a cry of triumph, the crowd bent to find more. Soon a rain of stones fell from the air around the small figure in the water. Stephen Haggerty saw one strike him.

Dackman clutched his head and then turned, his hands raised, supplicating. A cloud of stones curved through the air in reply. They showered down on his unprotected head and he slipped down in the water.

Haggerty clutched the balustrade.

Dackman was going under. One of his hands rose out of the water then sank down. More stones fell. For the last time,

306

Haggerty saw his face, the eyes wide and the mouth open. Then slowly he went under.

All around him, a widening pool of red spread on the turquoise water.